BLED OUT
Mark Simmons

Published in 2023 by Poe Boy Publishing.

ISBN: 979-8-9863099-0-3

DEDICATION

For Fava

ACKNOWLEDGMENTS

It would be impossible not to acknowledge Graeme Parker for all of his input throughout this entire creative process. It has been a challenging journey, but we got there in the end. I'd also like to thank Derek Schneider, and everyone else at Poe Boy Publishing. Jane Murray at Provoco Publishing has been nothing but supportive, her inciteful words have been invaluable in helping to make *Bled Out* what it is. Thank you to Hache Jones for her editorial prowess. My family and friends for believing in me and coping with my excuses for not seeing them at various social events.

For my wife. Thank you for all the love and support you have given me over the years. And for your tolerance of dealing with the gremlin in the corner working every hour under the sun. And most importantly I'd like to thank myself. Because as someone famous once said: *"If you can't love yourself, how the hell you gonna love someone else?"*

Chapter One

They find their favourite spot. A good vantage point to observe, just far enough away from the windows that they won't be seen.

It's a good night for it. Late summer evenings mean warm weather and deep shadows.

There were no guarantees, but then that was part of the thrill. What delights would tonight offer?

They bring the binoculars up to their eyes to get a closer look.

The shape of a woman is cast against pale coloured curtains. This stirs their yearnings, and they shift their feet, readying themselves with their free hand. The shadow moves and is gone.

Their shoulders slump, but their annoyance quickly subsides. This is part of the game.

On the floor above, the next set of curtains have been left wide open. Their heart starts to race as they touch themselves, waiting for that first glimpse.

Their patience is rewarded as a familiar blonde moves into sight. The length of her hair saving some of her modesty, but not much. The limited view only excites them more and this excitement grows in their hand.

She's been seen and finished over before, but her beauty is part of what keeps bringing them back, and they get to work.

Movement in the bushes disturbs their rhythm. Frustration courses through them as they look around. But they remember the family of foxes living in the undergrowth and raise the binoculars again.

Thankfully, she's still at the window. Her hair cascading over her breasts as she runs a brush through it.

Their excitement returns, their toes dig into the bottoms of their shoes, and they try to finish.

But the happy ending would have to wait. There is that sound again.

They feel a presence behind them, just in time to avoid the blow to their head. The strike was only glancing, but in their panic to get away, they lose their footing and their hold on the binoculars.

Another blow catches them on the shoulder as they scramble through the undergrowth to get away. Their clothes snag on some brambles bringing them to an abrupt stop. They glance back in fear, waiting for their attackers next assault, but no one is there.

Had their assailant been watching? Waiting for their chance to strike? They won't be scared off so easily though.

They'll be back; back to see that exquisite blonde one more time.

It was noisy outside again. But that was nothing new. It was what you got for leaving the window open. In this heat though, having any type of through draft was a necessity. The noise was probably the foxes. Or one of the pervs who came for a free show. Both were harmless, so she ignored them and went back to brushing her hair.

Stepping away from the cool evening breeze, she continued to brush her hair as she moved towards the bathroom. However, as she turned her back on the open window something didn't feel right. It felt as if she was being watched.

The floorboards vibrating beneath her feet as she heard the footstep behind her, and as she turned to confront the intruder, something struck her on the back of the head. The blow took her off her feet and the floor greeted her as she fell.

Chapter Two

Arriving at The Scenic Hotel, her feelings of anxiety began to well up. The customary bouts of nausea forming in the salivary glands and a layer of sweat across her scalp. These sensations were nothing new, just her body's way of telling her to be scared.

However, fear could be controlled. For what was there to fear?

The dead?

Detective Constable Lawrence knew that each new body was difficult in its own way. But there was no reason to be scared, after all, they were dead. You just had to treat every inch of the scene as evidence, and the deceased were no exception. She took a deep breath, swallowing down her fear.

Standing at the doorway of the hotel, she checked herself in the glass. She normally wouldn't have been so vain, but she'd been woken early for this one. Nightshift were swamped, so they'd been called in before their shift was supposed to start. When she said *they* what she meant was *she*.

In the streetlight, her complexion looked paler than usual. Her skin looking almost as white as her mother's. Her hair was under control. The frizz she'd inherited from her father hadn't worked its way out just yet. It was held close to her scalp, a few pins holding it in place at the base of her skull. Next to her pallid skin her hair looked jet black.

Her Egyptian blue trouser suit had come straight from the dry cleaners and looked neat and tidy. The white blouse she had on underneath looked orange in the artificial light. Her black shoes had been polished to a shine as they always were.

Happy with her appearance, she went inside.

To call it a reception area was a stretch. A fold-out desk in the hallway of an Edwardian mansion block, with a handwritten sign was what it really was.

A less than happy man stood behind the foldout desk. He was pointing a finger at a uniformed officer, his voice echoing in the open space.

'Just tell me how long?' the man barked.

'I can't answer that question, sir,' the uniform replied in a mild voice.

Lawrence assumed the barking man was the manager and with each step she got a better look at him. He was overweight, his belly poked out between his faded green shirt and stonewash jeans. His hair hadn't been washed, and his thick stubble had an unsightly gloss to it.

'You can't, or you won't?'

'I'm Detective Constable Lawrence,' she stated as she held up her warrant card. 'What's the problem?' Her question was directed at the uniform.

The manager seemed annoyed by the disruption, and his face turned red.

She could see what he was thinking, it was written all over his face. Who does this girl think she's talking to? He hadn't seen the warrant card, or the trouser suit, or the white cuffs gleaming out the ends of her jacket. All he'd seen was a black girl.

He wasn't the first to show his feelings like this, and he wouldn't be the last. She'd met the same face her entire life. But no matter how hard she tried to represent the upstanding member of society that she was, there were always some that just saw a black girl. Which was fine, she knew what she was, and most importantly, what her job was. Facing this type of prejudice was nothing new, it was her normal.

'I've got paying customers being disturbed,' the manager looked from one officer to the other, unsure who to address.

'And what appears to be the disturbance?' Lawrence asked as she took a step closer to the uniform.

'You lot.' He jabbed a finger at them. 'Bad for business.'

She gave the manager her best smile and stood in a more casual stance, 'I've just realised I don't know your name, sir?' She hoped that pleasantry might soften his mood.

'Sheehan.' he replied.

'Well, Mr Sheehan, are you able to confirm your role here?'

'I've already told this bozo.' He waved at the uniformed officer. 'Why don't you ask him?'

'I'd prefer to hear it from you,' Lawrence answered calmly.

'Would you now?' Sheehan looked her in the eyes, held her stare for only a moment, and then turned his gaze towards the hotel entrance. 'Is there anyone more senior arriving? Someone who's hit puberty perhaps?'

Normally there would have been a more senior officer with her. Her so-called partner, Detective Inspector Bambridge, should have been on site with her right now. She'd had the call telling her to get to the scene. He should have got the same call. But where was he?

She looked at the young officer who stood next to her. He was clean shaven and shared her youthful looks. But his babyface probably came from the fact that he was fresh out of the academy. Hers was probably a combination of luck and good genes.

All the years it had been since she was at the academy

seemed to stand for nothing, though. The way she was treated in her department she may as well have just graduated. The manner she was spoken to at times made her feel like her appointment was nothing more than a token gesture. Having a mixed race, black woman in the Homicide department ticked more than a few of the equality and diversity boxes for the bureaucrats. Having a mixed race, black woman who looked half her age was clearly a disadvantage when dealing with people like Sheehan.

She rolled her eyes. Regardless of her girlish features she was the most senior officer currently on scene and the manager would have just have to accept it.

'I'll take that as a compliment, Mr Sheehan,' Lawrence offered as she adjusted her footing and stepped back into the manager's line of sight.

'Weren't meant to be.'

'That's a shame,' she said with her best forced smile, 'but if you wouldn't mind answering my question, please?'

'Which was what?'

'What your role is round here?'

'I'm the manager,' Sheehan raised his voice again. 'So, how about answering my question? Seeming as your boy here won't give me an answer.'

'What question?' Lawrence ignored the manager and looked at the uniformed officer.

'Morning, Ma'am,' he said, with a nod. 'Mr Sheehan was under the impression we're distressing his customers.'

'Have they made a complaint to my colleague here, or just to you?' Lawrence asked as she turned her attention back to Sheehan.

Sheehan didn't like the question and gave her a stern

look. 'They came to me,' he answered as he leant forward across the desk.

'Well, if they have any issues, they're more than welcome to come speak to us directly.' She gave him her best smile again.

'Why would they want to do that? They've paid good money to stay here, and the last thing they want is to have to speak to you lot.'

'Why's that, Mr Sheehan? Do your guests have something against the police? Something that would cause them to complain about us doing our jobs?'

'It's just not great for business, is it, having you lot sniffing around?' was his belligerent response, as the sweat rolled off his flushed features. Whether his perspiration was from the heat hanging in the air, his lack of hygiene, or from being within the proximity of two officers, would remain to be seen.

'And how is business, Mr Sheehan?' Lawrence asked, as she picked up what looked like a diary from the desk.

'Give that back!' Sheehan snarled as he tried to take it from her. 'That's private property.'

Lawrence stepped back from him with the diary in hand and gave Sheehan her best smile.

'Privacy goes out the window when someone gets murdered in your establishment,' she stated as she flicked through the pages.

The diary read exactly as she'd suspected, a house with multiple occupancies, masquerading as a hotel with nothing but female names on the register. Add the general seediness of the place into the equation and she could only come to one conclusion.

'And you get even less privacy when the victim is a sex worker.'

Sheehan took offence. 'Now listen here...'

Lawrence dropped the diary onto the table and leant in close to the manager. The mild manners and smiles were gone, and only a stern stare remained. The smell of last night's booze hung on his breath as he shied away from her. 'All it takes is one call to a friend of mine in Vice, and they'll be all over this place. Be amazed what they can find.' She took a step back and the well-practised smiled returned. 'Now, let us do our jobs, so Vice don't have to do theirs.'

Sheehan gave a weak smile and then sat down.

Lawrence looked at the uniform officer. 'Can you show me to the scene?'

'Right this way,' he led her to the stairs.

'What we got?' she asked, as they reached the landing of the second floor.

'Victim is female,' the uniform began. 'She looks to be in her late twenties.'

'Have we been able to ID her?' Lawrence asked nodding at a second uniform stood outside the hotel room.

'Not yet,' the first officer replied. 'We did a quick sweep of the room, but we didn't find anything with her name on it. No mail, or driver's license that we could see.'

'Did she leave a purse or handbag lying around?'

'Yes, ma'am,' the second officer added. 'But there was nothing in it.'

'Nothing at all?'

'No, ma'am.'

'So, someone cleaned it out?'

'Looks that way, ma'am.'

'Did the manager find the body?' Lawrence asked as she looked at the door.

It had several dents in it and the lock was hanging from the doorframe.

'He said the victim's boyfriend stopped by and found the body,' the first officer replied.

'That's more than stopping by,' she offered as she pointed at the door. 'The boyfriend still here?'

'No, ma'am. Manager said the boyfriend told him about the body as he left,' the second officer stated as he moved from foot to foot. 'Mr Sheehan said he went to check and found her. Said he didn't touch anything and called it in as soon as he could.'

'How noble,' Lawrence replied, as she studied the second officer. He looked even younger than his colleague. He also looked extremely uncomfortable.

'I want a detailed description of this boyfriend from the manager,' Lawrence stated, as she looked between the two uniforms. 'If he doesn't give you much, just keep pestering him until he does.'

The first officer nodded and headed back down the corridor.

'Were you first on the scene?' she asked, turning to the officer stationed on the door, his features taut. She could tell he was green to murder scenes.

'Yes ma'am,' he said, snapping out of his empty stare.

It was clear the scene had disturbed him. But why was that? Was it because of what he'd found, or simply because it was his first body? Lawrence considered asking him but held her question back. Best to just leave him to his thoughts.

'Everything as you found it?' she added.

'I followed protocol, ma'am,' The uniform sounded confident. 'Kept my movements to a minimum. Forensics should only find my fingerprints on this door handle.'

Lawrence could tell he was telling the truth. This was the good thing about getting a newbie, they hadn't had time for the comfort of the job to sink in, and still had schooled routines fresh in their minds.

Reaching into her left trouser pocket she took out a pair of latex gloves. As she snapped the second glove on, she pushed the door open.

A rank odour greeted her as she passed over the threshold.

To the right of the entrance was a kitchen. Dirty dishes were piled up in the sink, revealing the source of the smell. She turned on her torch and shone it into the confined area. Apart from the unwashed crockery there was nothing of note, so she moved on.

Moving through the kitchen, down a small corridor, Lawrence noted the over trodden carpet lining the floor, various pairs of high heeled shoes were lined along the skirting boards to her left and right, and several coats hung off two hooks on the left wall.

She paused at what she thought was a door in front of her, but as she shone her torch at it the surface looked uneven. Light crept through multiple sections of the woodwork. Reaching out she touched the surface and a string of hanging beads parted. She stepped through the curtain and then let them go. The sound was thunderous in the small room.

Weak light, heralding the newly forming day cast through thin curtains to her left. Lawrence ran her torchlight across the room and felt uneasy. In just one sweep she had seen so much mess. The clean freak in her surfaced and an urge to tidy up bubbled to the surface. A deep breath helped remove any temptation.

A television sat on one side of an open window; dust caked across its screen. A coffee table sat between the tv and a worn-out sofa. The two-seater had begun to fray, thin and greasy from overuse. The cushions looked equally as uninviting.

On the right-hand side of the room was a double bed. Lawrence carefully worked her way over to it, making sure she didn't step on anything. The beam of the torch led her to dishevelled bedding, with a well-used look, and again, she had to resist the urge to fluff the pillows or rearrange the duvet.

To her right, a slither of light caught her eye and took her mind off the mess. She turned her torch away from the bed and found a door in the corner of the room. 'Must be in there,' she stated. She stepped around the bed and then pushed the door open.

A halogen light had been left on over the sink, its bulb struggling to stay lit as it flickered on the wall opposite the door. Next to the sink, the toilet was at an angle to the room, slotted in, at the end of the bathtub.

The tub's pristine white porcelain bounced her torchlight around the room. The light also danced on a small section of tiles on the floor next to the bath. There was a hint of bleach in the air. This felt odd, the sterile look of the bathroom, compared to the rest of the flat, but her attention was turned to the naked body hanging over the bath.

The victim's legs had been tied with rope at the ankles. The rope had then been wrapped around the metal shower curtain rail, before being tied off around the bath taps.

Lawrence ran her eyes over the body. The black and red rope had cut deep into the flesh of the dead woman's ankles, causing the feet to swell. The arms were tied behind her back with more rope. There were no signs of resistance or bruises on either arm. Her blonde hair had been curled up into a bun at the base of her skull. Which to the untrained eye would have hidden the injury she'd sustained on the back of her head, but Lawrence was anything but untrained. The blow must have been what incapacitated her. Followed by a single small incision made on the left side of her throat, which undoubtedly had been the cause of death.

'Where's the blood?' she said aloud, stepping closer to the body. There was no blood on the dead woman's neck or around the wound. None inside the tub. The whole area looked spotless.

Lawrence took a step back and looked around the rest of the small bathroom. Soap scum, and congealed toothpaste stained the sink. There was limescale caked around the bowl of the toilet. But the surfaces of the bath gleamed.

'They cleaned up,' she stated, as she drummed her fingers against her thigh. 'But why?' she asked, as she looked around again.

There was a clear line on the floor where the cleaning had stopped. The far end of the tub looked like it hadn't been touched either.

She shone her light into the plughole and leant forward making sure not to touch the body.

'Did they wash it away?' she asked as she stood up, her knees cracking from the exertion.

The clatter of the hanging beads in the living room drew her attention away from the scene. She took a step out of the bathroom to see who had joined her.

If any fashion label ever needed a posterchild for the "just got out of bed" look, Detective Inspector Bambridge was their man. For all the time Lawrence spent making sure she looked presentable, he had made no such effort.

His hair was normally a light shade of brown; however, it had been a while since it had been washed, which had turned it much darker. There was a hint of a beard forming along his jawline, but she guessed that it wasn't there intentionally. His eyes were sunken into pale features, and the bags underneath them betrayed his lack of sleep. The raincoat he wore, even though it was August, had once been a light beige colour. However, the rigors of time, and a lack of dry cleaning, had turned it a shade of dirty brown. The collar of his shirt was creased, and the top button was undone. A brown tie hung loose by his collarbone. His black trousers were too long in the leg and bunched over his scuffed brown shoes. He looked like if he had done any sleeping, it had most likely been in his clothes.

'Morning, Guv,' she greeted him with a smile.

'Mornin,' he grunted in response and then flicked on the lounge light. 'What we got?'

Lawrence stared at her partner for a second, he had just touched a part of the scene and wasn't wearing gloves. She wanted to castigate him for it, but she held her tongue. She'd already been yelled at by one middle-aged white man this morning. No point in provoking another; there was a body to be processed, and her senior officer to give the details to.

'Female victim,' she began. 'Hung up and bled out over the bathtub.'

'Was it one of ours that forced the door?' Bambridge asked, as he looked around the living room.

'Manager said he found it open.'

'Main bolt was locked when it was kicked in,' he stated. 'Someone really wanted to be in here.'

'The manager said that the boyfriend found her. Said he left in a hurry after finding the body. Looks like someone has gone through her belongings too.'

'What d'you think?' Bambridge asked, walking into the bathroom.

'Can't see the manager destroying his own property,'

Lawrence replied appearing in the doorway. 'But then kicking in a door would make a lot of noise. So, why didn't he come running as soon as heard the racket?'

'Could've been asleep?' Bambridge was standing in front of the body.

'It's possible. But it looks like he sleeps in the reception area, so he's bound to have heard it from there.'

'Manager's lying about something,' her superior officer stated, staring at the victim, his head tilted as he looked at her face.

Lawrence watched as his eyes moved all over her. His right hand rubbing his chin as he chewed on the inside of his left cheek. She wasn't sure whether she should tell him what she thought or let him assess the scene in silence.

This was one of the few times they had been at a scene together. They had been assigned to each other months ago, but only a few weeks into their partnership, riots had broken out across the city. Every department had been drafted into the policing of the disturbances and they had barely worked together since. This was due to Bambridge's wife losing her life during those crazy few days. He had been put on compassionate leave after her death. Although he had been back on shift for over a month now, he was rarely in the office.

'Looks like they cleaned up after themselves, Guv,' she offered, after the silence became too much for her to bear.

He nodded, turning on his own torch and shining it around the bathtub. 'Used bleach to wash it away,' he said, as he leant forward and looked down the plughole. He then took a closer look at the rope tied around the shower rail before moving his eyes to the victim's ankles.

'Knots are a bit shoddy.'

Lawrence took a step forward and had a look but couldn't see what Bambridge meant. 'Looks like they did the job,' she offered.

'They did,' he replied, 'but they didn't tie them off right.'

'Do you know much about knots?'

'Some.'

'How'd you learn that?' Lawrence was genuinely interested.

'Reading Melville.'

'He a knot expert?'

'No.' A single snort of laughter left his lungs. 'Looks like climbing rope.'

'Climbing rope?'

"Yeah, you know, for rock climbing.'

'Got ya,' she replied. She hadn't sounded convincing and waited for him to elaborate, but Bambridge seemed lost in his own thoughts. His eyes had glazed over, and his lips were pressed tightly together.

'You okay, Guv?' she asked.

'Seems excessive,' he said finally.

'What does?'

'All this,' he said, pointing to the ropes. 'Why go to all this trouble, just to wash all the blood away?'

'A ritual of some kind?' Lawrence speculated.

'Exactly that,' he offered with a wave of his finger. 'But rituals tend to have a purpose. A reason for the rigmarole.'

'I would have said it was to torture her, but there's no signs of it.'

'Just a single incision wound.'

'And the blow to the back of the head,' Lawrence offered, shining her torch at the back of the victim's head.

She could see that he was thinking it through. His eyes darting back and forth across the scene.

Was this the famed mind of D.I. Bambridge at work? The mind that had seen him reach top of his class in almost every field at the academy; that had seen him rise to the rank of Detective Inspector at a younger age than anyone in the history of the department. She hoped so, because in the time she spent as his partner, she'd seen nothing to back up that reputation. She had barely seen him do a full day's work, never mind solve any cases. The man was clearly going through some things, and in her opinion, shouldn't have been back on active duty. But who was she to make that judgement?

'She'd have bled out in no time,' Lawrence replied.

Bambridge nodded. 'Even more so being hung up like this.'

'Like she's at an abattoir,' she said absentmindedly.

'Exactly that,' he said, again, with another wave of his finger. 'Our suspect wanted her blood.'

'What for?'

Bambridge shrugged. 'Part of a ritual, like you said. Or to drink. To bathe in it. Could be anything. But I'd wager they took it with them.'

'There's a lot of blood in a human body, Guv,' Lawrence stated cynically.

'Never said the idea was perfect,' he replied and stepped out into the living room. 'Especially when our suspect didn't leave via the front door.'

Lawrence was about to press him on his statement when a new figure stepped through the beaded curtain.

'C.I.D.?' he asked.

'Yes,' Lawrence replied, 'D.C. Lawrence,' she added and held out her hand. 'This is D.I. Bambridge.'

Bambridge had moved across the room and was standing in front of the television. He ignored the new arrival as he squatted down by the window.

'Odell, forensic pathologist,' the newcomer replied, shaking Lawrence's outstretched hand. 'What we got?'

'Female victim,' Lawrence said, trying to hide her annoyance at how rude Bambridge had just been. 'Looks like she was hit over the back of the head. Strung up over the bath and then bled out from a puncture wound to the neck.'

'Thanks,' Odell nodded, and headed towards the bathroom. 'Anything stand out that we should concentrate on?'

'Check the plug hole,' Bambridge called over his shoulder. 'Need to know where her blood went.'

Two more forensic officers walked through the hanging beads carrying bags of equipment.

'Body's in here guys,' Odell waved to them.

'You'll need to check the window for prints as well,' Bambridge added as he examined the windowsill.

'We'll do a complete analysis of the flat, Detective,' Odell replied with a cold smile and then moved into the bathroom.

Lawrence moved closer to Bambridge, who continued to stare at the open single sash window. She tried to see what he was seeing, but nothing jumped out at her. 'What you got, Guv?' she asked.

'They went out the window,' Bambridge concluded as he stood up.

'How high up are we?' Lawrence asked as she glanced out the window. She could only just see the ground. 'That's a long way down.'

'Even further carrying a body's weight in blood.'

'You're that sure they took it with them?' Lawrence thought the idea a bit far-fetched, but Bambridge did have a point. Why string them up just to wash it all away? Forensics would hopefully shed some light on it.

He stared at her for a second and then shrugged. 'Let's check the alleyway,' he said as he pushed through the beads.

Downstairs, the uniformed officer looked about ready to punch Sheehan, and the manager's skin colour had changed to a deep puce.

'As I keep tellin' ya, I didn't get a good look at the guy,' Sheehan growled.

'Are you behaving yourself, Mr Sheehan?' Lawrence questioned firmly.

'This guy's a robot,' Sheehan replied, pointing at the young officer. 'What d'you know about the boyfriend? What d'you know about the boyfriend? Over and over. Like a fuckin' parrot.'

'What's out the back of the hotel?' Bambridge asked as he walked past the front desk.

'It speaks,' Sheehan sarcastically. 'Walked straight past me a minute ago.'

Bambridge stopped in his tracks and turned to face Sheehan. 'Answer the question,' he replied bluntly.

'How about you all answer some of mine first?' Sheehan said defiantly, his shoulders back and his head held high.

Walking up to Sheehan, Bambridge grabbed him by the collar and pushed him up against the wall. 'What's out the back of the hotel?'

Lawrence took a step towards them, unsure what to do. She had no love for Sheehan, but she had no tolerance for officers who abused their powers either. What Bambridge was doing could have been taken as police brutality. She glanced at the uniform, who looked just as uncertain as her.

'You can't treat me like this,' Sheehan said, as his pleading eyes danced back and forth between Lawrence and the uniform.

'Answer my question and I'll stop doing it.'

Lawrence could see Bambridge twist the collar, making it tighter around Sheehan's neck. She was just about to step in when the manager held his hands up in defeat. 'Alright,' he choked, 'alright, I'll tell you. There's a garden back there.'

'A garden?'

'Yeah, it barely gets used cos it's all overgrown. They're all like that.'

'What're all like that?'

'All the gardens on the block. None of them have been tended to. It's like a jungle back there.'

'Thank you,' Bambridge offered as he loosened his grip, but didn't let go. 'Oh, and is this your brothel?'

'It's not a brothel,' Sheehan shouted in Bambridge's face.

'There's no need to get aggressive, Mr Sheehan.'

Lawrence had seen enough and moved next to Bambridge with the intention of pulling him off the manager. But as she saw the fear in Sheehan's eyes, she decided to wait a moment.

'Look, I just run the place, alright?' Sheehan answered.

'Okay, so who's the landlord?' Bambridge asked as his gripped eased some more.

'Well, I am,' he replied flatly.

'And yet you say you just run the place. So, which is it, you run the place, or you own the place?' Bambridge pulled the collar tighter again.

'Both.'

'Both?'

'And neither.'

'Don't be playing with me,' Bambridge said as he pressed his hand into Sheehan's throat. 'The answers you give me now will define what kind of charges will be brought against you.'

Lawrence saw this as a good time to chime in. 'Help us find this boyfriend character,' she said with a soft tone, 'and we'll be able to be lenient with you.'

'But I didn't do anything.' Sheehan's eyes were everywhere. There was an inner turmoil he was having trouble with it. His lower lip taking a beating as he chewed on it.

'Well, help us out then,' she said calmly.

'We need the guy's name,' Bambridge added firmly.

'I don't know his name.'

'Don't give me that,' Bambridge snapped. 'He comes to your hotel all the time, and you're telling me you never caught his name?'

Sheehan remained silent, a worried look on his face.

'Your future is at stake here, Mr Sheehan,' Lawrence said.

'It's not that easy,' Sheehan blurted out.

'Seems easy to me. Tell us his name and you get to stay out of jail,' Bambridge said with a chuckle.

'You don't understand.' There was panic in Sheehan's words.

'Then help us to understand, Mr Sheehan,' Lawrence tried to sound reassuring.

'The people he works for…' he couldn't finish his sentence.

'What people?'

'He's just one of many,' Sheehan said, 'they change from week to week.'

'Who changes, Mr Sheehan?' Lawrence leant forward.

'If I tell you, I'm a dead man.'

'We can protect you, Mr Sheehan,' Lawrence added. 'We're the police.'

'You've no idea what they're capable of,' he shook his head. 'They've a whole network of people.'

'Organised crime?' Lawrence asked flatly.

'That's an understatement.'

'Yes or no, Mr Sheehan,' Bambridge barked.

'Alright, yes,' Sheehan barked back, his head hung as he accepted defeat. He took a deep breath before continuing. 'I let them have a room one time.'

'You let who have a room?' Bambridge pressed.

'Yeah, for rent. Then they wanted three,' Sheehan continued, ignoring the question. 'And before too long they'd booked every room.'

'Sounds good for business,' Bambridge commented.

'It was,' Sheehan sighed, 'at first. But then they started asking about the costs of maintaining the building. Next thing I know they're poking around the ownership rights. Before long I'm paying them to look after the place for me.'

'Were you threatened, Mr Sheehan?' Lawrence asked more softly.

'Constantly.' The fear was evident in his face.

'I guess that's why none of the guests will speak to us?' she asked in a more forceful tone.

'Of course, it is.'

'Are they all employed by these people?'

'I would have thought that was obvious.'

'That may be so but having your confirmation would help us with our enquiry.' Lawrence offered with a sympathetic tilt of her head. 'Need I remind you that a woman has been murdered.'

'I know she has,' he shrieked, his body shaking involuntarily. 'I'm trying not to end up in the same state.'

'We can help you with that,' Lawrence said. 'We just need to know if our victim was also employed by them?'

'Of course, she was.'

'So, who was this boyfriend character you spoke of?'

Bambridge asked as he loosened his grip.

'I don't know.'

'Don't give me that,' Bambridge replied. 'You must've spoken to the guy, on numerous occasions. What was he doing, collecting the earnings?'

Sheehan flinched at the comment.

'That's it, isn't it?' Bambridge stated. 'He was there to collect the earnings, and when she didn't answer the door, he kicked it in.'

Sheehan continued to cower.

'All we need is a name,' Lawrence offered.

'I don't know his name. I don't know any of their names.'

'They never called each other by name?' Bambridge asked suspiciously.

'They barely spoke English,' he replied.

'You need to give us something.'

'Look, they all worked for the Demir family, alright?'

'The Demir family?' Bambridge let go of Sheehan' collar and took a step back. 'The Demir family? You sure?'

'Yes.'

Bambridge started walking towards the exit again.

'Thank you for your time,' he offered over his shoulder. 'Constable, book him, under the Sexual Offences Act of 1956.'

'But…'

Bambridge cut him off. 'It is an offence to incite prostitution or control it for personal gain.'

'But I just run the place,' Sheehan pleaded.

The manager's whining voice was ignored as Bambridge carried on walking towards the door, leaving the young officer to start reading the Miranda rights.

'Surely, you could have handled that better, Guv?' Lawrence asked as she reached the front step of the hotel just behind him.

'Got an answer from him, didn't I?' he said over his shoulder.

Lawrence wasn't happy with his answer, or his methods. There had been a misuse of their powers, and they could get in trouble for it. But what was she to do, question a senior officer's procedures?

Should she report his actions to the Chief? What would that do to her reputation? Coppers who snitched on other coppers were usually shunned by their peers. She'd have to deal with the consequences if or when they came about.

Various refuse bins were scattered at the alleyway entrance. Lawrence followed Bambridge as he weaved his way between them. The end of the alleyway opened into a garden that looked just like Sheehan had described. He turned towards the building and looked up.

'That's a long way down,' Lawrence stated, as she followed Bambridge's gaze and found the open window belonging to their victim on the second floor.

'Yes, but the drainpipe runs right past the window,' he pointed out as he went down onto his haunches.

Even though the sun was trying to creep over the horizon, he still shone his torch down onto the floor. Aside from the weeds growing up between the paving slabs the area looked normal. But his beam soon rested on one spot.

Some of the plant life had been disturbed. One large weed lay on the slant, its thick stalk snapped halfway down.

'Something flattened this thistle,' he stated.

'Could've been someone who lives here?' Lawrence posed. 'Or when the bins were last collected.'

'No,' Bambridge pointed his torch towards a clear

path that had been trodden through the weeds, 'that's the regular route. Plus, this break is new. There's still moisture in the tear.'

'Okay, so, they dropped down from the window,' Lawrence conceded. 'Which way did they go once they landed?' She shone her torch in both directions.

Bambridge stood and turned to look at the surrounding gardens.

Unlike the horizon, the sun wasn't anywhere near making an appearance in the hotel's back garden yet. The buildings cast the gardens into more shadows than the time of day would have suggested. Yet, even in the poor light she could see just how overgrown and uninviting it looked. Bambridge started to walk into it.

'Guv, you sure you wanna be doing that now?'

What she really meant was, I don't want to be doing that right now. Give it a few hours, once the sun was overhead, and a change of clothes and she'd happily go searching through this micro jungle.

He got a few steps into the garden before his right foot slipped on something. For a second, she thought he was going down, but his arms went out and he managed to steady himself.

'We'll have a look later,' he said as he stepped back from the foliage.

'Maybe, we can get hold of some CCTV footage?' she offered as they stepped back round to the front of the hotel.

'Doubtful,' he replied, looking up and down the road, 'can't see any cameras.' He pulled his car keys out of his pocket.

'We done, Guv?' Lawrence asked as she looked down at the keys.

'Looks that way.'

'Can we have a run through everything before you head off?'

'Sure.' Bambridge was all business. 'Someone strung her up, bled her out, and then climbed out of window. Need to follow up on this boyfriend. My guess would be, he's her pimp. Probably who went through her handbag. We also need to investigate this Demir family.'

This was the most responsive she'd seen him since his return. Maybe the scene had sparked something? Awakening a lost curiosity, perhaps? However, there was one thing he'd overlooked that came to mind. The rope. If it was a specific type of climbing rope, then they might be able to track the manufacturer? Why hadn't he mentioned it?

Further down the street Sheehan was being escorted into the back of a patrol car. Maybe he knew more than he was letting on? It couldn't hurt to go with him to the station and see if she could get anything more out of him.

Bambridge opened his car door, and then paused. He looked up at the hotel and then dropped down into the driver's seat. 'Nothing scenic about it,' he mumbled to himself, then turned his gaze to Lawrence. 'You need a lift?'

She shook her head. 'I'm gonna get a ride with Sheehan,' she pointed to a patrol car. 'Might be able to get more info from him on the way.'

Bambridge nodded absently.

'You're welcome to join me at the station, Guv.'

He shook his head, a grimace on his face.

'I'll see you in a few hours then?' she asked, as he started to close the door. A nod was all she got before it shut.

Lawrence waved at the patrol car.

'Can I get a ride with you?' she asked. The two officers

in the front seats looked at each other, one of them shrugged, then so did the other. 'I'll sit in the back,' she added after they'd agreed.

'Just keep an eye on him ma'am,' one of the officers said as she sat down next to Sheehan.

'Oh, I'm not gonna get any trouble from him. Am I, Mr Sheehan?'

'I ain't got nothin' to say to you,' Sheehan replied as he stared out the window.

'Oh, come now, Mr Sheehan, you've been so helpful. Why stop now?' The hotel manager continued to stare out of the window ignoring her. 'We've got plenty of time for you to change your mind.'

The early morning light cast an eerily grey tone to everything. The sun's rays hadn't quite brought the city to life yet, but there were people about. There were always people about.

She had planned on pestering Sheehan for the whole journey. However, the rumble of the car engine made her instantly sleepy, so she closed her eyes for just a second.

Chapter Three

Bambridge watched Lawrence get into the patrol car in the rear-view mirror. As the vehicle passed by his window, he considered following them back to the station, but in truth he didn't want to.

Despite his years in homicide, and all the horrific things he had seen, this victim had sent a chill over his body. The scene had been nothing new, just another corpse, and even though the cleanliness had been a welcome change from the usual mess, something about the scene was off-putting. Was it the cleanliness amongst the chaos?

Deep down he knew it wasn't the spotlessness that had spooked him. It was something else. Something that had been occurring with alarming regularity of late. For the briefest of seconds, the body had looked like her, and even though he knew it wasn't her, panic had set in, and it had taken all his strength to not collapse on the floor of that bathroom.

Natalie had been dead for almost a year, but he still saw her.

He saw her in the colour of a passing woman's hair, or the way they wore a similar piece of clothing. The smell of a particular brand of deodorant, or the scent of their perfume. He would be reminded of her by a particular song on the radio, or the poster of a movie they'd seen together. On each occasion these memories came flooding back to him his pulse would race, and a smile would break out, before he realised that she was gone. The smile would be replaced by crippling feelings of despair and an overwhelming sense of hopelessness.

He'd been told it would get easier; that the pain he felt

would ease, and the emptiness would one day be filled, but he hadn't seen a change. Even in her absence, she continued to play a massive part in his life. If anything, her absence emphasised the empty vessel that was his life.

He'd also been told he should think about the good times, that he should find joy in all the moments they had spent together, but all he felt was sorrow, because those times were gone and wouldn't be coming back.

Others had said he should immerse himself in his work. Twelve months ago, he would have agreed with them wholeheartedly. Work had been something he'd thrived on for years. A reason to get up and leave the house every day. But now, it was just another thing that reminded him of her.

Natalie had been the original reason he'd joined the force. In the early stages of their relationship, she had decided she was going to sign up. With no real goals or drive of his own he'd gone along with her. From that moment they had shared a meteoric rise up through the ranks. A rise that had seen them both reach the very top of their respective areas of law enforcement. Him within the field of Homicide, and her investigating corruption within the corporate world.

But now, every second he spent at the station, or in a police car, or in the presence of anyone in the uniform, all he could think about was her. The hours spent around the police were torturous.

His life had been turned on its head, and he couldn't see a way out of it.

He had tried different ways to make him forget. Ways to numb the pain. To switch off the constant thoughts. But none of them had worked. Alcohol had just made everything worse, heightening the emotions tenfold. And even though it would have been easy enough to get hold of any drug he wished; he just couldn't bring himself to partake.

Tobacco on the other hand had found its way into his life. He hated every moment of it, but the process of rolling, lighting, and inhaling the dreadful substance was an effective way of diverting his attention. If only for a minute or two. The horrendous aftertaste, the smell it left on his person, and the ragged condition it left his lungs always felt like punishment. A way of bringing him closer to death. One cigarette at a time, nearer to Natalie.

The thought of smoking filled him with desire to pollute his lungs. The question was, did he have any on him?

His mind had been wandering so much lately that he couldn't even remember how he'd arrived at the scene. Clearly, he'd driven, but from where? And what had he been doing before?

He patted his pockets for a tobacco pouch but couldn't find anything. He did find a lighter though. He was pretty sure that he'd just bought some today. But was that today, or had it been another time?

Buying some more would have been the sensible choice. But deep down he didn't want to. He didn't want to smoke, but his body was telling him that he did. He must have been doing it for so long that his body now needed it. And it needed it now.

Cursing himself, he glanced down at the ashtray by the gearstick. Flipping the lid open he stared down at the pile of bent and broken cigarettes. None of them looked like something he could use, but he knew he needed to find something.

So, he began fishing around in the ash. With each sweep through of the grey powder he felt his heart start beating just that little bit faster. And with each stubbed out butt end he picked up and watched fall apart in his fingers his teeth ground harder together.

He dragged his fingers through the dirt again, and sure enough the remnants of a half smoked roll up appeared in his hands.

The joy he felt was swiftly followed by an extreme bout of self-loathing. He looked down at his ash covered hands and wondered what he had become?

He looked out of the car window at the building he had just left, and the streets surrounding it. They looked even bleaker in the early morning light. Another hideous corner of this vast city.

The ash on his hands, the dull morning streets, the body of a woman inside those walls, all seemed fitting. A visual representation of his current state of mind.

He needed to get away from this place, and never come back, but he knew that wouldn't be the case.

They would need to come back. He expected Sheehan to be unhelpful, especially now he was under arrest. Plus, he doubted they would get anything out of the people staying in the hotel. If the manager was telling the truth, then they would all be too scared to speak.

The only positive he could see was that the short street was relatively quiet. So, there was a chance with so many people living on top of each other, in such a noiseless environment, that someone may have seen or heard something. Time would tell on that thought process.

Getting away and lighting up were all that mattered right now. But where to go?

There were errands he could run.

Places and people he could look into.

Plenty of things to be getting on with.

Chapter Four

Lawrence snapped out of her snooze as the engine turned off. Her initial thought was whether she'd snored or not. Sat up straight, with your head leaning back was a guaranteed way of making some noise. Sheehan was sure to let her know if she had. But as they got out of the car, he remained silent. Perhaps she'd got away with it?

The paranoia she'd felt about her sleep was instantly replaced by a new bout brought on by the sight of the station. She knew that it wasn't the building which had her fretting, but rather the people inside it.

Since Bambridge's return from compassionate leave he'd managed to piss off most of the people in the office, showing a level of disdain for the job that hadn't been there before. Although even before she was assigned to work with him, she'd heard about his reputation of being a bit difficult; that his social skills left a lot to be desired. But he was a good copper, so that had all been overlooked. However, blaming the entire police department for the death of his wife, had not. Questioning the ability of the top brass, Bambridge had even gone so far as to yell at the commissioner during the funeral.

She and Bambridge hadn't been partners for long, and because of this, Lawrence didn't really know what to do when he had erupted. The partner thing to do would have been to side with him and have his back. However, as she hadn't felt that bond, she had kept quiet. Whether he resented her for it was a worry that she carried around with her.

The whole police force had gone through a tough time during the riots, and the subsequent issues that had occurred after. But his words at the funeral, even though they'd been cast from the lips of a grieving husband, had created an unpleasant atmosphere. One that followed them both around. People weren't aiming their malice at her; they were just avoiding her, because of her association with him.

Once she had overseen the booking in of Sheehan, she made her way to her desk.

As she entered her department, a new sense of dread started to rise inside her. This anxiety wasn't about being judged by passing officers, or about the whispered comments she'd hear. This was about the people she shared her desk space with.

Detective Inspector Canham watched her approach from over his gold framed glasses. The older man kept his appearance neat. His greying hair was cut close to his scalp, his face was clean shaven, and his breath smelt of the mints on which he was always sucking. He made a show of looking presentable and expected the same from his colleagues. His scrutiny of her outfits had a habit of making her feel uncomfortable. So much so, that it had made her put more effort into looking good. His gaze would regularly have her on edge from the moment she walked into the office. His old-fashioned methods were also disconcerting, and she'd often have to bite her tongue with some of his terminology. He was only a few years off retirement, so she would just have to tolerate him until then.

'Mornin, Lawrence,' Canham bellowed in his booming Scottish accent.

She could feel his eyes searching her wardrobe, trying to find something to criticise her about, and she hoped he wouldn't find nothing.

'Morning, Guv,' she replied, and waited for a remark,

but nothing came. 'Morning, Sarge,' she added to the man sat at the desk next to Canham.

Detective Sergeant Quinnell held his hand up in response and returned to his newspaper. It was nothing more than she expected from him. He clearly didn't care what Canham thought of him. His lackadaisical approach to his job must have driven the old detective mad. However, they had been partners for so many years Canham had stopped trying to adjust his mannerisms. The tall Sergeant's appearance was always presentable, albeit somewhat more lacklustre than Canham and Lawrence's efforts. It was this element, the neatness of the other man's existence that kept the Scotsman off his back.

'You catch an early one?' Canham asked, as he continued to stare at her.

'Something like that,' she replied and sat down at her desk.

With the mention of the early start, she could feel the lack of sleep in her limbs, but it wasn't anything unusual. Long nights and days, along with early starts were a regular occurrence.

'Chief wants to see you and Bams,' Canham added as he finally looked away from her.

Lawrence had sensed Bambridge hated that nickname, and she almost called Canham out on it, but she held her tongue. 'D'you know what about?' she said instead.

'You guys been roughin' up suspects?' Quinnell asked absently as he put his feet up on his desk and leant back further in his chair.

How could he possibly know that? She'd not long come back from the scene, and it had only been the two of them, the uniform, and Sheehan who'd seen Bambridge's scare tactics. She knew that word got around the department fast, particularly word about her and her partner, but this was just ridiculous.

Perhaps Sheehan had spoken to someone once she'd left? But even if that were the case, she had only just come from the booking in desk. How could that kind of information have reached Quinnell so quickly?

Had someone contacted him and shared the information? If they had, what was the purpose? To keep an eye on her perhaps, but to what ends?

She understood why the rest of the force might be giving her a wide berth, what with the company she kept. But why would members of own department be spying on her? If they even were spying. If she went with what was driving her anxiety, and creating such paranoia, it was because they considered her a token appointment. Someone that they'd been lumped with because she ticked all the right boxes. Being female and black sure did help with the equality quota. Because of this she assumed they wanted to keep an eye on her. Looking for the slightest error, so that they could get her moved on.

But were her anxieties warranted?

By her own account she wasn't anything exceptional. Nothing like the record-breaking prodigy Bambridge had been in his time at the academy. But then she didn't consider herself a fifth wheel either. Time would tell which one she was, and where her career would take her.

'And what does he really want to see us about?' she asked Canham, ignoring her sergeant's comments.

'Wouldnee say,' Canham answered. 'But that partner of yours best show up soon. Chief didn't look happy.'

Lawrence looked at the time. It was later than she thought. Worry started to form in her belly. She had spoken to the chief on a few occasions, but she had never been called into his office. Could she go see him on her own? That would only bring a series of questions as to where Bambridge was. Questions she couldn't answer.

What could the chief want though?

Quinnell's comments about being rough with a suspect were justified, whether he'd meant them or not. But trying to defend Bambridge's actions would be hard. Especially, if he wasn't present to help with the defending.

It seemed unlikely it was related to the new case. A murdered sex worker wasn't something the chief would get involved with. She'd find out soon enough.

Right now, though, she had to get Bambridge here. She pulled out her mobile phone and dialled his number. After the tenth ring tone she hung up.

Could she go and get him? That'd take more time than she had. Having one of them in the building was better than neither of them. She didn't know what to do.

As she considered her next move, her phone started ringing. The caller ID said Bambridge.

'Guv!' she answered, and without waiting for a reply continued, 'get down to the station as soon as you can. The chief wants to see us.' She tried to hide the concern in her voice but was unsuccessful.

On the other end, she could hear movement, but Bambridge still hadn't said a word.

What had he been up to in the past few hours? Had he gone home to get some sleep? Or maybe he'd fallen asleep in his car. The state he'd been in earlier would certainly suggest the latter.

'D'you need me to send a squad car over?' Still no answer.

Had he fallen back asleep?

'I'll get myself in,' he answered finally.

'How long we talkin' about, Guv?' Again, there was

silence on the other end of the line. 'Guv? You there?'

'Yes!' he replied, his voice going up an octave. 'Be there in an hour.'

The line went dead.

'An hour?' she was beside herself. What was she to do for an hour? It was a long time to avoid the chief. She'd also need to avoid the rest of the Homicide department. Listening to Canham and Quinnell berate her about Bambridge's absence sounded awful. But how could she kill an hour?

As she stifled a yawn, her stomach rumbled; an answer presented itself.

She could have gone to the canteen, but the coffee they served was an abomination. The food wasn't a whole lot better. The café round the corner at least served palatable coffee, it was miles better than the rubbish in the canteen.

She snuck out the building and made her way round to Sükür's. The Turkish owners were always very deferential to anyone they recognised from the station, and besides, Lawrence liked the thick, dark sweetness of Turkish coffee.

As she waited for her, coffee and a sucuklu yumurta, which everyone at the station just called the spicy sausage and egg sandwich, she knew her mind should be on the case. However, all she could think about was Bambridge, and what state he'd be in when he finally showed up.

He'd looked a mess earlier, but that could be overlooked due to the ungodly hour. She'd managed to do it though, and it wasn't the first time he'd shown up looking like that. She would have been happy with him just showing up in a clean shirt.

As she folded back the paper bag to take a bite of the sandwich, she put her partner to the back of her thoughts and started running through what she could look up at her desk. Most of the information they were waiting for would come from the pathologist, but there were a couple of things she could investigate.

Cynical eyes watched her as she sat at her desk with the remains of her breakfast.

'Any sign of him yet?' Canham asked, as he tapped away on his computer.

'He's on his way,' she replied, sitting down.

'It'll be nice of him to show up,' Quinnell offered from behind his paper.

Lawrence looked across at the detective sergeant. She wanted to mention how hard he was working; but what was the point? Quinnell knew how hard he worked and didn't care what anyone thought of it. Instead, she turned on her computer and typed into a search engine: climbing rope.

Her screen came alive with hundreds of choices. All assorted brands, colours, and lengths were available to buy online. She added black and red to the search and saw the options greatly reduced. However, there were still multiple options and all of them looked like the rope that had been used on the victim. That avenue would need a lot more research.

She changed windows and put the Demir family into the work database. The system gave its usual response and started buffering. The department's internal search engines left a lot to be desired. In hindsight, she should have done this search before she got her breakfast.

'Lookin fresh as ever, Bams,' Canham called out, as Bambridge appeared at her side.

'I see Hadrian's Wall failed again,' Bambridge replied without any hint of humour.

Lawrence knew that Canham was proud of his heritage and any jibes about it would shut him up. Like clockwork, the Scotsman turned and concentrated on his screen.

'How goes it, Guv,' she greeted her senior officer and turned to face him.

'Fine,' he replied as he looked down at her, confused.

She hadn't meant it as a question, just as a casual greeting, but he hadn't seen it that way. He stared at her waiting for her next question, which she didn't have.

Her computer pinged telling her that the search was completed. She felt relief as she turned back to her screen and opened the results.

Her hopes of getting a lead from the Demir family faded as she saw the list of casefiles. As she scrolled down the page and began to lose count of the open cases against the family, she knew that the boyfriend or pimp avenue was going nowhere.

'Not sure we'll get anything from the info Sheehan gave us, Guv,' she said with an air of defeat.

'Really? he asked as he leant on the table next to her.

She stopped scrolling so that he could read the multiple files on the screen. They ranged from drug arrests, assaults, suspected murders, possible connections to human trafficking and the sex trade.

Bambridge took control of her mouse and opened a file that was titled prostitution rings. Before he started scrolling through the file details, he hovered the curser over the warning at the very top of the file. In capital letters it stated that no officers should approach any Demir family members without informing their superiors, and that if they were to approach said crime syndicate that they should do it with back up.

'I knew I recognised the name,' Bambridge stated, as he let go of the mouse and stepped back. 'Not much point in speaking to them about a murder investigation.'

'There isn't?' she replied, cynically. Deep down she knew he was right, but she wanted to hear his reasoning for it first.

'Nope,' he offered with a shrug. 'Question them about a murder and they'll shut down instantly.'

She couldn't argue with him because she'd come to the same conclusion. The moment she had seen the pages of open cases against them, she'd known that path of investigation was dead.

'And besides, they didn't do it,' he added. 'Whoever went out the window did.'

'Where does that leave us then?' Lawrence considered mentioning looking into the type of rope their suspect had used, but she decided not to. If he continued doing what he'd been doing since his return to duty, then he'd disappear in the next few hours anyway. Why waste her breath telling him about something he'd just ignore? No, she would investigate that one on her own.

'Having to speak to the chief,' he answered with a sigh.

She caught a quick look at him. He was wearing the same clothes as earlier, which meant that he hadn't been home to change, and it didn't look like he'd been asleep, so where had he been?

She pushed Bambridge's wardrobe and movements out of her mind as she followed him to the office of Detective Chief Inspector Stone. Bambridge knocked on the door and waited for a response.

'Yes?' was the call from the other side.

Bambridge opened the door.

'Good morning, Chief,' he said once they were inside the office.

Stone was busy typing on his keyboard and didn't look up as they entered.

It was rumoured he never stood up from his desk. At only five feet eight inches, he had only just managed to get onto the force back in the day, and it had been something that he had been ridiculed about throughout his career.

He kept his head shaved and his face clean cut. The suits he wore were practical, his shirts were always pressed, and his shoes gleamed. The fact that he was obsessed with his work had got him where he was, and he expected nothing but the same from the people that worked under him.

'Good morning, Chief,' Lawrence added her own greeting.

'Good morning.' Stone shuffled some papers on his desk, glanced at his screen once more, and then looked at them. 'How'd your scene look, this morning?'

Lawrence could see tension in her superior's shoulders, and she presumed that it was about the way that Bambridge had handled Sheehan.

'Something wrong, Chief?' Bambridge asked. 'Manager make a complaint, did he? Because he was being a pain.'

'Just give me a summary.' Stone held up his hands and pointed to the two seats in front of his desk.

They both sat.

'The victim was restrained and bled out over the bathtub,' Bambridge said bluntly.

Lawrence knew that Bambridge had little regard for much right now but making the boss angry was a bad idea. Particularly, when she was sat opposite him.

'I'm going to need a bit more than that,' Stone replied, in sarcastic tones 'D.C. Lawrence. Perhaps you can give me your thoughts.'

'This wasn't your average murder,' she began, her

words sounding corny in her ears. 'The perpetrator was methodical in not just the way they killed the victim, but also in the way they cleaned up the scene.'

'They?' Stone asked. 'No theory on gender yet?'

'Not yet,' she replied. 'Although, the victim was strung up over the bathtub, which would require some strength. Not impossible for a woman, however.'

'Do many women frequent prostitutes?' Stone asked. 'Assuming the victim was a sex worker?'

'Looks that way,' Bambridge offered.

'Not as a rule, sir,' Lawrence replied to his first question. 'But it's not unknown.'

'They weren't there for sex,' Bambridge added.

'Evidently,' Stone replied, 'You got an I.D. on the victim yet?'

'We're waiting for the lab to get back to us on that,' Lawrence replied. 'The victim's bags had been emptied.'

'Lab should tell us if they took the blood with them,' Bambridge added.

'What makes you say that?' Stone eyed them both intently. 'Could the blood not just be down the drain?'

'That's what the lab results will tell us,' Bambridge stated.

'So why are you saying what you think happened before you have the facts?' Stone stared at Bambridge.

She knew that he was right. You could always theorise on what had happened, but until you had the facts, you should never let what you thought drive your investigation.

'Because that's what they did,' Bambridge answered.

'You're that confident?' Stone addressed Lawrence this time, but Bambridge answered

'Yes,'

'Would you care to elaborate?' Stone glanced in

Lawrence's direction. 'Or do you have magical powers that none of us know about?'

'You wouldn't go to all that effort just to wash it away,' Bambridge asserted, without waiting for Lawrence to speak.

'Oh, you wouldn't?' Stone snapped back.

'No.' Bambridge replied, seeming to not notice the annoyance in Stone's voice. 'It was a ritual. Why render someone unconscious, stringing them up, and then make a precision cut to the jugular just to wash the blood away? Why not just kill her on the bed? And why go to the trouble of cleaning up after yourself? '

'Could it just have been a sex act gone wrong?' Stone didn't sound convinced.

Lawrence wasn't buying it either.

'Not likely,' Bambridge slouched back in his chair.

'Why do you say that?'

'Because if it was an accident, why jump out the window? Why not just leave by the front door?'

'People do strange things when they're scared.' Stone shrugged, dismissively.

'So, why'd they clean up?' Bambridge persisted.

Lawrence could see the power struggle taking place between them. Their stares back and forth to one another could have cut through marble. She considered interjecting but decided against it. Being sat next to Bambridge was enough to get her into trouble.

'Guilt?' Stone offered with a shrug.

'Not likely,' Bambridge replied as he shifted in his chair. They continued to hold each other's gaze. 'What's the deal, Stone? Why so many questions over a dead pro? Just get to the point.'

'That's D.C.I Stone to you,' he kept his voice calm, but there was steel in the tone. 'And what point would that be, Bambridge?'

'That's D.I Bambridge to you, sir.'

Lawrence cringed at the retort.

They stared at one another again, and it was Stone who gave in first.

'Why were you so forceful with, Mr Sheehan?' Stone asked.

'He wasn't being forthcoming.'

'Yes, that can be somewhat tedious,' Stone replied with a cold stare. 'But to use excessive force isn't what we do here.'

'Got some information out of him though.'

'And is it anything you can use?'

The room went quiet.

Lawrence glanced at Bambridge and could see that he didn't have an answer, so she jumped in. 'Mr Sheehan gave us the name of the Demir family, sir.'

'The Turkish crime syndicates?' Stone asked cautiously.

'Yes, sir.'

'Well, that'll lead you nowhere. Under no circumstances are the Demir's to be approached or investigated in relation to this incident. I don't want any comeback rebounding on this division from either Vice, or Serious and Organised Crime units, do you hear? What else did you get off him?'

Lawrence had nothing to say, and Bambridge didn't answer either.

'So, you slapped someone around with little or no return?'

Again, Bambridge didn't answer.

Lawrence wanted to say something, but what? The chief was right, Bambridge had been overly violent, and they had nothing to show for it.

'The next time you raise your hands to someone, detective, you best have a valid reason for it. Because the last thing this department needs is a brutality lawsuit on our hands. So, do me a favour and be more reserved next time.' Stone waved for them to leave and turned back to his computer.

Bambridge groaned as he got out of the chair and walked out without saying another word.

Lawrence wanted to speak to the chief about her partner. She wanted to tell him that she thought he shouldn't be back at work. That he was clearly not in the right mental state to be back in the line of duty, but she didn't know how to broach the subject. Instead, she just followed Bambridge, closing the door behind her.

'What now, Guv?' Lawrence asked as they walked away from Stone's office.

He glanced at her, but she could see that he wasn't listening.

'Maybe the pathologist will have a name by now?' she added after a short pause.

'I doubt it,' he offered distractedly and strode off ahead of her.

She needed to do something. She couldn't leave it at that. Whoever that woman was needed some form of justice. Even if it was just to notify her family of her death. But that wasn't enough for her. Someone must have seen or heard something. She doubted she'd get anything out of the other residents at the hotel.

'Shall we head back to the hotel then? Start knocking on some doors?' she shouted as she jogged to catch up with her partner.

Bambridge nodded but she could see that he hadn't listened again. 'I've gotta run an errand, so I'll meet you there.'

Before she could respond, Bambridge had started walking away. She began to say something but thought better of it. What could she say to him? *No, we can't go separately.* She'd get more done without him anyway.

Now she just needed to get back to the Scenic Hotel.

Chapter Five

Taking a train north Lawrence was thankful that rush hour had passed. The space available with fewer people on board had helped to reduce the heat in the carriage. Yet, her shirt still ended up stuck to her, sweat rolling down the back of her neck.

There wasn't much difference in temperature once she was above ground. It wasn't as humid on the street, but it was still hot as hell.

The hotel looked different in daylight, just as unappealing, but different no less.

As she entered the makeshift reception area, she was greeted by the same uniformed officer she'd dealt with earlier.

'You still here?' she asked in a jovial manner.

He nodded tiredly and then returned her smile. 'My shift change should be along any minute.'

'Good,' she replied as she looked around the hallway and then at him. 'I've realised I never caught your name.'

'It's Hackford,' he answered.

'Good to meet you, Constable, I'm D.C. Lawrence, did you manage to talk to any of the other guests?'

Hackford shook his head. 'No, ma'am,' he stated. 'We knocked on every door, but no one answered.'

'No one?'

'No, ma'am. We tried each door multiple times and got nothing on each occasion.'

'And no one has left any of the rooms?'

'No, ma'am,' he said with a confident shake of the head. 'We were beginning to wonder if there was even anyone staying here.'

'That leaves us with nothing in the way of witnesses?'

'Yes, ma'am.'

The question wasn't aimed at Hackford, for she already knew the answer. Anyone staying in the hotel was being paid by the Demir's, and they were all too scared to do any talking. Fear would be keeping them silent.

She smiled at Hackford. 'Well, thank you, Constable. I guess I'll have to see if any of the neighbours saw anything,' she said with an air of resignation.

Door to doors had never been her favourite part of the job. In truth she hated them. Particularly, when they were in a rough neighbourhood such as this one. She could probably expect more than a few choice words from the residents. The abuse about being a police officer she could handle; it came with the job. It was the harsh words about the colour of her skin she knew were coming which were making her nervous. But she had to do it. They were an integral part of any investigation and cases had been solved with the help of eyewitness accounts.

Although, it would have been nice to have someone helping her, she knew that all she really needed was her notepad. It had saved her more than once. A detail she'd jotted down could spark a memory that had escaped her and help move a case along. So, by writing down a summary of each person she spoke to, the monotony of the day wouldn't be for nothing. She hoped.

But as she approached the building next door to the Scenic Hotel, she couldn't help but wonder what sort of errand Bambridge had to go on at this time of day?

There was no point stewing over it though, as he wasn't here, and all these doors weren't going to knock themselves.

She would have liked to say that the next few hours passed in a blur. However, that hadn't been the case. Each knock at a door and been just as excruciating as the last one. With each door getting their own little set of details in her notepad. She had considered leaving some of the more colourful language out of her writings but decided against it. She wanted to remember what each of them had said.

Sat at the end of the street, reading through the notes, she could sense that the eyewitness angle was about to go cold.

Block One: The Scenic hotel. No one is talking. Demir family got them all hushed.

Block Two:

Flats one through five no answer.

Flat six told to Fuck off through the door.

Flat seven no answer.

Flat eight. Magda Dabrowski. White Female. Polish. Early Twenties. New mother. Infant child on her arm. Husband at work. Moved here from Poznan. Complained about noisy foxes in the garden. Asked what we were investigating. Nice lady.

Block Three:

Flat one. Dedge. White Male. British. Mid Fifties. No first or second names given. Unemployed. Music playing too loud. Had bad hearing from listening to music too loud. Asked if we were investigating the hotel. Asked why he was asking. Said that he a lot of dodgy people come and go. Not his sort of buzz, but whatever gets you off. Pressed the issue. I ain't no grass.

Flats two and three no answer.

Flat four. No name given. Black Male. Teenager. Got called Pig and door slammed in face.

Flat five dogs barking through the door. No answer.

Flats six to eight no answer.

Midway through, her phone started ringing, it was Bambridge.

'Hello, Guv,' she answered, forcing a smile. 'How's it going?'

'Fine,' was his terse reply. 'Where are you?'

'Doing door to doors near the scene.' She waited for a response, but all she could hear was rustling on the other end of the line. 'Guv, you still there?'

'Yep,' came his response. 'Where specifically are you?'

'Sat outside the last mansion on the terrace.'

'Where?'

'The other end of the block from the hotel.'

'Be there soon.'

She stared at her phone for a moment, baffled by the actions of her superior. Firstly, by the fact that he was going to make an appearance at the scene. And secondly, that he was going to arrive after all the hard work had been done. Had she discovered anything then she might have been worried that he'd take all the credit for what she'd found out.

Maybe she did have something in the notes she'd made? She continued reading whilst she waited for Bambridge to show up.

Block Four:
Flats one to four no answer.
Flat five. Mandeep Deshmukh. Asian/Indian Female. Mother of four. Complained about the teenagers in the gardens. They make a lot of noise and use very bad language. Asked if we were investigating the teenagers. Thought they were in a gang. Cooking smelt amazing.
Flat six no answer.
Flat seven. George Opio. Black Male. Ugandan. Early thirties. Very tall. Body builder perhaps? Didn't give job description. English wasn't great. Asked what we were investigating. Tried to ask me out. Was quite forceful in his

approaches.

Flat Eight. No name given. Elderly White Female. Called me a Nosy Coon and spat at my feet. Wretched lady.

Block Five:

Flat one. Got called a Nigger Pig through the door.

Flat two. Got called a Dyke, a Nigger, and a Cunt through the door. Aggressive banging from inside the flat.

Flat three no answer.

Flat four asked to show ID. Didn't believe warrant card was real. Told to Fuck off.

Flats five to eight no answer.

Block Six:

Flat one. Sarah Goodwin. White Female. Early thirties. Shift worker. Stacks shelves at local supermarket in the evenings. Studying during the day. Lives with boyfriend who was at work. He is a trainee nurse.

Flat two. Howard and Elaine Schultz. Retired Jewish couple. In their seventies. Asked if we were investigating the disturbance last night. What disturbance? Sounded like there was a fight in the garden. Could have just been teenagers though. Sounded like punches.

Flat three no answer.

Flat four told to Fuck off through the door.

Flat five. Leon Wallace. White Male. Mid-twenties. Shift worker. Didn't say where he worked. Medical perhaps? Clothing looked like a nurse. Had badges on his shirt. Just got in from work. Asked about what we were investigating. Hadn't heard anything.

Flat six. Young lady. Didn't give name. Thought I was calling to fix the plumbing. Explained who I was, and she got scared. Clearly on drugs. Hallucinogenic of some kind. Didn't know what time of day it was. Made sure she was okay and moved on.

Flat seven no answer.

Flat eight. Samuel Jarvis. White Male. Early sixties. Retired

Police Officer. Wanted to talk shop. Asked about what I was working on. Asked if it was about the hotel. Knew that it was a brothel. Had called multiple times but nothing had been done. Angry at the lack of police presence in the area. Very angry.

Flicking back over the notes brought a few feelings out. Anger at first. But then she felt pity for them. Pity at how closed minded their lives were. The fact that people still spoke like that in such a multicultural city was baffling. She'd faced it her whole life and would most likely have too for many more years. She just needed to get a tougher exterior.

After a time Bambridge's car appeared at the end of the street and pulled up in front of her. Where had he been?

'So, what'd I miss?' he asked after he'd locked his car.

'Not a lot,' she replied. 'I haven't checked the gardens yet, but a few of the residents said the local kids hang out back there. Plus, a couple of the residents said they heard what they thought was a fight back there last night. Might be worth a look now that it's not five in the morning?'

'Worth a look,' he agreed, 'Anything else?'

She glanced at her notepad again. 'Sounds like there's foxes in the gardens as well.'

'Anything useful? What'd the residents have to say?'

'Well, the ones that weren't hurling abuse at me were all curious about what we were investigating. A few of them guessed that it was about the hotel.'

'They know what the hotel was?'

'Some,' she said with a nod. 'One in particular, a Samuel Jarvis. Said he was a former copper. Was pretty angry about a brothel being on his street. Said he'd called it in multiple times and had no response.'

'Worth looking into,' Bambridge said whilst staring

back towards the hotel.

'D'you recognise the name?'

Bambridge shook his head.

'Other than that, we've got a mixture of young and old people. Some of them employed, most of them not. A few crazies, but nothing out of the ordinary for a parade of houses like this.'

'What d'you mean by that?' Bambridge looked at the terrace trying to see what she meant.

'I grew up in a place like this,' she answered with a shrug. 'A much bigger place than this, but the residents are much the same. Angry people who think the world owes them something. When in truth it doesn't owe them a thing. You wanna make something of your life living in a place like this, there's only one way you do it. By your own willpower. Because no one around you is gonna help. They're more likely to rob you.'

'This negativity doesn't sound like you,' he replied, turning to face her for the first time.

'I'm sorry, Guv,' she offered with a smile. 'Places like this just take me back. And to nowhere good.'

'Can't let it cloud your judgment,' he replied firmly.

She wanted to ask him what right he had telling her about judgments being clouded, but there was no point. He seemed like he was currently in a good place, so it was probably wise to utilise him.

'You're right,' she said after a pause. 'So, like I said, the last thing to do is check the gardens.'

'Fighting could've just been the teenagers,' he stated in a tone that implied he didn't want to go back there.

'D'you not think it's worth following up?' She heard the change in her own voice and winced. Why was she getting angry?

'Any kid that lives here ain't talking to the police,'

Bambridge offered with a shrug. 'You lived in a place like this, you said. You should know.'

He was right, you wouldn't get a word from any of them.

'Should probably look back there anyway, right?' she stated, equally firmly.

Bambridge visibly shrunk with her words, but after some inner turmoil he agreed with a nod. 'Outside of the lab results, and this ex-copper, we've not much else to go on.'

'Shall we start from under the victim's window then?' Lawrence was already moving towards the hotel before he responded. For a second, she thought that he hadn't followed, and wondered if she'd be doing this on her own as well. But a glance over her shoulder confirmed that he was right behind her.

Back under the window the gardens looked just as unappealing in the light of day as they had in the early hours of the morning.

The lawn was mostly weeds that had grown to varying heights. A waist high wire fence separated the hotel's garden from next door, with the same fencing divided each garden on the terrace. The tall overgrowth obscured most of the fence, making the place look like one large area.

A path had been trampled through the plants closest to the hotel. It led to a part of the fence that had been pulled away from the wall. The same walkway had been created through each garden, with varying amounts of damage done to each of the fences.

Looking out over the whole area, she felt a sense of dread. It was a massive space that would need multiple officers combing it to find anything. But as she let out a breath of resignation, Bambridge walked into the middle of the hotel garden. His eyes were on the ground as he began looking at the foliage. What he hoped to find on his own was beyond her, but she joined him amongst the bushes anyway. Maybe they would get lucky?

'You see this?' he said pointing at a piece of grass near the back of the garden. It looked the same as the rest of the garden.

She shook her head. 'No.'

'It's been disturbed - look,' he pointed at the same spot again, only this time he moved his hand in motion that was supposed to show her what he meant, but she still couldn't see anything.

'Just looks like a bunch of weeds, Guv,' she answered. 'I think we're going to need a whole team in here.'

'Stone won't green light that, and you know it,' he replied, as he ducked down and moved further into the bushes.

She did know it. Money was tight, as it always was, and a full team going over this place would cost. Cost that she knew wouldn't be given out for one dead sex worker.

'You're right,' she answered. 'But I still don't see what you're seeing.'

'Come here,' he waved her over. 'You see how the stalks of the nettles have been flattened?'

Now that he had pointed it out, she could see something. Some of the plants had been disturbed and like he had said, they had been flattened to one side. Following in the direction they had been crushed, Bambridge moved further into the undergrowth. He went down onto his haunches and began studying the ground. Without pausing to push the nettles aside he disappeared into the undergrowth.

Lawrence wanted to follow him, but she was a city girl, and had never enjoyed being in or around nature. She started to take a step further into the brush, but a nettle stung her through her trousers, so she took a step back.

'You got any gloves on you?' he asked after a moment of him shuffling deeper into the nettles.

'Sure,' she said, fishing a pair out of her inside pocket. 'Why, what you got?' she asked, searching for him in the depths of the undergrowth.

His arm jutted out and she placed the gloves in his palm. It disappeared back between the weeds, and she waited again. With a groan, he stood up straight and then pushed his way out into the open.

'Someone's left something behind,' he stated, holding up a pair of binoculars.

Chapter Six

After handing the binoculars to Lawrence, Bambridge had ducked back into the bushes, but found nothing else. He'd then confidently declared they needed to get the binoculars to the forensics lab, and that they should speak to the pathologist at the same time.

At Bambridge's car Lawrence had been worried that his lack of hygiene may have spilt out into his vehicle. All manner of horrors formed in her mind as she moved round the passenger side of the vehicle. However, as she opened the door, her fears subsided. The footwell was clean, with only a few traces of dirt brought in on the sole of someone's shoe.

As they worked their way through the afternoon traffic, the summer pounded down onto the pavement, the tarmac, and the car, causing all manner of smells to rise into the air, creating a truly unique urban funk.

'How's the aircon in this thing?' Lawrence asked as her shirt stuck to her back for the umpteenth time.

'Hasn't worked in months,' Bambridge replied, his eyes on the road.

'You're kidding?' she hoped that he was, but there was no humour in his face. 'I'm getting cooked here, Guv.'

'Perhaps I could send for the fan wavers?' Bambridge said without a hint of mirth.

'I'd take anything right now, Guv.'

He looked over at her, and she expected a scolding to come her way. 'Wind your window down,' he replied finally.

Traffic fumes had always turned her stomach, a troublesome flaw to have when growing up in the middle of a city, but one she'd learnt to deal with. However, when you were stuck in London traffic there was no getting around breathing in the pollution. She decided that the heat was worse than the vapours and opened her window.

The traffic cleared for a stretch of road, and Bambridge put his foot down. The breeze that swept over her was warm, but it still felt good. She leant forward and let the wind pass over her back, the draught cooled her wet shirt if only for a moment.

When they arrived at the lab, Lawrence had recovered most of her equilibrium and was happy to feel no sweat sticking to her back. They were greeted by a very young-looking lab technician, who took the evidence off Bambridge.

'How long will it take, to get prints off those?' Bambridge asked as soon as the technician handled the binoculars.

'It depends on our workload,' the technician replied, flatly.

'Regardless of workload, what's the quickest you could get something off them?'

'Hour, hour and a half maybe,' he answered with a shrug. 'But like I said, our workload means I can't guarantee when this will get looked at.'

'What if I said that Detective Chief Inspector Stone wanted this pushed through as a priority?'

'DCI Stone?' The technician looked worried.

'That's right,' Bambridge answered firmly, 'he told us to bring it straight down here as it was part of a vital case.'

The worry on the technician's face increased and Lawrence knew that the binoculars would be worked on straight away.

One of the bonuses of having Stone as your head of department was that most of the other departments, including forensics, all feared him. Not because he was aggressive with the way he spoke to them, but because he was friendly with all the right people. Whatever he'd done throughout his career to get so many of his peers and superiors on his side was a mystery. The rumours were numerous. Ranging from he had dirt on all of them. That they all played squash together. They were all in the Freemasons. That they were all part of some illuminati cult. Or, the best one in her opinion, that they were all members of the same swinger's club. Although, she wasn't even sure if Stone was married. Whatever the reason, Stone's name was a good way of getting doors opened for you.

Bambridge knew this and was using it to their advantage. But what would happen to him if word got back to Stone that he was falsely using his name to get things done quicker? She just hoped that she wasn't there if it happened.

'We'll be back in an hour,' Bambridge stated as he walked away.

Morgues had never bothered Lawrence. For some, what was stored in them was an issue, but not for her. There was nothing to fear of the dead. And aside from some of the more gruesome ones, once you'd seen one body on the slab, you'd seen them all. Their victim was no different.

The pathologist didn't look how she remembered from the morning. But then they'd only had a passing conversation, and the lighting hadn't been great at the scene.

He was of average height. His hair was combed against his skull and was starting to thin on top. He had a well-groomed beard, its length just long enough to hide the excess weight he was holding in his chin. The design worked as his faced looked slimmer than the rest of his body. If she had to guess, she'd say he was in his late thirties or early forties. When he saw them approaching, he nodded and hung the clipboard he'd been holding on the end of the autopsy bed.

'Detectives,' was his greeting.

'Doctor Odell,' Lawrence smiled at him, hoping she'd remembered his name right. He didn't correct her.

'What you got on our victim?' Bambridge went straight to the point.

'We've been able to ID her as Tracey Collins. She was in the system for two priors for soliciting and one for drug possession.'

'Any next of kin?' Lawrence asked, making notes.

'None on the system,' he told her. 'Her medical records show her as an orphan. She was a UK citizen, lived her whole life in London. Preliminary examination shows she suffered a blunt force trauma to the back of the head. Followed by a single puncture wound to the right jugular. Which led to exsanguination.'

'Exsanguination?' Lawrence hadn't heard the word before.

'She bled out,' Bambridge told her. He was looking around the room as if he were afraid of something, or nervous, even.

Lawrence could tell that he wasn't comfortable. Maybe he was having trouble with this one? It happened. Some bodies just hit you differently.

'Exactly,' Odell said with a shake of his finger, bringing Lawrence back to their victim and the pathological report 'Aside from the blood still in her feet, she's been completely drained.'

'I couldn't see any defence wounds or bruising on her.' Lawrence said, looking at the dead woman's arms and legs again.

'That's because there wasn't any,' Odell replied. 'There is some bruising on her knees and elbows, but the bruising is old. Side effects of her profession perhaps?'

'So, our assumptions about her being a sex worker were correct?' Lawrence asked.

'She was booked for soliciting,' he repeated, with a sigh of impatience. 'However, she did show signs of recent sexual activity, and judging by the number of contraceptives, used and unused, found at the scene, plus, the multiple DNA samples found in and around the bed, it would be safe to assume so.'

'Any idea what caused the bruising to the back of the head? Lawrence aimed the question at them both. 'Anything that could indicate what type of weapon was used?

'No. Only that it was from behind and in a downward motion.' he moved around the body pointing at the area in question.

'She was hit on the top of the head?' Bambridge questioned as he turned his back on the table.

'Looks that way. A single blow that must have rendered her unconscious.'

'So, her attacker was taller than her?' Lawrence offered, as she watched Bambridge. There was nothing particularly harrowing about the body. If anything, she looked serene. So, what had him turning his back on her? His behaviour was odd. An inconsistence to the cool and collected person she'd seen in the garden of the hotel.

"Most likely.'

She nodded and smiled at Odell, who just stared at her blankly. 'Any trace of drugs in her system?'

'There's nothing unusual in her toxicology test.'

'Would a puncture wound like that be enough to bring

you back from unconsciousness?'

'Depends how hard you were hit, and how quick the incision was made.'

'Any idea on a weapon?' Bambridge asked as he walked away from the table.

'The incision was made with a very sharp object. A single thrust into the jugular. Although the cut wasn't as precise as a surgeon. It was accurate. Severed both the external and internal jugular veins, and the carotid artery were cut. She would have bled out in less than a minute.'

'What did they use to clean the body?' Lawrence asked, her eyes darting between the victim and Bambridge.

'They used a sodium hypochlorite'

'That something you get off the shelf?' Lawrence moved around the table to try and see what state Bambridge was in, but he had his back to her.

'It's in most bleaches, but the stuff they used was probably medical grade.'

'Precision cuts and medical cleaning products. Could our suspect have a medical background?' Lawrence leant forward and got a closer look at the cut.

Odell gave a shrug of indifference. 'It's possible. Going by the tools used. They knew where to cut, how to levitate the body to drain it out, and they cleaned the body clinically. Even cleaned under her fingernails.'

'What about the plughole?' Bambridge asked over his shoulder.

'We found traces of blood, but they'd been stripped of any DNA by the bleach.'

'So, could the blood have been removed?'

'Removed?' Odell didn't seem to understand the question.

'Yeah, taken away.' Bambridge took a step towards

the exit to emphasise his point. 'Taken with our suspect.'

He looked baffled. 'It's possible, but we've no way of knowing that for sure.'

'But you said there were traces of blood in the plughole,' Bambridge added. 'Traces to me implied only a little bit.'

'What are you getting at, detective?'

'I'm asking if you think the blood was washed down the drain?'

Odell looked exasperated and turned his attention to Lawrence, asking her to explain. When neither of them said anything, he shrugged and gave an answer. 'It's certainly possible,' he replied, with an inconclusive tone. 'But like I said the bleach stripped the materials of any DNA, and it also took away any hope of measuring the quantity of blood washed away.'

His words hung in the air.

'Any other questions?' he asked after the moment of silence.

'You get any prints from the window?' Bambridge asked as he took another step towards the exit.

"No,' Odell offered. 'But we got multiples from the rest of the flat. All of which we're still processing. Anything else?'

'No, that pretty much covers it.' Bambridge replied as he left the room.

Odell had started to say something but paused as he watched Bambridge leave. He looked at Lawrence and said it to her instead. 'If we get anything from the prints, we'll let you know.'

'Thanks,' she said with a smile. 'Is there a copy of her report available yet?' Lawrence asked, as she ignored Bambridge's rude exit and pointed at the clipboard on the end of the bed.

'I'll get it over to your department within the hour,' Odell replied, picking up the clipboard and turning to the workbench behind him.

Lawrence took this as her cue to leave and headed out the door after Bambridge.

She found him stood under an air-conditioning unit. His head tilted back, and his eyes closed.

'You alright, Guv?' she asked.

'Fine,' he replied calmly, but she could see that something had bothered him. Something in the morgue had shaken him and he was doing his best to hide it. 'Just enjoying the aircon,' he added.

Lawrence joined him under the cooling breeze, and for a second, everything was forgotten. Where she was, who she was with, the case, the heat, everything. Only the cold processed air mattered, and it felt fantastic.

'What now, Guv?' she asked, eyes closed.

'Where's that report lead your thoughts?' Bambridge replied.

'Well, it confirmed something we'd already assumed, that the victim was bled out,' she stated, opening her eyes. 'However, we can't confirm where the blood went.'

'They took it with them,' Bambridge, eyes still closed, was insistent.

Lawrence still wasn't sure about that, but why else would they have strung her up?

'Medical equipment,' Lawrence continued. 'Our suspect knew where to cut and used cleaning products not readily available. Where is our suspect getting them from? Maybe they work in medicine?'

'A good assumption,' Bambridge replied, 'But nothing to go on. We don't have a confirmed weapon. Could have just been a kitchen knife, and they'd looked up where to cut online. Plus, the bleach they used could be used in other professional fields. Not just medicine.'

'Why did they clean up so thoroughly?' Lawrence wasn't sure it was important. But the fact they only cleaned that small area bothered her. Maybe it was her own idiosyncrasies towards cleaning that was driving that question?

'They did a good job on the bit they cleaned,' Bambridge nodded. 'Might lead us somewhere.'

'Hopefully, we get something off the binoculars,' she said enthusiastically, 'as they're currently our best lead.'

'Agreed,' Bambridge replied, and opened his eyes. 'I think our killer dropped them.'

'Let's hope so,' Lawrence stated and then stepped out of the breeze.

'That all you got?' Bambridge glared at her.

His stare brought a heat across her body, and fear that she had overlooked something major crept into her mind.

'Nothing else comes to mind, Guv.' Even though she hated saying it, she really didn't have anything else. She waited for him to tell her what she'd missed, anxiety bubbling at the back of her thoughts.

'He's not as good as he thinks he is,' Bambridge stated finally.

It wasn't what Lawrence had been expecting. 'How d'you mean?'

'They tied her up, but the knot was shoddy. They knew where to cut; but the cut was uneven. They cleaned up, but only parts of the scene. The parts they'd soiled. They dropped their binoculars. Our suspect thinks they can do anything, and it looks like they can, but they're still learning their craft. That will change with more practise though.'

This was the most interest he'd shown in a case since his return, she thought. Perhaps the case was rejuvenating his passion for the job?

'You think they'll do it again?' she asked.

'Yes,' he said confidently.

'Why?'

Bambridge shrugged. 'Just the effort they went into with our victim. Screams of a perfectionist. And perfectionists are always striving to do better.'

Lawrence said nothing.

Bambridge stepped out from under the aircon and started walking.

She had so many questions about what he meant by a perfectionist, and why that would lead to them attacking someone else. But her first question was where was he going? He wasn't headed towards the building's reception area, and he wasn't moving towards the lab technician's desk either.

'Guv?' she called after him, but he didn't seem to hear her.

Could she be bothered to go chasing after him? He'd been distracted throughout Odell's report and clearly had other things on his mind.

'Detectives!' a voiced call from the corridor behind her.

Lawrence turned as the young technician came walking towards her waving a piece of paper. 'I thought you'd left,' he stated as he got closer.

'Not yet,' she replied as she glanced back towards Bambridge.

'It's good that you haven't,' he offered, handing her the piece of paper. 'We got a hit on those binoculars you gave us,' he continued eagerly, 'they've got a bunch of priors, so they came up straight away. Told you we were quick here.'

Bambridge appeared at her side and took the paper

from her. Without so much as a thank you he started walking towards the reception area.

Chapter Seven

Paul McNulty had a long list of previous arrests. All of them were related to voyeurism and indecent exposure. His priors had involved a variety of women. Varying in age, none of them minors, but all of them had either seen him at their window, or he had exposed himself to them in public.

Initially she had questioned whether he was the right guy, stating that most voyeurs didn't like getting close to their victims. The peeping was more than enough for the Tom. However, Bambridge had countered her argument, stating that the urges of a voyeur can escalate to home invasion, theft of the victim's property, and in extreme cases, assault. He named a few US serial killers who had started out peering through people's windows.

It hadn't taken long to get a search warrant on McNulty's home. Chief Inspector Stone had been almost happy at the prospects of a quick arrest. Another file off his desk.

As they approached McNulty's front door, with six uniformed officers in support, Lawrence still had her doubts that this was their guy. Something about his file details just didn't add up. But her uncertainty was soon overwhelmed by the anxiety she felt for the forthcoming raid.

A bonus about working in CID was that you didn't have to be the first through the door on these things anymore. That was the job of one of the uniforms. But even though she wasn't the primary through the door, she still was on edge.

'Police, open up,' the primary uniform called through

the door and then aggressively knocked. 'Paul McNulty! We have a warrant to search the premises. Open up.' He knocked again and received the same answer.

With a nod, the primary signalled for his colleague with the battering ram to step forward. The ram struck the door just below the handle and on the second blow it forced the door open.

The six uniforms entered the building, yelling the usual procedural phrases whilst Lawrence waited at the door with Bambridge. She tried to access what frame of mind he was in, staring at him while they waited. But his eyes were on the ground, his expression vacant.

She put him out of her mind and stepped through the door.

Aside from the mess made by the broken door, the hallway was tidy. There were no shoes left lying around, no mail scattered on the floor, or keys that had been discarded. The place was spotless. The cleanliness continued throughout the rest of the flat.

In the living room the sofa looked like it had never been sat on, its cushions plumped to perfection. The coffee table in the middle of the room gleamed without a speck of dust, with the same treatment to the television. The spotlessness was certainly in keeping with the clean-up job at the murder scene.

Lawrence found Paul McNulty in the bedroom, along with the two uniformed officers who had him face down on the bed, with his hands cuffed behind his back.

Lawrence waited for Bambridge to begin speaking to their suspect, but he just lingered in the doorway, the same vacant look in his eyes.

'Good afternoon, Mr McNulty,' Lawrence said after she got sick of waiting for him to speak.

'What's good about it?' he replied through gritted

teeth.

Again, the bedroom was pristine. The bed had been made perfectly. So much so, that the sheets had barely moved even with three bodies on top of them. Next to the bed was a desk, with a high-grade PC running on it. A decent camera with a long lens, was wired into it and the tower was humming with activity.

'Were we downloading something, Mr McNulty?' Lawrence asked, stepping over to the computer.

'Just some photos I took,' he answered.

'Mind if I take a look?' she said, as she tapped the spacebar.

'Do what you like,' he replied.

'Any idea why we're here today, Mr McNulty?' Lawrence asked turning towards their suspect.

'I haven't the foggiest.'

'Well, I'm arresting you on suspicion of murder. You do not have to say anything. But it may harm your defence if you do not mention when questioned something which you later rely on in court.'

'Murder?' McNulty exclaimed, as he was lifted to his feet. 'The fuck did I do?' he added with a confused expression. The uniforms bungled him out of the room. He could be heard repeating the word 'murder' and telling the uniforms they'd got the wrong man.

Bambridge was standing in the corner of the room, his eyes everywhere and nowhere at once. Lawrence wanted to ask him what he thought, but he looked so lost in himself that she wasn't sure what to say. Instead, she stood looking at the password bar on the screen, wondering if she could guess it.

After hovering over the keyboard for a few seconds, she conceded that she had no idea what it could be. 'Any thoughts on what his password might be?'

'Nope,' Bambridge replied, as he joined her at the computer. 'That's a job for the tech boys,' he added as he picked up the camera. 'But there might be something on this?'

He played around with the buttons on the camera until the small screen on the backside came to life.

Lawrence stood beside him as he flicked through multiple images. They were all different shots of women. All of them taken without their consent, with all the women in varying stages of undress. As the image changed again, and new face came into view, her opinion of whether Paul McNulty had killed Tracey Collins changed, as the face of their victim, caught through her bedroom window, came onscreen.

'Case closed?' Bambridge stated as he stared at the camera screen. 'Should have all the evidence we need on here.'

'Looks that way,' Lawrence replied. It didn't look good for Paul McNulty. However, there was still something that didn't sit with her. It was all a little too convenient.

'Interview will clear it up,' Bambridge left the room.

Lawrence knew that there were more items to check. There were shelves full of books and they hadn't gone through any of the wardrobes. They also hadn't looked in the bathroom. It was all well and good that McNulty had pictures of the victim on his camera, but where were the tools he'd used? Where was the weapon, and the rope, and the blood?

For the whole journey back to the station, and throughout the booking in process, Bambridge was distant. So much so that he left her to deal with it while he went to the bathroom. Surely, he didn't think this case was solved already. They hadn't even done the interview yet. Why was Bambridge so adamant that McNulty was their guy?

It was pretty obvious that he had lost all interest in the case, and that his mind was elsewhere. Thinking about more errands he needed to go on perhaps? But it was by no means case closed as he had stated at McNulty's flat. Pictures of the victim didn't put him in her room.

In the interview room Paul McNulty looked agitated. There was a layer of sweat across his pale forehead, over the top of his balding scalp, and across his top tip. His left knee was jiggling with nervous energy, and he bit at his left thumb. Next to him an appointed duty solicitor was saying something in his ear, but McNulty didn't appear to be listening.

'How d'you wanna do this?' Lawrence asked as they stared through the two-way mirror at the duty solicitor. She recognised him from previous suspects but couldn't remember his name.

'Point out what we've got him on and see what he says. The fact that he's got pictures of our victim, along with all his priors, should be enough to keep him locked up for a while,' Bambridge left it at that and left the room.

Once again Lawrence found herself confused and standing alone. She shook her head in disbelief and followed him into the interview room, where he was busy going through the procedural process of opening a new tape, slotting it into the recording machine and then making the usual declarations for the benefit of the tape.

'Good afternoon, Mister McNulty,' Bambridge offered, as the tape began to whirr. 'Do you know why we've brought you in today?'

McNulty looked at him, then at Lawrence with a dumbfounded expression, but remained silent. He folded his arms across his chest and leant back in his chair.

'Nothing to say, Mister McNulty?' Bambridge asked as he sat down opposite him.

Lawrence took her time to sit down, her attention on their suspect, measuring him to see how he was dealing with being under arrest. Through the two-way mirror she would have said badly. But now that there were people in the room with him, he seemed calmer. Calmer in that his leg had stopped jiggling. There was still fear in his eyes.

'Fair enough. You have the right to silence. But then looking at your record, you already know that don't you?'

McNulty just stared at Bambridge; his lips pressed tightly together.

'Okay then,' Bambridge added with a sigh. 'Let's do the official part. D.I. Bambridge and D.C. Lawrence present for the interview of Paul McNulty in connection with the murder of Tracey Collins.'

McNulty remained silent.

'Nothing to say?' Bambridge said with a tilt of his head. 'These are some serious charges you're being brought up on. Not the usual indecent exposure ones you're used to.'

'Do Mister McNulty's previous convictions have anything to with his arrest?' the solicitor asked.

Bambridge looked at him as if he'd insulted his grandmother, and Lawrence feared that he was about to lose his temper again. But he seemed to get himself under control before he answered with a stern no.

'Then I suggest you don't bring them up again.' The duty solicitor was firm.

The silence in the room was palpable, but McNulty just continued to stare at Bambridge with the same unimpressed face.

'You seem very calm for someone who's been accused of murder?' Bambridge said, ignoring the solicitor.

Lawrence wasn't sure where Bambridge was going with his scare tactics, but they weren't working. It was evident that McNulty had been in his fair share of interview rooms, and that simple threats were not the answer.

Could she tug on his heart strings? Or hit him with some moral standards that he should be adhering to? She hadn't read his file to know what strings to pull, and whether he had any morals. Whatever she was going to do she should probably chime in with it soon.

'Do you like taking photos, Mister McNulty?' Lawrence asked.

He moved his cold stare across to her, but there seemed to be a slight break in his facial features. As if something had caught his interest. However, he still didn't speak.

'I haven't the eye for it, unfortunately. But my other half does. He's pretty good at it. Manages to make a decent living out of it. I find it fascinating watching him load the shots he's taken up onto his computer. Takes ages, but it's exciting seeing what he's taken on a bigger screen.'

She could see that he wanted to reply to her, to talk about the hobby he was clearly interested in, but his instincts kicked in and he remained silent once more.

'Don't get it myself,' Bambridge added, and leant back in his chair dismissively. 'It's just capturing something that's already there.'

'It's so much more than that,' McNulty answered eagerly.

'I agree with you,' Lawrence replied, and shifted forward in her chair. 'The way my other half lines up his shots, is pretty amazing. The details that he manages to pick up look so good.'

'What does he photograph?' McNulty asked as he mimicked her and leant forward.

'He's a fashion photographer,' she answered, with a smile. 'Some of the models he takes pictures of are just stunning. Particularly the women.'

'They're so much more susceptible to good light,' McNulty replied, with his own smile. But then instantly retreated as the duty solicitor whispered something in his ear.

'They look even better when you don't have their permission, right?' Bambridge asked.

McNulty's demeanour returned to its closed former position, and he became silent again.

'That's what you're into isn't it. Creeping on unsuspecting women? But then I guess taking pictures wasn't enough for you. You had to get closer, didn't you? So much so that you had to climb in Tracey's window.'

McNulty shook his head, a scowl filling his face.

'For the benefit of the tape, Mr McNulty is shaking his head,' said Bambridge, and then, 'Only problem was, she didn't want you there, so you hit her over the head, and then you killed her.'

'Who's Tracey?' McNulty asked confusion all over his features. His solicitor offered more advice, and he looked even more confused.

'Blonde. Worked at the Scenic hotel,' Bambridge said, his voice sarcastic. 'You know, the one you strung up and bled out over the bath.'

'She's dead?' he sounded genuinely upset.

'Tends to happen when you slit someone's throat,' Bambridge added.

'But she was alive when I saw her last,' McNulty stated as his sadness increased.

His solicitor leant in and spoke again, but McNulty

seemed oblivious to his presence.

'When was this, Mister McNulty?' Lawrence asked in a softer voice.

'Last night,' he replied. 'Right before I was chased off.'

'Chased off?' Lawrence repeated.

'Yeah, someone smacked me over the back of the head, so I did a runner.'

'Did this attack cause you any injuries? Do you need us to provide medical support?' Lawrence knew that offering him a medic would cover their arses in case he collapsed in custody. Also, if he did have any visible bruising then it might prove his innocence. Which, if she was being honest with herself, she thought was the case anyway.

Where was the rope and the weapon? And looking at how thin he was, she doubted he would have been able to scale the drainpipe outside Tracey's window.

'No, I'm fine,' McNulty said with an absent wave of his hand. 'He just grazed me. Didn't even leave a mark.' He tilted his head forward to show them. 'See?'

'Again, for the benefit of the tape, Mr McNulty is displaying us his head where an alleged blow was struck by an unknown assailant. But you admit to being at the Scenic hotel last night?' Bambridge asked firmly.

'Well, yeah,' McNulty replied with a confused expression.

'Thank you, Mister McNulty, that's all I need from you right now,' Bambridge stated as he stood up.

'But I didn't do anything?'

'You just admitted to being at the scene of a crime on the night a murder took place. Not sure what you think you didn't do?' Bambridge brought the interview to a conclusion and nodded to Lawrence, to take care of the tape, before he stalked out of the room, brushing past the uniform who had been standing in front of the door. As Lawrence finished bagging the tape, she beckoned to the uniform to return McNulty to the cells.

She hurried after Bambridge. Surely, he didn't think that was enough evidence to put McNulty away for this crime.

Following him out the door, she ran to catch up with him and was about to tell him what she thought, when Chief Inspector Stone appeared at the other end of the corridor.

'Detectives,' he greeted them with his closest version of a smile. 'I hear you might have someone in custody already. That's a record, even for you, Inspector.'

'Just doing my job, Guv,' Bambridge was nonchalant.

Lawrence tried to hide her frown, but Stone must have seen it because he turned towards her. 'You don't agree, Constable?'

'No,' she lied, and then considered what she was going to say next. She could either keep her mouth shut and let the two of them live out the story they had created for themselves. Or she could voice her opinions about how she thought he wasn't their man. 'Well, yes, actually.'

'You do, or you don't agree?' Stone asked, confused.

'I don't agree,' she said more confidently.

'Why not, Constable?'

'Because I don't think we've got enough on him.'

'We've got his prints near the murder scene,' Bambridge interjected. 'A picture of the victim on a camera he owns,' He counted his arguments off on his fingers. 'Plus, we've just got him confessing to being at the scene on the night of the murder.'

'But we have nothing on him being inside the victim's flat,' she stated, in disbelief. Did Bambridge really think that they had enough?

'Forensics are still running the prints from the scene,' Bambridge retorted.

'Do you think they'll find our suspect's prints?' Stone asked Bambridge.

'Forensics said they'd found multiples and that it would take time. But I'm confident they'll find Mister McNulty's prints at the scene.'

'And if they don't, what then?' Lawrence could feel her anger rising. How could neither of them see the gaps in their case? Maybe neither of them wanted to see the gaps. They just wanted the case closed so that they could go back to their lives. Another gold star for the boys in blue.

'Then, Detective Constable,' Stone answered bluntly, 'if needs be, you and D.I. Bambridge will find more evidence. Such is your job to do.'

He looked at her with a challenging expression, which she took as her cue to shut up.

Stone turned his attention back to Bambridge who was staring down the corridor. Was he even listening?

'I'll look forward to reading your report on the matter,' Stone added and then strode away, down the corridor.

Lawrence watched him leave before rounding on Bambridge, who was still staring in the other direction.

'D'you really think this is our guy?' She made no effort to hide her annoyance. The more she was around him, the less respect she felt for him. Did he really not care about the job anymore?

'He ticks all the boxes,' he replied with a shrug.

'But it's not him. Surely, you can see that?'

'Looks like our guy to me, I think we've enough to charge him,' he replied and started walking away from her.

'So that's it?' she called after him, her anger boiling up again.

'For today, after I've spoken to the custody office about charging our suspect.'

'Guess I'll see you tomorrow then?'

He raised a hand in a goodbye as he disappeared round the corner.

Lawrence took a deep breath to steady herself as her hands clenched into fists. She closed her eyes and concentrated on her breathing. There was no point in getting mad about the situation, as it would achieve nothing. Much better to try and find other possible leads when the McNulty charges fell on their face, and she knew exactly who to look up.

At her computer she typed in Samuel Jarvis and waited for system to catch up. As she waited, she noticed Canham looking across at her.

'Hey, Guv,' she said with a smile.

'What you working on?' he asked, returning the smile.

'Just looking someone up.'

'Anyone interesting?'

She had always thought it was Quinnell that was the gossip of the partnership, but clearly Canham was just as nebby. 'An ex-copper actually.' It couldn't hurt to get his input on this one though. Chances are they may have worked together.

'Anyone I'd know?'

'Possibly,' she replied, looking down at her notepad. 'A Samuel Jarvis.'

'Jarvis? Aye, I knew him. Made a name for himself in Vice. Rumour has it he shut down more brothels than a Gonorrhoea epidemic.'

'So, he was a hard copper?'

'Aye, a real stickler for the rules. Nicest man you'd

ever meet off the job, mind. Wouldnee say boo to a goose off duty. But when he was working.' He left the sentence hanging.

'Why'd he leave?'

'Funnily enough, he got his leg crushed under a condom vending machine. It got knocked over on some raid he was on. Got a full sick pay, with early retirement from it, mind.'

'Was he a violent type? Someone who'd be out for revenge?'

'What, Sam? Na, like I said, passive as a lamb that one.'

Her computer pinged, telling her the search was complete. Glancing through his records, everything Canham had said was true. So much for other leads.

Her temper started to flare up, so she decided to call it a day and head home.

Chapter Eight

Bambridge needed to get away. Away from this city. From its memories and from the situations it kept presenting to him. But would that change anything? Would he still see her, think of her, or be reminded of her if he were somewhere new? All he knew for sure was that he couldn't carry on like this.

For a moment, and it had been a brief one, this new case had caught his interest. He had almost enjoyed it, going over the variables. The method of the execution, the cleaning of the area, the precision of the cut, and the whereabouts of the blood. And now they had Paul McNulty. Perfect.

It had ended up looking like an open and shut case. Although Lawrence seemed to disagree.

Whether she was trying to make a name for herself he couldn't be sure, but her enthusiasm for the job was commendable. Her youthful exuberance would have been infectious for him had it been a year ago. But now that kind of work ethic wouldn't rub off on him.

It wasn't just the way she approached the job that had caught his attention. She also was constantly checking up on him. Not in the same way that a nurse would, but more like a parent that was watching their toddler wobble across a room. She didn't look like she was ready to step in if he fell, but she always appeared to have one eye on him. Going by his current state of wellbeing, he couldn't really blame her. He would be weary of him and his actions as well.

Leaving Lawrence behind, he could feel tension forming in his muscles. His jaw was clamped shut, his teeth grinding so hard that his ears had started to burn. It was the thought of going home that brought these reactions to the surface.

Home was the worst place to be right now. Mostly because he had lived with her, there. And to all intents and purposes, it was where she still lived. She may have been physically gone, but she was still there, in her clothes, in her belongings, and all the things of her that were scattered around the flat.

Was it that he was scared to go home? That was the logical answer. But what alternative did he have? He could sleep in his car again. It wouldn't be the first time he'd done it, and it wouldn't be the last. However, he'd caught a lung full of his armpit earlier and had almost retched. Which meant that he needed to pay some attention to how he looked and smelt. He could have a shower at work, but he'd still be in the same clothes, and his dirty clothing was half the problem. The simple answer was he had to go home at some point. But not right now.

Right now, he had other things to be doing. Other places to go. Other people to observe.

The list he'd compiled wasn't long, but there were enough names on it to fill his time. Time that this recent case had taken up. Resentment had built up inside him about the wasted hours. Hours that could have been better spent. Somewhere out there someone was to blame. Someone that had caused the empty house he was frightened to go home to.

The person he had in mind this evening was across town. A solid lead that had the potential to cause progression. Someone who knew who had taken her away from him, and this person was as good a lead as all the others he had.

As he steered his way through the streets the tension he felt wasn't fading and he knew that he needed something to take the edge off. A smoke would see to that. However, he would need to roll one up.

Rolling whilst driving was an option. The road ahead was straight, and the traffic was moving slowly, so that seemed like a good choice. Reaching into his pocket, he pulled out his tobacco pouch. Inside was everything he needed, he just had to build the thing.

Ahead the brake lights turned red, and he was forced to stop, which gave him a second to roll. However, even with all the roll-ups he'd made before, he still hadn't mastered the technique of doing it quickly, and the traffic was moving again before he could lick the paper's resin.

He thought about pulling over to finish the job, but there was a bus lane to his left. He considered doing it anyway. A glance in his rear-view mirror showed him three buses weaving in and out of one another. The lane was far too busy.

With the half-rolled cigarette in his right hand, he used his left to steer. The engine soon started to scream at him, demanding he change gear. Pressing his right forearm against the wheel, he changed gear with his left hand, spilling some of the contents into his lap.

A road appeared on his left and he decided to make the turn. As he moved the wheel, he caught sight of a bus in his wing mirror and braked sharply. More of the tobacco fell from the paper and he cursed himself as he waited for the bus to pass.

Behind him someone's horn signalled their disapproval, but he ignored them and turned off the main road.

Parking on a double yellow line, he knocked the gear stick into neutral, pulled up the handbrake and left the engine running.

With help from the orange streetlamps, he was able to salvage most of the spilt leaves from his crotch and from the top of the steering wheel. Mission accomplished, he found his lighter and lit up.

The first drag, as always, was heaven. Knotted muscles released under his skin. The tension in his legs eased, and as he blew out the smoke, he started to feel normal again. He leant back into the chair, wound the window down a little, and took a second hit.

This second drag however wasn't so heavenly. As the smoke reached his lungs, it burnt and made him start coughing. With each hack, he felt a pressure in his head build as he struggled for air.

The pain cooking through his lungs took away all other thought, and for a second his mind wasn't on her. Eventually, he got his breathing under control though, and as he took in his surroundings, with the world slowly spinning, he knew she would be back.

He closed his eyes as a feeling of nausea washed over him and he sat for a moment.

He tried to concentrate on something that would help with how he was feeling, but the only thing that came to mind was Natalie.

All he could see was her battered body in the morgue. The defence wounds on both of her arms. The fingers of her left hand that had been bent out of their sockets, and then shattered in multiple places. The discolouration of her skin on her abdomen were most of her ribs had been cracked or broken. The swelling in the left side of her face where her jaw had been dislocated. How misshaped the back of her head looked from the blow that had eventually fractured her skull and ended her life.

He wished that what he saw were the good times, the

fond memories; he wished he could see her beautiful smile, the way her hair glowed in the sun, her eyes as she gazed longingly into his, the figure hugging dresses she would wear for a night out with her husband, but there was only her battered body. The good times were gone and a shattered corpse in a morgue was all he had left.

Rage welled up inside of him and the world stopped spinning.

Putting the car back into gear he swung out into the road, his vision still clouded by the bout of headrush, but he knew that his anger would help him to focus. To get him to where he needed to be.

The lights and sounds of the city passed him by, as he weaved his way through its streets. His attention was on the road as he fought to keep on top of his feelings. He needed to be calm. But he also needed retribution. The tobacco had made him feel good; briefly, it had made him leave the corpse in the morgue; but it couldn't find the right muscles to enable him to smile again.

Through a layer of sweat and heavily ground teeth he managed to reach his destination. However, he was still seething. Natalie's disfigured body flashing before his eyes repeatedly.

His person of interest would be passing by shortly. The routine they had carved out for their life predictable, to say the least. It had taken him only a short while to learn their day-to-day activities. So much so that he knew where to be on what day of the week. He just hoped all his investigating would prove fruitful; that he would be able to shed some light on what happened that day almost a year ago.

If this lead didn't pan out, then so be it. There were a whole bunch of other people who fit the bill. Several others that he'd investigated. Others that he hoped would provide an answer. The answer to what really happened to Natalie. And not the bullshit reports his superiors had written up.

Whatever this lead gave him, he hoped that it was something of note.

He was running out of patience. Running out of any form of desire. Running out of the will to carry on. Because what was there for him now? She had been his world, and now she was gone. There was nothing left. Nothing to keep him going. Nothing to make him smile and to make him laugh. Nothing to make him get up in the morning. Nothing to make him go out at night. Nothing to breath for. To live for. To die for. Nothing.

Chapter Nine

Lawrence had the conversation between Bambridge, Stone and herself bouncing around in her head all the way home. How could they possibly think they had the right guy? Yes, they had evidence that put him in the gardens outside the scene, plus evidence that he had been stalking their victim, but they had nothing on him at the scene of the crime.

Her two senior officers seemed to be riding their hopes on fingerprints, but she was doubtful. Everything about the scene made her think that their suspect wouldn't have been that sloppy. If the murder had taken place as they presumed, then there was no way the suspect would have left any prints.

It was all too meticulous. The hanging of the body, the draining of the blood, the cleaning up, and then the going out of the window, it all screamed of forward planning. And yet, there were elements of Paul McNulty that made complete sense. The cleanliness of his flat lined up with the way the body and area had been cleaned. The pictures of the victim and the fact that they'd found his binoculars outside her flat was in line with the forward planning notion.

But then, he could just be a pervy stalker.

Waiting at a pedestrian crossing, the traffic was frequent, even at this time of night, but she barely noticed, as her mind wandered. Her thoughts drifted away from the case to that of Bambridge's health. Both his physical and mental states.

Physically, he was a mess. He barely ever changed his clothes. She could only guess at how often he washed, and in this heat, he was starting to get ripe. But she was also worried about what shape he was in. She tried to get some exercise in at least twice a week. Even if it was just a thirty-minute run around the block, it was better than nothing. Bambridge however probably couldn't finish a run to the end of her road.

She had been told that once you join CID the amount of exercise you did in the job decreased, but she hadn't believed them. However, having been a detective for over a year now, she could see what they meant. Particularly in homicide. Because until you caught a case you didn't have a great deal to do. Unless you were working on something else, of course. Detective Sergeant Quinnell was a prime example of someone who'd got very comfortable in the role.

Bambridge, on the other hand, always seemed to be on the move but looked tired when doing it. He'd never pass any of the academy fitness tests were he to take them again. But then, who out of her department would?

The lights turned red, so she crossed the four lanes of traffic.

It was his mental health that really worried her though. Clearly, he hadn't come to terms with the death of his wife. He wasn't just absent in body; his mind was all over the place too. It was as if his attention span was non-existent. This case being the prime example. The way he'd dropped the whole thing, with the slightest hint of the case being solved, was astounding.

Walking home, the various independent shops down her street were still bustling this late in the evening. Their throng brought a welcoming distraction as the warm evening had brought everyone out onto the street. Tables and chairs had been set out on the pavement in front of restaurants, cafes, and bars alike. Laughter filtered out from a barbershop, its occupants enjoying whatever joke had been made in unison. A shopkeeper haggled over prices whilst stood amongst the fruit and veg on display out the front of his shop. But once she was past it all her mind returned to Bambridge.

She had been sure he was interested in the case. That the oddity of how the victim had been killed had caught his attention; but she guessed she was wrong. The way that he'd been so adamant McNulty was their guy had felt strange. As if the convenience of him being at the scene was all Bambridge needed. With his interest gone, he'd already moved onto whatever he was doing with his time.

'What the hell are you doing with your time?' she asked aloud. The question had been about Bambridge but fitted with her own situation. What was she doing with her free time? And what was she doing in the relationship she was in?

Stepping off the main road, the sound of traffic instantly decreased, and she soon found herself stood outside her rented home.

The small, converted church wasn't ideal. The ceilings were far too high, and it was a nightmare to keep warm in the winter, yet it managed to stay quite cool in the summer. It suited her needs for now.

'Suited her needs' was also a perfect way to describe her relationship with Craig. They had been together for about three years now, and if she were being honest with herself, they'd moved in together far too quickly.

When they had first started dating it had been great. He had been kind and courteous, so different than all her previous boyfriends. She put it down to the fact that he wasn't from the same part of town as her. He was from less than half a mile up the road, but the difference half a mile made in this city was vast. His family were by no means wealthy, but they weren't from a council estate like hers. And it was from the estate and its surroundings areas that all her ex's were from. So, when he'd greeted her with a *hello*, rather than a *what we sayin' girl* she had been impressed.

Craig had been a way out of her little corner of the city, and for a while their relationship had flourished. But then his bouts of jealousy had started to creep out. Only on occasion, at first. Minor comments about activities with previous lovers would leave him quiet for hours. She had just taken it as insecurity, it wasn't until they were living together that his questions about her ex's had started to surface. And with the questions came the bouts of jealous mood swings. Mood swings that would continue for days.

Entering the house, she wondered what mood she would find him in? But as she was greeted with his shoes kicked off by the door, rather than put in the shoe rack they lay next to, she felt her own mood change. What other mess would he have made?

She hated mess. Hated clutter, and things being left out. Everything had its place in her home and finding things out of place really wound her up. His shoes on the floor had already set off her OCD before she'd even stepped into the living area, where the soft sound of typing filled her ears. You could hardly call it a living room because it was on open plan space, with the bedroom on a mezzanine above it. A thin wall divided the rest of the area from the kitchen and bathroom.

Growing up in the city she was used to small living arrangements, but their flat left you with little to no place for time to yourself. The bathroom being the only room that even had a door.

All the lights were off apart from one small lamp on the work desk in the corner. With his back to her and his head hung over his keyboard Craig looked busy. She stood for a second and watched him, but then her eyes were drawn to his work bag open next to him, its contents strewn across the floor. She chewed on the inside of her cheek as she felt her anger rising.

He had his earphones on, his head darted between the screen, the keyboard, and the notes on his desk. In the top corner a loading bar was currently on 67%. Every few seconds the counter would go up and a new image would appear on the screen.

It was of a young woman dressed in a bright green tracksuit, her hair and make-up over stylised as she stood under a railway bridge. The grey walls a contrast to the lavish clothing. Another image of a beautiful woman came on screen and her own pangs of jealousy bubbled up.

To help fight her jealous thoughts she tried to recognise which bridge it was. But the next image came up, and another beautiful woman came onscreen she couldn't figure it out. Wherever it was it looked filthy. Which gave her some comfort, knowing that he'd been in just as unpleasant places as her, albeit with better presented company.

His head rose and he turned to face her with a smile. 'Hello, you,' he said, taking off his earphones and standing to greet her with a hug.

'How was your day?' she asked, as his embrace ended. She could have done with it lasting longer, and with a bit more pressure, but she was far too hot. Why hadn't he opened the window to let some air in?

'Hot as hell,' he replied, pecking her cheek.

She nodded in agreement. 'Did yours involve sitting in traffic for hours?' she added, taking a step towards the kitchen.

'No, but it smelt of piss under that railway bridge,' he pointed to the screen and then gave her a look that included a scrunched-up face. 'Were you stuck in the car with *him*?'

'What do you mean?' she asked. She could feel her anger rising. His question was probably meant as a harmless one, but she couldn't help but feel like it was an accusation.

'From what you tell me your boss's a mess,' he said, as he followed her into the kitchen.

In truth, she couldn't remember what she had and hadn't told him. Sometimes you just needed to decompress at the end of a shift, and words would come tumbling out.

She wanted to tell him about how much pain she thought Bambridge was feeling, and that he shouldn't really be working, but she decided to keep it light.

'His car doesn't have aircon either,' she offered instead, and then gasped as she saw the state of the kitchen.

Craig had made himself something to eat. Which would have been fine if he had taken the time to clean up after himself, but he hadn't. Whatever he'd made was partially splashed all over the hob. The peelings of the vegetables were still on the chopping board, and not in the green recycling bin they lay beside. The knife he'd used hadn't been cleaned and still had red onion residue all over it. Plus, his plate, cutlery, and the pan he'd used to cook were on the countertop, right above the dishwasher. And to cap it all, he hadn't left any for her, only the mess.

She wanted to yell at him, but what was the point, he'd never learn. He'd been raised in a house where his mother had waited on him, hand and foot. So, the bare minimum when it came to cleaning up after himself was what he was used to. Now was not the time to bring it up, though. Something to eat, and a bath was what she needed now.

'Is his hygiene still bad?' he asked as he moved a little too close behind her.

She couldn't remember telling him that. She needed to be a bit more mindful when downloading after work.

'It's not the best,' she said with a shrug.

'Guy's got issues though, right?' he asked as he put his arms around her. As he pressed against her, she could feel that he was aroused.

She didn't remember telling him that either.

'Yep' she conceded, as she felt the heat of Craig's body behind her. She wasn't averse to the idea of being close to him, but with the day's sweat still covering her, and with the heat his body was giving off, she didn't want him so close. She just felt unclean. Thinking of cleanliness reminded her of the murder scene again.

'He's grieving,' she replied, as she stepped away from him, her hackles up. She wanted to ask him why he had an erection, but she knew why. He always came home horny after a photoshoot. And looking at the pictures he'd taken she could see why. But she wasn't going to be used as a sexual release. 'His wife died. I can only imagine what he's going through.'

She wasn't sure why she was defending Bambridge. She had little affinity to the man, but she couldn't help it. It had been ingrained into her at the academy. He was a fellow copper and she needed to have his back.

She didn't hear Craig sigh, but she noted the way he stomped over to the fridge. He opened the fridge, took out a jar of olives and stuck his fingers into the brine.

'Use a spoon,' she said and opened the cutlery draw a little too forcefully.

He took one, oblivious to her annoyance, and started fishing another olive out. 'Maybe he came back too soon?' Craig offered, with his mouth full, as he leant against the counter, by the peelings he hadn't tidied away.

'They wouldn't let him back to work if he wasn't ready,' she almost snapped. But deep down she wanted to agree with him. He had returned to work too early and judging by his recent actions, there was a case as to whether he should come back at all.

'You sure about that?' Craig asked, as he put the lid back on the olives and threw the spoon into the sink. It clattered in the metal basin, setting Lawrence's teeth on edge. 'Sounds like you need all the help you can get,' he added, replacing the olive jar, and slamming the door of the fridge.

'What does that mean?' She could feel her irritation growing with his every word.

'Didn't you say people have been quitting left, right and centre?' he stated returning to the spot of the vegetable skins, his back to them once again.

First, he has a dig at her partner, then he starts laying into her place of work, she wondered if he would have anything positive to say this evening. But he wasn't wrong about the people leaving. Since the change to the pension scheme, the force had been losing staff on a regular basis, and she couldn't blame them. With that nice retirement money gone as an incentive, why would you want to stay on?

She could feel her blood boiling at his negativity and had to turn away from him. For a second, she assessed whether she could be bothered to speak to him at all, and if she should just walk into the bathroom and close the door.

'We always need more help,' she replied absently as

she grabbed a coffee mug from the cupboard and filled it up from the kitchen tap.

'Yeah, but, if your partner's not pulling his weight?' Craig left the question hanging.

Lawrence had no idea how to respond, so she just continued to drink her water. After he remained silent for what seemed like an age, she finally ran out of patience. 'What?'

'What do you mean 'what'?' he replied coldly.

'You made a comment about my partner that literally made no sense.'

'What d'you mean, it made no sense?'

'You asked an open-ended question, that I had no way of answering. What if my partner isn't pulling his weight? What would you like me to do about that?'

'You could report him to your boss?'

'He is my boss,' she answered sarcastically.

'Your boss's boss then.'

'And what would that achieve? We'd be down another body, and I'd be working alone in a department I've barely been in a year. A department that I'm sure doesn't want me there anyway. So, if I go grassing on my partner what kind of impression will that leave on the rest of the team? They'll kick me out. Then all the hard work I put in getting myself into the homicide department will have been for nothing.'

'But if he's not pulling his weight, then isn't it like not having him around anyway? So, what difference would it make?'

Her anger was making its way to the surface, and she could feel the tension in her jaw. She really wasn't in the mood to have this pointless conversation. All she wanted was a soak and a drink of some description. She ignored his comment and went to the fridge.

In the door was an unopened bottle of Muscadet. She took it out and then began searching for a wine glass. When she couldn't find any in the cupboard, she could only assume that they were all still in the dishwasher.

Teeth clenched, she opened the door and looked inside. The machine was clearly full and was ready to be turned on. 'Why've you not turned the dishwasher on?' she asked through her gritted teeth.

'We haven't got any tablets left,' Craig replied in a defensive tone.

'Then go round the corner and get some,' Lawrence bit at him.

'Don't shout at me,' he snapped back. 'I've been at work all day.'

'What, and I haven't?' she asked, as she reached into the cupboard for another glass. However, there weren't any. They must have all been in the machine. She shook her head and decided to continue using the coffee mug. It would play hell with her OCD, having to drink wine not from a wine glass, but it was a sacrifice she was willing to make.

'I didn't say that, did I?' he growled at her. 'Am I just supposed to know that we're out of tablets?'

She held her nerve as she pulled a draw open looking for the corkscrew. 'No!' she replied as she slammed the draw shut. 'But you've managed to make yourself some food and left your dirty dishes on the counter. I can only assume that you left them there when you saw the dishwasher was full.'

'Correct!' he barked.

'Right, so if you saw that it was full you must have gone to use it and discovered that we're out of tablets.'

'Brilliant deduction, Detective,' he offered sarcastically.

She ignored his childish remarks and carried on with her barrage. 'Then if you knew we had no dishwasher tablets, why didn't you go and get more?'

'From where?'

'There's a thousand fuckin' shops on the next street over,' she waved the coffee cup to emphasize her point. 'I'm sure you could find some in one of them?'

'Local shops are too expensive.'

'I think we can stretch the budget for one box of dishwasher tablets.'

'Don't start nagging me with your OCD cleaning habits.'

She wanted to throw the mug at him but held it together by concentrating on the bottle of wine. In doing so, she noticed that it was a screw cap. This relieved some of her tension and she steadied herself before speaking.

'Is keeping the place tidy too much to ask?' she asked in a calmer voice.

'No, it isn't,' he conceded. 'But you gotta understand that I work too. I might not be solving crimes, and running around arresting people, but my work is tiring. And you don't hear me complaining about it.'

'It was you that brought my work up,' she barked back, her anger surfacing again.

'No, I only brought up your boss.'

'Who I have to deal with at work.'

'It seems like he's more the issue than the work itself.'

He was right of course, but she didn't want to say so. She didn't want to say anything. But she knew that she had to if she wanted this argument to end. 'Seems like you've got more of a problem with him than I have,' she retorted, unscrewing the lid off the wine and poured a healthy measure into the coffee cup.

'The guy's a waste of space.'

'You've never even met him,' she added, stepping into the bathroom.

'I don't have to meet him to know what sort of effect he's having on you.'

'And what sort of effect is that?' she demanded, as she turned to face him in the doorway.

She could see he was trying to find the right words, the words that would explain his feelings towards Bambridge, but he couldn't seem to articulate them. She knew what it was.

'You really need to get this jealousy thing under control, Craig,' she told him, and she could see the annoyance swell inside him. As he stood dumbfounded, she kept the bottle of wine in her hand and closed the bathroom door.

She knew what she had said was petty, and as she started running the bath, she could hear him knocking on the door, but she ignored him. Instead, she sat on the toilet and drank her wine, listening to the water thundering into the tub.

Craig's jealousy was a serious problem. She'd been fine with all the bouts in the past because they were about her past life. It was a life she wasn't proud of, but those events had helped shape her into the person she was today. But if he was going to continue getting jealous of the time that she was spending with Bambridge, then the relationship was going to suffer.

Maybe she was wrong? Did Craig just want what was best for her and her career? He could see that Bambridge was bad for both, and he was just looking out for her. She wished that were the case, but his history of envious temper tantrums was all that she could think about.

Turning off the taps, she checked the temperature before getting out of her sweaty, fetid feeling clothes and slid gratefully into the bath, wishing she hadn't mentioned Bambridge at all. Her work problems were hers to deal with. There was nothing Craig could do to change them, anyway. He'd say it was good to talk these things through, but she didn't think so. He wouldn't understand, and he'd try to solve the problem for her. When in truth, whenever she did want to talk about work it was just to vent, not have an answer lectured at her.

'Baby, please can we talk,' he pleaded through the door.

At least he's talking now, she thought to herself. It was the stretches of silence, with him looking at his feet, that she couldn't bear. Invariably, it would be during an argument which he had started, and then expected her to finish.

'What is there to say?' she replied, as she poured herself some more wine.

'That you understand my concern,' he answered, with a hint of anger in his voice.

'You're concern about what?'

'About you,' he sounded sincere, at least.

'What about me?' she asked, draining the second mugful of wine, and pouring some more.

'About you, in this job.'

'It's the same job I've had since you've known me.'

'Yes, but you've changed departments.'

'The hours are the same.'

'But you've become a different person,' he countered.

'I got promoted,' she replied. 'It's what happens. You get a better job, and more responsibilities come with it.'

'But the people in this new department seem even more like arseholes than the last lot you worked with.'

Lawrence took that as a dig at the police in general, and she could feel all the irritation that the bathwater had eased building up again. She wanted to defend the arseholes she had worked with, and still worked with, but she just didn't have the energy.

What she really wanted to do was dunk her head under the water, but that would mean having to deal with her hair. She'd only recently had it straightened, and the bathwater was a guaranteed way of bringing the frizz back.

'What do you expect? It's a high stress job,' she said, after a while.

'Aren't most jobs stressful?'

She could sense that the conversation was about to be turned back around to him. That in some way his job was just as difficult as hers, and again, she considered submerging herself.

'Some more than others,' she replied, as she disregarded the cup and just drank direct from the bottle.

'What's that supposed to mean?'

And the conversation was back around to him. The question was, did she bite or change the subject? After another swig from the bottle, she chose the former.

'I hope you're not comparing our jobs?'

'Why, because yours is worthwhile and mine isn't?'

She wanted to reply frankly and just say yes, but she held her tongue. 'That's not what I'm saying.'

'What are you saying then?'

She sank deeper into the bath, contemplating the submersion idea again. 'What I'm saying,' she paused as she considered what she going to say. 'What am I saying?' she asked herself quietly.

'What was that?' he called through the door.

His petulance and insistence on an answer fanned her flames, and she decided not to hold back. 'What I'm saying is some jobs are more stressful than others. And if you want me to make the comparison between taking pictures of pretty girls under a bridge and assessing the details of a scene of a murder, then I would have to put processing bodies, rather than processing photos, as a higher stress level job. But that's just my opinion.' She finished and waited for him to respond.

She could see his shadow under the door. Then she heard something crash and decided that being underwater wasn't such a bad idea. She compromised and just lowered her ears below the waterline. The dull sound of her own breathing was the calming experience she had been looking for. She closed her eyes and tried to relax.

Chapter Ten

This number would be interesting.

Their routine had been studied and a suitable window had been found. It was astounding just how repetitive the numbers were in their everyday lives. Each day bringing the same activities week after week. So sad a situation for something with so much promise. So, infuriating that what was inside was being wasted.

It was these predictabilities that allowed the work to happen.

Not all of them were as predictable as this number, though. This number you could set an alarm by. So much so, the need to follow it had ceased some time ago. No need to keep track of where it was, or what it was doing, because it always did the same thing. Today was no exception.

These simple-minded numbers and the meaningless patterns of their lives!

They would all have meaning soon enough.

It was Wednesday evening, which meant only one thing, it would be consuming alcohol at a public house. It was the same outcome every other evening, truth be told. And it was always the same public house. The banality of this number's routine was partly the reason it had been picked. For one it was an easy objective. And secondly, it would get its number off the list. There were so many more interesting, and more deserving numbers. It made sense to pick this one now. The quicker the exquisite blood could stop being polluted the better.

Wednesday had presented itself as having the best opportunities. The public house was always half empty.

Only the hardened drinkers were present. In truth Monday or Tuesday could have worked just as well. But on Wednesdays the bus that the number took only ran every hour. Why, was a question for the person who'd written the timetable. The 'why' was irrelevant because it presented the best window of opportunity.

Unlike all the other nights, when the number would stumble home at any irregular time; on Wednesday, the bus timetable forced it to leave at the exact same time each week.

There was an element of risk, but then there always was. The risk was part of the process. Part of the anticipation. The excitement. Keeping count of the ins and outs of the public house was the best way to assess the risk. On this evening, the count had been low.

Assessing the location was also a vital part of the process. Having a complete understanding of your surroundings was key to success.

This location was quite fortuitous in many ways. Although it was on a quite busy road, the building itself was somewhat secluded. Which was probably the reason it attracted the clientele it did. Along with its seclusion, the building was also in a mild state of disrepair. This was beneficial. The exterior lighting down one side of the property wasn't working. Be it through poor maintenance or an act of vandalism. Again, the reasoning for said fortune was unimportant. It presented an opportunity. Albeit a risky one. But the long strip of darkness along the building was a perfect spot. And the dark was a friend.

With the number's bus due to arrive, it was time to get into place.

The expectation is intoxicating. Coursing through every vein, and into every muscle. Months of preparation, planning, studying of the number's movements have come to this. The chance to be in the presence of greatness. To take such a unique substance. A substance so unbefitting the host. But it would be purged soon enough.

Stood in the gloom, limbs taut, the wait was almost over.

Much the same as hunting or fishing, a lure is needed. A way to draw the number into the shadows. And what better lure than the vanity of the human spirit? Or put in simpler terms the use of the numbers name.

It would feel strange to say it aloud. For it was just a meaningless title. A title given by unknowing sires. Sires that had no concept of the being they had brought into existence. A being with so much potential. Potential that had been squandered.

Feelings of familiarity take hold, a side effect of the suspense no doubt, but they manifest all the same. The thought of the numbers name has caused it. Bringing more details to bare. Its full name. Its date of birth. Its home address. The colour of its hair, and the colour of its eyes. But most importantly the potency of its blood. For it is the blood that matters.

The door to the public house opened, the sound of its inhabitants spilling out into the evening, and a step was taken further back into the darkness. But the heartrate soon slows. It's not the number leaving. The person leaving stumbles down the road and are soon gone from sight.

Perhaps the timings are off? The number had definitely been seen going in, and it hadn't come out yet. But had the gun been jumped? Had the position been assumed too early?

Like clockwork, the number stumbled out onto the street, and the pulse races again.

'George.' The lure is cast.

The number stops and turns towards the shadowed alleyway. 'Who's that?' it asked as it swayed on its feet.

'Over here, George.'

It took a step into the alleyway, but not close enough. One step more would do it.

'What d'you want? I've gotta catch the bus.'

'I just need a word, George.'

They stared into the shadows, their eyes struggling to focus. 'What about?'

Another step closer would be enough.

Being so close to the number was thrilling. Seeing its spherical face from this distance stirring the interest. Its close-set eyes, under thick, formless eyebrows exploring the darkness. Its overweight body a prison for the wonderous substance inside. The heart drummed inside the chest and the fists clench at what is about to happen.

'About you.'

'I ain't got time mate,' it replied and turned to walk away.

It was time.

The blow to the back of the head was clean, catching it behind the right ear, and as planned, the number crumbled. There is a pause to see if the blow was enough. Whether a second one is required. But the number didn't move, so it can be moved. Grabbing the feet, it is easy enough to pull it further into the darkness. A second blow for good measure calms the nerves and the process can begin.

Unfortunately, the environment isn't ideal. The tools brought would help to appease some of the concerns. However, there was no getting around the awkwardness of a deadweight human body. This number could prove to be more cumbersome than the last. But then, these things had to be overcome.

For the blood was all that mattered.

A small amount of light is needed so that the rope can be tied, the number can be put in place over the receptacle, and the blade can be prepared for the incision. But most of all, so that the procedure can be observed properly.

Face down, with its head hung over the gathering device, its neck exposed, the knife feels heavy in the hand. These few seconds before the incision are always the most difficult, the hand shaking uncontrollably. Be it through fear of making a mistake, the anticipation of what has been asked for collection, or the excitement of seeing such a Godly substance. Whatever the reason, an intake of breath focuses the will, and puts a stop to these mild nerves.

With a steady thrust, the blade finds its mark, and the blood comes.

The exquisite blood.

The way it flows from the wound, exquisite.

Its colour in the artificial light, exquisite.

Dark at its core and yet light at its edges. The fashion at which it pulses from the lesion, mesmerizing. Coming fast at first, the heart pumping it out in the manner of a geyser. But as the body is drained, the stream begins to ease, flowing steadily before slowing to a mild leak, and then as per usual the experience is over far too quickly.

Lifting the number by their feet provides a means of getting the last few pulses before the cleaning process can begin.

Once the collection is finished, the container is sealed, and put aside.

Meticulously the tools are tidied. Each one, soiled or not, is washed in bleach. All traces of the spilt blood removed. Such an exquisite substance must not be left on display. Only the worthy are allowed in its presence.

The number is given the same treatment. All residual traces removed from sight before the number is discarded.

The container is rechecked. The exquisite blood is sealed inside.

The equipment is packed down.

The number can be crossed off the list.

The location vacated.

Chapter Eleven

Lawrence got up to the ear-splitting sound of her alarm, as she always did, but she didn't feel like she'd had any sleep. The arguing with Craig had continued long into the night, and still hadn't reached an amicable conclusion. Plus, she'd sunk a whole bottle of wine to herself, which hadn't helped her sleep pattern.

Normally, she would have tried to stir Craig, even if it were just to say good morning, but today she had no desire to. He could sleep all day for all she cared. Her patience had been seriously tested last night, and she had spent the early hours contemplating what she was going to do.

The relationship wasn't working, and neither of them was happy. But the question that kept running through her head was should she work at what they had, or call it a day? Currently, her gut was telling her to end it. It was also telling her that she shouldn't have drunk so much. The white wine and nothing to eat was washing around in her stomach.

Was that thought process just a side-effect of last night though? Would she feel different with a few litres of water, a handful of painkillers, and some food inside her? Maybe her attitude would change when she'd had some time away from him to cool off?

What had also annoyed her, was that she got her hair wet. It was her own fault; she should have just blocked him out. But something about his words had ground her down and submerging herself up to her ears had been the only answer. Regardless of what she had or hadn't done last night, she still might have to straighten her hair before leaving the house. With a little luck there wasn't too much frizz.

On her way to the bathroom, she heard her work phone vibrate, stopping her mid-step. She wasn't due into work for a few hours, which had her wondering what was up. But the phone would have to wait. What state was her hair in?

A quick glance in the mirror told her that her hair would be manageable for now. However, if the day got humid then it would start to go wild. A few extra hair pins would work.

Bladder emptied; she sought out her work phone.

The message told her that she was required at another scene. Two in such close succession was a rarity, even in this city, but that was the job.

Once she was dressed her next task was getting to the scene. But first, she needed some water, and to find some Ibuprofen. The water was easy, however, the box of drugs she found was empty. She'd have to grab some more, along with some food on the way. She just hoped she could keep them both down.

Looking at the location details, she realised that the area wasn't ideal for getting to via public transport. Which left her with only a few options. Take the train and then bus to the scene. Or head into work first and commandeer a vehicle from the station lot. Both would take time, and too long for her to get to the scene.

There was a third option of course. She could get Bambridge to collect her. But what was the likelihood of that happening? The fact that he'd even shown up to the last scene had been a miracle. There was no harm in trying, though.

She opened her phone and gave him a call. But as she had assumed, it just rang out. As she was hanging up,

Craig came down from the mezzanine. Lawrence wasn't sure what type of response she was going to get from him. He would either give a sheepish apologetic performance or play ignorant to last night's attitude. Whichever was coming, she wasn't in the mood for either.

He stood staring at her for a few seconds, words seeming to get caught on his tongue. Just as he was about to speak her phone rang, breaking the silence.

It was Bambridge. She tried to hide the shock in her voice that he had returned her call, but she didn't think she was successful.

'Morning, Guv,' she answered, as she glanced at Craig. She saw him roll his eyes before walking into the kitchen. Clearly, this argument wasn't over.

'You rang?' he mumbled.

'We caught another body, Guv.'

'I saw,' he was barely audible.

'Can you swing by and pick me up on the way? The location looks remote.'

The silence on the other end of the line was torturous, and she considered telling him not to worry, she would get herself there. But she heard him move around on the other end of the line and then clear his throat.

'I'll be there in ten,' he told her and hung up.

She was surprised that he'd said yes. He certainly didn't have to collect her. But then, he did live pretty close. Realistically, would he be there in ten minutes though?

Should she try and talk to Craig before Bambridge got here? Ten minutes wasn't going to be enough. She would have to try when she got home tonight.

'I've gotta go to work,' she called towards the kitchen, but got no response. Walking over she could see that the bathroom door was shut. 'I'll see you tonight then,' she added and left.

Standing outside, waiting for her lift didn't feel quite so appealing. The heat of the day was already cooking the streets and there was no telling how long Bambridge would be. She needed to do something about her hangover. She decided to grab a bagel and some coffee from round the corner.

Whilst she waited for her food she had one eye on her phone, waiting for him to call. But as the cappuccino was placed on the counter, along with her food, and an americano for him, her phone still hadn't buzzed.

She'd devoured the bagel before getting back to her building. Stood waiting another ten minutes she procrastinated about whether painkillers were needed. The food had helped, and each sip of coffee was also cutting through the headache. Just as she decided she was going to get some painkillers, his car appeared at the far end of the road.

'Thanks for this,' she offered as she got into the passenger seat. 'Got you a coffee,' she added handing him the cup.

He dropped it into the cup holder by the gear stick and had already pulled away before she'd put her seatbelt on. For the next few minutes, they travelled in silence. Lawrence just couldn't think of anything to say, so she drank her coffee instead, aware again of her headache, edging around her temples.

The silence made her think of Craig, and how he'd made an art of somehow staying silent whilst they were arguing. His ability to start a row and then stare at her as if it were her fault was something she'd never been able to understand. She was still pondering Craig's capacity for ignorance, when Bambridge broke into her uncharitable thoughts.

'Sleep alright?' he asked absently as he weaved between a bus and black cab.

'Not too well,' she answered, and wondered whether to bring up that she'd been arguing most of the evening. She decided against it and went for a more amicable answer. 'I can never sleep in this type of heat.'

'Not sure anyone can,' he replied, eyes on the road.

She looked at him side-on. He didn't look like he'd showered, and she was positive that he was still in the same clothes as yesterday. She took a deep breath to see if she could smell him, but all she could pick up was tobacco smoke. Which was odd because she'd never seen him smoke. Perhaps it was something he didn't like to do in public? The stigma of it had been ever present since the indoor smoking ban. Maybe he just didn't want anyone knowing?

'What do we know about this scene?' he asked after another bout of silence.

Lawrence got out her phone and started reading the sent information.

'White male. Found outside a pub this morning.'

'Drunken brawl?'

'Could be,' she replied. 'Says the staff from the pub found them.'

'They should be able to tell us more.'

His statement sounded final, so Lawrence sat in silence for the rest of the journey. The food and coffee had settled her stomach, but the motion of the vehicle was making her head rattle. Thankfully, it didn't take too much longer, and they were soon parked out the front of the pub.

The building looked like a thousand other public houses across the country. A hanging sign, that hadn't ever been cleaned, stuck out over the front of the property.

Someone had stolen an S from the letters plastered over the front of the building.

'The ilver Trumpet,' Bambridge said aloud. 'This the place?'

'This is it, the Silver Trumpet,' Lawrence replied and typed it into her search engine. 'It's got no reviews on the internet, and no pictures of the place either. The only information is the address, and a mobile phone number.'

'Seems legit,' Bambridge offered, with a hint of sarcasm.

Lawrence held back a laugh. 'Scene must be down that alleyway.'

The alleyway stretched down the side of the Silver Trumpet and looked just as bleak as the rest of the pub's exterior, a thin gravel path, barely wide enough to accommodate a car. The small stones that formed the pathway were so compacted down that it was practically dirt, and various weeds had grown up down its centre.

The scene had been cordoned off, with the victim lying face down between the various bins of the pub. A familiar figure was stood over the body.

Doctor Odell was busy making notes on a clipboard as they approached.

'You guys again,' he said, in what Lawrence thought was an attempt at humour.

She knew that the medical world had a morbid sense of humour, and she could only guess the things Odell had seen. In a way, people who'd worked the force probably had a similar taste in comedy, but for her, now wasn't the time to be using it.

'Us again,' Bambridge replied in a droll tone.

'What we got, Doctor?' Lawrence asked, getting straight to the point.

'Okay,' Odell said, as he took a step back. 'So, our

victim's name is George Stephens. Suffered blunt force trauma to the back of his head.' The purple and yellow bruising was visible through the victim's thinning hair, and the area looked swollen. 'He then suffered more bruising to the face probably from where he landed on the ground.'

'That what killed him?' Bambridge asked, going down on his haunches beside the body.

'No,' Odell shook his head. 'They suffered a puncture wound to the neck.'

'Caused by the fall?' Lawrence asked, as she moved closer to the body. The similarities of this victim's injuries were sparking her interest.

'No,' Odell said with a chuckle, knowing where Lawrence's mind was going. He read from his clipboard. 'This was done by a knife of some description.'

'What kind of knife?'

'A small blade of some description. But it was sharp.'

'Punctured the jugular again?'

'Could be,' Odell answered without conviction. 'I'll know more once I get him on the table.'

'So, they bled out?' Lawrence asked, as she got a closer look.

'Looks that way,'

Lawrence cast her eyes across the rest of the scene. The wound on the victim's neck looked clean. She then looked at the area surrounding the body, and a question immediately came to her. 'So, where's the blood?'

'Did it rain last night?' Bambridge asked, as he stood up. 'There's a drain just there.'

Lawrence glanced at the drain but was instantly suspicious. The area was bone dry.

'Hasn't rained for three weeks,' Odell interjected, confirming her thoughts.

As she leaned in closer to the body, the smell of bleach caught in her nose. 'The wound's been cleaned?' Lawrence asked, looking up towards Odell and then Bambridge.

'Looks that way,' Odell confirmed, 'but again, the table will confirm that.'

'Knife wound to the neck, cleaned with bleach, all sounds a bit familiar,' Lawrence stated as she stood up.

Odell nodded his agreement, but Bambridge had already stepped away from the body, and had started to walk towards the far end of the alleyway.

'Anything else?' Lawrence asked with one eye on Bambridge.

'Not really,' Odell replied. 'But I'm pretty sure he's been here a while.'

'Since closing time?'

Odell nodded again. 'Lay here all night, which gave the rats a chance to have a nibble at him.'

Now that he'd pointed it out, she could see that his fingers looked as if something had taken a bite out of them, along with the tip of his nose, and his right ear.

'And judging by the smell of booze on him, he'd had a skin full. But the tox report will confirm that.'

'Thanks, Doctor,' Lawrence replied, her attention on what Bambridge was doing, for he had disappeared behind the building. She went after him.

He was stood in an area behind the pub that was overgrown with weeds. Two picnic tables sat amongst the overgrowth; a makeshift pathway cut through the undergrowth providing access to what must have been the pub's smoking area.

'You okay, Guv?' she asked, wondering why he was back here. It would have been an opportune place to be sick. The thought of it sent a wave of nausea over her and she took a deep breath. It certainly wasn't the first time an officer had shown up to a scene still under the influence. But she really didn't want to pollute the scene. Another lungful saw her right.

'Fine,' he replied, keeping his back to her.

'You think we might find something in all this again?' she said, as she looked at the unkept garden. 'Another pair of binoculars perhaps?' She had meant for it to be a joke, but it just sounded like she was mocking him.

'The victim had no reason to come back here,' he said, more to himself than her.

'Why's that, Guv?'

'There's no way out,' he offered and then pointed to the high fence all around the small courtyard.

'Maybe he came out of the fire exit by the bins?' Lawrence said as she studied the courtyard more closely. 'If he were a smoker, he could have come out this way for one, and been nabbed out here.'

'Staff should tell us what he was up to,' he stated and then marched back out of the courtyard.

When was a good time to bring up that it was looking like Paul McNulty wasn't their guy? If this was the same killer, and she thought that it was, then they would have to let him go. She would get to it at some point.

Lawrence hadn't noticed when they had first arrived that the curtains were still drawn. The heat of the day was in full effect, and it must have been boiling in there. The thought of going into a hot, alcohol smelling pub turned her stomach.

'Looks closed,' Lawrence stated as they got to the door. She hoped that it was, as it would mean she wouldn't have to go in.

'Yeah, but the landlord should be home.'

'I suppose we'd better go in and interview the staff,'

said Lawrence, looking at the squat pub building with disgust.

'I suppose we must,' Bambridge agreed, looking every bit as reluctant as his detective constable.

'Would you drink here?' Lawrence asked, suddenly, hoping to break the tension she felt emanating from her superior officer. Was he tense because he had realised, he was wrong about McNulty?

'I'm not a big drinker,' he replied.

'I wouldn't be either if this was the only option.'

Bambridge grunted in what Lawrence took to be a laugh. 'Can't argue with that,' he stated and pushed open the front door.

Much like the exterior, the interior of the pub looked like a thousand others she'd been in. Although, this one looked somewhat more tired than others. The wallpaper was faded, the fabric on most of the chairs was threadbare, and the carpet hadn't been cleaned in a very long time.

As they walked towards the bar, she could feel her shoes sticking ever so slightly. The air was thick with the smell of old beer, old furnishings, and stale sweat. Her stomach swirled again, and it took every bit of willpower to not run straight to the toilet.

A man who was obviously the landlord stood at the end of the bar; his arms folded across his chest as he watched them approach. The man clearly wasn't happy. A death near the premises had forced him to close, and his regular drinkers would no doubt have been propping up the bar right now. But seeing the old bill outside would probably have scared regulars away anyway.

'Hello,' Bambridge stated and showed him his warrant card.

'Officers,' the landlord responded with a curt nod.

'I'm Detective Inspector Bambridge, this is Detective Constable Lawrence. We were hoping to ask you some questions about George Stephens.'

'Who?'

'Don't give me that.' Bambridge's smile quickly vanished. 'The murder victim in the alleyway beside your pub. Or does that happen regularly here?'

'No, we don't get many deaths,' the landlord replied, with a sarcastic undertone. 'I just didn't recognise the name.'

'I guess you can't remember the name of every patron you get in here,' Lawrence added.

'I remember everyone's name. It's that type of establishment. But no one round here called him George Stephens.'

'What name did he go by then?'

'Ayrton.'

'What's that?'

'Ayrton. As in Ayrton Senna.'

'Why that name, sir?' Lawrence asked, the joke completely lost on her.

'Because of a little car accident, he had a few years back.'

'What car accident was that sir?'

'Stupid idiot got drunk, tried to drive home, and reversed it into one of you guys.' the barman answered through a bout of laughter.

'One of us?'

'Yeah, backed right into a patrol car. Got a hefty driving ban for it too.'

'I don't get the reference,' Lawrence was mystified. She vaguely recognised the name from somewhere, but she had no idea what it had to do with their victim.

'Not a motorsport fan?' the landlord asked her, and

then turned his attention to Bambridge. 'I presume you're the brains of the unit?'

'I don't get what you mean, Mister...?' Bambridge appeared to ignore the jab at Lawrence.

Lawrence wanted to punch the guy and give him an earful of what she thought. An unusual reaction as she was normally so calm. She wrote it off as a side-effect of the terrible night's sleep she'd had and the sensation that was buzzing in both her head and her guts. Best to remain silent.

'My name is Foley,' the landlord replied.

'Well, Mister Foley, if we could get back to the matter at hand?'

'Which is what?'

'The body outside your establishment.'

'Right,' he stated with an absent nod of the head. 'What about it?'

'Were you the one who found it?'

'Yes.'

'And at what time was that?'

'This morning sometime,' he answered with a shrug.

'Could you be a bit more specific?'

Foley shook his head. 'Not really. I'd had a skin full last night and wasn't really paying attention to the time. I often have a pint or two with my regulars.'

'And how did you find the body?'

'What do you mean?'

Lawrence could see that Bambridge was starting to lose his patience. It was bad enough that she was getting angry, but to have him do it as well wasn't good.

'What we're asking, Mister Foley, is how is it you came about finding the body?' Lawrence added, in what she hoped was a cooling down manner.

'So, you're the brains then?' he replied, as he pointed

at Lawrence. 'Or do you take turns?'

She could feel her blood boiling again, but she kept it under control. 'If you could just describe how you found the body?'

'Well, like I said, I was a bit worse for wear this morning. I went to take out the bins.'

'Don't you do them at closing?' Bambridge interrupted.

Lawrence could tell it was a way of firing back at him. A way to show that he wasn't so smart either.

'I usually do,' Foley stated, 'but it must have slipped my mind last night. Which wasn't great for my hangover, as they'd stunk the place up. So anyways, as I goes to get rid of them, is when I came across Ayrton.'

'Do you use the fire exit when you take the bins out?' Lawrence asked.

'What other door would I use?'

She could have bitten back, have lost her rag with him, but what was the point. They were here for George Stephens, not this mildly annoying pub landlord. 'So, is that a yes?'

'Yes.'

'And how was George when you found him?'

'Dead, obviously,' Foley responded with a look of confusion.

'What I mean was, was he face down when you found him, or was he on his back?'

'Face down. At first, I just yelled at him. Telling him he needed to go home. But when he didn't move, I went over to check him, and that's when I saw the blood.'

'On the back of his head?'

'Right.'

'What did you do then?'

'I checked his pulse, then I called you guys.'

'Can I ask where you checked his pulse?'

'Why?'

'So, if we find a fingerprint in the same area, we can rule you out as a suspect.'

'Why would I be a suspect?'

'Just tell us where you checked his pulse, then you won't be,' Bambridge stated through gritted teeth.

'On his neck.'

'In the same spot of the wound?'

'What wound?'

Bambridge glared at the other man.

'Do you have any idea who might have attacked Mr Stephens?' Lawrence asked, stepping in to ease the tension.

'None whatsoever.'

'No one?' Bambridge was persistent. 'There wasn't anyone that George was arguing with last night. No drunken disagreements?'

'No,' Foley stated. 'Ayrton wasn't the sort.'

'How do you mean?'

'He wasn't the arguing type. Or the fighting type for that matter. If anything, he backed away from conflict. So much so that he also got called Frenchie at times.'

'Frenchie?' Again, Lawrence didn't understand the nickname.

'On account of him waving the white flag,' Foley replied. 'He'd rather step back and let things happen, than get involved.'

'So, you wouldn't say that he had many enemies then?' Bambridge enquired.

'I wouldn't say that he had any. His ex-wife got angry with him at times. They'd row a bit, but it never turned violent.'

'There was animosity between him and his ex?'

'I wouldn't say animosity,' Foley shrugged. 'She was pissed at him for getting done for drink driving. He had a job that involved a lot of driving. Salesman of some sort. So, losing his license meant he had to change his job. Hence, why she left him.'

'How long have they been separated?' Lawrence asked as she made notes.

'Pretty much since he lost his job. She took the kids with her as well.'

'You seem to know a lot about his personal life?' Lawrence added with a questioning tone.

'It's all he ever talked about.' Foley said, heaving a sigh. 'Loved a moan about his life.'

'Do you think his wife could have had something to do with his murder?' Bambridge asked.

'No,' Foley said emphatically. 'She was pissed at him about the job, and the fact that he was always in here, but she seemed level-headed enough to be getting on without him. Was probably better off without.'

'So, the man has no enemies, doesn't have any arguments on the night, and yet he ends up dead around the back of your pub.' Bambridge looked Foley in the eye. 'What do you think happened?'

'No idea.' Foley genuinely looked lost. 'He left through the front door, just before closing time as he always did.'

'So, he went out the front door?'

'Yep, regular as clockwork.'

'Why before closing time?' Lawrence asked. 'Didn't he get another drink in before time at the bar?'

'Needed to catch a bus,' Foley answered. 'Damn thing only runs every hour on a Wednesday, so if he missed the eleven o'clock one, he'd have to wait around till way after closing time for the next one.'

'Couldn't he just wait here until the next bus came?'

'Fuck no,' Foley stated, as he turned his nose up. 'When I shut, I shut. No hanging about. I wanna go to bed.'

'Did Mister Stephens smoke?' Lawrence added, as an afterthought.

'What?' Foley sounded confused.

'Did he smoke?'

'Not that I know of.'

'So, he would have had no reason to be in the alleyway?'

'None that I can think of.'

"And you didn't hear any commotion out there after he left?'

'Nothing.'

'We'll need to know the names of any regulars in here last night.' Bambridge said.

'Can't think of anyone, offhand,' Foley replied.

'No one?'

'Nope.'

'I find that hard to believe.'

'But it's true,' Foley stated with a smirk.

'We'll have to come back, then, when you re-open, Mister Foley. Take statements and confirm who was here and who wasn't.' Lawrence told him.

'You could try, but I doubt you'd get much out of them.'

'Why's that?' Bambridge asked.

'Folk's round here ain't in the habit of grassing.'

'I can't see how talking to the police about a murder investigation could be considered grassing,' Lawrence said cynically.

'Getting them to talk to you lot at all is your bigger problem.'

'Our lot?'

'Yeah, those of the police persuasion.'

'And why's that?' Bambridge asked, again.

'Let's just say there's been some questionable methods used by some of your colleagues in the past round here.'

'Did you make a complaint? Lawrence asked, as she felt anger swell up inside her again. But she wasn't sure if it was in defence of her colleagues, or because the same colleagues had given her profession a bad name.

'What's the point? The law don't come round this way often. Complaining about them when they do show up would only make them come round less.'

'Sorry you feel that way,' Bambridge offered but he didn't sound genuine. 'And thank you for your time,' he added as he turned away from the bar.

'I hope you find who did this,' Foley said to Lawrence as she started to follow Bambridge.

'You do?'

'Of course,' Foley said with a shrug. 'Under all the moaning about his life, Ayrton wasn't so bad. Certainly not bad enough to get bumped off like that.'

'We'll do what we can,' she said with a smile and left.

Outside Bambridge stood with his back to the entrance to the alleyway, his eyes searching the street. He looked one way, and then the other, before looking up at the tops of the buildings surrounding the pub.

'Everything alright, Guv?'

He grunted and continued to look at the tops of the buildings. 'No CCTV here either,' he said finally.

The word 'either' got stuck in her ears. To her it implied that he was equating this scene to the one at the Scenic hotel. Which meant that he thought they had the wrong guy in custody. Or was she was thinking too deeply.

'Ideal for snatching him off the street,' Lawrence offered, but then noticed the amount of traffic that was passing them by. 'Street's pretty busy, though,' she conceded as she did her own observation of the street. 'Would take some balls, and bit of luck to not be seen.'

'True,' he replied, but then pointed both ways down the street. 'It's the furthest point from either of the closest lampposts. Possible dark spot?' He looked back down the alleyway. 'And there's no lights down there.'

'Our victim looks like a big guy though. What is he, about six foot, 200 pounds?' Lawrence added, looking at the distance from where they were to the body. 'Wouldn't be easy to overpower him and then drag him all the way down there.'

'So, he must have been lured in,' Bambridge stated as he turned to face the alleyway. 'Could have been going for a piss?' he thought, after a pause.

'What, when the pub's toilet is just inside?'

'Trust me, I know the inabilities of the male bladder once it's had a few beers. Plus, they only needed to get him a little way into the darkness.'

'That's a long way to drag someone though.'

'Our suspect has already proved they're strong by hanging up our first victim.'

'So, we're excluding Paul McNulty from our investigation?'

Bambridge paused again. She could see that he was considering his words. 'How could he do this when he's currently locked up?'

'You think this is the same killer then, and it isn't Paul McNulty?' She had been thinking that from the moment she'd smelt the bleach, she just wanted to hear him say it.

Bambridge nodded as he stared off into the distance. 'Should have listened to you on that one,' he added as he walked back up the alleyway. 'The cause of death was a single incision to the right side of the neck. Just like our first victim. Plus, they cleaned up the body. And where's the blood?'

Inside, she was smiling. A moment of self-worth that she wanted to rub in Bambridge and the Chief's faces, but she held it in. Call it a professional curtesy, if you will.

'Chief's not gonna be happy,' Lawrence said, glancing at Bambridge.

'He never is,' he replied turning to her, deep in thought. 'Can't see a connection between the two victims though.' He let his words hang in the open before continuing. 'Dead beat pisshead, and a sex worker. Can't image they hung out in the same social circles.'

'I don't know, our guy over there seemed like a bit of a scumbag. Wouldn't have put it past him to visit someone like Tracey.'

Bambridge shook his head. 'They're not even from the same parts of the city. Invariably, people tend to stick to their own little pockets of life. They're too spread out over the map.'

'Okay, so what are the similarities?'

'Outside of the method of their deaths, nothing.'

'There must be something?'

'Like what? One's male. One female. Different ages. Different hair colours. From various parts of the city. Different lives. There's only one thing that connects them both.'

'Which is?'

'The blood. With both cases they took it with them.'

This sparked Lawrence's mind into gear. 'The bleach again, and another precision cut. Someone in the medical profession?'

'The taking of the blood points us that way.'

'Okay, so what can we do about that?'

'Nothing,' Bambridge replied bluntly.

'Nothing?' Her anger started to swell up again. 'What d'you mean, nothing? Doesn't that give us a lead?'

'It does, but what are we to do with it? What possible angle does that give us?'

He stood looking at her, waiting for an answer. An answer she knew she couldn't give because he was correct. They had nothing. Their suspect had made sure they had nothing by cleaning up after themselves. She conceded defeat by nodded in agreement.

'So, we've got nothing,' she said finally. But then a slim hope popped into her head. 'Is it worth speaking to the ex-wife?'

He walked out onto the street before speaking. 'I don't think we need to.'

'No?'

'No. By the sounds of it she had barely anything to do with him. And besides, she wasn't here.'

'Yeah, but maybe she'll know more about people he may have pissed off?'

'You think so?'

'Well, more than the landlord at his local boozer I'd say.'

He considered her words for a moment before answering. 'I don't think so. She kicked him out. What's she gonna know? He probably spent more time with Foley than he did with her anyway.'

So that was it then? She thought to herself. Another case opened, and just as quickly shut by Bambridge. What was his deal? Did he not want to do any work? It certainly didn't look like it. But why was he in such a rush to quash this case just as they'd realised that the two were connected? He either didn't care or had an ulterior motive. But what could that be? It seemed like he and the chief had wanted to sweep Tracey's case under the carpet. Would they have the same thing in mind for George? Until she spoke to the chief about this new case that question would remain unanswered.

'So, what now?' she asked in a huffy tone.

'I need to run an errand,' Bambridge answered, too quickly. 'So, where can I drop you?'

She swallowed her annoyance before replying coldly, 'Just drop me somewhere in town.'

He confirmed with a nod and started walking back to his car. Through gritted teeth she shook her head in disbelief, before following him.

Chapter Twelve

Lawrence had nothing to say throughout the journey back into town. She wanted to talk to Bambridge about why he was being so dismissive towards this new case. The same attitude he'd had towards the first murder. But how do you ask a superior officer why they didn't seem to care, without committing career suicide? She had concluded that the best course of action was silence.

'Where am I dropping you?' Bambridge asked after a time.

In truth, she had no idea. What she should be doing was going back to the station and investigating both victims. If she was lucky, she might find what connected them, other than the way they had been killed. She needed to have a poke around the internet about the blood itself. Specifically, why someone would be taking it and for what purpose.

For profit? For pleasure?

She also needed to follow up with both victims' families. She knew Tracey had been an orphan, so she wasn't sure how much she'd get from that angle. But George's ex-wife was worth following up on. She couldn't understand Bambridge's thought process on that one. Surely all leads needed to be followed up, no matter how fruitless they may prove to be? It was just another question about him that was running through her mind.

She should have been doing all these things, but what she really wanted to do was follow Bambridge and see where this errand he had to do took him. So, when she saw a taxi rack up ahead, she saw her chance.

'Just drop me here, Guv,' she answered as the line of

black cabs came alongside his car.

'Here?' he said, sounding confused, and something else, he sounded distracted.

'Yeah, this'll do.'

'Alright.' He pulled over.

'I'll see you later,' she said as she closed the door.

As soon as he pulled away, she jumped in a black cab and immediately showed her warrant card. 'I'm gonna pay you, don't worry, but can you follow that car.' The words felt so corny in her ears and as the driver pulled into the traffic, she felt embarrassed. But she was soon put at ease by the endless talk from the cabbie.

'What'd they do, officer?' was his first question.

'I'm hoping to find out,' she said as she sat behind him.

'Cleaning up the streets, one scumbag at a time?'

'Something like that,' she replied, with a small chuckle.

'Well, you've got my blessing. This town has got a lot rougher in recent years. What with all the knife crime and that. People seem to be ruder than they were a few years back. I blame the current government. Bunch of wasters, the lot of them. Only out for themselves. Take what they did with your industry for example. Changing that pension scheme of yours has put a strain on everything, am I right?'

Lawrence wanted to answer but he was already off again before she could speak.

'I mean, you guys have a tough enough job as it is. But you take away that pension incentive and the work suddenly becomes a lot less appealing, am I right?'

'You're not wrong,' she replied, but he didn't hear her, he was already ranting about the rise in crime, caused by the lack of funding to the police, and to public services.

His complaints about the current government

continued for the rest of the journey, but she barely listened. She was more interested in where Bambridge was going.

He was headed East, that much she was certain about. But where was he going?

As Bambridge wound his way through the streets, the area he was driving started to bring back memories for her, and none of them were good.

It all looked different from last time. For one she wasn't seeing it all through the acrylic face shield of a riot helmet, and the inhabitants weren't throwing rocks at her. With each second that they drove behind him, she realised that she hadn't been to this part of town in a year. Whether it had been on purpose, or just a subliminal turn of events on her part she wasn't sure. But as she remembered each street corner, a flashback to those crazy nights would come flooding back. Crowds of rioters throwing anything and everything at her and her colleagues on one corner. A bus engulfed in flames on another corner. Shop windows that had been kicked in and looted. She forced all of the memories into the back of her mind.

Ahead Bambridge's brake lights came on and he pulled over.

'Want me to stop as well, love?' the cabbie asked, as they came up behind Bambridge.

'No,' she blurted, 'Drive round the corner and I'll get out there.'

'Smart move. Just in case the guy sees ya.'

Lawrence reached into her pocket, ready to give the driver some money, but he waved her away.

'Your money's no good here, officer. Just make sure you go get your man.'

She thanked him and left the vehicle before she lost sight of Bambridge.

He had left his car, a cloud of smoke billowing in his wake. It amazed her that he was smoking. Because before the death of his wife she was sure that he had been a fitness freak. Or at least someone who took care of themself. Now he couldn't be any further from that person. But then she couldn't really blame him for it.

Bambridge took the first right, and then halfway down the next street ducked down an alleyway. Lawrence jogged to catch up and then paused at the entrance. A glance down the path between the buildings and she still had eyes on him. He got to about halfway down the alleyway and stopped. He took a drag on his cigarette, tilted his head back, and blew the smoke into the air.

Lawrence stood poised, waiting for him to make his next move, but he just stood there. She assumed that he must have been waiting for someone. Perhaps a dealer was coming to him? Drugs would explain his erratic mood swings. But then why come all the way out here to meet up? Could they not do that anywhere? She couldn't see any doorways along the alleyway, and there were no steps or fire escapes that she could see. So, what was he doing here?

His head was still lilted back as he took another drag, but with this inhalation he started to convulse. His shoulders shook as his head lowered, his legs wobbled underneath him, and he collapsed onto one knee.

What Lawrence had taken as convulsions were tears, and her first instinct was rush over and help him. But what would she say to him when she helped pick him up? That she had followed him to see what he was up to. No, she had to stay where she was.

With another wave of spasms, he fell backwards and landed on his bottom. The floor of the alleyway looked filthy, and she grimaced at the thought of what he might be sitting in. But as she saw his shoulders shaking again, she realised that he didn't care.

A break in the clouds brought the full force of the summer sun right down onto the tarmac, and Lawrence had to step into the shade. However, Bambridge just sat in direct sunlight. Still wearing his coat, he must have been boiling. He didn't seem to care though. Only his tears were what mattered to him. And in the quiet of the mid-afternoon Lawrence could hear his sobs.

Her personal phone vibrated in her pocket, and she fished it out. It was a message from Craig. She read the opening line and felt her stress levels rising. He'd opened it with: Can we talk? There were two more paragraphs after the initial words, but she had no interest in reading them. What was the point? Surely, the talk he wanted to have would include everything in it.

She hovered over his number, considering whether she wanted to talk, but now was not the time. Right now, she needed to know what the relevance of this alleyway was. Which meant she needed to get back to the office. She took a note of where she was and then went to find another cab to take her back to the station.

Throughout the journey, all she could think about was Bambridge, and the way that he had collapsed. There was no doubt that he looked weak, and more than a little bit malnourished, but it wasn't his physical state that had caused it. His emotions had done that to him.

She also hovered over Craig's number again, but still had no interest in speaking to him. Particularly over the phone. Whatever they had to say to each other needed to be done face to face. But then look what happened when they'd done that last night. A row had ensued.

Returning to the station the usual bouts of paranoia overcame her. Why had she been picked for the position?

There were a number of officers she could think of that would have been better suited to the role. However, each person that came to mind was male. No matter how hard she tried, she just couldn't shake the feeling of being a token appointment. She was the only woman in the department, and one of only four people of colour she could think of in the entire station. Sure, there were other female officers onsite, and they were good ones at that, but the other non-whites were definitely 'also ran's' in their departments. Was she the same as them? What was it Craig had once said; that she was suffering from Imposter Syndrome. For once, he may have been right. For the briefest of seconds, she had considered walking back out of the station. But she knew that wasn't the answer. What was she to do instead, go home?

With a deep breath, she went inside. However, before she went to her desk, she decided to take a detour to the bathroom. To check on what state her hair was now in. After using the toilet, she assessed the damage in the mirror.

She could see that the humidity of the day had started to work its way in, and there was a mild frizz starting to form. A readjustment of the pins and she was sure it would hold up for the rest of the day. Another check, this time on her clothes, and she was ready to face the scrutiny of Canham's gaze.

The examination from over the top of his spectacles started as she entered the room. His eagle eyes trying to pick out anything wrong with her. But she was confident that she looked good.

'Still hot out?' he asked, as she reached her seat.

'Unbearable,' she replied with a smile and sat down.

'Bams not able to handle it?'

'How'd you mean, Guv?' She really didn't know what

he meant.

'I've not seen him all day. Not seen you's either, but you're here now. Can't see him though. The heat melted him somewhere?'

She wanted to say that she had no idea where he was, and that she didn't really care. But she knew that would only get her into trouble. She also wanted to say that he was off on some errand that she knew nothing about, but that just wasn't true. However, she couldn't tell him the truth. That he was on the floor of an alleyway somewhere in tears. In the end she decided on somewhere between the truth and a lie.

'He's off doing an errand for the new case we just caught,' she offered absently, over her shoulder. 'I came here to do a data search on the victim. Dividing the workload, so to speak.'

'And you got handed the desk work?' Canham said with a mild chuckle. 'Your boy's either smart or stupid, traipsing around the city in these temperatures instead of sitting in the office. I'd say you got the better deal,' he finished and went back to looking at his screen.

Lawrence waited for some comment from Quinnell, but he just sat with his feet up. If she were to hazard a guess, she would have said he was asleep. The man had no dignity.

Opening her computer, she went straight to the search engine and typed in the address she'd followed Bambridge to. As always it buffered for a moment whilst it found any information. A single file came onto the screen and her heart instantly sank.

The report was about the death of Detective Sergeant Natalie Bambridge. She had been found beaten to death in that same alleyway. Due to the multiple injuries that she had sustained, the murder had been classed as a gang beating that had taken place during the riots. Like the two cases they were working on there was no CCTV in the alleyway, so no suspects had ever arisen.

Lawrence searched Sergeant Bambridge and did a quick scan of her details. She had started on the beat and, like her husband, she had risen through the ranks, progressed to CID, and was quickly promoted to Sergeant. But unlike her husband, who had gone down the Homicide career path, she had found her way into the field of economic crime. Primarily, working in a department that spent its time trying to connect organised crime with legitimate businesses, and how best to take down these fronts that the syndicates had set up.

She took a second to admire the talent that had been in their marriage. A marriage that was now no more.

As she flicked back to Sergeant Bambridge's case file, she caught a glimpse at the date of her death and her heart sank once again. It was one year to the day since her death.

Lawrence wanted to go back to that alleyway and comfort Natalie Bambridge's widowed husband. How she would have done it, she couldn't say, but she knew that she needed to help him in some way. All the negative thoughts she'd had about him fell away, and only a feeling of pity remained.

No wonder he had no interest in the cases they were working. Why would he possibly care about two dead strangers with the anniversary of his wife's death looming?

She'd always assumed that she would be working most cases on her own these days. But she now took it as gospel. There was no way she was going to get anything out of him for the next few weeks at least. She would have to solve these two on her own.

Finding a connection between Tracey and George would be a huge step towards solving either, or both cases. But like Bambridge had said earlier, the only thing connecting them was the method that their killer had used. And even that had varied a little.

Yes, they both had been beaten over the head and stabbed in the neck, but with Tracey they had taken the time to hoist her up, treating her like an animal for slaughter. The obvious reason for this was that they had more time with her. They'd attacked George in an alleyway next to a busy road and pub. Stringing him up hadn't been an option.

The main connection was that they had both been drained of their blood. But for what reason?

Was it a prize? The result of their murder ritual perhaps. A trophy that they kept somewhere. Or maybe they were taking the blood for something else. Not as a prize but as a product. Something that they could sell perhaps.

'How much money would you make selling blood though?' she asked herself.

'Not much,' Canham called from over his shoulder.

'What's that, Guv?' Lawrence asked, as she turned away from her screen.

'You asked how much money there was to be made selling blood, and I said not much.'

'How d'you know that?'

'Worked a case a while back,' he replied, looking at her over the top of his glasses, 'People getting kidnapped, having their organs removed and then sold on the red market,'

'The red market?' Lawrence questioned her hearing for a second.

'Aye, that's what they call it. Like the black market but

they sell biological products.'

'Products?'

'Aye, you know, organs, body parts, bone marrow.'

'But you're saying there's no money in blood?'

'No,' Canham said, as he took his glassed off. 'Unless you export it. But what's the point? Might as well get the stuff from closer to home.'

'There must be some money in it, in the blood, I mean?' Lawrence asked as her eyes danced back and forth between her two victims' names. She felt a lick of excitement through her body. Maybe Canham had something here.

'Not really,' Canham answered with a shrug. 'There's more to be made in plasma, which is a component of blood, or something. The real money is in the organs. Hearts, lungs, kidneys, and the like.' Canham leant back in his chair as he studied her. 'This your bathtub case?'

'Cases, yeah,' she replied.

'Did they take any body parts?'

'No, just the blood,'

'Then they're not selling it.'

'No?'

'Like I said,' he turned back to his own screen, 'there's no money in it. I thought you'd caught someone for that bathtub case anyway?'

Paul McNulty came back into her head, and she swore under her breath. They would need to let him go. With a sigh she stood up and made her way to the holding cells.

Chapter Thirteen

Everything was spinning. The floor moved in serpentine motion, causing the eyes to the lose focus. The walls danced, jolting up and down in a steady rhythm. The ceiling was breathing, dropping closer and then rising away. All these actions triggered cartwheels of the stomach.

What time was it?

What day was it?

How long had he been in this state?

These were all questions that ran through Bambridge's mind as he the world rotated around him. He had no doubts about what had caused him to reach this current state. An anniversary and a birthday. One was to be celebrated, and the other was to be grieved.

He'd never been one for celebrating birthdays, but Natalie had always gone at them wholeheartedly. So, in his own way he'd celebrated her birthday. Even though she wasn't with him. His honouring of his wife's birthdate might have been a touch more reserved were it not for the anniversary that came with it. Because like Shakespeare, she had died on the same day she was born.

A date that had brought so much joy and laughter in the past, would now only bring sadness and misery. It was this thought that stuck in his head and helped fuel the journey he had taken himself on. A haze filled trip into oblivion, which could have been going on for days, or even weeks.

It was just another inconsistency that was this part of his life. He'd been avoiding the flat for a while, with the very thought of going inside bringing him out in a cold sweat. And yet, he'd now spent an unknown number of days there. But then, where else was there to celebrate it?

Could he have gone and seen her family? That would have been the obvious choice. But in all honesty, he'd barely spoken to them since the funeral. It wasn't that he hadn't got on with her family, far from it, he was very fond of them all. It was just that the sight of them was excruciating and brought bouts of pain and sadness.

Much like everything else, he could see her in all of them. Natalie was a carbon copy of her mother, and her sister was just a slightly shorter version, but with longer and darker hair. Her father had the same laugh as her, but he couldn't imagine much laughter taking place. It hurt too much to be around them.

He had no family of his own to fall back on. Raised an only child, by parents who had been in their late thirties when he was born, he had always been independent. And it had been just him for several years now.

With no friends of his own to speak of, he'd never had anyone to lean on. His social circle had always been made up of Natalie's mates, and slowly, he had lost contact with all of them after her funeral. Maybe his grief had been too much to bear on top of their own? Or they just hadn't liked him? Had they put up with him because of Natalie?

Some would say that he should be seeking professional help, but he'd never been one to talk about his feelings. He'd always kept everything penned them up until it all boiled to the surface in a sudden burst of rage, and then he'd feel calm again.

Deciding to go to the place she'd last been alive had been a terrible idea. The thoughts of what had happened to her in that place had been excruciating. Going through the events of her final night, whilst sat on the baking concrete floor, had been the catalyst for his recent actions.

They still lingered in his thoughts now. Her injuries certainly were in keeping with someone who had been attacked by an angry mob, and her body had been found in an area that had been right in the middle of the troubles. He wondered, and not for the first time, why she had chosen to be on the streets during an outbreak of rioting? Had she wanted the cover of chaos to avoid detection? Had she been following up a lead? Meeting a grass? He would never know. The commissioner, and every other senior officer, laid the blame for her death solely on her shoulders. And it was these accusations that had caused his outburst at her funeral. He knew her better than they did, and he knew that she wouldn't have been out that night unless for some specific reason. To him, it was obvious that she had died in the line of duty and for the official report to blame his wife filled him with rage. Rage that one day, he would unleash, when he knew the truth. Something must have drawn her into that alley, and it was that something that he was spending all this spare time searching for. The truth.

So far, his investigations had come up fruitless, and the longer he went without coming up with a solid lead, the less likely it was that anything would come of them. He knew how quickly things could go cold, and with each dead-end, his hopes would sink a little deeper.

With his sinking hopes came terrible bouts of depression and self-loathing. He wanted to find some form of justice for Natalie. But when he broke it down was it really for her, or was it so that he would have closure?

In his mind he thought that if he were to find someone responsible for her death, then maybe the pain would go away. Right now, he would have taken it easing just a little, never mind going away.

But would it make the pain go away? It certainly

wouldn't bring her back.

The room intensified with its rotations and Bambridge realised that he needed to get up, he was going to be sick. However, getting up would also mean having to look at all the things that belonged to her. It was either that or be sick on himself.

With a grunt, he picked himself up off the floor and stumbled towards the bathroom.

A pull on the cord and the light came on, assaulting his eyes. His ears also took a beating as the extractor fan came to life along with the lighting. He stood swaying as both senses adjusted to the change. Eventually he was able to take a step forward and grab the sink with both hands. He closed his eyes as he rode the waves of nausea and his body's urge to adhere to gravity. But he kept himself on his feet and looked to the mirror for sanctuary.

The face that stared back at him was unrecognisable. Sunken cheeks and dark patches under his eyes. His pale and sallow skin was a cautionary tale for bad habits and poor dietary choices. He knew that his diet was all over the place. At one time, he had been regimented about his mealtimes, making sure that he got the right foods to help keep his body fuelled for the day. Now though, he couldn't even remember what his last meal had been, or, when he'd had it. His eyes, bloodshot and swollen, were a by-product of the lack of sleep he was getting.

His sleep pattern was now defined by two things. The first being that if he was asleep, then he wasn't out finding Natalie's killer. The second thing being that when he did close his eyes all he dreamt about was her. And those dreams were never pleasant.

There were grey hairs starting to appear at his temples that hadn't been there a year ago. He wanted to put that down to his age but knew that it was more to do with what had happened to Natalie. The grey in his stubble was more noticeable, and it was the stubble he concentrated on. It needed to go.

On more than one occasion in his life he had been recommended a cutthroat razor. His father had been the first person to mention them. As his facial hair had started to grow in, he'd bought a pack of disposable razors to get the job done. However, his father had stopped him, disappeared, and then come into the bathroom with his razor.

'This is the only razor you'll ever need,' he'd stated and had then given him a lesson on how to use it properly.

The other person had been Sergeant Nicholls at the academy. His words had been somewhat less encouraging and had been something along the lines of: 'Disposable don't do shit. Get a cutthroat.'

He hadn't told Nicholls he already had one, because the man had been a mean son of a bitch, and he would have been reprimanded for answering back. He had come up in the 70's and 80's when it was easier to look the other way when a suspect took a beating. Brute force had always been his methods, and that included the way he dealt with new recruits. The thought of Nicholls brought back all manner of memories, and none of them were good. But they had taken his mind off Natalie, if only for a moment.

His reflection vanished as he opened the cupboard door in search of his father's razor. It must have been a year since he'd opened the cupboard. He couldn't remember the last time he'd opened it. But he knew the razor was in there somewhere, he just needed to search through Natalie's stuff to find it.

All the products made him freeze, and for a second, he considered the electric razor he'd been using the past year. It would be a much quicker process, and was in the other room, so he wouldn't have to go routing through her things.

'The only razor you'll ever need,' he mimicked his father aloud, and started taking the products off the shelves.

The feminine hygiene items were not a problem, as there was nothing personal about their bright coloured packaging. And the reels and reels of dental floss were equally as impersonal as he had also used them in the past. However, the packet of electric toothbrush heads hit home hard.

It had always been a topic that he'd mocked her on. She had never been happy with her teeth, complaining about how they weren't straight, or how they were more a shade of yellow than white. She'd been obsessed with the dentist, making sure she had an appointment booked for every six months whether the dentist recommended it or not.

He didn't want to touch them, but he could see the razor was underneath. With his hand raised in front of the shelf he stood staring at the circular heads through the clear plastic of their packaging. Like so many other inanimate objects in the flat it brought a lump into his throat, and a welling up in his eyes. He closed his eyes and blindly reached for the razor. Everything clattered into the sink, and he was forced to open them.

The box had shattered into pieces, scattering the toothbrush heads all over the place. But in the middle of all the damage was the razor, its blade exposed by the fall.

'Always make sure you keep the blade sharp,' his father's words echoed in his ears, and he grimaced at the fact that he hadn't done so. He couldn't remember the last time he'd used it, never mind sharpened the blade.

He picked it up and examined the blade's edge. It looked blunt, so he pressed his thumb against it. The pressure felt good, and he held it there for longer than he should have, and a thin line of blood trickled out.

The blade was blunt, but not too blunt. It could still do some damage if he applied some pressure. Still sharp enough to pierce the skin. Still sharp enough to open a vein. But could he?

The question was coming up more often. And it was normally followed up with what was there for him now? What reason was there for anything?

She'd been all there was. All that mattered. So, what was there for him now? She had been his world, and now she was gone. There was nothing left. Nothing to keep him going. Nothing to make him smile and to make him laugh. Nothing to make him get up in the morning. Nothing to make him go out at night. Nothing to breath for. To live for. To die for. Nothing.

He had two options. Stay in the flat and face the blade. Or leave and face the streets. But which one was the right answer?

Chapter Fourteen

This number would be different.

Different in so many ways.

And yet exactly the same.

The repetition of its existence was no less tedious than others. At least this one's schedule held an element of variety to its proceedings. Enough activities, be they social or work based to keep things interesting.

It had taken somewhat more patience than the previous projects. Hour upon hour spent watching. Waiting. Anger would lead to frustration when the number wasn't where it was supposed to be. Disappointment would lead to self-doubt when it was missed by minutes. These feelings were weak. Meaningless biproducts of emotion. Emotions that served no purpose. Nothing more than a source of constant annoyance. Aspects of life that needed to be controlled. Needed to be overcome. Denied even. And deny them we must. For they were clouding the judgement. The way had been shown, and it was clear.

The number's routine had been learnt and the proper opening had been pinpointed.

Predictabilities would always allow the work to happen.

This number filled its spare time with exercise. Its primary method coming in the form of running. The thought of having to follow in its path had brought on more feelings. Those of dread and resignation. Dread of having to partake in such activities. Resignation that there was no other way. But emotions needed to be overcome as the work would always require some physical exertion.

Predictability produced the results needed.

After following the number a few times, it had become apparent that only one route was being ran. With careful observation and logical deduction, it was clear that a best time was trying to be beaten. A best time that took it on just one route. And one route was good. This revelation had brought with it joy. Joy in the form of a tingling sensation across the skin. But like anger, disappointment and dread, joy was just another emotion. An emotion that needed to be stayed. The course it had set itself wasn't particularly challenging, but there happened to be a rather steep gradient two thirds of the way round that had proved hard work. It was at the top of this hill that provided the opportune location. It would stop there. It always stopped there. For the run up the hill was hard.

The top of the hill had more than just its exhaustion creating plus points. There were plenty of trees and bushes at the crest. Plenty of places to wait. Another advantage was the playpark situated at the top of the hill. An area with ample objects to tie the ropes to.

Identifying the ideal moment had proven to be the next arduous task. Sometimes the number ran in the morning, sometimes late afternoon, sometimes at night. Finding out when it would be running at night had been the goal. Night-time is always the best time. In the dark. Because darkness is a friend.

The number worked at a hospital. A noble enough cause. Its blood deserved so much more though. More than the treating of the sick and the needy. But then, the blood of each number was being wasted. Wasted in such unworthy vessels.

Medical employment leant itself to shift work. Which explained the erratic exercise timetable. The staff were subjected to shift patterns. Four days on, four days off.

The hours would transition from daytime to night over a period of two weeks. Before moving back into day shifts over another fortnight.

The problem with this shift pattern had been figuring out how the process worked and learning when the number had days off. But more importantly when it had evenings off. This had taken a lot of care and attention. Including ventures into the hospital to see first-hand what routine was being dictated to the number.

Frustration formed in the corridors and waiting rooms, but it had all been worth it.

An opportune window would eventually present itself and this night was that moment.

A position has been picked out, right at the crest of the hill, where it will be at its slowest. Bushes thin enough to see through, and yet thick enough to hide behind form a perfect place to lie in wait. Now, it is just a matter of passing the time until the number arrives.

It is silent. The occasional evening breeze rustling the leaves in the branches overhead. The light wind was followed by a stillness. A stillness that must be mirrored. Any movement might give the position away. Through the silence the sound of footsteps echo from down the hill. It is coming.

Excitement flows through the body. Excitement that must be stemmed. Must be controlled. Must be overcome. Emotions are for the weak. And this work was not for the weak.

The footsteps are getting closer. Rising over the hill. Soon the work will begin. Heavy breathing accompanies the footfalls. This is good. The number is tiring as it always does at this point. The gradient is a gruelling one. It should be all that is needed.

Sure enough, it appears over the crest. Its bright

running clothing making it unmissable in the evening gloom. But instead of stopping as it always did, it kept moving. The continued effort at trying to beat a best time must have increased its fitness.

Panic grips the muscles, and a reassessment of the plan starts running through the head. But as the number comes alongside the bushes it stops. Breath ragged as its hands go to its hips.

It is just there. Stood but a few feet away. Its head tilted back as it gasps for air. The desire to reach out and grab it is intense, but discipline is vital.

Approaching it head on, would leave too much open for error. Too many factors that could cause failure. No, best to engage the number in the same way as all the previous numbers, from behind. That way it wouldn't be prepared for the ensuing blow. But with this one might require some leg work.

It starts walking again, moving past the hiding place, and the window of opportunity must be taken. A few quick paces must be made to catch it up before the blow to the back of the head takes place. It falls. The way it flops to the ground is fascinating. The sense of power that surges through the body is invigorating. But the work is not done, as it is still moving. A second blow to the back of the head sees that error corrected. Erring will not be approved. Must not be condoned. Must do better.

Soon it can all begin.

First, the number needs to be made ready. The playpark will cater for everything needed.

As always, the limp figure of an unmoving body proves cumbersome. Thankfully, all the running it has been doing has made it light, and easier to move than the others. The others had been fat, and lazy. The imperfections of the imperfect matter not. Only the blood mattered.

A climbing frame is by far a more effective apparatus than a shower curtain rail, and bath taps. And far superior to the floor of an alleyway. It provides a much sturdier platform from which the work can be processed. Where the blood can be extracted. The anticipation begins to form once the rope has been tied off.

With the number made ready; the process can continue.

Some light is required. Enough to prepare the tools. The feeling of expectation stiffens the muscles, all of them, and the excitement can hardly be contained. But it must be curbed. Focus is needed if everything is to go as planned. Calm and calculated movements are required.

Hung upside down, with its neck exposed, the knife is lifted from the toolbox, and the usual butterflies of the stomach return. Just like last time, the moment before incision proves to be the most difficult. Adrenalin flows, and the hand once again is unsteady. A deep breath and a squeezing of the fingers against the blade and the nerves are calmed. Keep the breathing steady and the hand will follow.

The insertion is clean, and the blood comes forth.

Such an exquisite sight.

The blood invokes feelings of power. Such a divine substance flowing from so small a wound. It's true beauty hidden by the artificial light.

Exhilaration overcomes all other sensations. All that can be seen is the blood.

It would never not be stunning. The way in which it leaves the cut, rapidly at first, but slowing as the heart gives its last beats. Its last few drops, mesmerising.

The sound of approaching voices fell on deaf ears. Eyes transfixed on the final pulses of blood overruled any sense of hearing. But the sound of laughter snapped everything back into focus. Someone was coming. Someone that had disturbed the work. The blade felt good in the hand and could quite easily be used again. Only if needed of course.

A look around identified the cause of the noise. A young couple, out for an evening stroll, were walking up the crest of the hill.

The heart raced as the realisation that they are approaching the playpark sets in. The hand tightens around the blade again, two quick slashes would see everything right. But would it be right? They were not on the list, and so were they worthy of the knife? Only those preordained were blessed with the kiss of the blade. They were not worthy.

They were approaching though, and panic set in. In a second of blindness, the foot catches the container filled with the exquisite blood. It topples over. The blood is spilt. Heart wrenching agony consumes us. The urge to scream fills the lungs, but everything must be tidied away. Swiftly, the light is extinguished, the equipment is packed down, and the location is vacated. A modicum of composure returns, but the mind races. The blood was gone. The area left unclean. The tools stuffed away untidily. A mess all round.

Nearby trees provide cover as a single scream sounds in the distance.

Chapter Fifteen

Lawrence had received the message about the latest crime scene at the worst possible moment. Craig had been mid-complaint when her work phone had sounded. He'd stopped midsentence and scowled at her. For a second, she'd considered ignoring it, but knew that she couldn't, it needed answering as soon as possible. His words about the job being more important than him had echoed in her ears on her way to the scene.

It was still playing on her mind as she walked through the park. People normally came to the green spaces of the city to get away from the heat of the day. But at night they were a different type of space. Some were safer than others, but they all had their dangers when you passed through them at night. It was still dark, but the sky was clear, and the moon had lit the way. Even in the lunar glow she could see that the summer heat had found everything that was green and turned it shades of yellow. The grass had been turned the colour of corn, and the ornamental flowers in the beds were wilted. Her shirt was starting to cling to her back as she came up the rise of a hill.

Blue and white tape surrounded a large play park. It had all the usual attractions, swings, a seesaw, a roundabout, two different sized slides, and what must have been a large climbing frame. She couldn't be sure because a white tent had been erected over a part of the park, but forensics mustn't have had one big enough, as part of a climbing frame poked out the top. On closer inspection she could see that it was actually two tents placed back-to-back. A makeshift cover for an awkward scene? The whole area was enclosed by a waist high black metal picket fence. A streetlamp in two of the four corners of the park would normally have kept the area lit, but technicians had set up multiple lights, bathing the site in brightness.

There were a few officers milling around the site, one was lingering by the tent, whilst another was stood with a young couple sat on a bench just outside the playpark. The couple looked distraught, and Lawrence presumed that it was they who'd found the body. One person she couldn't see was Bambridge. It had been over a week since she'd followed him, and he hadn't shown up for work at any point. Had it been any other time of year she probably would have chased him up. But knowing that it had been his wife's anniversary she'd just left him to it. He'd need to show up to this though.

Stepping inside the tents she instantly knew what she was dealing with. The black and red climbing rope was wound around the bars of the climbing frame and then tied off at the feet. The body was hung upside down, her throat opened up in the same spot. Their suspect had struck again. The only difference she could see was that the scene was a mess.

Blood covered the sky-blue soft play floor around the body, but the pattern of it was odd. It wasn't splattered underneath the victim as would have been the case if the throat had just been slit. Instead, it looked as though it had been spilt. Much the same as a can of paint had been knocked over.

A uniformed officer was stood to the right of the tent door, so she greeted him with a nod. 'What we got?' she asked as she gave the surrounding area a quick scan.

'Don't have an ID on the victim yet. Looks like she was out for a run and got jumped.'

'Who found her?'

'A couple of teenagers. Neither of them saw a suspect, but the young lad swears he heard someone running through the woods before they found the body.'

'Okay, thanks. I'll talk to them in a moment,' she said with another nod before stepping closer to the body.

It all looked familiar. The way that the ropes had been tied around the ankles, with the arms secured behind the back, the knot that held it all in place, it was the same as Tracey. This poor lady however differed in that she was fully clothed. The matching bright green spandex vest and running shorts a clear indication of what she had been doing when the murder took place.

The biggest glaring difference from the first two victims though was the colour of her skin. Her dark complexion was a stark contrast to the whiteness of both Tracey and George. Lawrence was no expert on genealogy, but she would have guessed that the victim had West African ancestry. She was also a lot younger than the other two. It was another abnormality in their suspects hunting pattern. The only connection between the three of them was the method. But then even this one was different as it looked like the blood was still here.

Also, unlike Tracey and George, the wound hadn't been cleaned. The blood had coagulated around the incision, and a trail ran down onto the victim's chin, with a few specks on her nose and cheeks. She checked the back of the victim's head and found traces of blood over an area that was swollen.

'Jumped them from behind again,' she muttered, as she got a closer look at the back of her head. It was more of a mess than the last two.

Now that she was closer to the puddle, it was clear that whatever container they used to collect the blood had been spilt. Looking at the pattern of the liquid there had been something in the way of the spillage. A clear line of the object was visible, followed by a series of droplets that led away from the scene. The blood must have pooled on the bottom of the object and then dripped as the suspect left the scene.

The trail led away from the body, multiple drops at first, but decreasing as they reached the park's fence. Lawrence had the urge to hop the metal structure right where the trail ended but thought better of it. The suspect may have left some trace evidence and she might corrupt the scene. They probably hadn't. They were far too cautious for that. But there was no point in being brazen just because she thought she knew their suspect. Plus, there were protocols that needed to be followed.

Once she had passed through the park's gate, she found the same section of fence and continued her search. Sure enough, the blood trail continued away from the park, and away from the tape that had been put out. However, the lights in the park only stretched so far, she'd need her torch to follow the rest of the trail.

'Constable,' Lawrence called over a uniform with a wave of her hand.

'Yes, Ma'am.'

'We need a new area cordoned off this way.' She traced a path towards a wooden area with her torch beam. 'Our suspect went this way.'

The uniform calling to one of his colleagues, but Lawrence wasn't listening, her eyes were on the floor. At first the blood was visible, its dark colour standing out amongst the dried grass. However, as she stepped off the mown areas into the rougher ground the search became more difficult, and she had to crouch down in the undergrowth.

She wanted to move further into the woods, but she had also just had this suit dry cleaned, and she knew that going further in would do some damage to the legs.

'Gotta start dressing more appropriately,' she muttered.

'Have you found something, ma'am?' the uniformed asked from behind her.

'Blood trail leads into the woods,' she replied as she stood up. 'Cordon this off until we can get more people to help search in here. Are the couple saying they didn't see anything?'

'I believe so, ma'am. But they're both in a bad way.'

'Okay,' she nodded, as she found the last drop of blood at the edge of the woods. 'We've got a blood trail leading from the scene to here. Once you've roped the trail off, I want you to see what you can find further into the woods. I'm gonna talk to the couple, see what I can get from them.'

'Yes, ma'am.'

She left him to his task and found the couple. The two of them looked distraught. The young girl was sat on a bench outside the park, her eyes fixed on a point in front of her. Her hair was in a topknot, held in place by a fluffy pink hairband. Her thin tracksuit jacket matched the hairband and so did the trim of the white miniskirt she had on. Her mascara had run, and her lipstick had smudged up the left side of her cheek. Signs of both were on her boyfriend's shoulder, his own tracksuit jacket a pale blue, with white trim. He had his arm around her and was trying to appear strong for her, but Lawrence could see that he was just as shaken. His eyes wouldn't stop moving. They would glance at his girl, at his feet, at the night sky, at the uniform stood by them. At anything except the playpark. His face almost matched the paleness of his clothing, his newly grown moustache, and slicked back black hair, the only colour in his young features.

They were both clearly of school age and would need looking after. Why were their parents not here with them?

'Hello, I'm Detective Constable Lawrence,' she told them, as she glanced at the uniform stood by them. 'Am I right in thinking you found the body?'

The young girl burst into tears, and her boyfriend held her tighter, his eyes taking on their own glazed look. Lawrence could see that this was going to be a tough interview. Neither of them was in a state to answer questions, but she needed to get something from them, even if it was just the outline of a figure, or the sound of the suspect leaving. She went down onto her haunches in front of them, her most comforting smile on her face.

'It's going to be okay guys; we're going to find the person who did this.' She let her words sink in for a second. The youngsters found focus on what she'd said, the male turned his attention towards her, but his arm tightened around his partner.

'What are your names?' she asked with a lighter tone. When neither of them answered she continued anyway. 'Well, as I said I'm Detective Lawrence, but you can call me Thia. And I meant what I said about finding who did this. One way that will help achieve this is if you can tell me anything you remember about finding the body.'

The young girl shifted in her seat at the word 'body' and her boyfriend's grip tightened further. So much so, that Lawrence could see that he was starting to hurt her.

'It's alright, you're safe now. No one is going to hurt either of you. All these police officers are here to protect you, myself included. So, how about you give me those names of yours? Seems only fair as I've given you mine.'

The young man heard her, and he released his

girlfriend. However, he still didn't say anything. She, on the other hand seemed to come alive as he let go, seeming to see Lawrence for the first time. Her eyes glittered, as more tears rolled down through her running makeup, but there was recognition in them as she took in her surroundings.

'Hi there,' Lawrence said with a smile. 'Are you okay?'

The girl nodded and sat forward. 'I'm okay,' she answered hesitantly, her cheap high heels knocking together as her legs twitched.

'We're a little shook up,' the boy replied, his hands going to his lap.

'I can imagine,' Lawrence said in a soothing tone. 'Do either of you need anything? A drink of water perhaps?'

'A drink would be good,' he answered with a nod.

'Constable, could we get...' Lawrence paused in a hope that he would say his name.

'Craig,' he said.

'Can we get Craig and...' It had worked once.

'Lara,' she said.

'Can we get Craig and Lara some water please?'

The uniform nodded and stepped away.

The sound of the young man's name on her lips made her think about her own relationship, and how her Craig also tended to hug her a little too tight. They'd need to figure out a way to loosen his grip if they were to have a future. But now was not the time for these thoughts.

'It's nice to meet you guys,' Lawrence smiled, as she stood up and then perched on the arm of the bench next to Lara. 'I know you've had a tough couple of hours, but if there's anything you can tell us about when you found what's in the tent over there, that would be really helpful.'

She didn't know why she had said 'us' instead of 'me'. A habit from having Bambridge around she guessed, but then he wasn't here, so why say it? She did know why she hadn't said 'body' this time, however. She'd managed to get Lara to open up a little and mentioning the body might make her clam up again.

'We'd come out for a walk,' Craig stumbled, something clearly bothering him. 'You know, just to get some air.' He subliminally reached towards his pocket. Whatever the real reason for coming to the park was in there and he didn't want Lawrence to know what it was.

'Hey, whatever your reason isn't important. I'm a homicide detective, all I care about is catching whoever did that horrible thing over there.'

Craig realised what she meant and stopped talking.

'I like using the swings at night,' Lara stated. 'Sometimes when there's no clouds, you can see the stars, if the light pollution isn't too bad.'

'The hill gives you a good work out, too,' Craig added, and then fell silent again.

'Okay, so you came up the hill, with your aim to go to the park. What did you see when you got here?'

Craig didn't seem to understand the question as he stared at her dumbfounded. However, Lara had something going on in her head, her eyes darting back and forth, and she considered what she'd been asked.

'Nothing at first,' she recollected. 'The hill had worn me out, and I had to catch my breath for a minute. I didn't notice anything as we got closer to the park. It wasn't until we were inside the playground getting closer to the swings that I noticed...' her words trailed off.

'It's okay, Lara. You're doing well. Craig, what do you remember?'

'Lara's right, you know, that hill's a killer.' He paused at his own words, grimacing for a second before he continued.

'You're doing great, Craig,' Lawrence reassured him.

Lara took his hand and smiled at him.

'It was dark, but I'm sure I saw something moving in the park, just for a second, but then it was gone,' he said, his eyes distant as he tried to remember. 'Then, when we were walking towards the swings, I'm sure I heard something moving around in the bushes. I was about to look when Lara found her.'

'In which direction did you hear the movement in the bushes?'

'Over there, I think.' He pointed towards the blood trail.

'But you didn't see anyone?'

'No. Like I said, it was pretty dark,' Craig said with a shrug.

Lawrence looked at him, then at Lara, who shook her head and then answered no. She swore internally. Having any type of description of their suspect would have been great. But with a little luck the spilt blood might lead them somewhere.

'Thank you for your time,' she said to the young couple as she stood up and left them.

'Detective,' a uniform called and waved at her. 'We've got something.'

Her pulse raced as she anticipated what they may have found. All she wanted to do was run as fast as she could across the field. To get to them as soon as she her legs would allow her. But she resisted the urge. She was the only detective on site at the moment and running over like a giddy schoolgirl was not the answer. She did move with haste but maintained a composed aura.

Reaching the uniformed officer, she felt excited about what they had found. And then instantly felt guilty for getting excited. A woman had just been murdered and she was getting thrills over what had been discovered close to her body. She contained herself as she watched where she stepped. But as a second call for her sounded across the open space she could not contain herself and ran.

Chapter Sixteen

It had spilt.

It had all spilt. The exquisite blood had been lost. Such a waste of something so precious. How could such an error occur? How had such carelessness been allowed to happen? What punishment would await? What pain would follow?

Panic had been the cause of the spillage. A panic that could have been avoided with a little more forbearance and a lot more courage. Courage to just scare off the young lovers, rather than run from them. But what was done, was done. No point dwelling. Except on the blood. The blood would need further considerations.

However, it was impossible not to dwell on the latest discovery. For upon inspection of the tools, one piece of the kit was missing. It was bad enough that the number hadn't been cleaned, but to leave something behind was inexcusable. There was no choice. Returning to the location was a must. Retrieving the tool was a must.

As expected, the location was awash with activity. The scream heard when exiting must have been from the lovers, who in turn must have contacted the authorities. Although, said authorities didn't seem to know what they were doing. They had cordoned off the area with their blue and white tape, covered the number with their makeshift marquee, but hadn't done much else.

Thankfully, it was still dark, and darkness was an ever-present friend. It creates a means to blend into the background. To almost disappear completely. It gives a chance to see if the lost tool was easily traceable. By walking slowly, and not attracting attention it may yet be retrieved.

Initial observations came up cold, as a perimeter around the location had already been established. And yet, the authorities seemed more interested in the number and the lovers than the surrounding area. Useful. The distraction will help to find the lost tool. Their slothfulness would create the time needed. Time to correct the carelessness.

As they hadn't appeared to have found it within the confines of the play area. it seemed logical it had been lost during the exit through the woods. All too hasty. Should have been more careful. More composed. More in keeping with expectations. Not a panic-stricken fool. A scan of the distance between the fence and the woods came up fruitless. Which wasn't to say that the tool wasn't in plain sight.

Circling around towards the woods without being seen might be troublesome, but not impossible. Careful. Must be careful. It was just a question of staying far enough away from any light sources to go unnoticed. But judging by the bumbling boys in blue, going unnoticed wouldn't be a problem. With an almost nonchalant air the treeline is breached.

This opinion soon changed as a new figure walked up the hill. She wasn't in uniform like the rest of them, and her eyes seemed to search the location in a different manner. As if she knew that he had dropped something, and she was looking for it.

Need to be alert. Be careful. But most of all don't panic.

The trees brought with them a cooling sensation, and an underlying peacefulness, which helped to calm the nerve. But finding the exact part that had been trodden earlier wouldn't be an easy task. Keeping the park in sight, more specifically the new authority figure, whilst also staying far enough from the treeline was the difficult part. Just keep calm. Move slowly. Become unobtrusive.

With the park directly ahead, it was now a case of moving one step at a time forward, with one eye on the plain clothed officer, and the other on the ground. With each step the cover of the trees became thinner, and the heart rate grew quicker. The lights brought by the authorities didn't quite reach the treeline, but they illuminated enough.

The last tree was within a few steps when a shimmer of light jumped up from the grass, and the heart rate jumped twofold. The tool in question was just up ahead. All it would take was a low run to where it lay, and all would be well.

Movement from the park caught the eye and brought the idea to a pause. The new officer had left the playpark and was looking at the ground. With each step she took she moved closer. Adrenaline raced through the body. Fear took hold of the limbs. But fear was just another emotion. An emotion that could be tamed.

A step backwards gave cover in the shadows, but all focus was on the tool.

The officer was looking for something. Maybe she did know about the tool after all? Because each time she progressed forward she would get closer and closer to it. Acceptance that it was lost would have to be dealt with shortly. But if fortune was onside today then this new arrival would be just as useless as her colleagues.

Another few strides forward and she had reached the edge of the cut grass. No more than ten metres away from the tool, and another five from the treeline. Time to go.

Flight was vastly becoming the correct option, but the need to tidy up the mess and retrieve the tool was great. Greater than the urge to run away though? The tool was important. The blood was so important. Leaving a tidy workstation was important. Being composed was important. All these things were important, and all of them had been forsaken. Forsaken because of one moment of panic.

The plain clothed officer lingered at the edge of the thicker grass, her eyes still on the ground, but she seemed to have stopped searching. Maybe the tool could be salvaged? However, that optimism soon diminished as a uniformed officer joined her. They spoke for a moment before she returned to the park.

Hope sprang once again but was swiftly quashed by the arrival of a second officer. Between the two of them they began moving into the longer grass, straight towards the tool. Frustration overcame all else. Emotion getting the better. Disbelief followed. Disbelief that so trivial a scenario as young lovers had caused this failure.

Fortune was not onside today.

As the location was left behind for a second time there was another call that passed through the trees. This one wasn't a scream though; it was the call of the authorities as they found the tool.

Chapter Seventeen

Walking in a straight line had proved to be an issue. More so than plucking up the energy to leave the flat. But by doing the latter he'd managed to partially achieve the former. He now just needed to find the scene.

Bambridge had lost track of several things. How long he'd been locked up in the flat. What day of the week it was? The last time he'd had anything to eat. Or even the last time he'd been to the toilet. Everything had been a haze for a while, but his work phone had bleeped, and he needed to be there, at the scene.

He had found the park easily enough. However, the exact location had proven to be more of a challenge. As he stumbled around the dark wooded area, he wondered whether he should have bothered. His mind was spinning. The constant thoughts of Natalie going through his head had got worse.

They had been bad for a while. But now that the anniversary had come and gone, she was, once again, all he could think about. So, locking himself in the flat he'd shared with her had been a bad idea. Just another terrible idea in a long line of terrible ideas.

The call from work had been a blessing in disguise. It had taken him away from the darker thoughts that had been stirring. Thoughts that had been lingering since he found his father's razor. Amongst the darkness of his waking moments, the idea of using the steel as an exit had been a very real one. How it had felt in his hand. It's weight. How the blade had felt against his thumb. Against the palm of his hand. Against his neck.

Right now, though, he'd have taken the flat with all its

memories, or the edge of the blade over being lost in a park at night. However, there was something familiar about where he was. It was all just grass and trees, but there was a nagging at the back of his head about the area. What was it though?

He found a footpath to guide him, and to help with walking in a straight line. There were wooded areas on either side of the path, and he could make out a clearing up ahead. In the distance he heard someone shout and used the sound as a focal point. He continued along the path.

He looked around for the person that had called out but couldn't see anyone. However, he could see that he was approached a clearing. The trees widened away from the path, and a bright light shone at him, beckoning him to enter the clearing.

He could see a few people gathered around a children's play area. Blue and white tape had been set up around the black fencing, with a white tent erected over some of the climbing frame. A modicum of privacy for the dead. Relief that he'd found the scene flooded over him, but he still had pangs of recognition trying to make their way to the front of his thoughts. Had he been here before?

He spotted Lawrence and was about to call out to her, but she started jogging away from the scene towards the treeline. For a second, he considered going after her, but he knew his body wouldn't be able to take the change of pace. So, he entered the scene instead.

With only a glance he knew that they had a third victim. The body had been tied up in the same way as before, and this one had been hung the same as the first victim. The type of rope they'd used was identical, and the knots they'd made were also similar. Although, these ones looked better than the first scene. They were getting better at what they were doing.

Maybe not too much better, he mused as he saw the blood on the floor, and down the chin of the victim. It had been spilt, not straight from the vein, the blood splatter pattern was too smooth. The blood had been collected, and then dropped. What a mess they'd created. A trail led away from the body. He followed the droplets of blood which led his eyes towards the area of woods where Lawrence stood with two uniforms.

Their suspect must have been disturbed. They were far to organised to have done something so stupid as drop the blood. But what had caused them to spill their prize? Probably the couple sat on a bench just outside the playground.

A third victim would have the brass sweating. Particularly as two of them had been killed in public places. There would be more heat heading their way without a doubt.

Bambridge joined Lawrence as she stepped back from an area of long grass. Her eyes were on the floor, but he could see a spark in them, with a knowing smile creeping into the corner of her lips. He followed her line of sight and saw the piece of metal.

'They drop something?' he asked, as he came up beside her. He could see her visibly flinch at the sound of his voice, and her face dropped. She turned to him with a different smile, this one was much more forced. A smile that he'd used in the past. A smile reserved for someone undesirable, or for a grieving family member. But which one did she see him as?

'Evening, Guv,' she replied after she appeared to compose herself. 'Looks that way. Must have lost it when they were fleeing the scene.'

'Young couple disturb them?' he asked crouching

down next to weapon.

It was a scalpel. The blade had a few drops of dried blood on its tip that had mixed with the dust from the sun scorched floor. The edge looked sharp. Much sharper than his father's razor. A far superior blade. Perfect for the task laid out for it.

'Looks that way,' Lawrence replied.

'They able to give a description?'

'Too dark to really see anything. The young lad told us he heard movement in the woods, though. And here we are,' she concluded as she pointed at the scalpel.

'The park not lit at night?'

'Yes. He just didn't see anything. Had his mind on other things I would imagine.'

'Definitely our suspect though,' he concluded, as he stood up.

Looking back at the playpark a realisation hit him. There was a reason he had recognised the area, why even in the dark the trees and pathways had seemed familiar. He had been here before. But more importantly, it was where they had been before.

It was their place in the park. Their place at the top of the hill. Their place with the bench with the great view. The bench the scared young couple now sat upon. The bench he and Natalie used to come to. The bench where they had first confessed their love for each other. The bench upon which he had asked for her hand in marriage. The bench.

The world tumbled as his body rejected his sudden movement. All he could see was a blinding light as he fell backwards. He waited for the hard ground to greet him but was instead enveloped by a pair of arms. He was caught and then softly lowered onto the ground.

He tried to get up, but his limbs wouldn't respond. His

fingers curled up into his palms and his toes clenched inside his shoes. His eyesight also gave up on him. Instead, the same image filled his vision. The image of Natalie on their bench. Everything was muffled, but he was sure he heard talking.

'Mustn't be well,' Lawrence said from above him. 'Let's get him away from the scene.'

He felt hands on him again and then the sensation of being lifted. There was a conversation about where to put him before he was once again laid down on the hard floor.

'Need me to get him some water, ma'am?' he heard one of the uniforms say, followed by the sound of footsteps.

'Continue locking off the blood trail and weapon. I'll take care of him,' Lawrence said as a hand rested on his shoulder. Her voice sounded clearer, which meant that his hearing was coming back. He blinked a few times, but the image wouldn't go away, he still couldn't see anything else.

'I'm alright,' he mumbled as he tried to move. However, his arms and legs still wouldn't react. Her smile filled his vision. The smile she'd made as he held out a ring to her. The warmth he'd felt as she embraced him. The love he'd felt in her arms. Natalie.

'Well, you're not, are you, Guv,' Lawrence replied by his right ear.

He turned towards her voice and her outline started to form. He also felt a tear roll down the side of his face. He just hoped she hadn't seen it.

'Just give me a minute,' he said as the feeling started to return to his toes. His fingers were still pressed into his palms though. He saw her face filled with joy as she looked down at the ring on her finger.

'That's exactly what I'm doing, Guv.' Her hand

tightened around his shoulder. 'Just lay still.'

Bambridge did as he was told. He took a deep breath and then let it out. Pins and needles started forming in his hands and feet, which told him that he was getting some feeling back. He now just had to bite down and take the pain. His teeth ground together as his extremities pulsed.

But the pain took her away. The agony of the blood running back into his hands and feet became all he could think about. The physical pain surged through him and vanquished the mental suffering. Natalie was gone.

Feeling started to return all over his body as his eyesight came back.

Lawrence was squatting next to him, her hand resting on him, a look of concern plastered all over her face as she looked out over the playground. They had moved him to a small clearing on the edge of the treeline.

'Has it been a minute yet?' he asked softly.

There was the slightest hint of a smile in the corner of her mouth that quickly disappeared.

'No, it hasn't. So, just lie there some more.'

'You do realise I'm your senior?'

'What by, rank or age?' she replied as she continued to look away.

'I'm not that much older than you.'

'No?' Lawrence looked down at him with a wolfish grin. 'But you are older.'

'And your senior officer.'

'That too. So, stop acting like my junior and stay still like I've asked.'

'Yes, ma'am.'

As he did what was asked, he watched Lawrence. She had stayed at his side, but as the crime scene technicians arrived, along with the pathologist, he could see that she wanted to get back to the scene.

'You know, you really don't have to babysit me,' he said as he tried to move his arms under himself, but his strength hadn't returned yet.

'I don't?' she replied with an air of sarcasm. 'You sure about that?'

He couldn't tell whether there was humour or malice behind the second comment.

'I can look after myself.'

She snorted a cynical laugh. 'My statement stands, you sure about that?'

Again, he couldn't judge her tone. 'Look, I can see that you're dying to get back to the scene. So, go, get back to it. I'll be fine here on my own.'

'The moment I leave, you'll try to get up and cause yourself more damage.'

'I can't feel my legs right now, I ain't going anywhere.'

Lawrence looked down at him, and he gave his most sincere look. She returned it with scepticism at first, but as she stared down at his body, he could see her assessing his words. She glanced back towards the scene, and he followed her gaze.

Doctor Odell was stood in the doorway of the tent, staring at the body. His technicians were already processing the climbing frame and surrounding area.

'Just go talk to the Doc, tell him what you think,' he said in his most humble voice. 'I'll be fine on my own. And besides, here comes that constable with my water.'

Lawrence stood up as the uniform returned with the drink for him.

'Can you keep an eye on him while I talk to the SOCO's?'

'Yes, ma'am,' the uniformed replied as he held the water out for Bambridge.

He tried to grab it, and his arm moved a little bit, but

then went limp again. 'You're gonna have to help me with that, constable,' he stated bluntly. 'My hands are still numb.'

'Of course, Guv. Sorry.' He unscrewed the cap and held it up to Bambridge's lips.

He drank greedily, and instantly felt the benefits of the liquid.

'You gonna be alright?' Lawrence asked him as she took a step away.

'Fantastic,' Bambridge replied after swallowing another mouthful. 'I'm feeling better already.' He gave her a false smile and then accepted another swig from the bottle.

'Good,' she told him, coolly before walking away.

He watched her go.

Another deep drink and he was able moved his arms. With a wave of his hand, he took the bottle off the constable and finished the contents. He could feel all his fingers and toes again and had full movement in all his limbs.

He could have quite easily got up and joined Lawrence, but he was enjoying the lie down too much. A breeze was blowing across the top of the hill, and it felt good against his damp skin. He put the lid back on the bottle, placed it under his head, and then lay back on the pillow of air. Resting for a little while wasn't such a bad idea. He'd close his eyes just for a moment.

Chapter Eighteen

They had caught a break. Their suspect had left their weapon behind. However, knowing the suspect's history, the likelihood of finding any prints on the scalpel would be slim. A mistake was a mistake, none the less. The main concern was what sort of reaction would they get from the suspect for making such an error?

Lawrence's other concern was what to do with Bambridge. She wasn't sure how he was going to explain his collapsing. Would he write it off as a side effect of the early hour? But then he'd shown up at a similar time to their first victims' scene, so she didn't think that excuse would stick. He could pass it off as still being under the influence of something, but she hadn't smelt alcohol on his breath, and his pupils hadn't looked dilatated. He did look a mess though. He always looked a mess, but this was another level. Wherever he'd been the past week or so hadn't been good for him.

Hopefully, the lie down would help. She left him to it as the sun came up and the scene was processed. Even at this early hour the sun's rays felt warm on her skin. It was going to be another sweltering day.

Doctor Odell had confirmed that the victim had suffered the same injuries as at the previous two scenes. The only difference being that it looked like this latest victim had more bruising on the back of her head.

'Why d'you think that is?'

Odell shrugged and then pointed at what the victim was wearing. 'She was in better shape than the other two victims?'

His comment made complete sense. The deceased had

clearly been out jogging and could well have been in full flow when she was attacked. Hence the multiple blows. She was also younger, so may have been able to avoid the first blow.

'Anything different stand out from the last two?'

'Other than this?' Odell pointed at the puddle of dried blood.

'Yeah, other than that.'

'Nothing. They were all bled out in the same way. The first two had only taken a minute or so to die. And once I get her on the slab, we'll be able to tell if her killer blow was as accurate.'

'Okay, so what about the blood itself?'

'What about it?'

'Well, I was looking into what our suspect could be doing with it, and I thought that they might be selling it. But a colleague of mine didn't think so.'

'This colleague a doctor?' Odell asked, frankly.

'No, but he said he'd worked on a case involving the red market, and that there was no money in blood.'

'Well, he's right about that. Plus, unless you get it on ice, blood doesn't keep for very long once it's out of the body.'

'Are there portable cooling containers that can be used for that?'

'Sure,' Odell replied absently as he delved into his work bag. 'Got enough ice you could use a standard cool bag that you'd use at a picnic. The other issue you'd have is making sure the container you put the blood in is sealed properly. Not sealed, and you've got maybe a day, probably less in this heat, before it spoils.'

'Any other things you can think of that they might be doing with it?'

'I don't know, drinking it?' he offered with a laugh.

'Although, if they are they'll still be thirsty after last night.'

'Any serious answers?' Lawrence asked, a hint of annoyance in her voice.

'Aren't you the detective?'

'Could there be similarities in the victim's blood?' Bambridge asked from the far side of the play park. He was leaning heavily on the metal fence, and there was a sheen of sweat covering him, but he'd managed to get back to his feet.

'I thought you were taking a minute?' Lawrence said through her teeth. He'd already fallen over once, and she wasn't sure she had the patience for it again.

'Change of plan,' he replied absently. 'Well, could there be?' He directed his attention to Odell again.

'What kind of similarities?' Odell asked, stepping towards Bambridge.

'Aren't you the Doctor?' Bambridge replied with a smirk, which Odell returned with an empty stare. They held each other's gaze, neither backing down, so Lawrence stepped between them.

'I think it's been hot enough guys,' she said calmly, 'no need to heat things up at this hour of the day as well.'

Odell eased up first, transferring his gaze to her, the cogs in his brain working on something.

'What you thinkin' Doc?' Bambridge asked, setting off towards the gate.

'I'm thinking I could run some tests on all their blood.'

'Is there enough left in any of them?' Lawrence asked.

'There was still a bit in the other two, and I'll be able to take samples from this one's feet.'

'What you gonna test for?' Bambridge called over his shoulder.

'Depends how much blood I can get out of them. But I

can test for diseases like HIV or hepatitis. Deficiencies in the blood like low iron or diabetes. I can check what blood type they all were. These are all things that could connect them, blood wise.'

'And you're sure you'll have enough blood to test for all three?'

'No,' Odell replied, 'but we'll see what we can do at the lab.'

'Any chance you'll be able to get an ID off her whilst we're here?' Lawrence asked hopefully.

Odell shook his head. 'Once we get her prints into the system at the lab, then we'll see.'

Bambridge had reached the gate and looked over at the other detective. He looked about ready to say something when his legs seemed to go out from under him again, only this time he caught himself on the metal fence.

'Thank you, Doctor Odell,' Lawrence said, walking towards Bambridge, hoping that he wouldn't fall again. 'Shall we go, Guv?'

Bambridge's face had turned puce. There was a sheen of sweat on his cheeks and strands of hair stuck to his forehead. He grimaced as he looked at his partner and forced a smile. 'Good idea,' he answered, standing up straight.

Lawrence got them out of the park, and more importantly, out of the glare from the sun in no time. She quickly made the decision that what Bambridge needed was more water, and something to eat. But would anything be open this early? Checking the time on her phone she realised that it was later than she thought. Hopefully, she wouldn't have to get a sandwich from a corner shop. He needed hot food, and if she was being honest with herself, so did she.

The nearest place she could find was an American style diner; Bambridge instantly quizzed her about why they were going there. She just ignored him and pushed him through the door.

The place looked like the set for a thousand American movies. Stainless steel counters were interspersed between red, white, and blue leather seats and U-shaped booths. The staff were all dressed in the traditional 50's uniforms, however, apart from the manager none of them looked like they wanted to be wearing them.

They were greeted by a waitress whose face went from misery to a fake smile in the blink of an eye. 'Welcome to Sleepy Joe's Diner, how are you doing today?' she asked, in a forced American accent.

Bambridge stared at the waitress like she'd questioned the lineage of his grandparents and looked about ready to lay into her when Lawrence spoke.

'We're good, thank you. Can we get a table for two?'

'Why certainly. Would you prefer a table or a booth?' the waitress asked, smiling falsely at Bambridge, and ignoring Lawrence, who bristled with indignation. Here she was shepherding a cantankerous middle-aged white man around, and it was her that was getting the cold shoulder. Was it something about her that people felt the need to ignore her? Perhaps it was because she was with an older man, and it was just ingrained into people that they should address him? Or perhaps it was simply to do with the colour of her skin? Either option had her fuming, making her question her decision to come into the restaurant.

He stared at the waitress with the same distain. 'What does it matter?'

'We'll take a booth,' Lawrence replied, hastily. Whatever the reason for the waitress ignoring her, she didn't fancy Bambridge kicking off.

'Sure. Right this way.' She led them through the half empty restaurant, to a booth in the far corner of the room and handed them a menu each. 'Would you like me to explain anything on the menu for you?'

'Why, is it different from other menus?' Bambridge asked as he took the laminated menu from her and sat down.

'No, we just do things a little differently here at Sleepy Joe's,' she replied, her smile still plastered to her face. Lawrence wondered how long she could keep it up for before she lost her rag.

'Different to every other restaurant in the world?'

'Look, let's just order, shall we?' Lawrence turned to the waitress and asked for a large jug of iced water and two glasses. 'We'll order food and drinks in a moment, thanks.

She knew bringing him here was a bad idea. Just how bad an idea it was would no doubt be revealed soon, judging by Bambridge's demeanour.

'You, okay?' she asked him, watching his face turn a waxen shade of beige, then he went very pale.

'I think I'm gonna be sick, gotta get out of here. The falseness of this place is nauseating.' He stood up and made for the exit. His hip knocked into one of the tables, causing the cutlery and condiments to topple onto the floor.

Lawrence followed him, apologising to the waitress on her way out. She saw him head up a side alleyway and judging from the retching sounds, Bambridge was, indeed, being sick.

'You still hungry?' Bambridge asked, as he joined her on the street, wiping his mouth with a stained handkerchief.

Lawrence tried not to look disgusted. He really was the most unsavoury character to be working with. He looked like a tramp. She wasn't really sure she wanted to be seen anywhere with him, let alone sit and eat in front of him, particularly with the danger of him puking again, but in truth, she was still hungry. She glanced down the street to see if there was an alternative to the diner where she could grab some food. In the distance she could see a pub, advertising food and live sports on the TV, which would have to do.

'I could use a drink, too,' she replied and started walking towards the pub, but paused when she saw that he hadn't moved. 'You coming? But her nerves, and empty stomach had had enough of him. She didn't wait for his answer and headed inside.

She found a table in the far corner, away from the TV screens and pool tables and sat down. For a second, she thought that Bambridge hadn't come inside, which would have suited her just fine. His hunched frame was soon silhouetted in the doorway. However, he couldn't have looked more lost. He gazed around the half-empty pub taking everything in as if he had never been in one before. Finally, his eyes met hers and he came over.

As he sat down, she stood up. 'Right, what d'you want to drink?'

'You not getting food?'

'I'll order that while I'm up there.'

He pondered her words for longer than she had the patience for. She was about to just walk off and order for him when he shrugged and gave an answer. 'A beer.'

She went to the bar and ordered a pint, a rum and coke, and two portions of chips. As the rum was put down in front of her, she finished it in one go and then ordered another. It felt like it was going to be a difficult couple of hours, so a little Dutch courage was necessary. Although, drinking that quickly this early in the day was probably a bad idea.

Dropping his pint down in front of him, she took up the seat opposite and studied him for a second. He sat staring at the pint, a look of mild confusion on his face. His eyelids looked heavy, as if he was having trouble staying awake. Which could have been attributed to his collapsing earlier. Whatever was causing him to be this way she felt she ought to at least know why. If nothing else to help her understand, and to see if she could help in anyway.

She could also smell him from across the table. It was a mixture of old sweat, overworn clothes, and tobacco smoke. The first two she was used to, she had been dealing with those for a while now, but it was the tobacco that bothered her. Not so much that he smelt of it, smoking was a common habit in the service, and she had more than a few colleagues that had ashtray mouths. It was more that he had started. He'd never shown an interest in it in the past. The bigger question was why was he smoking? Was it nerves? Was it something to do with his dead wife? What was going on in his head?

'So, what's going on, Guv?' she asked bluntly.

He looked at her from over the top of his pint glass, his eyes looked even more tired and lost than normal. He swallowed the beer in his mouth before answering. 'We're having a drink, aren't we?'

'Yes, we are. But what I mean is, what's going on with you?'

'I'm sat having a beer.'

'You know you can talk to me, right?'

'Isn't that what I'm doing right now?'

'You know what I mean.'

'I really don't.'

Lawrence took a deep swig of her drink and stared at him. He was either being stubborn, or he really had no idea what she was asking him. A different approach was in order.

'How do you feel after your fall?' she asked more softly.

'It wasn't a fall.'

'No? What was it then?'

'Just a little dizzy spell,' he replied as he took another sip of beer.

'A dizzy spell that caused two officers to stop what they were doing in the middle of a crime scene to help you.'

'Like you said, the heat got to me.'

'It was dark when it happened,' she said in disbelief. 'And besides, I never said that.'

'You didn't?'

'No.'

The silence that hung in the air was deafening. She decided the cut through the noise with the truth, she was tired of tiptoeing around him.

'I want you to tell me what's going on with you?' she took a deep breath. 'I know about last week. I know it was the anniversary of Natalie's death.' There. She'd said it. All she could do now was wait for his reaction; wait for him to start laying into her.

Instead, he tilted his head to one side and then studied her. 'Oh, you do, do you?'

She met his gaze with the same intensity. It was he who looked away first, his eyes dropping towards the table. 'Yes, and I'm so sorry. I can only imagine what it must be like, having to come back at work whilst dealing with your loss. It must he hard.'

'Oh, 'hard' is it?' he asked with a hint of sarcasm.

'Well, I expect it is, Guv,' she gulped, sensing she'd overstepped the mark.

'Oh, I expect it is, Guv,' he mimicked Lawrence's voice with an accuracy that made her cringe. She took a mouthful of rum. 'You've no clue as to what I'm going through. None whatsoever. You say you can imagine what I'm going through, but you can't. You. Have. No. Fucking. Idea.'

'I'm sorry, I shouldn't have said anything,' she was contrite, squirming in her seat, wishing she'd kept her big mouth shut.

'No, you fucking shouldn't,' Bambridge's voice was very low, almost a growl. His eyes bore into hers, their light blue iciness cutting into her and forcing her to look away. She looked at a poster on the wall, its details lost to her as she as she tried to avoid the pain and suffering behind his steely gaze.

'I'm sorry,' she said, again.

'I wish that were the case, but I don't think you're sincere. You're just like everyone else on the force, insincere, twofaced, disingenuous, and every other word in the Thesaurus that defines the police.'

Lawrence hoped that he didn't think that way of her. That they were just words of anger, or frustration, or whatever it was he was feeling. She wanted to reply, but everything froze in her throat.

'I'm sorry,' was all that she could repeat. She now knew how Craig felt, struggling to find the right thing to say to stay engaged in the conversation.

'I'd give anything,' his voice became almost conversational, as if he were telling her what he wanted from a drive thru menu, or what he'd had for breakfast that morning. If he'd actually had anything. 'Anything, to

189

be in her place. For her to be here and me not.'

'Don't say that,' Lawrence heard the croak in her voice, felt the sadness in her heart.

'Every fucking morning, I wake up, and she's all I see. Sometimes, I think she's still alive, you know, in that moment of bliss before reality kicks in. I barely stay in the flat, I sleep in the car or sometimes in the park, rather than be in a flat I used to share with her. With constant reminders of her all around me. The clothes she wore that still hang in her wardrobe, or on the hook by the front door, or in the wash basket that I can't bring myself to empty. I'm reminded of her by the bedclothes she bought that cover the bed I dare not sleep in; in case I rub away her scent by sleeping in them. By the furniture she picked that fills every room, the curtains that hung in front of every window, the toothbrush that's still sat on the sink. When I do go there, I somehow have to drag myself up off the floor and make it through each room. Each room that is filled with her. I struggle,' his voice faltered for a second. 'I struggle to know what day it is. What year it is. Some days are better than others. Sometimes I feel some semblance of normality. But then I'll hear a song she loved or see woman with the same colour hair as her or wearing a piece of clothing she used to wear, or hear someone say her name, they're not even talking about her, just hearing the name is all it takes. All it takes to lose it. Just fucking lose it. I collapse in on myself. Weep even though I have no more tears to give. Drink, even though I can't stand the stuff.' He chewed on his thumbnail as he stared into the middle distance. 'I went to that alleyway, the one where she was found, with the hope that going there might give me some closure. Some kind of respite from this constant agony, but it didn't work. It just made it worse. That park back there...' his voice broke, and tears rolled down his cheeks. 'That park was where we use to go when we both had a moment. It was our place. Our bench. I proposed to her on that bench. The bench that couple were sat on. Maybe that's why I collapsed? It was all just too much. I'd give anything. Anything to have her here for just one more day. I'd give up everything. Willingly give it up this very second. Give it all up just to be with her. Because living without her is misery. Abject misery. A misery that I sometimes consider ending,'

His words lingered in the air, and Lawrence took his meaning, or at least she thought she did. Did he mean to take his life?

'Don't say things like that, Guv,' she said with a wavering tone.

'Like what?'

'That you want to end it, cos that's not the answer. Please don't think like that.'

'But I do. I do have those thoughts. I've stood with a razor in my hand contemplating the meaning of it all. It's only cowardice that's stayed my hand.'

Lawrence felt her stomach drop. She's never considered him to be suicidal, but his words had really hit home. 'I know it's hard, Guv.'

'Hard? Don't tell me it's hard. You don't know the meaning of the word. You're too young to have even the slightest understanding. You're just a child. A young upstart that thinks she knows everything. But you know fuck all. YOU HEAR ME, FUCK ALL!'

He took a long swig of his pint and crashed the glass down onto the table. Lawrence jumped as she sat dumbfounded. There was a silence. Bambridge dashed his dirty coat sleeve across his eyes.

She didn't know what to do, but she knew she hated being called a child. Memories assailed her, people from the past, men who'd called her stupid, called her juvenile, who'd had no belief that she, Cynthia Lawrence, the little mixed-race girl whose black father had bailed on her worthless white mother before she was born, who lived in a dilapidated council estate in a shitty part of town, shouldn't have such aspirations as she did; they'd called her stupid and she'd proved them wrong. She felt like telling Bambridge her own story, biting back at his comments, even though she knew she should rein in her attitude, that she was technically still on the clock, and he was her superior, but she had grown tired of his neediness. She'd grown tired of all the men in her life. In fact, she was sick of all the people in it. Out of everyone though, was he really the person she needed to lose it towards?

Bambridge looked at her again and was about to say something when her phone rang. She tried to disregard it, but she knew who it was, and she'd already ignored three of his calls today.

Craig couldn't have called at a worse time. He always seemed to call at the least convenient moments. And yet, now was the best opportunity she'd had to speak to him all day. So, she pulled her phone from her pocket and answered it.

'Hello?'

'So, you are answering your phone,' he said in a mocking tone.

'I've been at work, Craig,' she replied, as she stood up and stepped away from the table.

'What, and you can't give up five minutes of your time to speak to me?'

'Not when I'm at a crime scene, no.'

'You've done it in the past.'

'Yes, and in the past, I wasn't dealing with murder

scenes.'

There was silence on the other end of the line. Lawrence could picture him processing her words. Much like she'd just done with Bambridge. He'd be rubbing his forehead vigorously whilst chewing on his bottom lip. 'You don't sound like you're at a scene now.'

She rolled her eyes and ran her tongue back and forth against her teeth before she replied. 'Well, we stopped to get some lunch.'

'We?'

She sighed internally as she could feel the argument brewing already. 'Yes, '*we*',' she replied, leaving her words hanging.

'You with that loser again?'

Again? She thought to herself. What did he mean again? Why would she not be with him?

'Well, of course I am,' she answered as she stared at Bambridge across the room. 'He's my work partner, I don't have a choice about it.'

'We all have choices, Thia,' Craig said, flatly. The fact that he'd used her name told her he was angry, and this argument wasn't going away unless she resolved it. Or just hung up. However, the latter option would only bring more strife.

'Yes, we do, Craig. However, when it comes to who you work with, choice isn't always an option.'

'Have you thought about what I mentioned?'

'What did you mention?'

'That you should put in a transfer request. Moving department maybe or try and get a different partner.'

Lawrence had no memory of him saying that. Which didn't mean he hadn't, just that she couldn't remember it.

'Even if I were to do that, it wouldn't be a quick process. Putting in a transfer request takes time. Getting a different partner takes time. Moving department takes time. Plus, I don't have any real interest in doing any of them.'

'But I thought you were going to do it? After the conversation we had I thought that was what you wanted to do.'

'Why would you have thought that?' Lawrence closed her eyes with the hope that doing so would somehow end the call, but it didn't

'Because that's what we discussed.'

'No. You talked about it, I listened, but I didn't make any promises.'

'But this new role is clearly not good for you.'

'What's clear about it?' she could hear her voice rise, octaves higher, as it carried across the pub.

'Well, look what it's doing to us.'

'It's not the job that's doing this,' she bit back.

'What's that supposed to mean?'

In the corner of her eye, she could see that the two plates of chips had arrived at the table and her stomach rumbled. 'You're a smart man, Craig, I'm sure you can figure it out.'

'You're blaming me for all this?'

She really didn't have the time or the energy to continue this talk. 'Look,' she sighed, 'my foods here, so I need to go.'

'So, food's more important than me?'

'Did I say that?' she raised her voice again, causing a few people in the pub to glance her way. She lowered it again as she continued. 'You're putting a lot of words into my mouth right now.'

'How d'you mean?'

'You've told me that I've promised to change departments at work, which I haven't. A department I fought hard to get into, I might add. You think that I think food is more important than this conversation when it isn't. You tell me that I'm not happy in my job, even though I've never said it.'

'You don't have to say it,' he interrupted, 'it's clear for everyone to see.'

'Everyone except me it would seem?'

'That's your opinion, not mine.'

'Seems like it's all your opinions at the moment.'

There was another pause on the line, one that seemed to last an age before Craig finally spoke.

'What time are you coming home tonight?'

The complete change of subject threw her, bringing a boiling rage to the surface that she tried her best to keep out of her voice. 'I can't answer that,' she hissed, through her teeth.

'You can't, or you won't?'

'I can't,' she snapped, 'because I genuinely don't know. We've caught an ugly one that is going to take a lot of our time.'

'You mean you and him?'

'Who else would I mean, Craig?'

'So, you'll be spending the evening with him?'

'We'll be going over the case, yes.'

'But you're with him right now, and will be with him all night?'

'He's my partner, Craig. What d'you want me to say?'

'I thought we were partners?'

'Is that what we are?' Lawrence knew that what she'd said was petty, but it had already left her lips before her brain caught up.

'What's that supposed to mean?'

'Look, I've got to go. Can we pick this up later?' She didn't wait for his response and hung up. She then put her phone on silent and put it back in her pocket.

Ignoring the looks she was getting from some of the punters, she went straight to the bar and ordered another rum, only this time without coke.

'Everything alright?' Bambridge asked as she returned to the table.

The neat rum she'd sipped before sitting down had stripped her throat and she coughed a few times before answering. 'Wonderful,' she offered finally, the sarcasm in her words thick in the air.

'D'you need to talk about it?' His tone sounded mocking.

'Not sure how you could help.'

'Relationship troubles?' he asked, only this time the mockery was gone, and he sounded concerned.

'You could say that,' she replied as she fought the heartburn the rum had brought on.

'Well, tell me about them,' he said with a smile, something Lawrence thought was impossible. 'I was in a relationship once; I might be able to help' That smile again. He'd been shouting at her moments ago, did he actually care? It seemed genuine. She returned it, and then distracted herself with the chips. The smell had made her mouth water.

She picked one up and bit into it. The heat from the inside was molten, and she had to bounce the hot potato from one side of her mouth to the other before she could swallow it. Cursing herself she blew on the other half of the chip, steam billowing out of the end, she knew she wouldn't be able to taste anything because of her burnt mouth.

'He's just a very jealous man,' she offered after her mouth cooled down a little.

'Jealous of what?' he asked as he took a chip, split it in

two and blew on the two parts.

'Of everything.'

'You'll have to be more specific than that.'

Lawrence shook her head as she tried to think about what Craig had shown jealousy over in the past, but it just seemed like he was always jealous. 'Of everything,' she repeated.

'Of what though? Of your career? The way you deal with your money? The complexion of your skin?'

'All of the above. Apart from the skin bit,' she answered honestly. 'He's in a minority there though.'

Bambridge ignored her insinuation of racism and pressed on.

'But there's got to be something that has bothered you specifically, otherwise we wouldn't be having this conversation.'

She wanted to tell him that it was him Craig was jealous of, but she dared not say. How would he take it? Would he think that she was taking the piss? Would he think that she thought of him in that way? Did she think of him in that way? He was by no means an ugly man, but the layer of funk that covered him had always turned her head away. She'd been with uglier men. Men that had made her grimace when she'd woken up next to them. But that was a long time ago, in a different life. Thinking of past lives gave her a subject to concentrate on.

'At the start of the relationship he was fine. We got on great, he was kind and considerate, and was clearly from a better stock than my previous boyfriends.'

'Better stock?' Bambridge looked genuinely puzzled.

'Yeah, you know, he was raised better.'

'How d'you mean?'

'Look, I grew up on an inner-city council estate, decent long-term partner material was slim pickings. So, you had to make do with what you got. Anyway, a few months in, stories of past conquests started to come out, as they tend to do, and he would have a real hard time dealing with what he found out.'

'How bad could it be?' Bambridge asked with doubt in his voice and written all over his face. 'You seem so grounded.'

Lawrence held up her glass and swished it around to emphasize her point. 'I used to do a lot of this,' she answered and then took a sip. 'Booze wasn't my friend and had a tendency of making me a bit loose. And loose Thia could get real wild.'

She didn't know why she was telling him this. He didn't need to know about things she got up to in her teens. The booze had started to loosen her tongue. She just needed to keep on top of it. But then when was the last time she'd drunk rum?

'Thia?' he said from over the top of his half-drunk pint.

'Yeah, Thia. It's my name.'

'Never heard that one before.'

She could tell that he thought it was something exotic, some name that had been handed down the ancestry line, and in a way it had been. Cynthia had been her grandma's name, but everyone had always just called her Thia. She'd been asked if it was African on more than one occasion, and sometimes she'd gone along with it. Telling them it was Greek and given to her after her white grandmother normally brought less of a reaction with it.

'You tell me yours, and I'll tell you the origin of mine.'

'Not important is what it is,' he said as he drank some more of his beer.

'Come on man. I'm sharing, so why don't you?'

He stared at her blankly. 'Because we're talking about your jealous other half.'

'Oh yeah, him.'

'Is it just your past he's envious of, or does he have a thing for how successful you are at work as well?'

'I wouldn't say I'm successful,' she said as she took another sip of her drink and realised, she wanted another. Old habits die hard.

'You're one of the youngest people I know to make the rank of homicide detective.'

'Not as young as you were though.'

'No, not as young as me. But you must be one of the youngest women to ever reach the role. And a woman of colour at that.'

'Why does my colour matter?' she could feel herself getting defensive.

'You tell me.'

She wanted to yell every reason why. Why she had to work twice as hard to get the same rewards as a white woman. The way she was often ignored in the staff canteen, yet the catering staff would happily talk to a white woman. The way Craig's family still hadn't really accepted their son's choice of partner. Of course, her colour mattered, but it shouldn't and that was why she got defensive, every time it was mentioned. But should she voice her opinion about how she saw herself as a token appointment? That was a whole other conversation that she didn't want to have right now. And besides, she was supposed to be grilling him.

'Okay, you make some good points there. But how old was your wife when she got promoted to Sergeant? I seem to remember her rising through the ranks swiftly.'

The minute she mentioned Natalie, she wished she hadn't. At the mention of his wife, Bambridge seemed to implode. His shoulders dropped, his head dipped low, and his skin paled. Lawrence wanted to apologise for bringing her up but judging by his previous reaction, this was the subject that she needed to push him on. There was no doubt that he was suffering from the death of his wife, and he'd just told her he didn't want to be around anymore. Maybe, if she was able to get him to talk about it, though, then maybe she would see some progress in him.

'You miss her.' she said, gently. It wasn't a question, but she hoped that it would create some kind of reaction from him. However, he just seemed to sink further into himself. 'I know it must be tough to talk about it, but I think it'll do you good.'

'Oh, you do, do you?' he said bitterly. 'Don't start that again.'

'I'm sure it couldn't hurt.'

'Hurt?' he replied, and then leant back in his chair. 'Hurt is all I've got.' There were tears in his eyes again, and he was biting down on his bottom lip. 'Perhaps hurting myself is the answer.'

This was not the reaction she wanted. He was moments away from breaking down in front of her again. She hadn't wanted this, she had just hoped to get some words out of him, not tears.

'It wasn't my intention to make you cry, Guv.'

'I'm not crying,' he replied, as his eyes welled up.

'Sure, you're not,' she offered reassuringly. 'And I'm sorry that I've made you feel this way.' She paused to assess what state he was in, and whether she should continue. She probably should have stopped; however, loose Thia had started to creep into her muscles, and she wasn't in the mindset for stopping something she'd started. 'I won't presume to know what you're going through but talking about it can only be a good thing.'

'I'm not much of a talker,' he said and then finished

his drink.

'Well, that's a lie,' she replied with a warm chuckle, 'I've heard you talk more than one suspect into a confession.'

'Different kind of talking.'

'How so?'

'It's not about me.'

Lawrence's phone vibrated in her pocket. She told herself that she needed to ignore it and let it ring out.

'Talking's talking though, right?' she asked.

'Do you find it easy talking about yourself?'

She considered his question, and her usual answer would have been no. But she'd had a drink, and the alcohol was now flowing through her system. 'Only when I've got some booze in me.'

'Perhaps that's what I need to do?' he said, his shoulders loosening ever so slightly, and the beginnings of a smile forming on his lips.

'What can I get you?' she asked as she stood.

'I don't really drink, and that pint has filled me up, so I'm good thanks.'

'You gonna let me drink on my own?' She stood over him, with one hand on the table, waiting for an answer, looking dominant and controlling Or at least that's what she hoped Bambridge was seeing. In truth, she'd got up far too quickly, and the rum had already gone to her legs. Holding onto the table was stopping her from falling over, too.

'I guess not,' he answered, with a shrug.

'Great. What're you having?'

'Like I said, I'm not a big drinker,' he said as he looked up at her. There was the tiniest spark of life behind his eyes. The most activity she'd seen there since before his wife's death. Maybe she was getting to him? She never paused to wonder why getting to him mattered so much to her. 'I'll have what you're having.'

'Great!' Lawrence said with a smile and headed to the bar.

Chapter Nineteen

Bambridge couldn't remember the last time he had felt this way. He would have said that he was happy, there was no getting around the underlying pain that still dwelled within him. However, the past few hours had been a welcome relief.

He'd tried alcohol as a means to numbing the pain, but it had only made it worse. He'd needed good company, though, he admitted, and someone who would listen. Lawrence had done both, although how much she'd remember was questionable. She knew how to drink.

With the drinks came a feeling of relaxation that he hadn't experienced in a long time. His muscles eased in a way that felt alien, causing him to sink deep into his chair. With this new sense of ease his tongue had also started to relax.

Lawrence's tongue, however, hadn't really stopped.

'You know you're real easy to talk to,' she offered after ranting about her football team for the past ten minutes. It had been the trend of the evening, Lawrence jabbering on about something for a while, before going completely off topic the next. If nothing else, it was amusing.

He wanted to contribute about the football, but in truth he'd lost interest in the sport years ago. His childhood club had been languishing in the lower leagues since he could remember. Plus, he just didn't understand the fervour that came with it.

'I guess I'm a good listener,' he offered unconvinced, his words sounding slurred.

'You are,' Lawrence replied, holding up her drink to toast him. 'But as I keep saying to you, I don't want you to listen, I want you to talk to me.'

She was also slurring her words, but she was in complete control of herself. As if this level of drunk was nothing new to her. She wouldn't have been the first copper that dealt with the traumas of the job with booze, Bambridge noted

'What d'you want me to talk about?' he asked.

'Everything,' she stated, putting her glass down and sitting back with her arms folded. 'Anything.'

'Like what?'

'Like, where you go with these errands of yours. Or, how you're feeling.'

'How I'm feeling? That's a bit vague. How I'm feeling about what?'

'About anything. About how you're coping with being back at work. How you're coping with the loss of your wife?'

Bambridge's stomach dropped at the mention of Natalie. Although, the feeling wasn't as bad as it had been in the past. He wrote it off as the booze numbing him to the sensation. Or maybe it was the company?

He was enjoying his time with her. Her company was welcome, and as he'd been watching her across the table, he had found her enthusiasm intoxicating. Or was it the booze? Whichever it was had made him realise just how lonely he was. Outside of work he hadn't held a conversation with anyone in a long time. So, the hours they had spent together was the most he'd talked to someone in over a year. And he had to admit that it felt good.

Aside from just now, when Lawrence had brought her up, he hadn't thought about Natalie for hours. He had been completely engaged. But now that she had been discussed he didn't know what to say, because the sense of doom had returned. The same feeling that had been enveloping him for the last year was back, and he had no desire to talk about it.

'I think I'd rather talk about footy again,' he said.

'Fuck me, I wouldn't,' Lawrence replied, her arms still folded. 'I've already got palpitations about next season. But you've gotta talk, Guv.' She sat forward with a look of sincerity on her face. 'If not to me, then to a professional.'

'I don't know, you seem like a professional talker from where I've been sat.' He'd meant the comment as a joke but couldn't gauge if she'd taken it as one, as the sincere look on her face continued.

'I'm being serious,' she leant over the table and looked him in the eyes. Hers were a deep shade of brown, with a lighter hazel at the edges. They were sincere. He could tell that she meant what she was saying. But he could also see the desperation. Had he driven her to it? To such levels that she was almost pleading with him to seek help. She had every right to. He had been a nightmare to work with this last year, and that wasn't likely to change any time soon. He could also see her own pain. Something more than just him.

'I know you are,' he replied with an attempt at a smile. He'd wanted it to look genuine, but he must have failed, she took his words to be sarcastic.

'Yeah right,' she replied, belligerently and shot him a scornful look. 'So why don't you do anything about it? Why do none of you men ever talk? Get things off your chest. Instead of being these pressure cookers that just explode when everything becomes too much.'

'I'm sensing we're not talking about me anymore.'

'What makes you say that?'

'I overheard your chat on the phone earlier. Boyfriend?'

'Oh, you "overheard" did you?' Lawrence added the quotation marks in the air, but there was no humour in them. She looked angry.

'Well, the whole pub overheard, actually,' he replied, with a grin, trying to defuse her annoyance. It seemed to work as a smile crept across her face.

'That was, kind of, about you actually.'

'He telling you to mind your own business?' Again, he'd meant it as a joke, but now she looked offended.

'Not even close,' she said after a pause. He could see that she trying to decide to tell him or not. 'More like change my business.'

Bambridge didn't understand the comment. 'What d'you mean?'

'It doesn't matter. The difficulties of my relationship aren't what we were talking about. We're supposed to be getting you to open up.'

'What sort of difficulties?'

She shook her head and a waved a finger at him at first. But then he could see that she wanted to talk about it. Something he knew he couldn't do. But her doing it would mean that he wouldn't have to.

'Come on, what difficulties?'

She shook her head again as she stifled a burp. It looked like the alcohol had finally started to hit her. But she refused to talk.

'Okay, how about you tell me your problems and I'll let you in on some of mine?' He had no intension of speaking to her about his issues, but she clearly needed to get them off her chest.

Her eyes lit up, and she moved around the table to the chair next to Bambridge. 'Deal,' she said, and held out her hand. He shook it and watched as she settled in to tell her story.

'Craig's a jealous guy.'

'Like John Lennon?'

'What?

'Never mind. What's he jealous of?'

Lawrence held her hands up as if she were showing him the size of a fish she'd once caught. 'Everything,' she answered.

'Of me?' His voice was incredulous. He looked down at his clothes and then glanced at his dark reflexion in the glass of a picture on the wall. 'What's there to be jealous of?'

'I think he just feels threatened.'

'He's never even met me.'

'Threatened by the fact you spend more time with me than he does.'

'Isn't that how partnerships work?'

'Yep,' she answered and then immediately paused and reached into her pocket. Bambridge could see the screen of her phone was lit up with a picture of a man that must have been Craig. She stared at the image for a moment, her jaw clenched, before she hit the decline button. As she was putting it back, he could hear it start vibrating again.

'Everything alright?' he asked but judging by the look on her face it clearly wasn't.

'We've just been fighting a lot,' she replied, her jaw still tight. 'And I can't be dealing with that conversation right now.'

'You'll need to talk at some point,' he offered.

'Not sure you can say anything about talking things through.'

He couldn't really argue with that comment.

'True,' he replied, 'but one of the best ways to keep a relationship going is to communicate. That was one of the things we got right.' He paused at the thought of Natalie, and the fact that he was going to speak about her. There were still butterflies in his stomach at the idea of it, but he continued anyway. 'If either of us had a problem with the other, we'd get it out in the open quickly. Both of us having very to the point personalities no doubt helped, but it doesn't pay to let things linger.'

She looked at him with what he thought was admiration, smiled and touched him softly on the shoulder. 'I couldn't agree more,' she stated, moving forward on her seat.

She was sitting pretty close. So close that he could smell her perfume. Or was it her deodorant? Whatever it was, it smelt good.

'The trouble I've got with getting it all out in the open,' Lawrence stated, as she moved her hand to his knee. 'Is that Craig always brings up the past.'

'Isn't that the point?' he said, looking down at her hand. 'You speak about things that have happened that hurt you.'

'No, but I mean in my past, before we were together.'

'Like what?' Her hand hadn't moved.

'Like, he still brings up a party we were at. A guy I was with one time came up and started speaking to me, oblivious that Craig was my other half. He starts speaking about what a great time he'd had and that we should do it again.'

'I can see why that would be a problem.' Her touch felt good. But he knew that it shouldn't.

'It was the detail the guy went into, right within earshot of Craig that caused the issue.'

'Detail? What, did the guy call it play by play or something.'

'Pretty much. I don't remember what the guy really

said, but Craig made sure to remind me the next day. And the day after that. And whenever we've argued since. I'm amazed he hasn't brought it up recently.'

'Can't have been that bad what the guy said?'

'Like I said, I don't remember what was said, but Craig reckoned he said something like 'my suck game was on point, with nothing but pure deepthroat'.'

'Jeez,' Bambridge hoped he sounded shocked. In truth the comment had stirred something in him.

'That's not all. He also said that I fucked like a porn star, that my pussy was the tightest that'd ever ridden him, and that he was washing the shit stains off his balls for days.'

Bambridge had to process what she'd said. The words were a lot more graphic than he'd been expecting, and he could see why they would have offended her other half. They would have incensed him as well. Hearing that said to any woman would have put him on edge.

The other problem he had was her words had put images in his head. Images of Lawrence doing the deeds described. Add the close proximity of her hand to his groin and he felt stirrings in his loins. He couldn't even remember the last time he'd been aroused. So, to feel it after such an unpleasant series of words made him worry. His worry increased and turned to fear that she would spot his arousal, and what she would do if she did see it.

'Pretty graphic choice of words,' he said, leaning forward to hide the bulge in his trousers. But by doing so he had moved closer to her, and her smell only enhanced his arousal.

'Like I said, I grew up around some rotten people. People who think that talk like that will get a girl's attention.'

'And Craig was different?' He hoped that talk of her

boyfriend would douse the fire in him.

Their eyes met for the second time. Only this time, rather than care and desperation, he could see uncertainty in them, along with something else, something he could decipher. As he held her gaze, he thought that it might be desire, but he instantly quashed the notion. There was nothing desirable about him. She shifted forward slightly, and for a second he thought she was about to kiss him, until her eyes looked down.

Her hand tightened around his thigh as her eyes rested on his crouch. He felt his cheeks go red with embarrassment and he was about to leave when she leant forward and kissed him. He backed away from her advance and once again looked her in the eyes. However, he barely recognised her. The look was like nothing he'd ever seen. There was a hunger in them that he had never experienced outside of a wildlife program. She had a predatory look about her that left him paralysed. Her hand went to his groin, and he froze.

'Is this a good idea?' he asked, through his clenched lips.

'Let's find out.' Her hand rubbed against him, and he felt himself get harder. Her lips met his again and her tongue slipped into his mouth. Her touch felt good, and he could think of no reasons not to continue. So, he kissed her back.

At first the sensation felt odd, like a long-lost feeling coming back from an age ago. But as their tongues connected, recognition set in, and he remembered how good it could feel.

Remembering the joy of kissing was followed by a sensation in his genitals. A sensation he hadn't felt for a year. A feeling that was being heightened by Lawrence rubbing her hand against his penis. The feeling grew to a pressure. A pressure that hadn't been released in quite some time. Not since Natalie. Her faced flashed before his eyes as he ejaculated into his underwear.

'I can't do this,' he exclaimed, pushing Lawrence away as he stood up. He could feel the dampness around his groin as he walked away from the table. Could feel the blood leaving his penis as it went flaccid. But mostly he could see Natalie's disapproving look, He could see the heartbreak in her face as he told her he'd been unfaithful. Now he could feel the pain in his own heart at what he'd done. The pain wouldn't cease. Would never go away. Natalie wouldn't let it.

Without looking back, he left Lawrence and the pub behind. He wanted to leave it all behind. Everything.

Chapter Twenty

Lawrence lay on her back, the room spinning from the sudden movement as she'd tried to sit upright. For a second she didn't understand what had happened. She had been into it, and it certainly felt like he had been. So, what was the problem?

He was the problem, she told herself, because she should never have ended up at this stranger's flat, in his bed, with him needing to prove himself. Prove that he could – how had he put it – 'go with a dark-skinned girl.' Well, fuck this guy, he hadn't been able to get it up anyway.

Why had she done it? Gone on the prowl. Why had she not just gone home when Bambridge had left her? Instead, of finding another drinking hole, seeking out some guy, and going back to his place. Deep down she knew why; because drunken Thia had been in charge.

The sound of vomiting came from somewhere in the flat, which told her that whatever his name was would be otherwise engaged for a while. Time to get herself together and head for the exit.

The old her had reared its ugly head. A part of her she thought was long gone, had surfaced, and was trying to ruin her career. Drinking off shift with her boss was one thing, jerking him off whilst sticking your tongue down his throat in the corner of a pub was quite another. What was it with men and no staying power tonight? More importantly though, what would she say to him? He would no doubt look at her like a slag from an estate, eager to put it about once she'd had too many drinks. An ugly truth at one point in her life, but not anymore.

However, those kinds of rumours spread like wildfire once the police got hold of them.

Why had she done it? She was in a relationship and prided herself on having never been unfaithful. So why had she been so willing? Was it the talk of those days that had coaxed those bad elements back to life? Or it was the booze that had brought them back? She'd been just as drunk in the past and hadn't acted this way. Was it because of her anger at Craig? Her lashing out in the worst possible way. It could have been any one of those reasons, or a combination of all of them. All she knew was that she needed to leave.

Slowly, she got up off the bed. She must've drunk more than she thought because she felt uneasy on her feet. She fought to stay upright and focussed on trying to find her clothes. Picking up her trousers, top, underwear, jacket, she dressed swiftly. Instinct made her check her badge; it was still in her inside jacket pocket. She stumbled towards the door which led to the hall, still listening to the unpleasant sound of retching echoing from a bathroom somewhere. She crept to the door, wincing at the noise the latch made as she unlocked it. Slowly opening the door, she stepped into the semi-lit, drab looking hallway and made for the door. What the hell had she done?

Outside, the humid night air did little to revive her throbbing head. Instead, the lack of any sort of breeze made her feel sick. She leant against a wall, taking deep gulps of air until she felt a little steadier. She straightened up, and then looked around to get her bearings. It wasn't a part of the city she was familiar with, so she started walking in the direction she thought they'd come from, but she couldn't be sure.

She began to feel better with each step. Just breathe, she told herself as her mind filled with all sorts of unpleasant repercussions from this evening. First, there was Bambridge. What was she going to say to him? How could she look him in the eye knowing what she'd done to him? Second, there was Craig. How was she going to explain getting home looking and smelling like she'd been out boozing and screwing around? She didn't stop to evaluate why she'd thought of Bambridge first.

The dull hum of an engine met her ears, and a black cab came trundling down the street. Throwing out her arm, she almost cried with relief when the cab pulled over and she could hurl herself safely inside.

'Where to, love?' the driver asked.

Lawrence knew she had to go home. She could hardly turn up to the station looking the way she did. She gave the driver her address, and sank back into the leather seat, resting her head on the cool glass window.

Suddenly, she felt her phone vibrate in her pocket. She supposed it was Craig and wondered how many times he'd tried to call since their last conversation. Peering at the screen, she realised it wasn't Craig, after all. It was Bambridge. What the hell did he want?

'Yes, Guv,' she said into the phone, as brightly as she could. Pretending none of earlier events had happened.

'You're one of the good ones, Lawrence, d'ya know that? And a decent copper too. Time to earn those three chevrons, Detective. Time to find out if your boss is a coward after all.'

She froze, all her drunken hang ups gone. There was something not quite right about Bambridge's voice. It was slurred, and slow in a strange way. She was instantly sober.

'Guv! Where are you? What's going on? What d'you mean by that?'

'You must always be listening, Detective, a single

word can be all it takes.'

'All it takes for what, Guv?'

'To crack the case,' Bambridge's strange, unfamiliar voice told her. 'Perhaps another clue?'

The line went dead.

'Guv!' Lawrence panicked and, in her rush, to call him back dropped the phone. Bending down to retrieve it off the floor her head swam, she may have felt sober, but the booze was still well and truly in her system. She managed to pick it up and was about to call him back when a message came up on the screen. It was from Bambridge.

She opened it and the panic she'd felt tripled. It was a picture of a cutthroat razorblade, clearly in Bambridge's hands. Her heart raced and her faced flushed. She needed to get to his place, and fast.

'Change of address, mate,' she called to the driver. For the rest of the journey, she kept trying to call Bambridge, but it would just go to voicemail. With each unanswered call her worries would increase. She considered telling the cabbie to step on it, but held her tongue, as he was already exceeding the speed limit.

They arrived outside Bambridge's place, she paid the driver, and jumped out. At the front door to his building, she pressed all the buzzers repeatedly until someone let her in. A glance on a wall plaque told her what floor he lived on, and she took the stairs two at a time.

At his front door her first thought was that she was going to have to force it open. But just before she started kicking, she paused and tried the handle. It open with a soft click.

Her detective instincts kicked in as it shouldn't have been that easy to get inside. She pushed the door open fully and stepped over the threshold.

'Guv?' she called into the dark corridor in front of her

but got no response. Ahead of her was a corridor with a door on the right halfway down, and an area that opened out into darkness at the end.

Should she just use the light switch? She didn't have any gloves on her, and if she were walking into a crime scene would she be contaminating it? She couldn't find her torch either, which made her mind up for her. Time wasn't on her side, so with her rolled up sleeve she turned the lights on.

'Guv, you there?' she called again, and moved down the corridor.

She had expected the place to be a mess. It would have been in keeping with Bambridge's appearance. But she was surprised to find the hall was pristine, with a number of coats neatly hung on hooks, and a tidy shoe rack underneath. She could clearly see women's clothing and footwear amongst them. They must have been the clothes he'd said haunted his every waking hour.

The door to the right was closed, so she used the sleeve method to turn the handle. Again, it swung inwards with a soft click. The light from the corridor told her it was a bedroom. She hit the lights again. The double bed was in the middle of the far-left wall, its sheets tucked neatly in place, not a single crease in sight. The curtains on the far wall were closed, the colour of their trim matching the cushions on the bed. There were no pictures on the walls, and nothing on the bedside tables, Underneath the window a washing basket was overflowing with clothes. The only part of the flat so far that was untidy. Opposite the window, on her left was a wardrobe, with one of its doors open. It was full of women's clothes. A whole rack of jackets, suits, shirts, and blouses hung over a shelf piled with different shades of folded denim, and various types of jumpers. Lined along the bottom of the wardrobe were all styles of shoes, ranging from slip-ons, trainers, dress shoes, heels and running shoes.

Nothing seemed out of the ordinary, but there was something about it all that didn't seem right. She just couldn't figure out what. She shook herself. What was she doing thinking about anything except Bambridge. She needed to find him.

'Guv, where you at?' she shouted as she left the bedroom.

The corridor opened out into a living area, with a kitchen diner area on the right, two more doors past the kitchen on the right wall, and a living room with a double sofa, coffee table and television in front of her.

From one of the rooms, she heard a clatter, and then a moan, but she wasn't sure which. As she moved closer to them the sound of movement returned, and she pinpointed where it was coming from.

She took a deep breath, before trying the handle. It turned with ease and slowly she pushed it open.

The bathroom wasn't as well-lit as the rest of the flat. It's only light coming from a single strip light above the sink at the far end of the room. Most of its glow was blocked by Bambridge who was leaning on the basin.

Lawrence could see that his shoulders were shaking, and there was an ever so slight sound coming from him. Was he crying? It didn't sound like crying, but there was a low moan coming from him. She paused for a second while she considered what to do. The urge to speak hung in her throat, and just as she was about to say something he moved.

His left arm slid along the edge of the sink and the light caught on something. A dark substance that covered his hand.

All feeling of drunkenness had left her body as she realised what it was. It was blood. This time her words didn't get caught.

'Guv?' she said with some trepidation.

He flinched at the sound of her voice, and she heard his breathing become heavy, rattling in his chest. His left hand slid back out of sight as he slowly turned towards her.

Lawrence had one eye on the cutthroat razor in his right hand, and the other on Bambridge. His eyes were glazed from the tears running down his face, and his lower lip trembled as he looked straight at her. However, her eyes soon moved from his face to his left arm as he raised it for her to see.

Blood was pouring from the wound he'd cut into his wrist with the razor.

Her caution swiftly changed to panic as she took off her jacket, wrapping it around her arm as she stepped towards him. He raised the razor in front of him in what she took as an attempt to ward her off, but there was no strength in the movement and the blade dropped out of his hand. Lawrence put her foot on the razor and pushed it behind her. Dropping her jacket, she grabbed his left arm and lifted it above his head.

'What did you do?' she asked in disbelief as his blood ran down her arm.

He didn't reply. Instead, he tried to fight her, trying to lower his arm so that the blood would flow better. But she was having none of it. She used her hip to press him against the sink whilst she held his arm up as high as she could, applying pressure around the wound.

'Just let me die,' Bambridge cried in her ear. 'Please.'

'Not gonna happen,' she replied through gritted teeth.

He continued to resist her, weakly trying to lower his

arm. She readjusted her footing and got a firmer grip on his wrist. Just as she felt like she had control over the situation his legs gave out from under him, and he fell into her. She caught him under his right arm and slowly placed him on the floor.

With him sat with his back to the sink, she stood with her feet either side of him and his left arm in both hands assessing the damage he'd done to himself. She ran her thumb across the wound, clearing away some of the blood and making the injury more visible. The incision was small, running about a centimetre down the wrist, just below the thumb; however, it looked deep. She took the cut between her thumb and forefinger and pressed it closed. He called out in pain, and tried to move, but she pinned his right shoulder against the sink with her thigh and continued to hold the wound closed.

'You've gotta let me go,' he shouted. 'I let her down. I wasn't there for her. I wasn't there when they killed her. I wasn't there. I need to go; I need to be with her. I don't want to be without her anymore.' His emotions were raw as he sobbed.

'The only place we're going, is to the hospital.'

'NO!' he shouted, and again tried to break free, but he was weak now, his energy spent. 'No hospitals,' he said, with less conviction. He started to shake, but she couldn't tell whether it was from tears or from an adrenaline rush that had come post injury. Whatever it was, it was working in breaking her fingers apart, and if he were successful, he would start bleeding again.

'Okay, okay, no hospitals,' Lawrence replied in a soothing tone. 'But you've got to stop moving around alright? Otherwise, you're going to bleed to death.'

'That's the point,' he told her. Then there was silence.

'I know it was, but if you'd meant it, you wouldn't

have contacted me,' she stated firmly.

It probably wasn't what she should have been saying, but she didn't care. All manners, talking down etiquette, and pleasantries had gone out the window. Keeping him alive was all that mattered.

'Why won't you just let me die?' he pleaded, just as Lawrence considered screaming with frustration. Her silence was getting to her, but she couldn't think of anything to say.

'Because.' It was all she could offer in response but knew how weak it sounded. She had to give him an answer, but what was it? Some platitude about how life was worth living. She'd seen where his life was, and honestly didn't think she could sell him that one. Instead, she went for how she was feeling. 'Because I don't want your death on my conscience.'

'Why would that be the case?' he asked as his head pressed against her leg.

'Because I came on to you last night, when clearly that wasn't the right thing to do. You're grieving and having a drunk work colleague feel you up in public is the last thing you needed. So, I'm sorry if I led you to this,' she said calmly. 'And I don't want that to be the reason you end it all. I couldn't live with that.'

'But I failed her.'

'You've not failed her.'

'YES, I HAVE!'

'You've not, Guv. Even after she's gone, you're showing her more love than some people experience in a lifetime. Love that I would kill to have. Affection that anyone could only dream of. Just because she's gone doesn't mean that you can't keep loving her. But you can't keep loving her if you're dead.'

'But I miss her so much,' he sobbed, guttural, heart

wrenching sobs.

'I know you do,' she replied, her voice breaking as she tried to keep her own tears at bay. 'I know.' She gritted her teeth as a single tear crept down her cheek. 'But is this really what she would have wanted for you?' She let her words linger for a moment before continuing. 'I didn't know your wife personally, but she loved you and wouldn't want this for you.'

'Natalie,' he wept, 'her name was Natalie.'

'I didn't know Natalie,' she corrected, 'but I'd heard about her and what a strong minded, powerhouse of a woman she was. And I can only guess that this life you're leading isn't what she would have wanted for you. If she loved you half as much as you love her, then it would break her heart to see you like this.'

Lawrence could start to feel her fingers getting numb, but she dared not separate them in case the wound opened again. She'd just need to hold on for a bit longer.

'How do you know what she'd have wanted?' he asked, his voice sounding weaker as his body started to relax under her.

'I don't,' she replied, as she looked around for something to wrap his wrist in. 'But surely you do. And this isn't it, right?'

His body sagged underneath her, and she hoped that he was done fighting with her. With her fingers still pinched she moved closer to a hand towel that hung next to the shower, grabbed it with her free hand, and then lay it on side of the basin.

Cautiously she lay his arm across the towel and then let go of the wound. She waited for the blood to start flowing again, but when nothing happened, she started to wrap his wrist. Pulling the material tight over the cut, brought a grunt of pain out of Bambridge that she ignored until she had finished.

As she let go of his arm, it started to drop down at his side.

'Keep that above your head,' she ordered, as she turned the tap on and started washing her hands.

Bambridge did as he was asked, balancing his left arm on top of his head. He shifted on his backside away from the sink and leant against the glass wall of the shower cubicle.

Lawrence used her hands to wash away all the blood in the basin, and around its edges, before she started taking the thick of it off her upper arms. The whole time she had one eye on Bambridge.

'You're still adamant about not going to the hospital?' she asked as she got her elbows under the running water. The blouse she had on was short sleeved, but the blood had soaked into most of the right sleeve and there were multiple droplets down the front of it. It wasn't the first time she'd got blood on something she owned, but the damage done to this top was severe. She made an executive decision and took it off. There was blood down her chest and soaked into her right bra strap, but she had no intention of removing that. Not in front of Bambridge anyway. Dropping the blouse into the sink she wondered whether it could be saved, although saving Bambridge was far more important.

'No hospital,' he replied, but his voice was weak.

She looked down at him and could see that he was losing consciousness. 'Hey, Guv, let's get you into a chair before you fall asleep,' she said, drying her hands on her blouse.

He did as he was told and tried to stand up. She could see that he wasn't going to do it unaided, so she grabbed him under the arm and helped him up.

Heading for the living room, with Bambridge leaning heavily against her, she guided him to a chair next to the double seater sofa. She made sure his left arm was still above his head before she sat down on the sofa.

His eyes instantly started to droop, and he was just about to nod off when he spoke. 'You're a good person, Lawrence,' he stated and gave her a half smile before his chin dropped down onto his chest. 'Not sure why you're half naked in my lounge though,' he added, and within a few seconds his breathing became slow and steady.

Looking around she could see that this room was also covered in dust. Not to say that the room wasn't tidy. Far from it. There was a neatness to the place that she could appreciate, it just looked like no one had been in the room for a long time.

She glanced over her shoulder and had a look at the kitchen area. All the sides were clear of any dishes or pans. The sink was empty, and the draining board had only a solitary sponge next to the tap. But again, there was a layer of dust over everything.

Bambridge was still asleep, so she took in the rest of the living room, with the hope of not falling unconscious herself. She needed to be on guard duty, to make sure he kept his arm levitated, and that he didn't try it again.

It all looked normal, apart from the various loops of paper bunting hanging from the ceiling. There were letters within the colourful bunting that spelt out *happy birthday*. Lawrence's heart sank as she realised that the party decorations must have been up for a year, and for the second time that morning she held back her tears.

He really loved his wife and the pain he must have been feeling was unimaginable. She had lost someone in the past, but by the time they had died, their relationship had long been over. To lose the one you loved in such awful circumstances must have been horrendous.

The desire to keep him safe swelled as she looked up at the decorations. She just needed to stay awake. She also needed to find something to wear. It wasn't cold in the flat, but she felt exposed in just her bra. She knew she should go into the bedroom and pick something out, but the sofa was extremely comfortable. Sitting for a just a moment couldn't hurt.

Her head rolled back against the sofa as she nodded off for what she thought was just a second, but when she looked across at Bambridge, his chair was empty.

'Guv,' she called out and stood up.

Her first instinct was to head back into the bathroom, to make sure he hadn't gone for the razor again. But he wasn't in there. A panic fuelled search around the flat told her one thing, Bambridge had gone.

Exasperated, she knew she should follow him, but where would she start? Plus, there was something odd about the flat. Every sinew in her body was telling her to look around. So, she went with her gut. First, she headed back to the bedroom at the front. Now that she wasn't in a panicked rush, she had chance to examine the rooms proportions. The ceiling was high, and behind the drawn curtains was a large bay window. The double bed on closer inspection was king-sized, and there was still plenty of space around it. There was a television mounted on the opposite wall. The only item on any of the walls. She looked again in the wardrobes containing her bosses' dead wife's clothes. Only this time she was looking for something to wear. She found a thin V-necked grey jumper in one of the draws. It went with her suit trousers, so she put it on.

As she stepped away from wardrobe her attention was drawn to the floor. She had left footprints. At first, she thought it was from the thickness of the carpet, but it was actually dust which lay thick across the floor.

Looking back into the wardrobe she realised what had been wrong with the clothes. They too were covered in a layer of dust. It was on everything. Looking back down at her feet she could see the pathway her feet had created. Had Bambridge not been in this room for a year? If so, then where had he been sleeping?

She followed her footprints out into the hallway, but they were lost amongst the multiple prints that filled the corridor. However, the edges of the hallway, the areas that hadn't been walked through had the same layer of dust.

Back in the living room the same path had been carved through the powder, but it only went in one direction, to the bathroom, and the door next to it. The kitchen surfaces, sink, and white goods all had the same amount of dusting, as did most of the living room, the only exception being the seats she and Bambridge had sat on.

Curiosity driving her she opened the other door.

Originally, the room had been used as an office. There was a desk along the back wall, with a computer and keyboard on one side, and a pile of paperwork on the other. In front of the desk was a swivel chair, with a filing cabinet on the left.

A pile of clothes had been left on top of the cabinet, with more hanging off the back of a chair. On the floor was a crumpled duvet and a single pillow.

As she looked around the small room it became apparent that Bambridge had been sleeping in it. She couldn't see anything to suggest he'd been eating in there as well, but that didn't surprise her, as he seemed to barely eat these days. He'd struggled with the portion of chips they'd eaten in the pub. However, empty tobacco pouches and rolling papers were littered around the edges of the room, and there was an ashtray that was mounded with cigarette butts. It stank of old sweat, ashtrays, and Bambridge. Suddenly, she realised that he was sleeping in this unused, spare room because he couldn't bear to sleep in the bed he'd shared with his wife. The realisation hit her hard, bringing tears to her eyes.

She tried to picture the room being used in happier times. As a home office, she thought, Bambridge's office. She imagined him working away at the desk, Natalie shouting him to get into the kitchen, dinner was ready. Or maybe vice versa, as they were both formidable officers. Then something caught her eye, taking her mind off her musings, and snapping her detective's brain awake.

It was an investigation board on the wall behind the door. A long list of names had been handwritten down one side of the board, with lines drawn from each name that expanded into more information. These lines currently led out from four of the names, that were all spread out across the list. There were also a few names that had already been crossed out. She tried to read the names underneath, but the marker pen had done a good job of covering them.

Lawrence could only assume that this was the list of people he suspected of killing his wife. It was a very long list, which made her understand more clearly why he'd been so pre-occupied and vacant. If he'd been looking into each of these people, then no wonder he hadn't been around. Although, the way that the names had been crossed out did concern her. There was a disorder to it that seemed so much more manic than the order of the rest of the board. Almost as if there was an anger behind the erasing.

She tried to take in all the information on the board,

but none of it would sink in. Turning away from it she noticed some things hanging off the back of the door that looked familiar.

She'd never been climbing before, but she recognised the equipment. There were two harnesses hanging off one of the hooks, each one had a small chalk bag that hung lower than the rest of the black strapping. And on the hook next to them were a few coils of rope.

Lawrence's heart went into her mouth as she stared at the same red and black rope that had been used on their victim's. Adrenaline started pumping through her veins. Her heartbeat quickened.

Had she been stood beside the killer all this time? Was Bambridge capable of doing these things to another person? He certainly seemed unhinged enough, but did he have the strength to do what had been done? Her immediate thought was no. He could barely stand up at times, let alone lift a lifeless body up. But then, where had he been going on all these errands? Why had he been so badly affected by each of these killings? The way he'd had to look away from Tracey in the morgue was almost as though he were guilty. She stood in the foul-smelling room horrified. Maybe Bambridge was the killer? What should she do? She had no idea how to handle this thought process.

She moved back to the board to see if she could decipher what names had been scribbled out. To see if Tracey Collins, or George Stephens were visible under the black marker. But he'd done too good a job.

Reeling with her own deduction, she backed out of the office into the living room. Was she now in the lair of a killer? A killer that had already dispatched three people, that they knew of. There were more than three names crossed off his list, so there was no telling whether more would be found.

But as she stood in the living space he and Natalie had shared, the footprints in the dust highlighted by the lights, the cynic in her started to wake up, and her detective brain began to pull apart what she'd discovered.

Yes, he had the same rope as had been used at their scenes, but if her memory served her correctly, she'd looked up the rope online and realised that it was a very common product. It could just have been a coincidence.

That was it, she thought, a coincidence. But still, even after she picked her bloodied clothing up from the bathroom sink, and her jacket off the floor, then made her way back to the front door, something niggled her. Bambridge's behaviour, his anger, his going missing. The reaction he had to each of the killings. The way he had commented on how the killer hadn't tied the knots in the rope correctly, was that him, reprimanding himself? And what about his reaction to the third killing? He'd told her that park was where he and Natalie had spent time together. Where he'd proposed to her. But was he telling the truth? Only his wife could answer that, and she'd been dead over a year now.

Deep in thought, she almost leapt out of her skin when her phone vibrated in her pocket. Heart thumping, she peered at the screen and sighed. It wasn't Bambridge, as she had hoped. It was Craig, and she knew this time, she would have to go home.

Chapter Twenty-One

Blood had been spilt and a tool had been lost. There would be no rewards for such carelessness. The tool was replaceable. There were dozens of them to hand. The blood, however, could not be replaced. Such a waste of so precious a substance. Pray there be no repercussions for such wasteful activities.

Must not let it be distracting. Mustn't dwell on the error. For we are only mortal. And there are still so many numbers on the list, numbers that needed to be harvested.

One would be required soon, as penitence. Penitence for such wasteful failures. Failures that needed to be rectified. Precisely and swiftly, for there were no reprieves for losing so much blood. No second chances.

All would be made well with the next number. For there were elements of its routine that looked promising. It had been studied, and a prime point had been pinpointed. There was a method in mind. A way to ensure compliance. It would just require a certain level of sacrifice. But then, didn't they all? It was why we have been chosen. Work like this could not be entrusted to just anyone. Only we were worthy. Worthy of his praise. Of his blessing. Of him.

This one however would require more. More than had been given before. It would involve changes. Changes to outfits, changes to the way it should be done, changes of character. Along with quite a considerable stretch of principles. But then adjustments are always necessary when preparing for the removal of such a high prize. For it must be done. Thy will be done.

Courage was also a requirement. Courage to do what

was needed to complete the list, and to deal with any obstacles that were thrown in front of us.

Most of all it required planning. With the movements of this one observed it was easy enough to put everything in place, ready for the blood to be let. The only thing that was different this time was the lure. The simple call of a name wouldn't be enough for it. Nor would waiting for the number to get tired after a run. No, no. This time we were to be the lure. Our physical presence would need to be used. And it was this that would stretch the principles.

As it turned out, all it took was paying for drinks all evening, which in turn had made the number pliant to suggestions. With little persuasion, other than the alcohol, we were soon leaving the establishment it frequently frequented and returning to its abode. Exactly as planned.

Thus came the disagreeable part of the lure. Actual physical contact with the number. Though it held greatness inside its veins, its physical being left a lot to be desired. Much like the previous numbers, the impurity of the life it had chosen must be overlooked if a successful harvest is too be achieved.

Deflection of its more probing attempts at coupling had been essential until we reach the location. A playful batting away of its hand when it got too close. A sidestep to avoid its arm around our shoulder. A quick turn of the head to elude a kiss. All of these tactics were used, whilst also maintaining a sense of allure during the journey to the number's residence. Once inside it proved easy to direct the number towards the bedroom. A few more seconds of circumventing its advances and it soon looked comfortable on the bed. The heart raced with anticipation of what was about to come. But first we pull the sheets over its head and keep striking it until its movements stop.

Due to the disagreeable methods of the lure, a convenient place to store the tools had been necessary. Thankfully, they were where they had been left. Another element of the routine that had needed to be changed. But with the right planning everything had worked out perfectly.

Now, the work can begin.

After the usual preparations the number has been hung, the tools have been prepped, the ropes have been tightened, and the receptacle has been put in place. The harvest would soon begin.

Emotions, as always, take hold. Excitement and expectancy take over. But emotions must be control. Tempered.

The hands shake, eagerness to see the exquisite blood, getting the better of us. A deep breath, and a calming thought steady the nerves. This act is not for us. It is for him. For he has chosen us to do his work. And his work is essential.

We have complete privacy, and all the time in the world. Another breath is taken to slow the heart rate, then we can begin.

The blade is heavy in the hand, but an adjustment of the fingers sees to that slight issue. With the hand steady, the right amount of pressure is applied to the correct location and the blood pours. A quick redirection of the flow with the thumb and the container starts to fill.

It is mesmerising. The way the blood drains from the number. Each beat of the heart forcing more of the dark liquid out of the body. Liquid that should have been moving towards or away from the head, was now exiting the wound, down the number's chin, into a funnel, and then into the receptacle. A much more appropriate place for such exquisite blood.

With the last pulses running out of the incision, preparation for leaving the location can begin. First, the cleansing of the tools.

From further inside the building a door opens, and the sound of voices follows.

Panic rushes through the system. To be disturbed a second time is infuriating. The unease intensifies as the easy option to escape, like last time, is not available. There is only one way in or out.

The noise from the other side of the door increases, but the work is far from done. The moment calls for a split decision, finish what has been started, or abandon another harvest. The two options bring forth a new emotion. Despair.

There is a moment of confusion as the mind struggles to process the situation, struggles to come up with an instant solution. But once again it is just a matter of controlling our emotions. A steadying breath helps to remove the feeling of hopelessness, bringing with it clarity and a subjective decision.

With the lock on the door engaged, the cleaning process can be completed. We just need to stay calm and continue as originally planned.

A thumping comes through the wall. Some music has started to play, far too loudly, somewhere in the building. This is a blessing as it allows for a noisier cleansing to take place. But we must still work fast. Fast is what is needed. We must get everything done. We must get out, and fast.

A knock at the door indicates that the work needs to happen quicker. The door is heavy, and the lock is solid, so there is still time, but not much.

The tools are stored correctly. The receptacle is made ready for transit. The location has been cleansed. Not to the usual standard but judging by the second more vigorous knock at the door, our time has run out. It will have to be good enough. The cleanse will hopefully be good enough. We strive ourselves on more than just good enough. Only the best will do for his work. But everything is done. It is time to move. Time to go.

With everything stored and ready for transit it is necessary to take one last look around the workstation. Not for memory's sake, but to make sure nothing has been left behind. No more lost tools. No more mistakes. Happy with the state of location, the number is checked one last time before we take a deep breath, pause, and listen at the door.

There are multiple voices on the other side, as well as the rhythm of the music. A party.

Another knock at the door startles us, and a breath is required to steady the heart rate.

Are we ready? To face the music, so to speak? A quick exit may be required, and some brute force. Should the blade be retrieved from the tool kit? No. Speed will be the key. Speed and an element of camouflage. Not on us, but on the number. The people on the other side are most likely weak. Weak of will. Weak and unable to cope with the sight of the harvest.

We are ready. We open the door.

A man smelling of tobacco and wine stands in the way.

'Thought you were gonna be in there all night,' he slurs, and then pushes his way into the room.

A crowd of people stand in the way. Their bodies swaying to the sounds of the music. The heart races at the anticipation of them all turning in unison, but none of them seem to notice. Their thoughts and attentions drawn to the music. Fogged by their inebriation. So, with the harvest reaped, the throng is casually weaved through, the front door is opened, and the exit is complete.

The expectation of screams, or the sound of chase increases with each step away from the location. But as the cool evening air blows over sweat soaked clothes neither event occurs.

Another number off the list. Another imperfect routine: but there would be room for improvement. There always was. And plenty more numbers.

Chapter Twenty-Two

Lawrence barely slept.

From the moment she left the flat, wandering the streets, hopelessly wishing she would find Bambridge, trying his phone multiple times. Each time it went straight to his voicemail.

When she got a strange look from a passer-by, that was followed by a look of concern, and then a question asking if she was okay, she knew it was time to head home. The bloodstain blouse she was holding had them concerned, but she reassured them that she was fine.

Craig had been awake when she got home. His face was thunderous, as he started to confront her but had instantly softened when he saw the blood. She spent the next hour trying to calm him down. Explaining to him that it wasn't her blood. But she hadn't bothered telling him whose it was. That was a whole conversation she didn't want to have. Reassuring him that she was fine had been enough of a challenge.

She had taken a shower and spent the rest of the early hours worrying about where Bambridge was, what he was doing, if his wound would re-open, and if he would try and take his own life again.

Sleep must have come at some point because she was woken by her work phone. There had been another murder, and this one had caught the media's attention. She sat staring at the screen for a second; the thought of Bambridge speaking on camera sending a shiver down her spine. A sentiment shared with the brass no doubt.

Thinking of Bambridge brought back what she had found in his flat. The climbing rope on the back of the door was almost identical to what had been used at the scenes. Granted, that type of rope was very common, but it had got her wondering. And now that there had been another murder the same evening Bambridge had disappeared. Her suspicions about him heightened.

Could he account for his whereabouts at the time of each of the previous three murders? What were the names that had been scrubbed off the list he had on his wall? Where had he really been when he said he was running errands? Perhaps the victims were all related in some way to Sergeant Bambridge's death? She was cynical of that last thought, but then, who were the names that had been crossed off?

Her work phone went off again, only this time it was Bambridge ringing her. She sat staring at it for a moment, unsure about whether she should answer. It seemed mad to stay up worrying about him all night, only to then ignore his call. So, she answered.

'Morning, Guv,' she said in a tone that implied everything was okay.

'I'll pick you up in twenty,' he replied and hung up.

She couldn't gauge what tone he had used. Had he been angry, or sad? Tired or wide awake? She had no idea and spent the next twenty minutes stewing over what she was going to say to him.

Lawrence knew that the journey was going to be awkward, even before she got into the vehicle. She had no idea how she was going to begin a conversation, and what subject to start on? His suicide attempt. The rope in his flat. The list on his wall. Her worries about what he'd been up to on his errands. She didn't want to talk about any of them. But they were all she could think about. That and whether she would be getting into the car with a killer.

As she got into the passenger seat, her eyes were

drawn to his left wrist. He had his arm rested on the wheel, however, his sleeve covered where the razor injury was, so she couldn't tell what he'd done with it.

She had multiple questions on the tip of her tongue, but she couldn't bring herself to ask any of them. So, she just sat in silence, fighting the urge to fall asleep. However, a difficult conversation would have to happen at some point. Another one. She felt as though she had accumulated a collection of difficult men, and it was her job to keep them all in check. When had she become a mother to two grown men?

Her mind went back to Bambridge. Did he even remember what had happened last night? He had stated that he didn't drink much but had also said that he had been drinking to dull the memories of his wife. Which one was it? Whichever one it was he'd seemed pretty drunk when he'd left her at the pub. But there had been something different about the way he'd spoken to her on the phone. A distance that hadn't sounded like drunk talk. Something strange.

As they pulled up outside the scene, Lawrence could tell the atmosphere was different to the previous cases. Not because of the number of uniformed officers onsite, and not because they were in a more affluent part of the city. There was an energy in the air that hadn't been present previously. What a difference location and social status did for getting crimes dealt with.

Bambridge turned the engine off and looked at her for the first time.

'You okay, Guv?' she was finally able to say.

'Did someone important die?' Bambridge asked, as he watched the activity outside the scene.

'Not sure,' she replied. 'But if they live in this part of town, they must have a bit of cash.'

'You're not wrong,' he agreed, as they got out of the car.

As they approached the scene, Detective Inspector Canham walked out of the front door. He saw them and greeted them at the base of the steps.

'They call you two in on this as well?' he asked, with a look of confusion.

Lawrence was just as confused as the Scotsman. Why would they need three of them at the scene. Plus, if Canham was here, that meant that so was his partner. Sure enough, Quinnell came sauntering out of the building, his mannerisms equally as unenthused as when he was sat at his desk.

'What're we dealing with in there?' Bambridge asked as his eyebrows raised ever so slightly.

'Real PR mess,' Canham began. 'The victim is a member of some socialite family. And he's one of three that live in the flat. One of the other two being the daughter of a member of parliament, and the other is some banker's daughter. Very big in the city.'

'Is it the same MO as our other cases?' Lawrence asked, getting her notepad out.

'Looks that way,' Canham replied. 'Killed whilst hung over the bath. But what's adding to the PR issue is that it looks like they had a party here. First uniforms on scene found all sorts lying around. As well as a certain commissioner's daughter passed out on one of the sofas.'

'That's not good,' Lawrence stated. 'Is she okay?'

'Ambulance came and took her to hospital. Sounds like she's going to be fine, just partied a little too hard.'

'What heat are we getting from the MP?' Bambridge asked.

'Nothing yet. But it'll only be a matter of time,' Canham answered with a sigh. 'The family of the victim will also be a problem.'

'Why, who are they?' Lawrence asked.

'Big construction family,' Quinnell answered from over Canham's shoulder. 'Owned and built property in London for generations. Friends in very high places.' Quinnell looked towards the house, where D.C.I Stone was talking to a number of people. 'Higher than him, even. Mix with royalty, I believe. That's the sort of profile they have, so, I can only guess what kind of grief we'll get from them.'

'Chief want us to keep a low profile on this?' Bambridge asked, sarcasm dripping through his words as he looked around at the media, already starting to line up behind the blue and white tape. Like vultures to the carcass, Lawrence mused. Always out for a story no matter the level of tragedy.

'As much as we can,' Canham replied, as he followed Bambridge's line of sight.

'Didn't see this circus for a dead sex worker,' Bambridge muttered, walking towards the scene. 'Standards get amended depending on who's dead, I guess.'

'Lower your voice, man,' Canham called to Bambridge's back

Bambridge ignored him and walked in the front door.

Lawrence started to follow but was stopped by Canham.

'Try and keep him in line.' He looked her right in the eyes. 'Careers can be made and lost when certain people are looking on. And trust me, people are looking.'

'I can only do so much,' she told him, as she started to step around him.

'Just do what you can, ha.'

He stood aside and she took the steps up two at a time.

The sights and smells of a party were evident the moment she walked through the door. A mixture of alcohol, and burnt tobacco hung in the air. Empty glasses, cans and bottles were on every surface. The disrespect for such high-quality furnishings put her on edge, and she had to stop herself moving a half-drunk cocktail that was leaving a clear watermark on a beautiful Ercol sideboard. The mess reminded her of a different time in her life when a party in someone's flat was a weekly occurrence.

However, the flats she'd partied in had looked nothing like this place. The size of the hallway alone was bigger than the flat she'd grown up in.

In the living room half a dozen partygoers were all congregated around the sofas. They were all dressed like they had been to a dinner party, rather than a drunken blow out at someone's house. They were all in various states of shock or dealing with their hangovers. Two uniforms were with them. The number of people in the living room couldn't have made this much mess, so clearly some had made a sharp exit when the body was found.

Bambridge ignored the living room and headed straight for the bathroom. Lawrence hastily went after him.

The size of the bathroom made Lawrence's jaw drop.

The whole right side of the room was dominated by a floor to ceiling mirror. Which probably created the illusion that the room was bigger than it was. However, the bathroom was still enormous. Along the back wall, underneath a large, tinted window, was a deep marble double butlers sink. Empty glasses teetered on the edges of both basins. Amongst the mess she could see handwash and lotion from Harrods, and a bar of soap from Creed. To the left of the basins was on old drawstring cistern toilet, its dark green seat matching the tiles around the bottom half of the room. The top half of the room was tiled in an off-white colour that matched the sink and bathtub. The floor was chequered in the same colours. Matching hand and bath towels hung next to the sink and bath.

The bath was next to the toilet. It was deeper and wider than any she'd seen before and looked to have been sunken into the floor. The taps alone looked more expensive than her whole bathroom, and she was quite sure there were Jacuzzi jets in the sides of the tub. A showerhead the size of her shower cubicle at home hung over one end of the tub, with the victim over the other end. There was a shower curtain that had been half ripped off hanging into the bathtub just next to the body.

It truly was the opposite of the bathroom belonging to the first victim. However, the deceased looked much the same, albeit this one was male.

Bambridge squatted down next to the bath and began studying the body.

Lawrence moved next to him, ready to catch him if he fell. She still wasn't sure what state he was in, and it wouldn't look good him passing out on the floor of a crime scene. She also wanted to see what he had done with the wound on his wrist, but his sleeve still hid that from her.

When she was sure he wasn't going to collapse, she tried to see what he had noticed, but nothing jumped out at her.

'What you got, Guv?'

Bambridge ignored her and turned his attention to the tub, leaning in to look more closely. As he started to rise, he stopped and looked at the back of the victim's head. He pointed to behind the left ear. 'They didn't clean up as well this time.'

Lawrence followed his finger and could see the small amount of blood. 'Perhaps they didn't feel like they needed to? Place is a mess from the party.'

'Cleaned the last place. That was far worse.' Bambridge stood up and had another look around the room. He paused as he saw something on the ceiling. 'They missed another bit.' He pointed to a small amount of spatter over the doorway.

'Getting sloppy?' What Lawrence really wanted to say was *are you getting sloppy*, but she knew she couldn't make that sort of allegation at this time. All she'd really found at his place was some climbing rope. The same rope tied around the body in front of her, but her thoughts went to how common the rope was.

'Possibly,' he replied. 'And yet, the knots they tied this time are better. Still not great, but better.'

Knots you tied better.

Lawrence stepped closer to have a look at the bath. 'There's more in the corner here.' She pointed to a smear of blood that ran along the side of the tub up onto the tiled wall behind it. 'A lot sloppier it would seem.'

She moved away from the bath and began to ask him what he meant about the knots being better, when she saw something on one of the dark green tiles. More blood, and by the looks of it someone had walked through it.

'Partial footprint maybe? She offered, squatting down to get a better look. 'The mess they've left doesn't make sense. Why go to the trouble at the first scene, only to not try at all at this one?'

'Maybe they were in a rush,' Bambridge answered and then left the bathroom without another word.

With a shake of her head, she went after him.

Bambridge approached the partygoers, giving the uniform officers a nod, before sitting down opposite the group.

'Morning, ladies, and gentlemen, I'm Detective Inspector Bambridge. I need to ask you some questions.'

There was a bunch of grumbled replies and pained nods.

However, one of them let out a deep sigh. 'Haven't we just done that with these two?' The young man pointed to the uniforms. His pink Yves Saint Laurent shirt had at least one stain down the front that had transferred down onto his black jeans. Whatever he'd spilt down himself there had been a lot of it. His tanned face was clean shaven, and his dark hair was styled into an elaborate quiff. He looked exhausted, but his eyes were alert. A narcotic of some description was still in his system.

'I'd like to go over it again, please,' Bambridge proposed, with a smile.

There was no feeling in the smile. Lawrence had seen him use it before. It was empty and would crack quickly. She'd need to keep an eye on the young man. He obviously saw himself as the alpha of the group and wanted to prove his worth.

'Who found the body?' Bambridge was keeping his voice calm, but Lawrence could tell that the alpha had annoyed him.

'His name is Stephen,' the alpha replied.

The smile broadened, dangerously. 'Who found Stephen?'

'Hilary did,' came his response.

Hilary, the poor girl, jolted at the sound of her name. She appeared to come out of whatever stupor she'd been in. Her blue eyes blinking away the fog from between her smudged mascara. She nervously tucked her blonde hair behind her ears, the motion causing her earrings to swing from her lobes. Lawrence recognised they were Tiffany by their unique green shade. Her white thigh-high Gucci dress matching her Bottega Veneta heels. Expensive clothing to be wearing for just a house party. Whether it was from booze, drugs, or the shock of finding the body was unclear, but the mention of her name had brought her back from the void.

'And what can you tell me about that, Hilary?' Bambridge gave her another smile, and this one seemed genuine.

'What can she tell you?' the alpha asked loudly. 'What sort of question is that?'

'I'm sorry sir, I didn't catch your name,' Bambridge replied calmly.

'That's because I didn't give it.'

'Yes, I know!' Bambridge's voice had an unpleasant edge to it. 'And yet, you give hers freely.'

Lawrence held her breath as she waited for Bambridge to start laying into the young man. But she could see the restraint on his face, which was quickly followed by another smile.

'I know you're all upset, and you're feeling the effects of the party and the events that have taken place. But I'm trying to help Stephen. The more information you can give, the better.'

The alpha was trying to stay angry, but Bambridge must have hit home, because he slumped back down in his chair and began to chew on his fingernails.

'Any details could prove vital.' Bambridge said, his words seeming to wake Hilary up some more, and she shifted forward in her seat.

'What do you want to know?' Hilary asked.

'How was the room?'

Hilary looked puzzled by the question and leant forward further. 'How do you mean?'

'Anything unusual?'

'What kind of a question is that?' the alpha piped up again.

Lawrence kind of agreed with him. She had no idea where Bambridge was going with the question. Was he just saying these things to mess with the alpha?

'Will you be quiet, Daniel!' Hilary snapped. 'You're helping no one with your comments.'

'I just want to know when we can go,' Daniel said, ignoring his friend.

'You can go when we're done with you.' Bambridge's tone changed, and the calm, smiling face was gone. But only for a moment, then his attention returned to Hilary. 'Let me rephrase the question, Hilary. When you found Stephen, were you the first person at the party to use the bathroom?'

'This is just ridiculous now,' Daniel snapped, and rose to his feet. 'What did you say your name was?' He pointed at Bambridge.

'Detective Inspector Bambridge,' he replied coolly.

'And you've been in this job for how long?'

'Do you mean in the service, or do you mean working on Homicide? Because both answers are more years than you've been out of school. But perhaps school is where you need to go. It might teach you some manners.'

Lawrence flinched at the comment, and so did the rest of the room. She hoped that Daniel wasn't the son of either the MP or the banker. That he was just a friend, and that some of the other dazed socialites sat before them were said offspring. If he was, then he may have just landed himself in real trouble. But would she also be fingered for the misdemeanour?

'How dare you!' Daniel's face went red. 'Do you have any idea who my father is?'

245

'I couldn't care less. Because I'm not interested in your father because he's not here. You are. And so is Hilary. And the sooner Hilary tells me what I need to know, the sooner you can go and deal with your comedown.'

The mention of a comedown got Daniel looking panicky, and he backed down again.

'I can't have been the first person,' Hilary replied to his question. 'The party had been going for a while before I went to the toilet. We had to make sure all the guests had a drink, and there were plenty of nibbles around the room.' She nodded towards one of the other women. 'So, I'd been busy for a while.'

'Any of you use the bathroom before Hilary?' Bambridge looked at each of them. His eyes lingering on Daniel, before resting on Hilary.

It took a moment for the question to settle in, but as it did, all of them raised their hands, including Daniel.

'And none of you noticed a body hanging over the bath?' Bambridge raised his voice. 'A body of a so-called friend.'

They all looked at each other and none of them could give him an answer.

'So, my original question stands, was there anything unusual about the bathroom?' They all stared at him dumbfounded. 'Your friend hanging over the bathtub, for example?

There was a collective gasp, and some of them looked offended, but the offence soon changed to guilt as they all realised what they had managed to overlook in their various states of inebriation.

Lawrence could see that Hilary was running things through in her head. What looked like recognition formed, and then her eyes widened before she spoke.

'I went to sit down on the loo,' she told them. 'And I

lost my balance, so I reached out and grabbed at the shower curtain. Nearly pulled it off the hooks. But I fell onto the toilet anyway. It was when I got back up that I noticed him.' Tears welled up in her eyes and she bowed her head.

'That's really helpful.' Bambridge's voice was soothing.

The group appeared to relax in unison, each of them seemed to visibly grow less tense.

'Was Stephen at the party with you?' Bambridge asked and they all tensed up again.

One of the other women answered. Her green Versace dress an equal to Hilary's in price and in beauty. Its matching Manolo Blahnik heels had Lawrence envious. Both outfits were stunning, and she'd have given an arm and a leg to own all four items.

'No.' she said slowly. 'He had his own social circle.'

'So, it's possible he was home before you?'

'Possibly. He kept himself to himself most of the time.'

'And not so much at other times,' Daniel added.

This made half of the group smile, whilst the other half looked angry. Hilary glowered at him.

'What does that mean?' Bambridge gave Daniel a piercing stare that would have turned most people to stone, and the young alpha was no exception. His eyes turned to the floor and Lawrence could see him physically deflate.

'He means that Stephen was gay,' Hilary answered, shooting Daniel a look that matched Bambridge's glare. 'He hung out at very different places to us.'

'He wasn't at the party,' Bambridge concluded, bringing a close to that part of the conversation. 'Anyone else in the flat when you all arrived?'

The question was greeted with a series of 'no's'.

'Was there anyone at the party you didn't know?'

'Plenty,' Hilary said, and gave the rest of the group a disdainful look. 'I told you all not to invite so many people back.'

'So, there were a lot of people here, who came back with you for the party?'

'Yes,' Hilary replied.

'Any of you see someone leaving the bathroom in a rush?' Bambridge waited for a reply that he never received. 'Someone you didn't recognise walking through the flat?' Blank faces greeted him. 'Anyone leaving the flat in a hurry?' None of them could give him an answer. 'And what time did you go out last night?'

'I went out straight from work,' Hilary answered, followed by similar responses from the rest of the group.

'Stephen could have been home all day then?'

'Well, he didn't exactly need to work,' Daniel remarked. with an air of jealousy.

'Why's that?' Bambridge was curious.

'Because he's a Bushell,' Daniel said and rolled his eyes. 'He can dine off his name alone in this town.'

From the entrance of the flat footsteps sounded on the wooden floor, and on cue several people in sharp suits entered the living room, walking directly over to the group of partygoers.

Lawrence saw the confidence in the young alpha return, and his chest puff up as the new arrivals surrounded their clients.

'This conversation is over,' said one of the suits, handing Bambridge a business card and then another to Lawrence. She glanced at the card and recognised the law firm's name. Bushell & Co. And also made a note of her name Jemima Herbert. The fact that they were representing one, or all of these young partygoers didn't surprise her. Having money always came with legal backup.

Bambridge stalked back into the bathroom.

Lawrence watched the group deflate again. She was trying to see if any of them looked like they'd got away with something. But they all just seemed tired and in desperate need of sleep. Happy that none of them were hiding something, she went after Bambridge.

She could see something was going on his head. He paced back and forth in front of the body, his right hand rubbing the stubble on his chin.

'What's on your mind, Guv?'

Bambridge paused and looked at her. 'They were disturbed again.' He pointed to the ceiling and finally the footprint in the blood. 'Would explain the lacklustre cleaning.'

'Okay, so they were disturbed. By what? The rest of the flatmates coming home?'

'Let's say they're in the middle of their ritual as those guys come home. They get put off and must rush the cleaning process.'

Lawrence ran the scenario through in her head and couldn't find any flaws in the idea. 'It certainly seems plausible,' she replied.

'They quickly clean up and, in their hurry, they missed a few spots.'

You mean, you missed a few spots?

'Too be fair, Guv, they could have missed some spots in the other place. It was filthy.'

'I don't think so,' he replied. 'They had more time. I'm pretty sure they were interrupted here. That's two in a row. Either they're getting sloppy, or more adventurous?'

'Then someone must have seen them leave the bathroom?' Lawrence stated. 'There's no way they weren't seen.'

Lawrence looked out of the bathroom door. There was a wide corridor leading from the bathroom, past the living room to one side and the bedrooms on the other. Judging by the mess of the place, the partygoers had spilled out into this area too, so getting to the door without being seen was impossible.

'If anyone did see them, they're long gone,' Bambridge offered. 'And that lot out there can't or won't help us.'

'Maybe, forensics will catch a fingerprint?' Lawrence didn't like where Bambridge's thoughts were headed. She didn't want to believe that they had reached another dead end. But then maybe he was leading the case that way on purpose? It was the perfect way to cover your own tracks.

Bambridge shook his head. 'Not a chance. They got the cleaning wrong, but nothing else. They're too meticulous.'

'Different sort of victim again,' Lawrence added.

Bambridge nodded as he looked at the body. 'Same end goal though, to take the blood. Although, looking at that bruising over his eye, the method of restraint was different. Hit them in the face, rather than the back of the head.'

'They were face to face?'

'Looks that way. How did they end up here though?'

'How d'you mean?' asked Lawrence, looking perplexed.

'Well, our first victim was working, so that was a possible way in for our suspect. Our victim at the pub was probably lured into the alleyway. Our jogger was accosted in a park. So, what's the deal with this victim? How did our suspect end up in the victim's flat? There're no signs of forced entry, which implies that they were invited in.'

'So, we're looking for signs of a struggle? In this?' She pointed to the empty cans, bottles of champagne and glasses littered around the bathroom.

'Not here, but maybe in the bedroom?'

Bambridge marched into the living room and walked straight over to the partygoers and their lawyers.

'Can I ask which of you live here? he asked, as he looked at each of the youngsters in turn.

Hilary instantly raised her hand, followed by the woman in the Versace dress. One of the suits placed a hand on Versace's shoulder and then whispered in her ear. She lowered her hand and then looked at the floor. A lawyer also said something to Hilary, but she ignored him and stood up.

'I do,' she answered proudly.

'Great,' Bambridge mirrored her enthusiasm. 'Did you go into Stephen's room much?'

'You don't have to answer that,' one of the lawyer's cautioned, her eyes fixed on Bambridge.

'No, but I want to,' Hilary replied to the lawyer and walked towards one of the bedrooms. 'This was his,' she added, as she pushed the door open.

The bedroom was large, but then Lawrence hadn't expected any less. She was less surprised by the soft creams and pale pinks of the walls. Stephen had a similar taste in furnishing to herself, and her envious observations of the flat continued. There was a wall of oak wardrobes down the left side of the room, with a double bed underneath the bay window. A pale cream sofa sat at the end of the bed, opposite a built in L shaped desk arrangement, in matching oak. Lawrence couldn't help but admire the dead man's choice in soft furnishings. He'd had obviously been a fitness freak, because there was a series of weights beneath a second, smaller window, on the right of the room and a yoga mat laid out in front of a huge floor to ceiling mirror. Lawrence moved over to the desk, noticing a corkboard with various pieces of paper pinned to it, and scanned all the information. A few of the logos were familiar, but she was so tired that her brain couldn't process what they were. So, she got out her phone and took a few pictures of it all for future reference.

'Did you come in here often, Hilary? Bambridge asked as he moved further into the room.

'You do not have to say anything,' the same lawyer stated, as she appeared in the doorway. It was going to be a morning of envy for Lawrence it would seem, because she couldn't help but appreciate the suit she was wearing. She didn't recognise the make, but it was quite clearly tailored, and its dark grey tone really complimented the lawyer's pale complexion.

'Oh, give it a rest,' Hilary replied with a sigh, her features stern. 'I'm not under arrest,' she turned to Bambridge with a softer expression. 'I'm not, am I?'

'No, you're not,' Lawrence answered, 'just helping with our enquiries.'

'Thought so,' she said, with an affirming nod. 'Stephen and I often work out together. He's a fitness nut and knows so many good ways to work out.'

'So, you have been in here often?' Bambridge repeated his question.

'Yes.'

'Okay, so, is there anything that seems odd in here? Anything out of the ordinary?'

Lawrence watched the confidence leave Hilary again, and the young woman in shock returned. But she looked around the room regardless. At first it seemed she wasn't going to find anything, but then she stopped next to the bed and pointed at it.

'He's not made the bed,' she said.

'Is that unusual?' Bambridge asked.

'Absolutely. He was meticulous with how he made his bed.'

'Why was that?'

Hilary shook her head. 'No idea. Something to do with the way he was raised, I guess. The Bushell family are a regimented bunch.'

'I'd watch your words, Miss Cartwright,' the lawyer interjected.

'Oh, do be quiet,' she said over her shoulder and then pointed at the dishevelled sheets. 'This just won't do, would be what he'd say about this. Even if I just sat on the bed whilst we worked out, he'd have to readjust them.'

Lawrence moved closer to the bed and leant down near to the sheets. She could see a blood stain amongst them. 'Got blood here, Guv,' she pointed at the spot.

It all became too much for Hilary as a whimper left her throat, and she stepped out of the room. The lawyer glared at Lawrence and then followed his client.

'So, this is where they were incapacitated. Then they were dragged to the bathroom and dispatched,' Bambridge surmised.

Well, you'd know.

'Looks that way,' Lawrence replied. 'Can't see us getting much more in here, Guv, or the bathroom. Like you've said before, our suspect is too thorough. Someone at the party must have seen them leave, though,' Lawrence added.

'Or something!'

Bambridge headed towards the front door before he'd finished speaking. She went after him, following him down onto the street. He stopped at the bottom of the steps and was looking at the tops of the houses, and at each of the lampposts.

'What are we looking for, Guv?'

He pointed at a camera on the corner of a building. 'That.'

Chapter Twenty-Three

Lawrence knew what Bambridge was about to suggest, even before he pointed at the CCTV camera, because she had thought the same thing.

Their suspect had left at some point, and with luck they had been picked up by the camera. A benefit of the scene being in an affluent area perhaps? She wished it weren't the case, and that every part of the city was just as safe as the next, but money paid for safety, as well as cameras outside expensive houses.

As Bambridge walked towards the camera, Chief Inspector Stone waved at them from close to the blue and white tape. He was clearly stood with two of the lawyers that had entered the flat. They must have left when Hilary had shown them around Stephen's bedroom. Whatever they had been saying had him flustered. Had Bambridge's harsh words finally got the better of him?

'Detectives,' Stone called out as he moved to intercept them. 'A word.' It wasn't a request.

Bambridge veered off from his path towards the camera and followed Stone to an area away from all the crowds. When Lawrence joined them, Stone let rip.

'What the hell are you playing at?' Stone demanded, taking a step closer to Bambridge.

'What d'you mean?' Bambridge replied, glaring at his boss.

'Since when do we make idol threats at possible witnesses?

'What threats?'

'At that young man in there. Do you have any idea who his father is?'

The fear that Lawrence had been dealing with since Bambridge's return was about to come true. Punishment for the way he spoke to people. She only hoped that she wasn't implemented in this mouthing off.

'Someone important?' Bambridge asked petulantly.

'You're damn right he's someone important. I can only pray that what you said in there isn't taken too seriously.'

'He's just a kid,' Bambridge said with a shrug.

'A kid whose father has a massive say in what does and doesn't happen in this city. Like whom does or doesn't get a pay rise this year. What departments do or don't get a decent budget for next year. Am I making myself clear?'

Lawrence could see both men were ready to lay into each other, and for a second, she thought she would need to step between them.

'Crystal,' Bambridge offered through gritted teeth.'

Stone got his temper under control and looked at her for the first time.

'Initial thoughts?' Stone asked, as he pointed a thumb over his shoulder towards the scene.

'We've got a fourth victim,' Bambridge replied, his own anger seeming to have subsided.

'You sure?' Stone looked cynical. 'Completely different type of victim to the last three?'

'They're all different,' Bambridge answered back.

'If they're all different, how can you be sure it's the same suspect?'

'It's our suspect,' Bambridge replied flatly, 'and we think they were disturbed by the flatmates coming home.'

'So, the housemates found the body?'

'One of them, yes,' he said with a shrug, 'but none of them in there are any use.'

'What makes you say that?'

'They were all off their tits,' Bambridge said in a mocking tone as he folded his arms across his chest.

Lawrence could see that he was anxious, and there was a sweat starting to form on his forehead. He was probably feeling the effects of their bender far more than she; or, he just didn't want to be around Stone.

'Why would that make them no use?' Stone asked, continuing to stare at Bambridge.

'None of them saw a thing.' Lawrence replied.

The senior officer's attention turned to her. 'How is that possible?'

'It appears that there were more people at the party than we have upstairs, a lot more. It's quite possible our suspect slipped out of the party unnoticed. And if anyone did get a look at them, they're long gone.'

'So, there's no reason to keep the residents any longer?' Stone asked, watching Bambridge again.

'I guess not, sir,' she replied, but wasn't sure.

'They couldn't tell you what day it is,' Bambridge said, as he turned away from Stone, his posture resembling some of the people they'd just interviewed, hunched, and looking like they wanted to be someplace else.

It wasn't the booze, she realised. It was the after-effects of his attempt to end his life with its subsequent blood loss that was beginning to take its toll. She would need to get him away from the chief before he passed out.

'It appears the suspect drew the shower curtain in front of the body,' Lawrence stated, to distract Stone from Bambridge. It worked. 'It wasn't until someone tripped and pulled the curtain back that the body was discovered.'

'I'm surprised they saw anything,' Bambridge said over his shoulder. 'Can't see beyond their own noses.'

'I'd advise you to watch what you say,' Stone replied

coldly. 'They're the offspring of some highly respected members of society.'

'There's no doubt about that,' Bambridge said cynically. 'But do they deserve the same respect?'

'Why would they not?'

'Because they're not the ones that need respecting. They're just a bunch of snotty kids.'

'From highly respected families no less.'

'Are the drugs they're on so highly respected?' Bambridge faced Stone with a challenging gaze.

'What they do with the recreational time is not our business, Detective. Murder is our business, and I suggest you keep your mind focused on such things.'

'We should interview the victim's family next,' Bambridge said, firmly, seeming not to hear Stone's words at all. 'See what they can tell us about the victim.'

'Canham and Quinnell will deal with the Bushell's,' Stone answered sharply.

'Don't trust me to be civil?' Bambridge joked.

'Exactly that,' Stone snapped back. 'There's a lot of big names involved in this, names that I don't want you pissing off.'

'Glad you think so highly of me. So, what are we to do? Sit back and let those two take over our case?'

'Exactly that,' Stone offered with a stern face. 'I think it best that you take some time off, Inspector Bambridge. It's quite clear that you have come back to active duty far too soon.'

Lawrence couldn't believe what she was hearing! Was he really taking them off the case?

'And what about D.C. Lawrence?' Bambridge said, supressing a mocking laugh. 'Has she come back too early? Or is she still allowed to work the case?'

She felt annoyed that he had spoken for her. But if

truth be told she wasn't sure what she would have said to Stone anyway.

'I think, with all the media attention we have for this one, some more senior officers would be best working the case.'

'You mean officers that you've got on your side. Ones that'll toe the line with what you tell them to do?' Bambridge added, his words still filled with laughter. 'Just like what the Bushell's, have got you doing, toeing in line? Why are we really being taken off the case, sir? Is it because they told you to?'

'Take it as you will, Inspector. But I'm pulling you both from it none the less.' Stone seemed filled with well controlled anger as he bit out his instructions to Bambridge and Lawrence. He left them without another word.

'Bit touchy, don't you think, Lawrence?' Bambridge jested.

Still in shock at being pulled off the case, she turned to Bambridge angrily. 'Well, you pretty much just accused our boss of being in the Bushell family's pocket. That kind of talk isn't gonna do anyone any favours! What the hell were you thinking?'

Bambridge just shrugged. 'A hunch,' he replied, watching his senior office disappear into the flat. 'One it'll do us well to remember.'

Lawrence didn't know what to say. She'd been moved off cases before, but that had been early in her career when she didn't know anything, and not in such a brutal manner either. She could understand why the chief wouldn't want Bambridge around this one, especially given the exchange that had just taken place, but she felt that she could still be of use. Stone's words about wanting more senior officers on the case rang in her ears.

Was she just a token appointment after all? A body added to the department to appease the equality figures. A black woman in the team was a great way to keep HR happy. Diversity targets achieved! If only she'd been gay, then she would have ticked all the boxes. She gave a mirthless laugh. All these thoughts were spinning around in her head so fast, that she didn't notice Bambridge had walked away from her.

He had moved across the road and was stood looking up at the camera. She moved to his side but could see that sweat had soaked through the back of his suit jacket. His fingers were clench into his palms, and his eyes were blinking continuously.

'You okay, Guv?' Her concern was genuine, he didn't look well.

'Fine,' he replied, but he sounded pained.

'Anything I need to worry about?' She watched him think for a second, before he shook his head.

'Your thoughts on in there is what I'm after.' Bambridge nodded his head back towards the crime scene. The sweat had started to run down his temple.

'I think we're being shafted,' she tried to hold back her anger, but she knew she sounded annoyed.

'Never mind that.' Bambridge waved away he concerns. 'What do you think about the scene?'

'What does it matter? We're off the case anyway.'

'Fuck that, I'm still gonna work it.'

'Really?'

'Absolutely. You think Canham and Quinnell will solve it?'

She pondered the question for a second before shaking her head.

'Exactly. There'll be another half a dozen deaths before those clowns get anywhere near catching the killer.'

'But the chief said…'

'The chief can kiss my ring piece. The only way this guy is gonna be caught, is if we catch him.'

'Him? You think they're male?'

Bambridge nodded. 'Those toffs in there implied Stephen was gay, and I'm guessing our suspect used that to their advantage, and that was their lure for this victim.'

Bambridge pointed at the camera. 'And right now, our best lead is ringing that number.' He looked at her implying she should be the one calling.

With a nod she pulled out her phone and dialled the number.

'P & B Security Services,' a voice answered.

'Good morning,' Lawrence replied. 'I'm Detective Constable Lawrence. We were hoping to get access to footage from one of your cameras?'

'Do you have a warrant for the footage?' The voice didn't even pause to consider the request.

'No, I don't have a warrant,' she replied, 'but it's in connection with a murder investigation, so, any help from you would be greatly appreciated.'

'I can't provide any footage from our archives to the authorities without a warrant, I'm afraid.'

The reply sounded rehearsed. Which made Lawrence wonder how often P & B Security Services were asked for their footage.

'I guess I'll come back with a warrant, then.'

'Have a good day now,' the other end of the line went dead.

'Sounds like that went well,' Bambridge offered. 'Just the type of firm the management company of a posh private estate like this would employ.'

Lawrence must have been distracted when they arrived because she hadn't noticed, but now that she had been made aware, she could see that the street and its surrounding buildings were all within an estate. The road leading in and out even had an archway over it.

'Shall I get a warrant over the phone?' Lawrence asked.

He shook his head. 'They're just stalling; besides, we'd need to get authorisation from Stone for such a thing. You got an address?'

Lawrence opened her phone, typed in the company name, and an address came up. She smiled. 'They're on site.'

'Really?

'Yeah,' she opened the address in her phone's Satnav and showed it to Bambridge. 'It's just up the road.'

'Let's go say hello,' Bambridge started walking.

'Should we not be trying to get a warrant anyway?' she asked as she jogged to catch up with him.

'From Stone? We're not supposed to be working this case, right? I'm sure we can just wing it,' Bambridge was adamant. 'Which way was the security office?' he asked over his shoulder.

P & B Security Services had their office two streets from Stephen's flat. Their premises looked like a bungalow, which had been converted. Lawrence could tell it had been designed that way on purpose. The idea being that the security office blended into its surroundings, even though it was the only bungalow in the whole complex.

Bambridge tried the office front door, but it wouldn't open. He saw the intercom next to the entrance and pressed the button. There was no answer.

Bambridge tried the buzzer again.

It crackled into life.

'Hello?'

'Police, open up,' Bambridge ordered.

'Who?'

'The Police, open up.'

'Do you have an appointment?'

'No, don't need one. Open up.'

There was another pause before the lock clicked, and Bambridge pushed his way inside. They passed through a second unlocked door that took them into the reception area.

It was a minimal space but luxuriously appointed. Lawrence could feel her shoes sinking into the carpet, which she couldn't remember happening in any other reception she'd been in. Nor could she remember seeing plush, leather chesterfield sofas and club chairs arranged around a walnut coffee table, upon which sat an array of today's newspapers and hardback books Lawrence couldn't afford. They all looked a little too highbrow for her reading tastes. The smell of fresh coffee drew her attention to a sideboard upon which sat a percolator and what looked like a Clarice Cliff coffee set. The only thing that hinted the room was anything other than a pleasant and expensive sitting room was the counter, on the far side of the room, which bore the company logo. An immaculately dressed, blonde haired receptionist sat behind the counter and smiled a corporate smile at them as they moved towards her.

'Good afternoon officers,' she chirped. 'How can we help you today?'

Lawrence checked the clock on the wall, it was indeed now the afternoon. As they approached the desk she could feel her stomach grumble, reminding her that she hadn't had breakfast, and it was now lunchtime.

'Good afternoon. D.I. Bambridge; this is D.C. Lawrence.' He showed his warrant card. 'We want to check some CCTV footage from yesterday.'

'Does D.C. Lawrence have a badge?' the receptionist asked, her smile fading a little. *Was it because of my skin colour,* thought Lawrence, *that she doesn't believe I'm a detective?*

She produced her identification, all her insecurities and feelings of inadequacy briefly rising to the surface as she gave the receptionist a false smile.

'Can I see a warrant for the footage?'

'Why d'you need a warrant?' Bambridge asked leaning against the reception desk.

'It's company policy.'

'Even if it hinders a murder investigation?'

'Our customers privacy is our priority at P & B,' the receptionist chimed, her words sounding rehearsed.

'Well, that's nice,' Bambridge replied. 'You come up with that?'

'I didn't come up with anything, detective. It's just what we believe here.'

'Here's how it's gonna go,' Bambridge leant further over the desk. 'You're gonna find the person who produced that slogan, and you're gonna bring them to see us.'

The receptionist looked shocked by the abruptness and sat with her mouth open.

'Now would be good,' he said as he snapped his fingers.

She smiled at them both, and then picked up the phone. There was a pause, before she spoke quietly into the receiver, then hung up. 'Someone will be with you shortly. If you'd like to take a seat?'

Bambridge smiled back at her, and then walked towards the waiting area, but didn't sit.

Lawrence also remained standing.

She'd been taught that when you greeted people from a seated position you began the conversation at a disadvantage. Who it was that had taught her she couldn't recall? But it was a wise choice to make as she was pre-empting a difficult interaction with whoever was coming.

Alex Parkhurst wore a slightly distracted expression on his pale face as he barrelled through the door on the far side of the room. Barrelled was the right word to describe how he moved. His six foot-and-the-rest frame was stocky, he was well built, reminding Lawrence of a rugby player. Not the kind of player that got stuck into the ruck though, his face was far too pretty. This rugby player was wearing a tailored suit, and he was wearing Lobb handmade shoes. Security obviously paid more than police work.

After exchanging greetings and introductions with the two police officers, Alex took Bambridge and Lawrence through to the private area, where the building took on the appearance of professional offices rather than someone's lounge. 'How can we be of help?' Alex looked from Bambridge to Lawrence, whilst leaning on the corner of a desk, arms loosely folded in front of him, and a pleasant smile on his face.

'We need to look at some CCTV footage,' Bambridge answered.

'Oh. I'm not sure we are able to do that,' Parkhurst replied, the smile wiped away by a closed and cautious look.

'Yes, you are,' Bambridge replied. 'If you're security, you'll know there has been a major incident on site overnight and that we could be investigating a murder. We'll need footage from outside Mr Bushell's house from all yesterday and this morning.'

'I'm afraid I'm not able to provide that, sir, unless you

have a warrant.'

'Rubbish,' Bambridge told him. 'You're a security firm. You should know that any footage on public highways can be viewed at any time by the police if they ask. We don't need a warrant and I'm asking.'

Parkhurst looked embarrassed. 'I'm afraid, with respect, sir, this is a private estate and the security cameras and equipment belong to the Bushell family, whom we work for. Therefore, as the estate is private property and the cameras in question belong to private individuals, I am not at liberty to let you see any footage. You'll need a warrant.'

Was Parkhurst's smile smug, thought Lawrence, or was he just proud he was doing his job properly. Or did the Bushell's have something to hide? A glance at Bambridge told her he felt it was the latter.

Mention of the Bushell's gave her an idea. It was a bad idea, and one that might get them into trouble, but by being here they were already disobeying a direct order, so what further harm could it do?

She pulled the Bushell & Co card out of her pocket and waved in front of Parkhurst. 'We've been sent here by the Bushell's to check the footage.' She could see Parkhurst process what she had said and the card in front of his eyes. He took the card off her and studied it.

'They send both of you?' he asked Bambridge from over the top of the card.

Bambridge fished around in his pockets before producing the same card. He held it up with the same front of house smile the receptionist had given. 'We're on the same team,' he said, placing the card in Parkhurst's other hand.

Lawrence thought that he wasn't going to buy it, and that they would be marched out of the building. But

Parkhurst smiled at them and handed back the cards. 'Good. I'd received word that someone was being sent. Didn't tell me it was going to be the police though. Please forgive our receptionist for being so blunt, she takes her job very seriously, and wasn't aware that I knew you were coming.'

'Not a problem,' Bambridge waved the comment away. 'However, we are in a bit of a rush, so if we could see the footage as soon as possible.'

'But of course,' Parkhurst replied, and started walking. 'If you'll follow me.'

Lawrence gave Bambridge a look that said, 'that was close', which he returned with a knowing smile, and together they went after the security representative.

Bambridge was right. They did need to hurry. Particularly if the Bushell family had sent someone to view the footage. But would the actual viewers show up before they had got what they needed?

Parkhurst stopped at a door with the words 'Surveillance Lounge' written across the black glass. His eyes told Lawrence all she needed to know. He and his company were under the cosh and the residents would be riding them hard. Or the Bushell family were. Either way, Parkhurst's job would be under the microscope.

The surveillance lounge was eerily quiet. It pressed down on Lawrence. Whether it was the low ceiling that was doing it, or if they had sound suppression equipment built into the walls, she couldn't be sure. Whatever it was, the change of atmosphere from the rest of the building was noticeable.

The lighting was also different. All the light was focused on the screens along the back wall. Away from the multiple screens the rest of the room was cast in shadows.

'Solomon,' Parkhurst said to the man sat in front of the screens. 'Solomon, two detectives are here to investigate the murder of Mr Bushell.'

Solomon nodded at them but remained in his seat. Even from his seated position Lawrence could tell that Solomon wasn't very tall, but his shoulders were wider than the back of the chair he was sat in. If Parkhurst was a rugby player that didn't get in the ruck, Solomon definitely was. He was bald, the lighting dancing off his dark skin. His face was round, but there wasn't an ounce of fat on him. The thin moustache on his top lip strangely making him look younger than he probably was, and his eyes were piercing, but there was a kindness behind them.

'Don't think him rude detectives, it's company policy that Solomon remains at his station the whole time he's on his shift. Something Solomon takes very seriously.' He placed a hand on Solomon's shoulder. 'Anything they ask for, please provide it.'

'Of course,' Solomon said as he swung his chair back around to face the screens.

Parkhurst took a few steps back but stayed in the room.

'We need all the angles you have of Mr Bushell house. From yesterday and this morning,' Bambridge stated.

'The whole day?' Solomon asked, his tone implying that it would take a long time to go through all of it.

'Let's take it back to 10pm of the night before,' Bambridge replied, moving next to him.

Solomon tapped on the keyboard and then pointed to one of the screens. 'This is the feed,' he said, and typed something.

The screen went black and then showed a wide shot of the house. A timecode in the top corner of the screen read 21:58 as the picture started moving. The clock went up at two second intervals, going from 22:00 to 22:02 and so on.

'It's not a constant feed?' Bambridge asked.

Lawrence could see Solomon twitch at the comment, and then his eyes moved towards Parkhurst, who answered.

'On the cameras by the entrance, no,' he said. 'The further into the complex you go, you'll find better quality equipment. The houses on the edge of the complex don't contribute as much to our upkeep and maintenance. They're mainly let to families and professionals. The houses in the inner circle, they're all owner occupied.'

'Jesus, even the rich have a hierarchy,' Bambridge said with disbelief.

'Keeping the feeds on constant is expensive. By having two second feeds we save a large amount of server space.'

'How long do you keep the footage for?' Lawrence asked.

'We have a back log on about a week. Our servers can't cope with much more than that.'

Bambridge and Lawrence watched the screen. At 00:38 two figures walked into the complex and then up to the house.

'Can we zoom in on that at all?' Bambridge asked as he moved closer to the screen.

'Sure,' Solomon replied and then tapped on the keyboard. The image got bigger, but the quality of the picture got worse.

'Can you clean that up at all?'

He hit some buttons and the picture got marginally better. 'That's the best I can get for you,' he said, with a glance in Parkhurst's direction.

'Thank you,' Lawrence said as she stepped closer to the screen.

'Can you run up to the moment they enter the house?'

The footage showed the two men step up to the front door, one hanging back whilst the other opened it. 'That must be Stephen,' Bambridge said as he pointed at the figure opening the door. 'Can you run it back to when they first appear?'

'Sure.'

The footage rewound too the couple's arrival.

Lawrence watched intensely to see if either of the faces were highlighted, whilst also followed the figure that she knew wasn't Stephen. Was it Bambridge? She tried to see if the posture or the way they walked was the same as him, however, the picture just wasn't clear enough. They got to the front door again and the footage froze. Did she want it to be Bambridge? Part of her said yes, as it meant she already had her suspect in her sights. But at the same time, she was praying that it wasn't him.

'Keep going,' Bambridge stated. 'Until the flatmates come back. If you can make it play a little faster, that'd be great.''

'Sure.'

The clock moved along at a quicker pace, with the picture mostly staying the same. The odd car passing through the image. Lawrence watched the clock, waiting for the flatmates to come on screen. But she was surprised when the front door opened, and a figure walked down the steps.

'Pause it,' Bambridge ordered. 'Who is that?' He moved closer to try and get a better look, but the image was bad again.

'I can't tell,' Lawrence replied, glancing at him side-on to see if the image looked like him.

'Let it run,' he said as he moved even closer to the screen.

The figure stopped at the bottom of the steps and then

turned into the front garden. He ducked down out of sight behind the wall and then reappeared with something in his hands, which he slung over his shoulder, and then went back inside.

'What the hell was that?' Lawrence asked, taking a step back from the terminal.

'His tool kit, perhaps?' Bambridge replied, tapping his finger against his lips. 'How often do the bins get collected?' He asked after a pause.

'Once a week,' Parkhurst replied wearily. 'They would have been picked up that morning.'

'What you thinking?' Lawrence asked, ignoring Parkhurst dumbfounded expression.

'He dropped off his tool kit,' Bambridge replied. 'Stashing it by the bins. But if the bins were picked up yesterday, he must have stored it that day. Can we run the tape backwards from 10pm?' Bambridge asked, moving closer to the screens.

The timecode wound back to 22:00 and started counting down. At 19:30 someone appearing at the house steps.

'Stop there,' Bambridge barked.

Solomon did as he was asked.

'Wind it back a bit. Until that figure first comes into shot.'

The footage wound back and then started just at the figure left the frame. As it played, they came into shot with a bag over his shoulder, ducked down behind the bins, then reappeared without the bag and walked off. With the daylight the picture was much clearer, and they were able to make out a lot more detail.

'Tell me you can clean up that image?'

Again, Solomon looked at Parkhurst, and this time there was a pleading looking in his eyes, as if he wanted to tell them something but needed his manager's permission.

'Only what we could do last time,' he answered.

A look of annoyance crossed Solomon's face that only Lawrence noticed. Clearly there was more to it than he was letting on.

'Okay, never mind. Forward it until the housemates come home.'

The clock ticked forward again and at 01:36 a group of people walked up the street. Lawrence tried to count the numbers, but there were so many that they became blurred on screen.

'How many'd you count, Guv?' Lawrence asked as she studied the footage.

'Over twenty.'

The group of people had all filed inside. Again, Lawrence concentrated on the clock in the corner and at 01:48 a lone figure exited the front door with a bag over his shoulder. She waited to see if anyone from the party followed him out, but as he moved down the street and then out of shot no one came after him. That niggle was there again. Was it Bambridge? Or was it someone else?

'Do you have any cameras on the main street?' Bambridge asked. 'Can we see where this person went?'

'We have a couple,' Solomon replied. 'But they're even lower resolution than this.'

'That's okay. I just wanna see where he went.'

Solomon did as he was asked, and two separate images came up on different screens. One of them pointing up the street, and the other pointing down. Both showed the same time in the top corner of the screen. The camera pointing up the street remained empty, apart from a bus working its way down the street. The camera in the other direction however, showed the figure moving quickly along the pavement. As both feeds played out the figure picked up his pace just as the bus moved into the same screen.

'He ran for the bus, look,' Lawrence stated and pointed at the screen.

Sure enough, the figure picked up pace, darting across the road so that they could flag down the bus at the next bus stop. The footage was extremely blurred, but there was no doubt that the figure got onboard.

'That's our man,' said Lawrence, firmly.

Bambridge shrugged. 'It could be, but we've seen a guy go into the apartment building where Stephen Bushell lives, with Stephen. Then we've seen him leave. It may be something, it may be nothing.'

Lawrence looked at Bambridge incredulously. 'It's the best lead we've got!' she sounded indignant.

'It's a shame you don't have any clearer footage. We'd no doubt get a look at this guy.'

Again, Solomon looked like he was going to say something, but stopped himself when he looked at Parkhurst.

Turning to Parkhurst, Bambridge said, 'I want a copy of that tape, untampered.'

'They will be released to the Bushell family through the usual secured lines,' Parkhurst said firmly, pressing a hand on Solomon's shoulder. 'Surely, they told you this before they sent you here?'

'Yes, they did, must have slipped my mind,' Bambridge replied, feigning ignorance.

Lawrence could tell that their time here was up. She could see the mistrust starting to form in the corners of Parkhurst's eyes. However, there was still a look of care and willingness to help in Solomon's, was he someone they could lean on?

'The usual channels will do just fine,' Lawrence replied. 'Well, I think we've seen all we need to see,' she added, as she subtly reached into her pocket for one of her cards.

'I'm glad we could be of help,' Parkhurst said with a broad fake smile and turned towards the door.

Lawrence placed the card on the table in front of Solomon, looked him in the eye and mouthed 'call me.' She then stepped after the head of security. Bambridge looked at her as if she'd gone mad, but she just winked at him and followed Parkhurst out of the door.

They exchanged pleasantries with Parkhurst and were outside the building in no time.

'What are you playing at?' Bambridge moaned as they walked away from the bungalow. 'We need to get closer look at that footage.'

'Everything's under control,' she said confidently.

'What does that mean?'

'I'm pretty sure I may have another way to get the footage.'

'What makes you say that?' Bambridge sounded confused.

'I've got a hunch,' she replied as she walked ahead of him.

'About what?'

Before she could answer her phone started ringing. She didn't recognise the number, but she had a pretty good idea who it was going to be, so she answered it. The voice on the other line made her smile.

Chapter Twenty-Four

Lawrence felt excitement. But then she also had a little bit of fear and quite a lot of anxiety buzzing around inside her. Excitement about who they were about to meet. Fear about what the meeting might uncover. And anxiety about doing things she shouldn't be doing.

Solomon had been very brief when he called her. Giving a place and a time that they should meet. A greasy spoon café about a mile away from where Stephen Bushell had lived in relative splendour.

'I know the owners,' he said, when the two detectives had arrived, and Lawrence ordered coffees for them all. 'We should be fine here.'

Lawrence found his words ominous. Just who were this Bushell family? They must have had some sway if they had one of their employees so paranoid. And by the way Parkhurst had been so edgy around them it was a sentiment shared by all who worked for them.

'Why would we not be fine?' Bambridge asked.

Solomon didn't answer the question. 'Let's just keep this brief,' he said instead and slid a USB stick across the table. 'That should give you all you need.'

'What's on it?' Lawrence asked as she picked it up.

'Better quality footage,' Solomon stated, his eyes constantly darting towards the door. 'We have two separate feeds running in that part of the complex,' Solomon answered. 'The one we showed you on site. And another, better quality one.'

'Why?' Lawrence's heart rate increased with anticipation. The footage they'd watched earlier had been surprisingly good, but its details were undefined. With this new footage she was sure they'd have a face. But what face would it be? The man sat next to her?

'The people who pay more wanted it,' he said, looking at them.

'Why?' Lawrence and Bambridge asked in unison.

His eyes went to the door as it opened for a new customer. 'Because the picture quality of the original cameras wasn't good enough.'

'So, why not just get them all updated?' Bambridge stated.

'Because they didn't want the other residents knowing that they had access to the better-quality footage.'

'What do you mean by access?'

'Some of them receive the same feeds as we do into their homes.'

'Why?' The two of them asked in unison again.

Solomon shrugged. 'They wanna know what's going on in their neighbourhood.'

'And why are you helping us? Couldn't you lose your job over this?'

'Fuck that place!' Solomon said, leaning back in his chair. 'I've been meaning to leave for a while now. Plus, no one deserves to go out the way Stephen did. He was a nice guy. Always had time for you. Would say 'hello' if he saw you on the complex.'

'Place must pay well though?' Lawrence asked, worry for Solomon creeping into her bones.

'Not as well as you'd think,' he replied with a shrug. 'That's the thing about the rich, the money only gets shared out amongst themselves.'

'Aren't you breaking the law by giving us this though?' Lawrence waved the USB at him.

He shrugged again. 'I can find another job. My skill set is varied and can be applied to any number of industries.'

Without another word Solomon stood up and left.

'You know this is going to be inadmissible, don't you?' The question was directed at Bambridge, who shrugged.

Why was he being so lackadaisical? Was it because by knowing it was inadmissible, he wouldn't be in trouble when his face showed up on the footage? She almost didn't want to watch it, but she knew that she had to.

'Where's best to watch that?' Bambridge pointed at the device.

Where, indeed? They could take it to the station, but there was no privacy there. If Stone, or Canham, or anyone that the Chief had on his side saw what they were doing then they'd both probably be on the wrong side of a suspension. That level of punishment was on its way most likely anyhow, but why tempt fate? They could go to her place and use Craig's computer. But would he be there? And if he were, what kind of reaction would she get bringing Bambridge round? Or, there was Bambridge's place. She'd definitely seen a computer in the study, but did she fancy going back there? And did she really want to watch the footage when Bambridge's face appeared onscreen whilst stood in his flat?

Could it really be him? But then why would it be him? She thought of how unbalanced he was right now, and how the anniversary of his wife's death had affected him. It was reason enough to justify his mental instability. His suicide attempt was an example of just how unstable he was. Did that make him a killer though? Had he been deliberately putting her off the scent, to cover for himself? She needed to examine the evidence. His mental state, his habit of not being around whenever a body was discovered, the list of names in his flat, some scored beyond recognition with a black marker. Was he crossing them off once he'd killed them? And then there was the rope, the same red and black rope used to tie the victims up. Rope that you could get in many places. Her mind raced, along with her heart as she stared at him across the table.

'Well?' he pushed for an answer.

But which one should she give? The station. Her place. Or his. She chose safety first.

'We can use Craig's PC.'

Bambridge looked sceptical. 'You sure?'

'Yeah, why?'

'Your fella won't mind you using it? I mean, won't he be using it?'

'You got an alternative?' She knew what he was going to say, but she really didn't want to go back to his place.

'There's always mine,' he offered, but then looked unimpressed with his choice.

'You don't seem too enthused about that idea.'

'No, it's fine. It's just that I'm not sure I remember the login details. It was Natalie's computer really.'

'We'll just go to mine,' she stated, relief flooding over her.

She had never felt so uncomfortable entering her own house. Yes, her and Craig had been bickering a lot lately, but she had never felt physically threatened by him. Not like she was feeling with Bambridge stood behind her with the keys in her hand. Did she want Craig to be there or not? He would certainly be a deterrent for Bambridge if he were to be revealed. But how awkward would it be if he was home? Either way the next few minutes were going to suck.

Craig wasn't home, so Lawrence wasted no time getting the PC started up and the USB stick inserted into the drive. Bambridge stood behind her whilst she typed in the password. His presence pressing down onto her back.

She concentrated on the job at hand and found the USB in the file directory. Opening it she could see that there were two files on it. One named Day and the other Night.

'What d'you wanna look at first?' she hovered the cursor between both video files.

He leant closer. The proximity of him made her edgy. 'Let's look at them arriving at and leaving the scene.'

She opened the 'Night mov' file and pressed play. Again, Stephen and his killer arrived at the scene. The picture quality was definitely better, but the killers face was still shrouded in darkness.

'Thought that guy said this was clearer footage?' Bambridge voiced her feelings. Yes, the rest of the street was less pixilated, but they still didn't have a face.

'Maybe, we'll get him as he leaves?' she hoped.

The killer picked up his bag from the front garden, but they managed to keep their face hidden. Lawrence could feel her frustration starting to rise. Had their trip to P & B Security and the subsequent meeting with Solomon been for nothing? As the last moments of the Night file played out, with their suspect leaving the scene, his face covered the whole time, her thought was that it had been. Beneath her suit and shirt, she began to sweat. And she hoped that her hair was still in place because she hadn't checked it in a while.

'Darkness is this guy's friend,' Bambridge offered as he took a step back.

She nodded her agreement. 'Let's see how he gets on in daylight though,' she added with optimism and played the other file.

The footage once again showed them what they'd already seen, but with so much more clarity. They approached the front steps with their bag, dropping it by the bins, and keeping their face hidden. However, as they left the front garden the face of their suspect was crystal clear. Lawrence paused the video and stared at a familiar face. But where did she know it from?

Lawrence experienced a number of emotions all at once. Delight that they had someone. Confusion as to where she'd seen them before. Relief that the face she was looking at wasn't Bambridge. Guilt at having ever considered that it could have been him. And then excitement again, as the case was now wide open.

'I think I know who he is,' she blurted out. 'I know that face, I know it!' But from where, she could not recall, yet.

'Who is he?'

She stared at the face for ages, racking her brain as to where she knew him from. She studied his features, trying to spark something, but it just wouldn't come.

'Lawrence?' Bambridge said, after the silence went on too long.

'Yeah, I'm thinking,' she answered, her eyes fixed on the man in front of her. If she'd had any sleep, it would have come to her instantly.

'Would I know who he is?'

'Doubtful,' she said sarcastically. 'You have to be around to meet people.'

'Bit harsh.'

It was a bit harsh, but it was true. If he'd bothered showing up at all for the past year, then he would have been present for so many more events. Been around when she had spoken to grieving loved ones, or when interviewing possible suspects, or doing door-to-doors.

'Door-to-doors, that's it!' she said aloud, and reached in her pocket for her notepad. She scanned through the pages until she found what she was looking for and then stood up. 'Time to go,' she added as she pulled the USB out of the drive.

'Go where?'

'Back to the Scenic,' she stated, once she was already halfway towards the front door.

Lawrence's blood was pumping. They had a lead. And a possible someone to detain. In her rush to get to Bambridge's car she almost didn't see Craig walking down the street towards them. The sight of him changed her mood instantly, and she started to think up excuses as to why they were there. Craig looked up from his phone and initially there was happiness on his face, but when he saw who she was with, the joy vanished, and mistrust took over. Did she have time to deal with him right now? Not really, and not in front of Bambridge. But she also didn't want him dwelling on why the two of them were leaving their home. She chose the truth.

'Hey hon,' she greeted him with a wave, 'just used the PC to look up something. Sorry if I left it running. Gotta go. We're about to go arrest a murderer.'

She hadn't meant to sound so excited with her final statement, but in truth she was. She didn't wait around for Craig's response as she was already rushing away from him towards Bambridge's car.

Sat in the passenger seat she was bouncing with anticipation, however, Bambridge hadn't started the engine. He was sat looking at her with a pained expression on his face.

'What's up?'

'Do you always speak to your fella like that?'

She didn't know what to say.

'No wonder you're having issues,' he added as he started the engine. 'Where we going again?'

Guilt ridden she gave him the address.

Chapter Twenty-Five

Lawrence's guilt continued throughout their journey.

'So, who is this guy?' Bambridge asked, after a long silence.

'I interviewed him whilst doing door-to-doors after the first victim.'

'Where was this?'

'On the same street that Tracey was killed.'

Bambridge turned his nose up and then shook his head. 'A bit close to home, don't you think?'

'How d'you mean?'

'Serial killers do tend to hunt in areas they know. However, hunting on the same street they live on seems a bit of a stretch.'

'True,' Lawrence replied. He was right it did seem odd to go after someone so close to their home. But maybe he had chosen his first victim out of convenience. And what was more convenient that five doors down? 'But it was definitely the same guy.' She waved her finger to emphasise her point. 'I recognised him.'

'But we've only got him dropping off something in the garden. Not leaving the flat and running for the bus. The footage of our suspect isn't with the victim. They might not be our guy.'

'So, who is he then and why was he at Stephen Bushell's flat?'

Bambridge went silent for a moment, considering her questions. He tilted his head to one side, and then the other, shrugged a couple of times and then answered. 'Could be an accomplice?'

Lawrence hadn't considered that. 'Is that a common

thing?' She had to admit she hadn't researched too much into serial killers. Some people had a weird obsession with them. An obsession she didn't possess.

'Some of them do. Take Rosemary and Fred West for example. They murdered at least twelve young girls together. So, it could be that the lure they've been using was the accomplice?'

'So, this guy?' She pointed to her notepad. 'Mr Leon Wallace, could just be the distraction for our actual suspect?'

'It's possible. What've you got written down about him?'

'Uhm…Leon Wallace. White Male. Mid-twenties. Said he was a shift worker, but didn't say where, or in what field of work. He'd just come home from his shift. May have been in scrubs of some kind. He had a badge on his shirt. That badge!'

The thought of the badge sparked something that made her put the notepad down and take her phone out of her pocket. Opening the picture library, she found the images she'd taken of Stephen's corkboard. On a flyer in the top right corner of the board was the same badge Wallace had on his uniform. She zoomed in on the image and read the name under the logo aloud. 'Blood donation badge of honour.'

'What's that now?'

'The badge this Wallace was wearing when I met him, was on a piece of paperwork stuck to Stephen Bushell's pinboard. It's a blood donor badge.'

'So, all our victims are donors?' Bambridge mused.

'What, and this Wallace is taking more than he should?

'Quite a lot more.'

'Didn't we ask Doctor Odell about possible

connections between the victim's blood? Damnit, how could I forget?' Lawrence asked as she closed down the picture library and dialled the pathologist. She put the phone on loudspeaker as he answered.

'Hello Doc, Bambridge and I have come up with a theory that maybe the link between our victims is they're all blood doners,' she said.

'Yes, that would make sense due to their blood types.'

'What d'you mean by that, Doc?'

'Well, they all had rare blood types,' Odell stated as he shuffled some paperwork. 'AB Negative blood to be precise.'

'All four of them?' Bambridge contributed.

'Yes, all four. Tracey Collins, George Stephens, the young lady in the park, Candice Okeke, and the latest one Stephen Bushell. That one sure has stirred up a fuss.' Odell's voice changed to an enquiring tone with his last sentence. Was he fishing for gossip?

'It sure has,' Lawrence replied, and then went back on topic. 'And AB negative is rare?' Lawrence asked.

'The rarest of them all,' Odell stated, his voice returning to a more formal manner. 'One percent of the population have it.'

'So, would it's rarity add a value to it?'

'Not really,' Odell said with a sigh. 'There's no money in blood. Organs is where you'll make a profit.'

'Thanks, Doc.' Lawrence hung up. 'So, we've got our reason for why he's taking their blood. Now we just need to know what he's doing with it.'

'We'll find out soon enough.'

They drove past the Scenic hotel and parked opposite the sixth building on the block.

'Do we need to call for back up?' Lawrence asked, excitement coursing through her.

'Doubt we'll get any,' Bambridge replied as he turned the engine off. 'We'll need a warrant to search the premises though. Technically.'

'So, what do we do?' The excitement she'd felt instantly started to subside as the process of getting a warrant to search someone's property came to mind. They'd never get one quickly, if at all. And even if they did it would be Canham and Quinnell kicking in the door.

'We're going anyway.'

'Without a warrant?'

'We're just knocking on a door,' he replied calmly, but there was an edge to his voice.

Her pulse raced. She was anything but calm. They were close, and they both knew it. But she also knew that she needed to not let her expectations overcome her again. She'd done that too many times before. She just had to stay focused.

Looking back down the street, Lawrence was astounded at how close it was to the scene of Tracey Collins murder. It was on the same parade of houses. The Scenic was on one end of the parade, and the home of Leon Wallace was at the other end. These factors made her doubt herself. Was this their guy? Or had she seen what she wanted to see, because she didn't want the figure in the footage to be Bambridge?

'Like you said, Guv, it's a bit too close to Tracey,' she expressed her doubts. 'I mean it really coins the expression, shitting on your own doorstep.'

'As I said earlier, most serial killers hunt close to where they live,' Bambridge replied. 'This, however, pushes that ideal to the limits. But the evidence has led us here. So, here is where we go.'

His words gave Lawrence some reassurance. 'Okay.'

'You ready?'

'I think so.'

'Let's go over everything before we go knocking.'

'Okay.' She opened her notepad again. 'So, the guy gave his name as Leon Wallace. Whether that's his real name though? Said he had just come home from a nightshift, didn't specify where he worked.'

'Did you ask?'

'I don't think so,' she grimaced. 'Should I have?'

'Probably, but what's done is done. What else did you put down?'

'He asked about why we were going door-to-door. And about what crime we were investigating.'

'Sounds like he was fishing for information,' Bambridge stated. 'The need to know what the police know is a common trait. Be it sick fascination with themselves, or the need to know if they are going to get caught. What did you tell him?'

'That we were investigating a murder in the area.'

'And what did he say to that?'

'He had guessed that something had happened at the hotel.'

'Did you ask him why he was so curious?'

'No.' Looking back over the notes Lawrence could see that she had done so many things wrong when speaking to Mr Wallace, and she was annoyed with herself. 'I just told him that I wasn't allowed to give out any information at that time.'

'Which was the right decision,' Bambridge said with a comforting smile.

'It was?'

'Yes.' He looked at her with a stern face. 'How were you to know this was our guy? If you go over your notes from that day most of the people, you spoke to would have asked the same questions. Hindsight is a beautiful thing, Lawrence, but don't let it dampen what you are doing now.'

'Yes, Guv.' She still felt annoyed even after his words.

'Hey!' He clapped his hands together. 'We're here now. Let's concentrate on that. You ready?' He didn't wait for an answer and climbed out of the car.

Lawrence let out a deep sigh, took another breath, and then let it out, and got out of the car.

'What number flat is he?' Bambridge asked, as his hand lingered over the buzzers.

'Five.'

Bambridge pressed the right button and they waited for a response, but no one answered.

'Maybe he's at work?' Lawrence said to help relieve the tension she was feeling. 'What's the likelihood of everyone in the block being at work though?' she asked leaning forward and pressing all the buzzers.

Bambridge gave her a puzzled look. She just shrugged, and then smiled at him as the door release sounded and she pushed it open.

'Neat trick,' Bambridge said, admiringly, as they entered the building. 'You done that before?'

'Once or twice,' she replied, and then started to climb the stairs.

Up on the second floor they found flat five and her memory of the conversation with Leon Wallace became clearer. So did what he had looked like.

He was pale, and not just in complexion. The light brown freckles across his nose, cheekbones, and forehead helping to emphasise just how white his skin was. Add to that his sandy blond hair, and his piercing blue eyes he couldn't have been more Caucasian if he tried.

Bambridge knocked and then stood back.

The silence in the corridor was painful in Lawrence's

ears. When no one answered she knocked herself, more forcefully. But it did no good, no one answered.

Bambridge tried again. 'Police, open up,' he called out, and then banged on the door once more.

Still there was no answer.

'Did you bring your baton with you?' Bambridge asked and then planted his foot into the door. It cracked but didn't give way.

'What are you doing, Guv?' she said as panicking she stepped in his way. 'We need a warrant before we can force entry.'

He stopped what he was doing and stared at her. At first, she couldn't see any semblance of understanding in him, he looked like kicking in the door was all he wanted to do. But as her hands rested on his chest and she smiled up at him, the firmness around the corners of his eyes softened, and he blinked a few times. Finally, he nodded his agreement and took a step back.

As she took a step back, he lunged forward and kicked the door again. This time it swung inwards.

Lawrence pulled her baton off her belt and extended it.

'Police, we have warrant to search the premises,' Bambridge shouted as he walked over the threshold.

Lawrence winced at his words. Not only had he kicked in the door, but he'd also lied about the warrant. They were inside though, and she followed him.

She wasn't sure what she had expected to find inside. Whether she had watched too many Hollywood horror movies and had been anticipating a Texas Chainsaw Massacre style living space, she couldn't be certain. But as Bambridge slipped his hands into a pair of latex gloves, he flicked on the light switch, and she saw it wasn't horrific at all.

The place was spotless.

A short corridor from the entrance led into an open plan living area. There was a kitchen to the left, with a breakfast bar separating it from the rest of the room. Past the kitchen was a closed door, with another on the opposite side of the room.

Between the two exits was a big empty space, with a double sash window looking out over the communal gardens behind it. What should have been the living room had nothing in it. No table or chairs. No sofas. No entertainment. Nothing.

As they moved through the flat, she noticed it smelt of recently being cleaned. But not with your usual scented household cleaning products. The place smelt of bleach, reminding Lawrence of Tracey Collins's bathroom.

Bambridge moved towards the door furthest from the kitchen, so Lawrence moved towards the other. She paused in front of it as she put on a pair of latex gloves before turning the handle.

It was the bathroom.

Like the living and kitchen areas it had been cleaned to a very high standard. The porcelain of the bathtub shone in the halogen light, and the smell of bleach hung thick in the air. On the sink was a toothbrush and a travel sized tube of toothpaste. There was also a travel sized shampoo and a small bar of soap in a dish at one end of the bath. No towels. No bathmat. The place looked like it had barely been lived in.

'No one's here,' Bambridge called from the other room.

'No, they're not,' Lawrence said to herself. The disappointment in her voice echoing off the tiles.

'I've got something though,' Bambridge stepped back into the living room, and waved her over.

She did as she was asked and moved over to the bedroom.

It was just as flawless as the rest of the flat, and just as empty, apart from a single cot bed in the middle of the room. The sheets made up to military precision. And a basic, fold out table against the wall next to the door.

Similar to Stephen's room, there was a cork pinboard dominating the wall. Unlike their latest victim's board, that had snippets of his daily routine pinned to it, this one did not.

Along the left side of the board was a list of names and addresses. Each one had been assigned a P number that was printed in large letters before their details. Five of them had a single red line through them. The fifth crossed out name, worried Lawrence. Was there another body out there somewhere?

'That's interesting' Bambridge was staring at the board. 'Who's the fifth name?' He learnt forward and read it aloud. 'Soren Christensen.'

'This is interesting, as well.' Lawrence stated, studying the other contents of the board.

Bambridge shook his head. 'He must be out there, somewhere. Christensen, I mean.'

'Look at this, Guv. I think it's his next intended victim.' On the other side of the board was a series of pictures, string linking some of the images together. They were mostly of a man in his mid-forties. Taken from different angles, at different times of the day, and at multiple locations. At the top of the board was the number P81 and the name Vincent Grosso.

'We need an APB on this Vincent Grosso.' Bambridge added.

Lawrence called it in. Giving dispatch his name and the address on the board, warning that he was a target for their suspect. When she finished, she could see that Bambridge was staring at all the paperwork on the table. It was all in neat piles with multicoloured sticky notes jutting out the sides of each pile. Leon Wallace had been busy and judging by the many names still on his list, plus the stacks of paperwork he wasn't even close to being finished.

'APB is out on Mr Grosso, Guv,' she said, moving next to him to get a better look at the table.

'Good,' he replied absently as he rifled through one of piles.

She did the same, looking at the pile nearest. For a brief second, she felt hope. Hope that the answer was about jump out at her. But nothing did. However, as she looked at what must have been accounting paperwork, a name kept repeating in the top corner of each piece which seemed familiar. Her heart skipped a beat. However, she needed to confirm what she thought she was seeing, so she opened her phone and went to the picture library again. Sure enough, the company name on the flyer on Stephen Bushell's pinboard was the same as the paperwork.

'Take a look at this, Guv,' she said as she lay her phone down next to the piece of paper.

Bambridge examined the two pieces of information.

Both had the name The Clean Blood Clinic on them.

'Do you have a rare blood type?' Lawrence read aloud from the image of the flyer. 'If the answer is yes then you could be eligible for a clinical trial at the Clean Blood Clinic.'

'What kind of money we talking?' Bambridge leant closer and for the first time she caught a glimpse of his wrist. It was wrapped in a bandage that looked like it hadn't been tied off properly, and there were blood stains over the wounded area. Judging by the looseness of the bandages he hadn't been to the hospital.

'Four figures,' she replied, as she recovered from the distraction.

'I thought there was no money in blood?'

'Maybe there is in AB negative blood?'

'Would explain why he's draining people,' Bambridge offered. 'There's a whole bunch of letters here with various Bushell company names on it. Looks like it not just blood he's been collecting. And he's been meticulous about all of it.'

'If he's so meticulous, why's he just left it all out on the table? If he's collecting dirt on the Bushell's then wouldn't you secure this all away somewhere?'

'Probably why these are all photocopies,' Bambridge said, pointing at some blotching in the top cover of one piece of paper. 'The originals are probably secured like you said.'

'But why?' Lawrence couldn't hide her confusion. 'What's this all have to do with our murders?'

Bambridge shrugged. 'I've no idea. But if this is our guy where's the blood? And where's the tool bag we saw him with at the last scene?'

He was right. Apart from the few items in the bathroom, the bed and the pinboard there was nothing else in the flat. They hadn't checked all the cupboards yet, but she had a feeling that they wouldn't find anything.

'They leave town?' Bambridge asked, as he stepped back into the living room.

'Place has been cleaned professionally by the looks of it.' Lawrence could feel that she was gritting her teeth. 'Which is normally consistent with a new tenant moving in. But most cleaning crews wouldn't use such strong-smelling bleach. So, did we miss him?'

'Possibly,' Bambridge stated. 'But this level of cleaning is consistent with the scene a few doors down. And why leave all this paperwork?'

'True, but where are all his clothes? And like you said, where's the blood and tool kit?'

Bambridge shrugged. 'Maybe, he got spooked? Getting interrupted twice gave him a reality check?'

'So, why go to the trouble of cleaning the place? Wouldn't you just leave?'

Bambridge shook his head. 'This guy is too meticulous. I bet he's still stewing about losing the blood and his knife at the playpark.'

'So, what do we do now?'

'Is there a number on that flyer?' he said as stepped back into the bedroom.

Lawrence kicked herself for not thinking of this! She dialled the number.

'Good afternoon, you're through to the Clean Blood Clinic, how can we help?' The voice on the other end of the line sounded enthusiastic.

'Good afternoon, this is Detective Constable Lawrence, I have Detective Inspector Bambridge on the line with me, we were hoping to speak to a manager of some description?'

'But of course. Can I ask what it's regarding?'

'By the looks of it, a list of your patients that has fallen into the wrong hands,' Bambridge replied.

'I will put you straight through,' the voice replied, with some urgency.

They were on hold for only a second or two before a new voice spoke.

'Hello, you're through to Doctor Salmon. My colleague has advised me that you're police officers and that may have found a list of our patients?' Her voice was calm, but Lawrence could sense a mild tone of worry at the edge of her words.

'Yes, hello Doctor, I'm D.I Bambridge. We're currently looking at a list of names that we think may have come from your company.'

'A list of patient names?'

'It looks that way.'

'With the patients addresses included?'

'That also looks like the case.'

'Can I just ask how you're sure the list came from one of our facilities?'

'Well, we're not one hundred percent sure that it did. However, your information was with the list, and we thought it prudent to contact you immediately.'

'So, not to sound too much like an A-hole detective, but how can you be sure the list belongs to us?'

'How about I read off some names and you tell me if they're in your system?'

'That's confidential information I'm afraid.'

'That's fine. You don't have to confirm or deny that the names I give you are in your system. I just want you to have a look for them. If their names are there, then I'm sure you would agree that we should carry on talking.'

There was silence on the other end of the line for a moment before Doctor Salmon responded. 'I'm listening, detective.'

'Okay, so some of the names we have are Tracey Collins, George Stephens, Stephen Bushell, Soren Christensen, Vincent Grosso, Candice Okeke.'

'Okay, detective, you got my attention,' Doctor Salmon said with a sigh. 'How is it you've come about this list?'

'We found it at the home of a suspected murderer.'

There was an audible gasp on the other end of the line.

'Please don't tell me the names you read out are dead?'

'I'm afraid some of them are.'

'Good lord. Then how can I help, detective?'

'I just need you to confirm a few things for me.'

'But of course.'

'Great. And as before, if any of my question breech your confidentiality terms then feel free not to answer. So, the Clean Blood Clinic is a blood bank, is that correct?'

'That is one of our functions. The blood donated is then distributed to multiple hospitals across the country.'

'Do you take all types of blood?'

'We do,' Doctor Salmon said with an air of pride. 'We're always happy to take any types.'

'Including AB negative?'

'Especially AB negative. The more we can get of it the better. It's an exceedingly rare blood type you see.'

'I'm aware of its rarity. Is that why you were offering money incentives to get people to donate AB negative blood?'

'Money incentives? I'm not sure I follow, detective. All our donations are voluntary. We get paid by the facility who needs the blood. That's how we make our money.'

'So, why am I looking at a flyer, with the Clean Blood Clinic's name on it, stating that your company will pay four figure sums to anyone that is willing to donate AB negative blood?'

'I don't rightly know, detective,' Doctor Salmon went quiet.

'Okay, so, can I ask you something else?'

'You may.'

'Do you have an employee there called Leon Wallace?'

The line went quiet for a while, as if the Doctor had put them on mute.

'Hello?' Bambridge said after the silence had gone on

for a while. 'Are you still there, Doctor?'

'Yes, I'm still here, detective. I was just checking our records for that name.'

'And how did you get on?'

'We used to have an employee by that name, but he hasn't worked with us for over a year.'

'Oh. Why? What happened?'

'We had to let him go.'

'And why was that, Doctor?'

Again, the line went quiet, before Doctor Salmon started speaking. 'Unfortunately, we had to relocate last year, and his contract wasn't renewed.'

'What was unfortunate about the relocating?'

'We were one of the unlucky companies to fall foul to an arson attack during the riots last year. The fire did irreparable damage to the building, so we had to move. With the cost of moving location, we were forced to lose a few members of staff. Mr Wallace was unfortunately one of them.'

'Seems a bit odd that a blood bank would be one of the buildings set alight?'

'They were some crazy days. Some of the data and raw materials we lost were irreplaceable.'

'I'm sure they were,' Bambridge replied. 'Do you recall the address of that building which burnt down?'

'Of course,' she said, and proceeded to give them the address.

Bambridge thanked her for her time, nodded at Lawrence, and she hung up.

'Time to go look at a burnt-out building,' Bambridge stated and then left the flat.

Chapter Twenty-Six

It was getting late in the day as Bambridge drove east across the city, towards the previous address for the Clean Blood Clinic. Lawrence could feel her eyes getting heavy. But as certain streets became recognisable, and images from a year ago started appearing in front of her eyes, her tiredness went away.

Lawrence had never been able to explain the cause of the riots a year ago. Some experts had blamed it on economic downturn. A violent flare up from the public after years of recession. A recession caused by the banks that had received a very public bail out from the government. Others thought it was backlash from the same governments constant misuse of public funds. Funds that were crudely displayed in the shape of lavish properties being built in areas of the city that clearly the residents couldn't afford. One disastrous political policy after another had led to dissent. The everyday working man had had enough, and they took their anger out on the very streets they lived in. Disorder had reigned for five days straight, with the police left to try and bring order to the chaos. Every single officer had experienced some form of trauma during those times. Some much more than others.

'Oy! Officer, no sleeping on the job. Get on that phone of yours and see what you can find out about this clinic.'

Startled out of her daydreaming, Lawrence knew he was right, the more they knew about this place before they went there the better.

'Sure thing,' she replied, as she opened her phone and started searching. She found their home page easily enough, however the site was limited in the information it gave out. 'So, they're a blood bank, like the Doctor said. They're a member of the blood donor's award scheme.'

'Which is what?'

'The more you donate, the more badges you get. Bronze after ten donations. Silver after twenty-five. Gold after fifty.'

'No mention of payment for it though?'

'No.'

'So, what was that flyer about then?'

'The Doctor seemed oblivious to the money offer.'

'She did,' Bambridge said as he chewed on the inside of his cheek. 'But that doesn't mean she didn't know about it. What else you got?'

'They're a registered organisation that works with the NHS. As well as several other private companies.'

On the search engine screen one of the alternative questions was: Can I sell my blood for money in the UK? She clicked on the link and had an answer appear on screen.

'That's interesting. Says here, it's illegal to pay blood donors in the UK.'

'Doctor Salmon must have known that,' Bambridge mused. 'I think we'll need to go pay her and her company a visit after this.'

'There's no information online about the fire she was talking about though.'

'Contact base and see what they can send you about it. If it's a reported arson case, then we should have something.'

A quick call and she soon had the file appear on her phone.

Lawrence was instantly surprised by just how little information was available. The file gave her the name of the company: The Clean Blood Clinic. The company's address, which they already knew and were headed for. A brief summary stating that the building had suffered fire damage a year ago. Suspected arson/vandalism during the riots last summer. And finally, the investigating officer had closed the case: Detective Sergeant Bambridge.

'Should I be suspicious about the fact that the investigating officer was your wife?' Lawrence asked, in a tone that implied much more.

'Really? Doesn't sound like something she would have worked on.'

'What it says on the file. Case closed by Detective Sergeant Bambridge.'

'But she worked on major crimes. Why would she be looking into a blood bank?'

'If they were buying blood, then she may have been working on it perhaps?'

Bambridge shook his head. 'She was going after corrupt bankers, not blood bankers. What else does the file say?'

'Not a lot,' she answered with a sigh.

The lack of details was annoying. However, seeing Bambridge's dead wife's name on the file had her worried. She had seen him tense up at the mention of her name. Would knowing she had possibly worked on the same case send him down that destructive path again? Also, something else was grasping at the edges of her memory. Something important. She wished she knew what it was.

'Odd place to get torched,' Bambridge said idly, looking at their surroundings.

He was right. Most of the buildings that had been damaged during the riots had been places of interest for looters. Sportswear and electrical goods stores had been the most targeted. A blood bank didn't seem in keeping with everything else.

'Yes, it is,' she answered. 'Maybe it was next door to something of note?'

'We'll find out soon enough.'

They soon pulled up out the front of the building and Lawrence checked that she had entered the correct address.

'We at the right place?' Bambridge voiced the same concerns she had.

The place didn't look like any medical facility she'd ever been to. It was a warehouse with a ten-foot-high razor wire fence, on a remotely placed industrial estate just outside of town.

'Satnav says we've arrived.'

'Definitely not next door to something,' Bambridge said absently.

'No,' she replied, jutting her bottom jaw out. 'A single structure in the middle of an industrial estate.'

Bambridge gave a groan of uncertainty. 'Insurance job?' he asked.

Lawrence had the same thought. 'Sounds about right, Guv. Plus, we're nowhere near any of the flare up points. For the riots, I mean.'

'So, that means the story about being targeted in the riots is bullshit. Alright,' he said with a sigh, 'let's look around.'

They got out of the car and walked down the ramp that led into the warehouse's courtyard. As they passed through the front gate Lawrence noticed that the lock was broken, and both sides of the mesh metal were dented.

'Looks like something came through here,' she said as she pointed at the bent metal.

Bambridge stopped to look and then nodded in agreement.

They moved closer to the building. The smell of burnt materials was still in the air. There was a set of metal shutter doors that, like the gate, had taken some damage. Whatever had come through the gate had also hit the shutters, as the bottom two thirds of the door had ripped away from the runner.

'Doesn't look like any clinic I've been too,' Bambridge stated as he went down onto his haunches and looked through the deformed shutter door.

Lawrence bent down next to him turning her torch on. The interior was blackened by the fire. She could make out the metal frames of shelving units with piles of burnt crates around them. Next to the shelves was the shell of a forklift truck, and directly opposite the shutter was the frame of a van that had been completely stripped by the fire.

'What type of blood bank needs a forklift?' she asked herself.

'And has van's driving through its warehouse door?' Bambridge shone his torch at the remains of the vehicle and highlighted the front of the framework. It was crumpled against the back wall.

Turning his light off he stood up. 'We need to find another way in.' He moved around the to the side of building and pointed at a sign on the wall that said 'Reception'. 'Maybe we'll get more luck this way?'

The door to the reception area had warped from the heat, with the metal at the top and bottom having buckled outwards. Bambridge tried the handle and with a screech it opened inwards. He pushed against it a few times before it opened wide enough. He ducked inside, but Lawrence lingered outside for a moment.

She didn't have her best suit on, but neither was it her worst. Either way she knew that it was going to get covered in ash going in there. What choice did she have though? With a shrug of resignation, she followed Bambridge inside.

Everything was a charred mess. Immediately to the right of the door was a line of metal frames that had at one point been chairs. The plastic seats had melted onto the floor and then resolidified on a pool around the chair legs. Part of the ceiling had collapsed in the back corner, blocking off most of the room. To the left was a small office area. Again, the intensity of the fire had melted the acrylic barrier that had separated the office from the waiting area. Inside the office the remnants of a computer, telephone, filing cabinets and a chair were now just blackened shells.

What worried Lawrence the most was that Bambridge was nowhere to be seen. Shining her light around the debris, she could see what looked like a pathway through it all. It wasn't definite, but the floor seemed clearer, and it led away from the reception area further into the building.

'Guv?' she called out quietly. Why she was whispering she wasn't sure, but the place had her on edge. She pulled her baton from her belt and extended it. 'Guv, where'd you go?'

Following the makeshift path, she headed to the far end of the room and through a door on her left. She found herself in a corridor that ran the entire length of the building. Apart from a few fallen ceiling tiles, and the burn marks on the walls, the corridor seemed to have not taken as much fire damage, although the air was acrid and stank of smoke.

To her left, a store cupboard. The outline of a metal

bucket visible amongst the ash. She headed to the right, the beam of her torch barely giving off enough light in the dusty gloom.

'Guv?' she called, loudly. Her voice carried along the empty space, but she received no answer. The eeriness of the place started to weigh down on her as she began to wonder where he was, and if something had happened to him.

She'd only lingered for a second, how could he have got so far ahead of her so quickly?

Did he know where he was going, or something? Her worries about finding the rope in his flat came flooding back. Was that why he'd disappeared? Because he knew where he was going. But they had identified Leon Wallace at the scene of Stephen Bushell's murder, so it had to be him. It had to be Wallace. She shook her head to rid herself of the doubts about Bambridge. Although, as Bambridge had said, they only had Wallace arriving at the scene earlier in the day. Which didn't prove anything, except that he had dropped the bag off. Was he the person who Stephen Bushell had taken home before the party began? Or was that someone else? She shivered. Was Wallace just a mistaken identity? Was the person who'd been bleeding people out the same person who was investigating the crime? Her doubts returned as she scanned around the eerie, darkened interior. Had he lured her here to make her the next victim?

Sergeant Bambridge's name on the file came to mind and her worries thickened. Was Bambridge who they'd been looking for all along? He'd found the warehouse easily enough and hadn't asked for directions once. The warehouse that his wife had been investigating. But why? Why was she interested in a blood bank if she was part of a major crime unit? Suddenly, in the pall of semi darkness that enveloped her, she had a flash of inspiration. The something that had been niggling her fell into place. The two other occupants of Stephen Bushell's flat had been the daughter of an MP, and a banker's daughter. Add in the Bushell's and you had some powerful people all rubbing shoulders. Shoulders that if rubbed the wrong way, would attract the attention of a certain major crimes division. Was the blood bank a front for a major organised crime? A means to launder money perhaps? It would explain the arson. The fire would have destroyed some crucial evidence. Evidence that maybe Natalie Bambridge had stumbled upon. And now she was dead. The same evidence they'd found in Wallace's flat perhaps. A shiver ran through Lawrence's body, as she considered also, that Natalie's husband knew all this.

She had to stay objective, and focused. Everything she'd just thought about was speculation. The only truth they had was that Wallace had been seen arriving at the scene of the crime and had left the bag the killer had used.

Lawrence took a deep breath to steady her nerves, but found the air filled with ash and had to hold back a coughing fit. Whatever was going on with Bambridge, he was up ahead somewhere and may or may not need her help. Should she try to find him and share her thoughts, or should she keep them to herself, just in case? *In case of what*, Lawrence shook her head and moved forward.

The corridor opened out into a large space that was obviously the main warehousing area

Much like the corridor, apart from multiple tiles that lay scattered across the floor, the warehouse was relatively empty. However, at the edges of the open space were more fire damaged goods. A quick examination of the burnt objects showed her that they were beds. Lots and lots of beds that had been cooked almost to an unrecognisable state. What the hell had been going on in this place?

In that far corner there was a flight of steps that had collapsed under the weight of a structure. Lawrence assumed it had been the foreman's office, as it would have offered a great view of the whole room. The room may have formed part of the blood banks donating area. Which may have explained the beds. But still, it was a large area, and a lot of beds. Just how many donations were they getting?

More importantly, where was Bambridge?

'Guv,' she said, her voice sounding massive in the large area.

'In here,' he called from somewhere on the far side of the room.

Lawrence walked in the direction she thought his voice had come from but paused as she still couldn't see him.

'Where abouts?'

'Over here,' he spoke again, which was followed by the light from his torch bouncing off the far wall.

She found him a small room, his torch glimmering off all the surfaces. The place had been cleaned. The same smell of bleach hung in the air and told her they were on the right track. Bambridge was stood in the far-left corner, his attention on the large refrigerator that dominated the wall. There was little fire damage here.

The wall opposite her was filled with more acrylic. Two doors were in the middle of the wall that gave you access to the two laboratories behind the reenforced glass. The lab nearest the door looked like it had taken some fire damage, as most of the glass was blackened, but the other one look untouched.

'What you found, Guv?' Lawrence asked as she

cautiously entered the room. The evidence to suggest Bambridge was their suspect was minimal, but she didn't want to take any chances. So, she crept towards him whilst still keeping her distance.

'It's the same list,' he stated as he pointed to the front of the fridge.

It was indeed the same list, with the same names crossed out. It could have been a printed copy of the one in Wallace's flat, but there was no denying that it was all handwritten. The diligence was frightening, but then they had been saying all along how meticulous their suspect was.

Moving next to Bambridge, she could hear a hum coming from the fridge. 'Is this thing on?' she asked as she took a step closer.

'Yes,' Bambridge replied as he rolled up his sleeve to open the door.

As it opened, she was hit by a wave of cool air. The thermostat must have been turned all the way down, as it felt much colder than her fridge at home.

'How do they still have power? Surely the electrics were fried in the fire?' Her question was a general one that she didn't expect an answer to. Nor did she care if she got one, as all that mattered was the cool air pumping out.

Comfort breaks over, she investigated the well-lit compartment. It was filled with plastic jars. Each one had a dark red substance inside them. Identical white labels were stuck to the front of each container, with a series of numbers and letters written in the same handwriting as the list.

On the front of each shelf were more labels. If there was a sequence to the logos, she couldn't see it. There were two labels per shelf, with the top two-and-a-half shelves filled.

'These numbers must coincide with the numbers next to the names on the list,' she stated, and then pointed at the jars on the top shelf. 'These labels tally up with the front of the shelf.' Her finger pointed to P18 and then to the jars P18-1, P18-2, P18-3. 'They're sequential.'

It was clear that the jars were full of blood, and that it was most likely the blood of the victims they were investigating.

'That fifth name still has me worried,' Bambridge said as he took a step back from the fridge.

Lawrence closed the door, and for a second suffered from light blindness. It was in this second that she saw movement. A figure stepped out of the burnt laboratory and struck her across the face. The blow didn't knock her out, but as she fell backwards her head struck the wall and everything went fuzzy.

Chapter Twenty-Seven

Lawrence fought for air.

She tried breathing through her nose, but it was blocked. The blow she'd suffered must have broken it. Opening her mouth, she took a deep intake of breath, and her eyes began to focus. Her hearing returned next, and the sound of feet shuffling on hard floor filled her ears.

With her lungs full, she rolled onto her front and tried to lift herself up. She swayed, her head spinning, her ears filled with a sharp, high pitched ringing sound. She put her arm out and used the wall behind her for support as she got to her feet.

A glance to her left reminded her where she was and that she wasn't alone. The same figure was moving towards her, and she would need to act fast. Thankfully, she had managed to keep a hold of her baton, and its weight was comforting in her hand. She lifted it so that it was between her and her assailant while her balance returned.

In the poor light she could make out where the person that attacked them was, and her training kicked in.

'Leon Wallace,' she said, her jawbone grinding. She thought he'd hit her in the nose. 'You're under arrest.' She stopped as a wave of nausea came over her, and for a second, she thought she might pass out. With a deep breath she kept her head, and more importantly, kept her balance. Taking a step sideways she readied herself for his attack.

The figure moved in front of her, the small amount of light making it difficult to see who it was as they took a step to the side. Was it even Wallace?

'We remember you,' he said, in a charming voice, but there was no warmth in the words. 'You came calling the other week.'

'Yes, I did,' she replied, as she tried to take in more oxygen. If she could keep him talking, then her head might clear some more.

'And how is your investigation going?' he asked with a snigger.

'You know how it's going, Mr Wallace,' she offered as she kept her baton pointed at his head. If only it was lighter. Where had her torch gone? And where had Bambridge gone?

'But of course, you are here.' He held up his hands to emphasize the point. 'In the very heart of our workshop.'

She had wanted to mock him about his idea of what a workshop was but was more concerned that he'd used the terms *we* and *our*. Perhaps he was the apprentice? If he was, where was the master? 'Did you know her?' she asked, hoping to play on their heartstrings.

'Who?' he asked quietly.

'Tracey Collins,' Lawrence reiterated. 'The woman you murder in the Scenic hotel.'

The figure stopped moving.

'Come now, Mr Wallace,' she said, trying not to goad him too much, 'last time we spoke you even made a point of saying someone was going to die in that hotel.'

'We don't remember that,' he replied, taking a step towards her.

'I think you do remember,' she answered as she took another step to keep him at a safe distance. 'I think you knew her. Maybe not directly, but you would have studied her. Because that's what you do isn't it, Mr Wallace. You stalk people, get to know them, and then you murder them for their blood.'

'Everyone knew everyone in that place,' he stated, with another step forward. His movement was slow and steady, but she knew he was quick, and very strong. 'I'm sure it had a heart of gold.'

'So, you did know her then?' Lawrence mimicked his movements, taking another step back, and refusing to refer to her as *it*. Was that how he dealt with the guilt, by treating them as objects? If she carried on moving sideways though, she'd run out of room. There always the warehouse. Which would be a much better option, as it would give her much more space. However, she didn't know where Bambridge was, and she dared not leave him.

'Maybe we saw it on the street?' His voice was pleasant, as if he were chatting with an elderly relative, but there was no joy in the words. 'But we wouldn't have spoken to it.'

'Why not?'

'We find it best not to interact with people who have taken certain career choices,' he said in a mocking tone. 'But then we all have our own paths to follow.'

'You didn't approve of what she did?'

'We couldn't care less.' He took a step sideways trying to get between her and the door.

'No?' she asked in a provocative tone and took another step back. 'So, killing her wasn't because of what she did?'

Even in the dull light she could see them shake their head. 'Choosing that life is, of course, disappointing. Particularly, with the potential inside it.'

'What potential?' She was running out of space, and she could see she was being shepherded towards one of the laboratories.

'To live forever.' The voice changed with these words. It took on a distant tone, as if quoting a script. The reverence ever so evident.

Lawrence tilted her head to the side. The movement was in part an attempt to feign interest in what he was saying, and a test to see how her skull was feeling. The neck roll had felt fine, and there had been no dizziness. So, she prepared to make her move.

'Live forever?' Lawrence made sure the mockery in her voice was obvious. 'Don't be ridiculous.'

'You would mock eternal life?'

'I'm not mocking it.' She grounded her feet ready to make her move. 'Just questioning it. Now, put your hands on your head and turn around.'

Even through the gloom she could see the smile. Not a friendly grin. This was a maniacal smirk that had an uninviting intent behind it. He held his palms out and started to move them towards his head. But stopped at shoulder height. 'We're not going to do that,' he replied, 'We've too much work to do.'

'What work?' she asked as she readjusted her grip on the baton.

Lawrence could guess what he meant. The names on the list. He was taking the blood from them and keeping them in the fridge. But she didn't understand why that was considered work.

'God's will.'

'God's telling you to kill the people on that list?'

'You know about the list?'

The surprise in his voice threw her off guard. 'Only what you've got pinned up on that fridge. And what you have back at your flat,' she replied with a hint a mockery.

'You shouldn't talk down about God's work.'

'Fine,' she said bluntly. 'Leon Wallace, I'm arresting you on suspicion of the murder of Tracey Collins. And the murder of Stephen Bushell. And George Stephens. And

Candice Okeke. You do not have to say anything...'

'Good,' he interrupted and rushed towards her.

Lawrence only had a moment to think, but it was all she needed.

Dropping her left shoulder, she swung the baton in her right hand at a downward angle. The hard metal struck just above the right knee. She ducked out of the way, avoiding outstretched arms, as his leg buckled, and he fell.

Straightening up, Lawrence turned to face him, the baton raised in case he came at her again. She started to read the right to silence again. 'You do not have to say anything. But it may harm your defence if you do not mention when questioned something which you later rely on in court.'

He pushed up off the floor in one swift motion. 'You don't know what you're doing,' he called angrily and dived towards her. She stepped back and caught him on his left arm with the baton. The blow knocked his hand down to his side and he backed away.

'Anything you do say may be given in evidence,' she finished as the figure stood in silence facing her.

He wobbled a little, as his leg tried to take his weight, but he was now between her and the only exit. 'You're going to spoil years of work. Important work.'

'Important for who?'

'For God, of course,' his words were soft again. As if the very mention of the name brought serenity.

'The God I know wouldn't want you killing people.'

'That's because he hasn't spoken to you. Only the worthy get to convene with him.'

'And you think you're worthy?' She made no effort to hide the scorn in her voice.

'I HAVE BEEN CHOSEN,' he screamed and came at

313

her again.

This time his shoulder hit her in the ribs, lifting her off her feet, and forcing her baton from her grip. She wrapped her arms around his head, but her gripped instantly loosened as they collided with the fridge. She linked her fingers together behind his head and locked her elbows around his ears. As he took a step back, she wrapped her legs around his waist. If she could limit his movements, she might stand a chance. But when he couldn't break her hold, he tried a different strategy, breaking her back.

He slammed her into the fridge, again, and again. Each time, she felt the air leaving her lungs, and the strength in her arms weakening. The list, along with the board, fell behind her, clattering in the small space.

Another blow and his head came loose from between her arms, exposing her neck. His lips peeled back over his teeth, and she knew what his next move would be. She let her arms and legs go loose and dropped like a stone. Her chin caught on the top of his head, bringing stars in front of her eyes, but his teeth didn't make contact.

They broke apart, but he was still towered over her. She brought her arms up, pressing her elbows together and pushing her fists up under his chin. She felt her knuckles pop, but she pushed him further away. As he reeled from the shot, she drove her knee up into his groin. He groaned but clamped his thighs around her leg and thrust his head forward catching her on the bridge of the nose. She blindly swung an elbow that caught him in the stomach, and with a cough he stumbled backwards.

Lawrence took a step back, her shoulder bouncing off the fridge. She needed to find her baton, as she could feel fatigue setting in.

'Give it up, Wallace,' she said through the blood running from her nose, 'We've got back up on the way.

Best to just surrender yourself before you get in even more trouble.'

'You don't get to tell us what to do. Only God gets to do that. And you're getting in the way of his work.'

'Your work is done,' she stated and then spat blood.

'It'll never be done,' he replied with an air of pride, 'It'll go on forever.'

'Where you're going will feel like forever,' Lawrence replied as she took a sidestep.

The laughter that filled the room was terrifying. 'And where is it you think we'll be going?' he asked and took a step forward.

Lawrence glanced around the room trying to find her baton, but it was too dark.

'You're going to prison, Mr Wallace,' she said with confidence, to hide how exposed and vulnerable she actually felt. He clearly had the advantage. 'For multiple murders, for the attempted sale of human blood, and for the assault of two police officers.'

'We'll just have to see about that,' he replied and snapped into action.

He was quick, but Lawrence was equal to his movements. As he stepped towards her, she stepped aside and pulled the fridge door open. The force of the blow was thunderous. She caught the door as it swung shut and hit him again. He stumbled backwards and she pushed the door open.

The light from the refrigerator filled the room and she used it to spot her baton. It was just to her right. No more than a few steps away. But she would have to turn her back on Wallace to get it. She kept her eye on him and stepped towards it.

Wallace snarled at her; his lip busted open. He was paler than she remembered, but then it could have just been the artificial light bleaching his skin.

'You need to stop now, Mr Wallace,' Lawrence stated as she took another step backwards, sweeping her heel to try and locate the baton. 'Before you do yourself more harm.'

'You mean before we do you more harm?'

'Take it as you will,' she said as her heel connected with something. She put her weight on the object, ready to pick it up.

'You won't stop our work, it's far too important,' Wallace replied and came at her.

He tackled her in a single stride, and they crashed into the wall. Her back hit some shelves, knocking more objects onto the floor. She hooked a leg behind him, pushed off the wall, and the two of them fell to the floor.

'You can't stop us,' he howled as he rolled on top of her. 'He has set this task, and it must be completed.'

His elbow came down into her neck, and Lawrence felt the bones in her throat groan in protest. She twisted, forcing his arm off her throat, and the two of them rolled onto their sides. She got a hand free, and it rested on something solid. She grabbed it and smacked it into the back of Wallace's head. The plastic jar shattered, his grip loosened, and she pushed him away.

Rolling up onto her knees she reached to her hip and took out her handcuffs.

Wallace also came up onto his knees, the left side of his face a crimson mask. 'Now we're angry,' he said through gritted teeth.

As he came at her she wrapped her cuffs around her right hand and swung at him. The cuffs dug into her fingers, but the makeshift knuckleduster did its job. He fell backwards. Lawrence stood ready to strike him again, but his eyes were unfocused. She grabbed and cuffed his left wrist. But as she tried to cuff his other hand, he grabbed the second cuff and fastened it to her right wrist. They were now cuffed to each other.

Wallace tried to get up, but Lawrence took a swing at him. He returned fire with his own right hook that caught her in the ribs. All the air left her lungs, and another blow caught her on the jaw. She tried to return the blow, but his elbow caught her in the eye, and she fell on her back. Wallace was on top of her, his free hand around her throat. She tried to pry his hand away, but her strength had left her. Everything was starting to go black.

Suddenly, the pressure stopped, and she could breathe. Wallace stood up and started dragging her across the room. She tried to dig her heels in and reached out with her free hand to try and grab hold of anything, but she kept moving.

Wallace stopped, and she lay limply behind him. She shook her head trying to focus. But as the sound of metal scraping against concrete was followed by the sparkle of a blade in the refrigerator light, she wished that she had remained groggy. Staying that way would have stopped her from seeing the bone saw Wallace had just picked up.

Panic followed and she tried desperately to move away from him, but the handcuffs did their job, for she couldn't get away. Her struggles were cut short by Wallace's boot hitting her in the temple. The blow whipped her head sideways and blurred her vision.

She could feel her cuffed arm being lifted up and then the teeth of the saw biting into the skin of her thumb, but she was too dazed to do anything about it. As the metal scraped against bone, she accepted that she was about to lose a thumb.

A foot scuffed on the floor to her right, and a shape appeared out of the darkness. It barrelled into Wallace, sending the saw spinning, and him to the floor. The movement twisted Lawrence's arm to an odd angle, and she felt something pop, but at least she still had her thumb.

'You can't stop us,' Wallace called out as he lay on his back. 'God gave us this project. The harvest must be completed.'

Bambridge came down on top of him with a series of punches. Each one connecting. Each one bloodying Wallace's face more and more. An end to the attack wasn't coming. Lawrence could see the blind rage in Bambridge's face. The unbridled fury that came with each strike. If he didn't stop, he was going to kill their suspect.

'Guv?' Lawrence said, her voice weak, but just audible.

His hands faltered, but he continued to punch Wallace.

'Guv, you there?' she said as loud as she could.

He paused, but his eyes burnt into the bloody mess of a face below him.

'I'm here,' he replied finally, as he lowered his fists.

Beneath him Wallace continued to smile, through the blood and cracked teeth.

'You can't stop us,' he whispered as his smile broadened.

'We already have,' Bambridge gasped, uncuffing Lawrence. He rolled Wallace onto his front and cuffed his hands together at the small of his back. He turned his attention to Lawrence.

'There you are,' she said, as he knelt next to her.

'Yes, I'm here,' he replied taking her hand. With his other hand, he moved some of the blood-soaked hair out of her eyes.

'Did we get him?'

'We got him.'

'But you'll never keep us,' Wallace called out. 'The work is too important. He'll release us. Release us and put us back to work.

'He?' Lawrence said as she tried to sit up.

'Just lay still,' Bambridge ordered as he laid a hand on her shoulder. 'We've got him is all that matters.'

Chapter Twenty-Eight

Back up, with an ambulance and an armed response unit had arrived, followed by Stone and a full parade of uniforms and plain clothes officers. Bambridge barely noticed. He only had eyes on Lawrence, and he didn't leave her side until the paramedics had confirmed she was going to be okay.

They had told him that he should also be going to the hospital, but he'd insisted they stitch up his wrist and let him get on with it. Lawrence however needed to go with them. As she was taken away on a gurney, the severity of her injuries was unclear.

He wanted to go with her. To be sat next to her in the ambulance. There was an element of responsibility he felt for the state she was in. After what she'd done for him the other night there was no denying, he owed her. He also felt something else for her, but he didn't want to analyse that right now.

There was also a desire to stay close to Leon Wallace, who had also been patched up, but he would not be going to the hospital. His injuries had been classed as noncritical, so he would be going to a cell.

Bambridge was also concerned that he and Lawrence had disobeyed orders. They'd still been investigating Wallace for the murder of Stephen Bushell when the chief had taken them off the case. So, if he was to leave Wallace then it was likely he'd not get a chance to interview him. And there was no way that was happening, chief's orders or no chief's orders.

Bambridge managed to catch a ride back to the station, making sure he knew where Wallace was at all times.

Only once he knew he was in a cell did Bambridge start to relax. But he knew that Stone had returned with them and would want an update.

It was almost as if thinking about the Chief Inspector made him appear, because as he stepped away from the holding cells, Stone greeted him in the corridor, with Canham and Quinnell lingering over his shoulder.

'Inspector,' Stone offered as a greeting.

'You alright, Bams?' Canham asked from over the chief's shoulder. 'You look like hell.'

'Got into a fight,' he answered absently. It was a vast understatement. Got in a fight to the death was a closer description.

'And how's our girl?' Quinnell asked.

'Our girl?' Bambridge made no effort to hide the bitterness in his voice. Quinnell couldn't care less about Lawrence; he just wanted more details for the gossip mill.

'She going to be alright?' Canham added.

That question, however, did sound genuine. No matter how little you thought of another officer you never wanted them to come to harm in the line of duty. And even though Canham was a miserable old bastard, he still wanted the best for his own.

'She's tougher than she looks. She'll pull through,' he said, more to encourage himself than answer Canham.

'I hear you caught someone?' Stone interjected.

'Lawrence caught him,' Bambridge corrected. 'She was the one who recognised Wallace from the Bushell party.'

'What state's he in if he put her in the hospital?' Quinnell joked.

Bambridge found no humour in his question, and he considered ignoring him, but what would be the point? Might as well give him something to gossip over.

'He's still able to talk,' he replied.

'Yes, but we need to take a moment before we do,' Stone stated calmly.

'Why?'

'You've just been assaulted by him,' Stone replied with a little less calmness.

'That doesn't bother me,' he waved a hand absently.

'Plus, have you seen yourself?' he didn't sound angry, just concerned.

He hadn't, but he knew it wouldn't be pretty. He shook his head as a response.

'He also put your partner in the hospital. You also assaulted him, from what I can gather. He's in the cells screaming wrongful arrest. So, whether it bothers you or not, those details mean you've an emotional connection. And that emotion could spill out in an interview room.'

'I'm fine,' Bambridge replied, anger starting to rise in him. 'I need to be in there for the interview.'

'As I just said, I don't think that's wise.' Stone looked at him with a steady gaze. 'You might not think you're emotionally attached to this case, but you are. It's too big a risk to put you in there.'

'So, what, you're gonna send these two in instead?'

'They're the detectives leading the case,' Stone said, pointedly reminded Bambridge of the fact.

'And I'm one of the detectives that caught the guy.'

'Regardless of that, it's still their case.'

'My collar, my interview. And the way I see it is you've got two options,' Bambridge retorted, defiantly. He knew what he was going to say might be a bad idea, and maybe Stone was right, his emotions were getting the better of him, but he didn't care. 'You either, let me go in there, or you send me home.'

The Chief Inspector looked at him for a long time.

'Alright,' Stone said finally. 'You can interview him. But I've got some conditions of my own. Firstly, I'll do all the talking.'

'You'll be doing it with me?' Bambridge couldn't hide the shock in his voice.

'You didn't think I'd let you in there alone with him?' His words had a tone that implied there was no room for discussion, and Bambridge knew he should stop talking. 'My second condition is you go tidy yourselves up.'

Bambridge contemplated having a shower, but the chances of the dressing on his wrist getting wet was pretty high, so he decided against it. Instead, he just freshened up in one of the sinks, rolled up his sleeves, removed his tie, and washed the dirt off his trousers. As he looked at himself in the mirror, he could see the water stains all down his legs.

'He's not gonna be looking at my trousers,' he stated and left the bathroom.

Leon Wallace sat at the table, a mild smirk at the corner of his mouth. He didn't look like someone who'd killed multiple people. But then what did that look like? He also didn't look like someone who had been beaten half to death. Yes, there were cuts and bruises on his face, and his lower lip was swollen, but he almost looked unharmed. The paramedics had done an excellent job.

His demeanour was calm, as if he was enjoying himself. His attention moving between the two cameras in the room, and the two-way mirror in front of him. His smirk broadening into a smile as he looked at himself in the mirror. He seemed oblivious to the lawyer sat next to him talking into his ear.

Bambridge stood watching from the other side, gently flexing the fingers in his left hand. As he stared at Wallace's pale features, the fury he'd been feeling started to subside. He knew he had to keep his own emotions in check or Stone would remove him from the interview. He just had to make sure that smirk didn't cause him to lose it. He stared at the lawyer for a second, he swore he knew her. But then she could just have been another duty solicitor appointed to Wallace, and he'd seen her around the building.

Quinnell made a whooping sound as he looked through the glass. 'You really did a number on him,' he stated and pointed at Wallace.

'As I said, I'll lead,' Stone said firmly, ignoring Quinnell's comment. 'I'm sure he'll try and taunt you in some way. So, maybe Inspector Canham and I should go in?'

'No way,' Bambridge replied just as directly, 'I'm gonna be the one sat next to you.'

'You sure you want to do this?' Stone asked sounding less harsh. 'Inspector Canham has said he's happy to step in.'

'I bet he has,' Bambridge laughed. 'Be a nice collar to add to the CV wouldn't it, Hamish?'

'I only offered...' Canham held his hands up in defence.

'Save your excuses, I know you're only doing what you're told, but this is mine and Lawrence's case, regardless of what anyone else thinks,' Bambridge glared at Stone. 'So, it's going to be one of us that grills this guy. Thank you for your offer, but no thanks.'

Stone stared at him for a moment. Again, the gears were turning in the chief's head, assessing how to respond. 'Like I said earlier, you've been assaulted by that man. I don't care how strong willed you are, that will influence you and how you behave towards him. I'm only giving you the option to step back as a reassurance that you won't let your emotions get the better of you in there.'

'If anyone should be stepping back it's you, chief,' Bambridge said coldly.

'Now, listen here, Bambridge,' Stone started but was cut off.

'No, you listen. I'm going in there and I'm gonna interview my suspect. You wanna throw the book at me for it, then fine. But when you do, throw it at me, and me alone. Lawrence has just been doing what I told her to do. You wanna deal out punish when we're done, you just punish me.'

The room fell silent. Canham and Quinnell both looked shocked by his outburst, but Stone just stared at him blankly.

'You ready then?' Bambridge asked as he stared into the interrogation room.

'After you, Inspector,' Stone replied through gritted teeth.

As the door opened, Wallace turned towards them with a welcoming grin on his face. 'Good evening,' he said as his smile widened, his attention on the doorway. When Stone closed the door, his smile changed to a grimace. 'Where's your partner, detective?'

'She's fine, just off duty,' Bambridge replied through a fake smile. He was waiting for Wallace to start bragging about what he'd done, his blood already starting to boil. Stone had a point. He shouldn't be in here so soon after witnessing and doing what he had.

'We never meant to hurt you or your fellow officer,' Wallace added, his smile broadening.

'What were you meant to do then?' he asked without thinking and instantly felt Stone's hard stare.

'We'll get to all that soon enough,' Stone said as he glanced at Bambridge briefly, before returning his stare to the detainee. 'First, we need to deal with the formalities. Detective Chief Inspector Stone, and Detective Inspector Bambridge residing over this interview with Mr Leon Wallace, with his legal representation also present. For the records, please state your name.'

'From the very start I want to it on record that we will be filing for unlawful arrest,' the lawyer stated. 'My client was assaulted by multiple officers, and we will be seeking to have the maximum punishment brought down upon said officers.'

'We will take that into account, counsellor,' Stone said calmly. 'If you could please state your name,' he asked, turning again to Wallace.

'But of course, it's Leon Wallace.'

Stone nodded his approval. 'Do you know why it is you've been detained?'

'You do not have to answer that,' the lawyer answered for him.

'We can make an educated guess,' Wallace replied warmly, ignoring the lawyer, and giving Stone a smug grin.

It was bugging Bambridge where he'd seen the lawyer before. There was nothing remarkable about her. Her hair was tied back in a neat bun. Her make-up was minimal, with just a little bit of eye shadow and mascara. However, it was her suit that he noticed. There was no denying it was expensive. If her suit was expensive, then so were her services. She clearly wasn't a duty solicitor. This woman had been purposefully hired. But where was she from?

Stone was waiting for Wallace to continue, but his beaming features were all he got. As the silence dragged out Stone shifted in his chair.

'Care to share with us what that guess might be?' he asked politely.

'No,' Wallace chuckled.

'Well, I can inform you, Mr Wallace, that you are going to be charged for the murders of Tracey Collins, George Stephens, Candice Okeke, and Stephen Bushell.'

'Who?'

Bambridge didn't like how casual Wallace was acting. Or the way he looked so happy. With all the bruising on his face it was surprising he wasn't in pain with such a broad grin. But what concerned him the most was just how in control he seemed. As if he already knew the outcome of the interview.

Stone ignored his previous answer and continued. 'What is it you do for a living, Mr Wallace?'

'Working for a medical research company,' he answered straight away.

'And what company is that?'

'The Clean Blood Clinic.'

'And why did you lose your job at the clinic?' Stone continued without a change of tone.

'We didn't,' Wallace replied sceptically.

'Not according to the Clean Blood Clinic, Mr Wallace. They say you haven't worked there for over a year,' Stone said, shifting forward in his seat.

The lawyer whispered in Wallace's ear, which seemed to agitate him slightly, but as she continued to speak, he mellowed.

'Well, you know how incompetent Human Resources can be.' He answered finally.

'Do you know the address of your place of work?'

Wallace shrugged.

'For the benefit of the tape, Mr Wallace has shrugged, and given an impartial response. Mr Wallace, I only ask because you were apprehended on the site of your former place of work. A location that last year sustained fire damage from a suspected arson attack. A location I might add that held blood samples of the four people previously mentioned.'

Bambridge was pretty sure they hadn't confirmed the blood belonged to the victims yet, but he hoped that it would be the case. If not, that statement could hurt them down the road.

'We also found a list with the same names at the location. A list we also found at your home.'

'Our home?' Wallace seemed surprised.

'Yes, we searched your premises early today.'

'Can we see the warrant for that search,' the lawyer asked, and that same smile crept across Wallace's face.

Bambridge grimaced internally. They hadn't got a warrant. The chief taking them off the case had left him a little hot-headed and he had decided to just kick the door in. That would negate any evidence they'd found. Never mind. They had him on so many other things.

'We could add trespassing on private property to the list of charges if you like?' Stone stated, as if he'd read Bambridge's mind.

'Trespassing?' Wallace asked with another smirk. 'Where have you dug that charge up from?'

'The location you were arrested is property of the Clean Blood Clinic.'

'Yes, it is,' the lawyer added, 'So, I'll need to see the warrant for entering that building as well.'

More internal grimacing. They hadn't got one for the clinic either. Who was this lawyer? Where did he know her from?

'If it's a CBC site then how is it trespassing? We're an employee?'

'But you're not an employee according to them.'

'Did you speak to HR?'

'We spoke to a Doctor Salmon, who assured us you haven't worked with them since the fire.'

'So, you didn't speak to HR.' Wallace said with a shrug. 'That's fine, we'll come back to that when you've spoken to them.'

The audacity of that comment almost brought a laugh out of Bambridge, but he managed to hold it in. Stone fixed his suspect with a cold stare that Bambridge was happy he wasn't on the other end of.

'I'll be the one dictating how this interview goes, thank you.'

Bambridge winced again. Stone had just shown Wallace that his words had annoyed him. But how would he use that information? And how would the lawyer?

'But of course,' Wallace replied. 'Please, proceed.'

His lack of fear was interesting. Whether it wasn't the first time he'd been in an interview room, if the lawyer gave him confidence, or if he were just a cool character, Bambridge wanted to know.

'What sort of work do they do at the clinic?'

'We're a blood bank.'

'A specialist blood bank?' Bambridge chimed in for the first time.

'You could say that,' he offered with another smile; this one however had an element of mystery behind it. Like he wanted to tell them but chose not to.

'What does that mean?' Stone asked.

Wallace held Bambridge's gaze for a few seconds before returning his attention to Stone. 'What it means Chief Inspector Stone, is that we have a number of different clients, that deal in all manner of biological products. Including blood.'

'Such as what?'

'Such as if someone needs a liver transplant for

example. Or a kidney transplant. Or a heart transplant.'

'All above board?' Stone asked firmly.

'What relevance do these questions have to do with my clients arrest?' the lawyer interrupted.

'I only ask because it seems like you had a lot of blood stored. But it didn't seem particularly legal.' Stone said ignoring the lawyer again.

'What blood?'

'The blood in the building you were arrested in, Mr Wallace.'

'You have no proof this blood you speak of, and my client, have anything to do with each other,' the lawyer said.

'The blood in the room you were arrested in,' Bambridge added, as he leant forward in his chair. 'In the fridge. Along with your list and all of your planning. All in the room you assaulted DC Lawrence and I in.'

'Assault is it, Inspector?' Wallace mocked, with a bitter smile. 'What exactly does constitute assault in your eyes? A punch to the face? Two punches to the face? A multitude of punches to the face of a man flat on his back?'

Another whisper in his ear, and another angry reaction. Bambridge got the impression that Wallace didn't really want the lawyer there. And judging by the area he lived in, and that he didn't have a job, he wondered where he was getting the money to pay for her.

'Why do you ask, Mr Wallace?' Stone said in a calm tone.

Bambridge could tell what Wallace was implying, but he didn't like the way Stone had answered. With their track record, Bambridge knew Stone would be happy to get him out of his department. An accusation of excessive force was a clever way to get rid of him. It would be a struggle to talk his way out of the beating he'd given

Wallace. The red mist had formed, and he done what he had.

'We're simply curious. But not about what you think, Chief Inspector. We want to know what Inspector Bambridge thinks about what constitutes assault?'

They stared at each other for a long time, neither of them saying anything, but a conversation was happening none the less. It involved Wallace goading Bambridge into admitting that he'd assaulted him. But he was having none of it.

'By law assault is defined as any act by which a person intentionally or recklessly causes another to suffer or apprehend immediate unlawful violence,' Bambridge spouted the words that were burnt into his brain.

Wallace sat nodding as he considered the statement. He looked at both cameras again, and then at the two-way mirror before speaking. 'Intentionally causes another to suffer,' Wallace repeated, with a soft chuckle. 'Now, that's the interesting part of the rhetoric. Don't you find it interesting, Inspector?'

'I've never really considered it,' Bambridge replied.

'No?' Wallace held him with a questioning stare. 'You seem to know it well, and yet you've never considered the words?'

'We learn a lot of things in this job,' he answered. 'What the words mean are not important. How you deal out said words according to the law is what matters.'

'And how do you feel you dealt out those words a few hours ago, Inspector? Do you think you interpreted them correctly?'

'We'll be the ones asking the questions, Mr Wallace,' Stone interrupted.

'But of course,' Wallace replied, lifting his hands off the table offering his surrender. He smiled but there was no joy in the muscles in his cheeks. No warmth at the corners of his mouth. And nothing that resembled life behind his eyes. The smile was cold.

'Where did you get the list of names, Mr Wallace? From the Clean Blood Clinic? Because if you did that's another crime you're going to have to answer for. Theft of confidential information. Your former employer is going to have a field day in court with you.'

Wallace stared at Stone with a bewildered expression.

'Mr Wallace?' Stone said.

'Yes?'

'The list. Where did you get it from?'

Wallace snorted, shook his head in disbelief, and then started staring at Bambridge. 'From God,' he answered.

The lawyer leant close again, her movements a little less casual than her clients.

He'd admitted to obtaining the list, which was why she'd got a bit jumpy. They still didn't have anything incriminating on him. And the lack of warrants was a real worry.

'The Lord speaks to you?' Stone asked, matter of fact.

The way he'd asked made Bambridge think that Stone was a religious man. It was possible. A lot of people kept their beliefs to themselves on the force. Along with their political views. When it came to policing the public, you had to leave both of those things at the door.

'We spoke to our Lord,' Wallace corrected him, 'not your Lord.'

'Is there a difference?' Stone asked as he sat back into his chair. There was only interest in his words now. All his scorn and puzzlement were gone.

The smile returned to Wallace's lips, followed by a look of pity. 'Our Lord is not some commoner martyred by the Romans.' Wallace sat up as he spoke, his chest puffed up with pride. 'He's an immortal. Destined to walk the earth forever.'

'Or, a more likely story, is you found that list at work and took it upon yourself to start killing the people on it. Killing them for their blood,' Bambridge added, his voice scornful. 'Blood that you knew had value and could get you some money.'

'God does not need money,' he said with a sigh.

'But you did get their names from the database at the Clean Blood Clinic?'

'You don't have to answer that, Leon,' the lawyer piped up. Her eyes burning into Bambridge. 'Where is your proof of this theory, Detective?'

'Pinned to the wall of his flat.'

'A flat that, so far it seems, you entered illegally.'

Wallace mimicked a sad face and shrugged his shoulders.

'Did God work at the clinic?' the Chief added.

Wallace laughed at the comment. An empty laugh that was mocking in a cruel way. He shook his head whilst his cackle rattled in his throat. 'God, does not work.'

'Was it you that burnt down the clinic?' Bambridge asked. Had he done it to cover his tracks? But then why had he gone back there? Because all the facilities he needed were there perhaps?

'You don't have to answer that.'

'No, that was an act of vandalism,' he said, with a smirk that told Bambridge otherwise. 'We liked working there. We were sad when we heard what had happened.'

'But you know who did it right?'

He laughed and then leant back on the chair.

'What's so funny?'

'When you're dealing with Gods,' he began, shifting in the chair so that he was sat up straight, 'it is important to understand that they work outside the boundaries of society. They do as they please. And sometimes things go wrong quickly.'

'So, you do know who burnt the place down?'

'The authorities, we would imagine.'

'You're blaming us now?' Bambridge offered with a laugh.

'Not you,' Wallace said with a slight chuckle. 'The authorities.'

'We're the Police, Mr Wallace,' Stone offered, pride soaking his words, 'what more authority do you need?'

'You're just sheep in the herd,' Wallace replied with a nonchalant wave of his hand and then leant forward again, this time he looked at them both. 'We're talking about the real authorities. The ones that run everything.'

'And who is that?'

'Gods,' Wallace said with the same distant voice.

'Gods?' Bambridge mocked.

'Yes, Inspector Bambridge, Gods. Or Immortals if you want to use a different adage.' Wallace snapped; his face filled with thunder as he growled at him. A primal snarl that showed the monster he really was. But just as instantly, his serene expression returned.

'Why would God set fire to a blood bank?' Stone asked, his own tone just as mocking as Bambridge's last question.

'There are many Gods in this world, Chief Inspector.' he rebuffed, holding his gaze. 'Not just Jehovah and the son he sacrificed. We must choose which ones we serve. Or be consumed by them.'

'How very philosophical,' Bambridge ridiculed. 'Next you'll be telling us the earth is flat, and lizard people are in charge.'

'No, not lizards, Inspector, Gods.' Wallace shook his

head. 'Haven't you been listening?'

'Yes, I'm listening,' Bambridge answered. 'Believing is quite another thing.'

'It's fine that you don't believe,' he said with a smile. 'It's actually how they want you to be.'

'And how is that?' Bambridge asked coldly.

'Oblivious.'

'You keep saying we and our,' Stone stated, 'Are you saying you didn't work alone?'

'You don't have to answer that. And I'd advise you both to start rephrasing your questions. You are both trying to lead my client.'

'What do you think Inspector?' Wallace tilted his head as he stared at Bambridge.

'You are our only current suspect in these murder enquiries.' Bambridge waited for a response, but Wallace remained silent. A knowing grin on his face.

He had briefly discussed the idea that there was an accomplice with Lawrence, but the two of them hadn't dwelled on it. Perhaps they should have? The way he was talking, maybe there was more than one accomplice. Should they be looking into the Clean Blood Clinic more closely? Without question. But that would have to wait for now.

'I think you work alone,' Bambridge said confidently. 'You're too much of a perfectionist to have someone else helping you. Which is why you kept screwing up.' He let his words settle in Wallace's ears. He could see that they had had an effect, as he sunk into his chair, and his eyes narrowed. It was an angle to start pushing on. 'It was the way you tied off the rope on the bath taps that first caught my attention. You know when you hung Tracey Collins over her bath. Very shoddy.'

'You don't know what you're talking about,' Wallace

replied, but the confidence from earlier was gone.

'Yeah, real shoddy. You used a half hitch knot, instead of a taut-line hitch knot.' Bambridge had no idea what knot he'd used, or which one was best for hanging a body. But he could see that it had royally pissed off Wallace. 'Then, you don't even bother to hang poor old George Stephens up. What's up with that, just being lazy?'

'Detective, I'd advise you to change you tone,' the lawyer demanded.

'Why? He's fine with it. Aren't you, Leon?' He waited for a response but got a maniacal stare instead. 'But the real screw ups came with the third and fourth ones, didn't they?'

Bambridge could see the rage building inside his suspect. His jaw was clamped together, and the veins in his neck were standing out. If he could feed into that anger, then maybe he could get him to make a mistake.

'Yeah, that third one was a right mess.'

'Detective, I've warned you.'

'We're just talking, right Leon? Just shooting the breeze. Trading old war stories. Only your stories are about failure of late.'

'Failure? What failure?

'Leon, please…' the lawyer started.

'Silence,' he hissed back at her. 'You will speak when I need you to speak.'

The lawyer pressed her lips together, but Bambridge could see she was still paying attention to what was happening. She was ready to bail her client out of whatever mess his mouth was about to get him into.

They had definitely met before. He knew he knew her, but from where?

'Spilling that blood for one,' he added. 'The way it washed out all over that playpark. What a waste. Can't have been good for the old profit margin.'

'Profit margin?'

'Yeah, you know, when you were going to sell Candice Okeke's blood.'

'Right, I want this interview to stop, right now!' the lawyer began to stand, but Wallace's hand grabbed her wrist and held her in place.

'Mr Wallace,' Stone said in a firm voice. 'Please let go of Ms Herbert's wrist. Now.'

Wallace did as he was asked and removed his hand from hers. If Ms Herbert was shaken by the brief encounter, she showed no signs of it. She remined calm and continued to sit next to her client.

How did Stone know her name? Bambridge couldn't remember her ever giving it.

'Okay, so, you weren't selling it. But spilling so much blood, and losing your knife, must have been infuriating. If not more than a little idiotic. What happened? That young couple put you off your flow.' He waited for Ms Herbert to interject, but it looked like she was done speaking. 'And don't even get me started on all the bits you missed when cleaning up after Stephen Bushell.'

'We do as he wishes,' Wallace blurted out.

'We?' Stone interjected. 'There you go using the plural again. Who is we?'

'His flock. We do as he asks.'

'Including murder?' Bambridge added bluntly.

'We do as he asks,' Wallace repeated.

'And does this God of yours forgive you for taking those people's lives?' Stone asked.

'He doesn't forgive.' Wallace held back a laugh. 'But he does reward those that serve him well.'

'And that's what you've been doing?' Bambridge asked, 'Serving him? You can't have been serving him that well if you kept screwing up.'

'He asks, so we give.'

'You give what?

'Only the purest will suffice for God.'

'Some of your victims didn't seem that pure to me,' Bambridge replied.

Wallace gave him a cold stare. All humour left his features and Bambridge felt a chill on his skin. He'd given that same look in the burnt-out building. The memory reminded him just how much he hurt all over from the fight.

'Are you mocking their sacrifice?'

'Not at all,' Bambridge replied, the feeling of almost having him was very real. He could sense he almost had him. 'I'm just wondering if we have different interpretations of what pure means?'

'Would you like me to use a word that better suits, Inspector? Would; only the best, be more to your liking?'

Bambridge stared back at Wallace, the initial chill now gone, and only a grim determination to send this guy down remained.

'The best what?' Stone interjected, breaking the interaction.

'Or the rarest is perhaps a better choice,' Wallace added as he looked at Stone.

'Like type AB negative?' Bambridge asked, but he already knew the answer.

Wallace's eyes widened, and a welcoming smile filled his face. 'The blood of the chosen,' he whispered with a sycophantic fervour.

He'd used the word blood, but it wasn't enough, they needed more.

'Why are they the chosen?'

'Because of the blood.'

'And that's why you chose them?

Wallace remained silent, his eyes glazing over as he stared into the middle distance. If they could get him to admit to just one of the murders, then that would be enough for a conviction. He just needed to steer them away from the talk of Gods and Immortals.

'Do you not feel any remorse about killing those people?' Bambridge asked casually.

'You don't have to answer that,' Ms Herbert stated and got a cold look from Wallace.

'Remorse is for the weak.'

'The weak?' Stone replied, and then started yelling, his voice drowning out all other sounds.

Bambridge could have laughed. Stone had told him to stay calm, and here he was, losing it in an interview room, veins bulging in his temple as he berated Wallace. But he didn't really hear what the Chief was saying, because he was staring at the file, trying to find something to pin the murders on Wallace. Something that he could use to coax a confession out of him. He was currently more than happy to talk. It was just a case of getting him to say the right words. But what were those words?

Nothing in the file jumped out at him. All the crime scene photos left him with just as little as when he was actually at the scenes. The information on Leon Wallace was minimal, with only a single page of details available.

There wasn't even anything in the photos of the laboratory that he could use. The fight between Lawrence and Wallace had left the place in a state. The only thing recognisable was the list of names. But there was something about the list that caught his interest. No, not something. Someone.

'You knew Tracey Collins, didn't you?' Bambridge said with belief, cutting through Stone's full flowing rant.

He hoped for a reaction from Wallace. A notification that he knew what he was talking about. Something that he could work with, but he just stared back at him blankly.

'Who?'

There was no subterfuge to his response. Well, none that he could see. The blankness in his features seemed genuine.

'Tracey Collins,' he repeated. 'The woman you killed in the Scenic hotel.'

'You don't have to answer that.' The lawyer's voice again.

Wallace's features remained emotionless, and he shrugged at her. 'I don't know who that is.'

The list stared up at him. The five people with a line through their names calling to him. His lingered on the P numbers they'd each been designated. The same numbers allotted to the containers full of blood in his fridge. These numbers hadn't been crossed out. He looked at Tracey's details and decided to try something.

'And what about P52?'

'What about it?' Wallace replied offhandedly.

'They were your neighbour, were they not?'

'P52 was too good an opportunity to overlook.'

'Leon,' the lawyer barked, and then started whispering in his ear again. He ducked away from her, growling inaudibly.

'Is that why you chased Paul McNulty away?' Bambridge knew that he was onto something. 'Because she was too good an opportunity to miss?'

'Who?' Wallace asked confused, as he slumped onto his side, away from the lawyer. 'You keep giving me all these names, and they all mean nothing.'

'The man you chased away from under P52's window?'

'He was a pervert, who needed scaring off.'

'And by scaring him off you were able to kill P52 for their blood?'

Wallace sat up straight, looked him in the eye and smiled. 'You know all this already. So, why are you getting me to repeat what you already know?'

'Why would I know all this already, Mr Wallace?'

Wallace smiled at him, only this time it wasn't cold, or empty, or emotionless, it was warm and friendly. 'I may not have seen God's face, but I know his voice,' he said, with tears forming in his eyes. 'And it sure is beautiful.'

Bambridge wasn't sure what he meant, so he ignored the statement and carried on with his plan of attack. He found George Stephens on the list, and then found the number Wallace had given him.

'So, what was the deal with P18?' he said as he looked for Candice and Stephen's numbers.

'A creature of habit,' Wallace stated absently, his gaze transfixed on Bambridge.

George had been a creature of habit. His daily trips to the Silver Trumpet brought on by his alcoholism had seen to that. But Wallace still hadn't admitted to anything.

'And P7?' Bambridge asked referring to Candice Okeke.

'Another creature of habit.'

'Failed to get her blood though, didn't you?'

Wallace was clearly annoyed.

'P64 was where you went wrong,' Bambridge continued as he looked at Stephen Bushell's name. His surname specifically. 'Stephen Bushell, or P64 as you call him, was significant too. A person of too much significance in this world for your works to go unnoticed.'

'Significant for his blood. Nothing else.'

'Stephen was a known member of society,' Bambridge

said in defence of the dead. 'Some would say because of his family name, and nothing more. But you can't kill someone with a name like Bushell and get away with it.'

'Names are irrelevant. Only the blood matters.'

'I'm sure the Bushell's would disagree.'

'God cares not about the bleating's of the herd. P64 bled out just as easily as the others.'

They had him. A confession to the murder of Stephen Bushell.

'Right, I want you to stop talking now, Leon,' Ms Herbert stated as she stood up. 'This interview is over. My client is clearly not in a sane state of mind. I recommend that he be assessed by a psychologist. I also would like a statement about what caused the injuries to his face. Because to me that looks like excessive force used to detain my client. And until I see the warrant for my client's home and for the Clean Blood Clinic, all your evidence is inadmissible. Now, I want the two of you to leave, and I want the microphones turned off so that I can talk to my client in private.'

'But of course,' Stone stated, pleasantly, as he stood up. 'Come along now, Inspector Bambridge. Best leave Ms Herbert and her client to it.'

Bambridge sat dumbfounded as realisation of where he'd met Ms Herbert came to him. She had been stood in the doorway of Stephen Bushell's bedroom, advising his flatmate Hilary not to say anything. She was part of the Bushell's legal team. Why was she here, defending the man that killed Stephen? What kind of secrets had Leon Wallace uncovered? The piles of paperwork in his flat came to mind as he sat staring at the two of them across the table.

'Why are you still sat there, Detective?' Ms Herbert demanded, her eyes burning into him.

'Time to go,' Stone said politely as he opened the door. 'Detective Bambridge!' He raised his voice. 'Come on.'

'What are you doing?' Bambridge asked Ms Herbert as he begrudgingly stood up.

'Defending my client, Detective.'

'You're not gonna get away with this, Wallace. D'you hear?' Bambridge stated, anger filling his words. 'You'll pay for your crimes. Mark my words.'

A hand landed on his shoulder and tried to pull him away, but he resisted, and tried to take a step forward. More hands landed upon him, and he was dragged towards the door.

'Remember, Detective, you're just sheep in the herd. Sheep in the herd.'

Stone, Canham and Quinnell all let go of him once they had themselves between him and the interview room door.

'What the actual fuck?' he said to Stone.

'What's the problem, Detective?' he replied, as he adjusted his suit jacket.

'What's the problem? What's the problem? That's a Bushell lawyer in there.'

'That's correct.'

'A Bushell lawyer that's gonna make sure our guy walks. A guy that just killed a family member of the very company she works for.'

'He just confessed to four murders; he's not going anywhere.'

'Oh, don't be so naive. He's gonna walk, and then this Bushell family are gonna make him disappear.'

'Disappear? How are they going to do that, Detective?'

'You tell me, Chief,' Bambridge replied. He wanted to ask him how much? How much the Bushell's had paid him to let what just happened happen. Wanted to ask how long he'd been on their payroll, but what was the point? There was no getting around what had occurred. He shook his head in disbelief and walked away from Stone and his lackies.

'Get yourself home, Bambridge,' Stone called after him. 'We'll talk about how the arrest went when you're back in tomorrow.'

Bambridge didn't even respond. He had no interest in talking to any of them. And he had no interest in going home either. There was only one place he wanted to be right now.

Chapter Twenty-Nine

Bambridge woke with a start. His limbs were stiff from the odd angle he'd been sleeping. The chair next to Lawrence's bed was small and less than comfortable, but he managed to nod off in it no less.

Shifting in the seat he'd felt better. At first, he thought it was the way he'd slept, but as he moved about, he realised that it was because of the fight he'd been in. He was in better shape than Lawrence though.

She had been in and out of consciousness the whole time he'd been with her. Each time she had opened her eyes he'd thought that she was going to speak. But there would be no recognition in her eyes, and she had fallen back asleep.

Whenever a member of the nursing staff had been in the room, he'd asked after Lawrence. Each time they'd told him she'd be fine and would be conscious soon. But as the hours ticked by, he'd started to doubt their expert advice.

His hand lingered over the television remote, but he couldn't actually remember the last time he'd watch TV. Never mind during the day.

He looked around the room and realised just how sterile and empty it felt. Which had him worrying that he should have brought her a gift. However, in his rush to get here, he hadn't considered that. Some flowers, a card, or a box of chocolates would have been a good idea. But then he thought of her poor face, and her broken jaw and dismissed the chocolates.

'I didn't expect company,' Lawrence croaked from the bed.

Bambridge turned to face her with a smile. 'Been here all night,' was the only answer he could muster.

'What've you been doing?' she asked as she tried to rise onto her elbows but didn't seem to have the energy. She fell back against her pillows with a cry of frustration.

'I fell asleep for a few hours,' he replied, with a wince.

'That dull, huh?'

'The conversation was pretty slow.'

She chuckled at the comment and then groaned in pain. 'Don't make me laugh.'

'Sorry,' he said sincerely. 'Where does it hurt?'

'Where doesn't it hurt.'

'So, where does it hurt the most?'

'Everywhere,' she said and tried not to laugh, but it came out anyway.

He joined in with his own low chuckle but had trouble finding humour in her words. 'Staff here think you're going to be okay,' he reassured her. In truth it was more to reassure himself.

'Well, that's a relief. Right now, though I'd just take something to numb the pain.'

'Surely they can give you something?'

'They could,' she said with a forced smile, 'but then we wouldn't get to finish our conversation. Plus, pain means things are healing.'

Bambridge looked down at her and couldn't think of anything to say. He'd never been one for small talk and trying to hold an idle conversation with a hospitalised work colleague wasn't an easy chat to have.

'So, d'you come here for a reason?' Lawrence asked, her tone light. 'I assume we caught our guy as we're both still here.'

'We caught him,' he answered. Although, there was no joy in his words.

'You don't seem happy about it.'

'It didn't go how I would have liked.'

'What'd he have to say?'

'A lot of things. But also, nothing.'

'Who interviewed with you?'

'The Chief.'

Lawrence visibly flinched and he knew why. 'How was he?'

'He asked the right questions,' Bambridge said with a hint of irony.

'But didn't get the right answers?'

Bambridge paused to consider his own answer. 'We got answers, just not when the Chief was asking.'

'So, you led on the interview?'

'No, the Chief led. He just wasn't as in tune with the ins and outs of the case. Plus, he got a bit flustered when the topic of God was raised.'

'He a religious man?' Lawrence asked as tried to turn towards him and instantly stopped, a look of pain on her face.

'You alright?' Bambridge asked, the talk of work forgotten as he leant forward and rested a hand next to hers.

'Fine,' she offered. 'It just hurts to move. They discussed religion?' she asked after a pause.

'Not religion. God. Well, Gods to be precise.'

'They argue over which of theirs was better?'

'There was no arguing,' he said with a shrug. 'Just Wallace talking about his God, and how his God made him do it.'

'So, we got a confession?' she asked in a positive tone.

'Yes, but there was a snag.'

'What snag?'

'He lawyered up.'

'How'd that guy afford a lawyer?'

'The Bushell family sent him one.'

'What the fuck?' Lawrence tried to sit up again, but the movement made her grimace, and she flopped down onto the bed with a cry of anguished pain.

'Are you alright?'

She nodded at him, but the pain clearly wasn't subsiding. 'I'm fine.'

'Well, you're not, are you?'

'I'm fine,' she said again, through gritted teeth.

'Any idea how long you'll be in here?' he asked with a frown.

'Until I'm not in agony,' she said with a groan. 'And stop changing the subject. What d'you mean the Bushell's sent him? Didn't he kill their son?'

'I don't understand it either. But what I do know is we've gotta watch our backs. These Bushell's are into a whole lot of shit.'

'Like what?'

'Like the pockets of our colleagues.'

She stared at him, her drug fogged mind clearly trying to process what he'd said. 'I thought it was you, you know.'

He smiled. 'Yes, I know you did.'

'You were never around, whenever any of the murders took place.'

He shrugged. 'Unfortunate timing,' he told her and then looked her straight in the eye. 'I've been paying for counselling. I'm supposed to see a grief counsellor to help with the loss. But every time I go, I just sit in my car. I'll actually go inside one day.'

Lawrence was quiet for a long time and Bambridge thought she'd fallen asleep.

'I'm truly sorry for your loss, Guv' she whispered.

'Going to the counsellor will help.'

He shrugged again. 'I know. It just takes everything out of me, trying to pluck up the courage to go inside. Maybe one day.'

Her small, bruised hand reached for his. 'I'm happy to go with you. If you need moral support.'

'That's very kind of you. I'll think about it.'

'What's the vibe from Stone?' she asked, suddenly snatching her hand away and becoming as businesslike as she could from where she lay.

'About what?'

'About us disobeying his orders and staying on the case?'

'Nothing,' he answered with a shrug.

'He's not gonna chuck us out of the unit?'

'Why would he?'

'Chuck me out then?'

'Why would he do that either?'

'Seems the logical choice if you were gonna punish someone. Punish the rookie by moving her to a different unit.'

'Never gonna happen.'

'No?' Lawrence didn't sound convinced.

'D'you know how hard I fought to get you into that department?'

The shock on her face made him smile.

'Why would you have done that?'

'Because I want the best to be working with me.'

'Is that why Canham and Quinnell are in the department?' she asked with a wicked smile.

'Leftovers from the old regime,' he stated with a shrug. 'But I'll get them out the door soon enough.'

A knock at the door cut Lawrence off. It opened and Craig entered. He looked Bambridge up and down with an uncertain gaze before stepping into the room.

'Hey, you,' Lawrence said and tried to sit up again, but her strength wasn't there.

'I'll leave you two to it,' Bambridge said, sidestepping past Craig to the door.

'Thanks, Guv,' Lawrence said as she glanced back and forth between the two of them. 'Just one question though?'

'What's that?'

'It might be the painkillers messing with my head, but did we get Wallace locked up, or not?'

Bambridge gave her a determined stare, and with a confident nod said, 'We will.'

He closed the door on his way out.

ABOUT THE AUTHOR

Mark Simmons has been writing thrillers and horror recreationally since a young age, finding a passion for classic and modern literature from the local library and the books suggested to him by his older siblings.

Born and raised on the coastline of Suffolk, England. Mark also found his creativity stimulated by the rolling countryside and coastal emptiness of East Anglia.

After twelve years of working in various areas of the Television Broadcasting Industry across the UK, he has returned to his roots, and now lives on the banks of the River Stour with his Epidemiologist wife, The Doctor.

It was her love of crime books that was the catalyst for his Detective Inspector Bambridge series of novels. Creating an unorthodox character that operates in his own dark world.

Bled Out is the first in the series of DI Bambridge novels, where we delve into the darkest recesses of the minds of both the killer and the detective.

Ingram Content Group UK Ltd.
Milton Keynes UK
UKHW020717210423
420559UK00017B/1204